The Love of
Geli Raubal

Brenda Squires has worked extensively in education and psychotherapy but has always had a passion to write. Her first novel, *Landsker*, won the Romantic Novelists New Writers Award. *The Love of Geli Raubal* draws on her experience as a student of the German language and from the time she spent living and working in Berlin. She divides her time between west Wales and London and is actively involved in promoting writing and literature.

The Love of Geli Raubal

Brenda Squires

PARTHIAN

Parthian, Cardigan SA43 1ED
www.parthianbooks.com
First published in 2016
© Brenda Squires 2016
All Rights Reserved
ISBN: 978-1-910901-50-2
Edited by Richard Davies
Cover designer: Robert Harries
Typeset by Elaine Sharples
Printed and bound by Printed in EU by Pulsio SARL
Published with the financial support of the Welsh Books Council
British Library Cataloguing in Publication Data
A cataloguing record for this book is available from the British Library.

London, 1932

London, 1975

One

Max Dienst sat at his desk, pulling his thoughts together for his next journalist dispatch to Berlin. The phone juddered, breaking his concentration. '*Ja, ja. Am Apparat,*' he said. The line crackled and rasped, there were several clicks, and then Wolfgang Seifert, his editor at *Die Tatsache*, was speaking.

'Sorry… early call…' The line went dead, then picked up again. 'I wanted to speak to you – urgently. It's like this, your reports are sound, more reliable than most, but I need you back here.'

'In Berlin?'

'That's right. I can't go into details. You have to take my word for it. Things are moving fast here. I need to get this sorted… in the next forty eight hours.'

'That doesn't give me much time—'

'Max, as I said, this is vital.'

By now Max's head was spinning. He pictured *Die Tatsache* office, a square block in treeless Wilhelmstrasse. With its high ceilings and portraits of dignitaries it had had an imposing aura. He'd first seen it nine months ago at his interview. The editor, busy fielding phone calls, had barely glanced at him. He found it hard to recall exactly what the man looked like. It had all happened so quickly.

Seifert had said they wanted more reports from London. Knowing Max's English was fluent and glancing at the letter of recommendation he'd waved his hand, agreeing to give Max a trial run. No guarantees, he'd added: they would judge him by his writing alone.

Being foreign correspondent would be perfect, especially

3

in London. Rhiannon would be delighted. After all, that had been part of their agreement. He'd been at a loose end: he had just submitted his book on alcoholism amongst Rhine bargees to a publisher in Hamburg but had not been hopeful. Though the book was well researched, booze-ridden bargees drowning at midnight were not a burning issue. Viewed in the cold light of economic necessity he knew any writer of serious social commentary would struggle to make a living.

So Max had seized the moment.

Now the same editor wanted to uproot him and rein him in: 'I'm offering you a chance to develop your ideas from the heart of the country.' Again the voice was lost, then 'I need someone with an objective eye.'

Max's pulse quickened. 'What? I can't hear very well!' he yelled, drawing a reproachful look from the colleague he shared a corner with. He raised a placatory hand, straining to make sense of the fluctuating signal. Max pictured Rhiannon, his wife of one year, drifting in her inimitable way round their rooms in her red dragon dressing gown. Or she might be curled up on the sofa, picking her way through a tome on Victorian London. What would she have to say about all this?

'Well?' urged his editor impatiently.

'I need to think about it.'

'Be quick about it. It can't wait.' The line crackled again and then went dead.

His colleague, Jean Luc, a French foreign correspondent, stopped typing. 'What's up—? Want to talk about it?'

'Not now.' He needed to think. Before the call he'd been carefree, whistling as he cut across Highbury Fields. He was getting used to London: there was a gentility about the place that suited him. Cities, prone to anonymity, are forgiving and London with its myriad waves of immigrants, was especially so. People were getting used to seeing him around.

The newsvendor at Highbury Barn, knowing he was German, had shouted: 'How's it going then, Fritzie?' When Max waved in response the man added with a grin: 'Never mind – we won the war anyway!' At that Max shrugged good-naturedly, realising he had a long way to go before understanding English humour.

At lunchtime he left the office with Jean Luc. They headed towards the saloon bar of the Jester's Hat in Mitre Court. Jean Luc pushed a pint of stout towards him. 'I haven't seen you look so worried in weeks?'

Max sipped his drink. 'I got a call I wasn't expecting from my editor. He wants me to go back to Berlin.'

'I thought he said you were doing a good job here.'

'He was being cagey, said he wants me for something specific. All very mysterious… wouldn't say more.'

'Sounds a bit strange to me. I would have thought you were more use to them here than there. They'd have to start all over again with the next correspondent.'

'I know. I started to say that but the line was bad.' Max thought back over his time in London. He'd spent the first weeks showing just how graphic his reports could be and what unusual facts he could serve up for the discerning readership of the solid Berlin broadsheet. For eight months he'd been cabling and phoning through his reports on the British social and political scene. Seifert had increased his column space, though not his fee. 'London is fascinating – especially now. People are drinking and dancing to their hearts' content. It's all a bit mad and frantic. I love it.'

'It may look innocuous but things are changing under the surface,' said Jean Luc.

'I know.' Max paused over his glass. 'They say the social fabric and the class system are fractured. That nothing will

ever be the same. I disagree. The ruling class will find a way
back…'

Jean Luc took another swig from his beer.

'I did a piece the editor liked on the Disarmament
Conference and British attitudes towards it.'

'Can you say no?'

'The more I think about it the more I want to go. I'm
curious. How could any decent journalist resist the challenge?
But it's not just up to me. I don't think Rhiannon will be all
that keen…'

'What am I to do for company if you slope off to Germany
again?'

'I know. Still don't trust us, Johnny Foreigner and all that…'

Just then the bell for last orders rang and Jean Luc glanced
at his watch. 'Better go. I'm interviewing in half an hour.'

'Who is it this time?'

Jean Luc smiled at him.

'Why so secret?'

'What are you up to?'

'Bits and pieces for my next dispatch. Rhiannon suggested
we meet for tea. She's in the West End shopping. I've been
working late so we've hardly seen each other lately.'

Jean Luc shrugged, downed his beer and then headed for
the door. Max watched him disappear through the dim bar
out onto the bustle of the street.

He waited for Rhiannon in the Lyons Corner House on the
Strand. He was anxious, excited. The call had shaken him. He
was halfway through his second cup of tea when she arrived,
fifteen minutes late, looking breathless as though she had
been running. He watched her struggling through the door
with parcels under her arm, her hazel-green eyes glowing,
her dark auburn hair flying about her neck.

'Sorry, I forgot about the time. Have you been waiting long?' He opened the door for her.

She gave him a wide smile and slipped down onto the seat opposite. 'You've already ordered. Is it cold?'

'I can order some more.' He reached over and tucked a wisp of straying hair behind her ear.

Her pale, open face with its intelligent, questioning eyes turned towards him. 'I got a letter from Aunt Vicky. She's up in town. I'm going to see her later. She's been elected chair for the whole of south Wales.'

'That's good, no?'

'She'll be insufferable now.'

'Will she want you to help her out?'

'Oh, I doubt it. She's got plenty of local support.' When Max said nothing Rhiannon asked. 'You're very quiet. Are you annoyed with me for keeping you waiting?'

'Not at all.' His eyes searched hers. 'I got a call from Berlin. The editor wants me back there.'

'You've only been working for them for six months.'

'Eight.'

'Eight then.'

'The editor likes my dispatches.'

She was tilting her head to the side in that bemused way she had.

'He says I have a good eye…'

The waitress arrived with a fresh pot of tea and arranged cups and saucers on the small round table.

'We've only just settled in London. Found a place to live.'

'But we did say we would go back to Germany. That was always part of our plan.'

'You make it sound as though you have no choice in the matter. Like it's some military order. I thought you were more of a free spirit than that.'

7

'I could go alone. Just for a month or two. To see how it works out.'

'We *are* married.' Rhiannon thoughtfully stirred her tea.

'It's sooner than we intended, but this is an opportunity,' he stressed. 'He wants to hear back from me as soon as possible.'

'Oh does he indeed!'

'He *is* the editor. And I'm the one they need. We don't have a lot of time to play with.'

'Things are never that simple and then there's…'

'There's what?'

She hesitated, spoke almost in a whisper: 'Starting a family. Children.'

He sat back with a sigh. That had completely escaped his mind. They had indeed spoken along those lines. A night or two ago in the early hours they were murmuring pillow talk, after making love, and she had slipped the idea between them. In the flush of satisfaction it seemed a natural one, an outcome of their tenderness. Now in the clattering teashop, where they had to strain to keep their conversation private, it became the worst possible idea. He did not want to be fettered.

Rhiannon caught his discomfort. For a moment she looked wistful then set about tidying herself and her parcels. She looked away before speaking. 'I'm starving,' she said. 'I'm going to order a plate of scones. Want to join me?'

Aunt Vicky, in her tailored navy suit and with well-coiffed hair, was the epitome of the New Woman: engaged, fashionable and quick-witted with the air of too many things on her plate. She kept an office in Smith Street near Westminster Square. 'Sit down, won't you. I don't have a lot of time to spare, though of course I'm delighted you called by. How's Max, by the way?'

Before Rhiannon could respond Vicky was off again. 'My

head is aching from all the meetings I've had to sit through in the last few days – whether or not the Women's Institute should support the miners' hunger marches on London. Not that we'd get involved directly, you understand, only in terms of support. If only Westminster could see reason…'

'I was delighted – and of course honoured – to be elected chair but we have such a battle ahead of us. Things are not going the way we hoped. There's resistance to soft-pedalling with the miners. The country is up against it, they say.'

Lost in her own thoughts, Rhiannon struggled to take it all in. Something about Vicky's impatient, broad-sweep way of seeing things made her hold back. But who else could she speak to in the family? 'I know how busy you are… '

'Do sit down, Rhiannon, and stop hovering by the window. You're blocking my light.'

Rhiannon groaned in irritation and pulled out a chair opposite her aunt's desk. 'Max has been recalled to Berlin. I thought you should know.'

Vicky took off her reading spectacles and looked across at her niece.

'This morning he got a call from his boss. They want him back there.'

'Things are none too clever in Germany right now, Rhiannon. Opinion is divided. But it's all very unpredictable.'

'We have to decide one way or another. I am finding it impossible…'

'Come on Rhiannon. Show a little grit.'

Rhiannon got up and walked back to window, careless as to whether or not she was blocking her aunt's light. 'For me it feels very sudden.'

'You don't want to go?'

'I am not sure. If he doesn't go his career prospects will be affected. It's a good move for him.'

'What do *you* want?'

Rhiannon felt heavy. 'I want – I want what most women want – fun, a bit of stability. He'll be miserable if he stays.'

'I wouldn't recommend Germany… Wait a year to see how things work out there. It should be clearer then.'

'He can't wait. *We* can't.'

Even as she spoke she had a sense that things were moving beyond her control, like a persistent trickle of a stream gathering force and carrying her along. When she saw her aunt fidgeting again with the report on her desk she got up to go, saying she'd let her know once a firm decision had been made.

That evening they had been invited to a party in Highbury Barn, close to their apartment, but infinitely more fashionable. They'd made a pact while getting ready not to mention 'his posting,' as they were now calling it, in front of anyone else.

Rhiannon put on a swirling dress of pink satin – the straight, boyish line of the Twenties long-since ousted by a more feminine, flouncy look – while Max's only concession to fashion was to wear the dark blue lounge suit he'd bought when they first arrived here. She applied lipstick and a touch of rouge, leaving her hair loose and untidy around her face. Tonight she would forget the future and her part in moulding it. Tonight she would laugh, drink champagne, dance and glow.

It was a damp evening with the first breath of autumn in the air. They walked past the looming church and its closely huddled trees. The house sparkled. Through its large picture window she caught sight of glittering chandeliers, women splendid in pastel dresses beside men in Oxford bags. Could they really be on the point of leaving all this behind? The door swung open and a rush of 'Oh my darlings,' and 'How amusing, how sweet!' filled the air, even newsmen and their wives affecting the manners of the voguish upper classes.

Max was stopped in the hallway. In his reports he'd been exploring the corners of the country where unemployment was hitting hardest. Men with centre partings and eager eyes surrounded him. 'Is it as bad as they say it is?' they asked.

Rhiannon entered the main reception area alone. Dancing had broken out – a riot of bodies twisting to the beat of the jazz musicians at the far end. She was asked to dance by a tall man she recalled from a previous bash and they were soon moving along with the others. The French windows had been thrown open. Couples wandered down the steps into the terraced garden, where an ornamental fountain, illumined by gaslight, threw strange shadows. Her dance partner went off to fetch her a cocktail which, when she drank it, made her giddy and happy all at once. They danced and danced again.

Her dance partner noticed her looking over her shoulder. 'Is anything the matter?'

'I was just wondering where my husband was. He's such a talker, he rarely gets to dance.'

'You're married to that German fellow, aren't you?'

'Oh, do you know Max, then?'

'Not directly. I've seen him in one of the Fleet Street pubs. He works for a German newspaper, doesn't he?'

'That's right – as foreign correspondent.'

'Now, there's a country with a future.'

'What do you mean?'

'I was over there last year. Went to one of the Nazi rallies. A great show they put on. We could so with someone like Hitler over here. He'd kick a bit sense into people – all the loafers and moaners. Just like Mussolini. He's doing great things for Italy. Got to have a firm grip.'

A sliver of sweat trickled down his brow onto his full,

complacent cheeks as he spoke. Rhiannon felt an intense, irrational dislike for him. She made her excuses and went in search of her husband.

Encircled by intent listeners Max was holding forth. 'Crisis...' she heard him say. 'Balancing payments...and unemployment...' he was well away. She sidled up to him and laid her hand on his arm.

He looked startled. 'Ah, it's you. I was wondering where you were.'

'Want to dance?'

'Why not?'

The others broke their circle to let them pass.

'Enjoying yourself?' he murmured into her ear.

'So-so.'

'There are some people I want you to meet— Jean Luc you know of course.' She smiled towards the handsome Frenchman, whose lean face and dark eyes reminded her of a portrait of Marcel Proust she'd once seen.

'—And Antoinette and Marie Claire.'

Rhiannon shook hands with Jean Luc, his wife and her sister.

'I hear you're off to Berlin?' said Jean Luc.

Max shifted awkwardly from one foot to the other.

Rhiannon turned and walked away towards the garden. Max found her sitting on a stone seat, staring into the shadows. 'You broke your promise,' she said, drawing her stole about her shoulders.

'He was there when the call came through. He just spoke out of turn.'

She watched the falling water change colour. 'Max, we need to decide this together.'

He frowned. 'Let me get you a drink.'

'Diversionary tactics?'

Later she was drifting among the revellers.

'Dance? We were going to dance.' Max nudged her towards the dance space.

'Are we friends again?'

'I don't know about that.'

Max's hand was light on her waist. 'We need to come to a decision.'

'What – here?'

After a few minutes they slipped away, walking through the darkness without speaking, their footsteps crisp on the flagstones.

Back at home they were sitting on the sofa in their living room. 'Sometimes we can will something, do everything to make it happen, but things block us. Circumstances coalesce and gravitate in a certain direction, almost despite ourselves.'

To Max, Rhiannon's high-pitched voice seemed more excitable than usual. Was she trying to convince herself that what would be would be, so the burden of personal responsibility was lifted from her?

'The party made me restless,' she added.

'I don't believe in fate but I believe in seizing opportunities when they arise. And this is one such an occasion...' he replied slowly.

'My head is going round.'

'Shall I make some tea?' he asked.

'No, I'm fine.'

More than ever Max was aware of the decorations and bits and pieces she had created to make the place into a home, like the embroidered grey cushions, now tinged silver in the light of the standard lamp. Yet the room seemed suddenly narrow, a strangers' room, or some hotel room they'd washed up into.

Must we stay here? he wanted to ask, but stopped himself, knowing it would only upset her.

She was a believer and he was not, or rather the things she placed credence in were planets apart from his beliefs. Yet without her he lacked the ability to ground himself. 'It will all work out,' she was fond of saying, whereas he relied less on the fundamental rightness of things.

'If we take up this offer – do you know how long it will be for?' she asked.

'No, I don't.'

'At the party I was dancing with some fellow singing the praises of the Nationalist Socialists...'

'Erskine, was it? Don't mind him. Fancies himself as a minor aristocrat.'

'But what if it doesn't work out there?'

'That's a risk we'd have to take.'

Max took hold of her hand. 'I think you will like Berlin.' He linked his fingers through hers. 'You could get a lot out of going.' She looked at him. 'You need to make your own way. Create your own life.'

'I know.'

'I'll work hard... It won't be forever.'

She went through to their bedroom. Sensing she needed to be alone with her thoughts, he let her be. There was no point in rushing her. She would make up her own mind. He rubbed his palm over the place she had just vacated. He could feel the warmth of her body, fading slowly. He sat there for several minutes. She left the lamp in the bedroom on, waiting for him.

Berlin

Two

'Opening session of Reichstag with Hermann Göring as Reichstag president. Adolf Hitler orders Nazi deputies to vote in support of Communist motion in order to bring down Chancellor Franz von Papen. Reichstag dissolved and new election set for November 6th'
Joseph Goebbels' Diary: September 12, 1932.

Across the mahogany desk Max attempted to assess his editor. Wolfgang Seifert was a stocky man in his mid-thirties. He was said to be tough, a devil for weeding out weak stories, but his face was round and good-natured.

Max was determined to push past formalities. He was still unclear why his boss had been so adamant that he return to Berlin. Wolfgang Seifert had seemed too busy to stop and explain. The chair creaked as Seifert leaned forward. On the desk was a silver-framed photo of a laughing blonde woman and two young girls. Max nodded towards it. 'Your family?'

'Astrid is from Sweden… We lived there for several years.' Max was already aware of this. He had also learnt that Seifert was an Internationalist and a connoisseur of wine and Expressionist paintings. On one of the walls Max noticed a photo of Marlene Dietrich. From the back rooms over the inner courtyard he heard the hammering and clatter of rollers and heavy metal presses.

'I'm relieved to see you. We've been stretched.' Seifert had a Bavarian lilt Max had not noticed before.

'I'm delighted to be here… Sorry to mention it, but can I just check you got my note about the resettlement money?'

'Where are you staying?'

17

'At *die goldene Krone*.'

'When did you send the note?'

'Before we left London.'

'We'll get something sorted out.' Seifert looked at Max so directly that he felt reluctant to pursue the matter. 'What does it feel like to be back?'

Max shrugged. 'I'll tell you in a month's time.'

'When were you last here?'

'Nine months ago, for my interview.'

'Of course.'

'I notice you changed the pictures.' Max pointed to the sultry Dietrich.

'She makes me smile. Sometimes I need that. I assume you've been keeping abreast of things?'

'I've tried.'

'Whatever impression you formed in London, I can tell you it's worse.'

'The street fights, you mean?'

'The economy has hit rock bottom. Most of it you will know – in general terms: it's all very fragile. When the Prussian parliament was dissolved out went democracy. Now…' He paused, raised his hands in a gesture of questioning uncertainty. 'The country is being run by presidential decree. You may not have realised that in London.'

'I listened to the wireless, read the newspapers. In the last few days I've seen enough swastikas for a garden fete.'

'Not everything gets reported. It's getting vicious. And now yet another Reichstag election…'

'Press restrictions? Anything new I should know about?'

'We can still report what's going on. But who knows for how much longer?'

They were interrupted as a secretary juggled the door handle and a pile of files. Max got up to help her. The editor nodded to her to put the files on an adjacent table. After she had left Seifert said: 'Some say civil war is inevitable.'

Max had heard this before and assumed the claim was exaggerated, just some subeditor flaunting a strong headline. Yet now, coming from the editor of a mainstream paper, the words had substance. A hint of anxiety flashed across Wolfgang Seifert's face.

'The soul of Berlin is being fought over. A third of Germany's Jews live here. The Nazis must win here if they're going to succeed. But the Communists will fight for all they're worth.'

'That *does* sounds like a drama.'

'It's no cocktail party.'

'I'm sure it's not.'

They stared at each other. 'I am still not clear why you called me back,' said Max.

Seifert leaned back. 'I like your approach. The pieces you did on disarmament. You get the facts. A journalist has to get out there. I'm tired of slogans.'

'What *is* the job?'

'You're replacing Kurt Stein. Now he writes for *die Vössische Zeitung*. He was one of our best.'

'I see.'

In London Max had enjoyed himself sending up the English when he felt like it, picking up snippets from pubs and parties. 'What I wrote as foreign correspondent was different. It was from the standpoint of an outsider.'

'In some ways you're an outsider here. Just what I want.'

'The English say the Germans have no stomach for democracy.'

Seifert smiled at Max. 'Ah, do they indeed. Who in particular?'

'The man on the Clapham omnibus.'

Seifert waited for an explanation.

'It's an English expression. Mr Average, you might say.'

'Are they that interested in us?'

'I mix with all sorts.'

'Democracy is under siege. The Republic is getting it from all quarters. There's a need for impartiality. A need to find out the facts and present them. Let people make up their own minds…'

'And for us?'

'If the Nazis get in they'll shut us down. Now they've started appealing to students and intellectuals, businessmen. The more we expose them – based on fact – the better. When the Press goes, it's the beginning of the end. This coming election could be vital.'

'You want me to focus on unearthing stuff about the Nazis?'

Wolfgang Seifert concentrated on the wall behind Max as if examining it. 'It's not a matter of fabricating anything. There's plenty happening, lots of stories, but people don't recognise what's going on. I want you to take a closer look at the leaders, especially Hitler. Avoid left-wing rhetoric. No Communist clichés.'

For a moment Max was uneasy. 'Did you know I used to be a Communist – as a student?'

'I may have done. I'd forgotten. It's not relevant now. You're not involved with them any longer, I take it?'

'I broke with them.'

'We were all young once. Keep away from them now. You don't want to get yourself compromised.' The editor opened a drawer and put some papers into his briefcase. 'Take the next week getting a feel of the place. By Monday, a thousand words say. I'll show you where your desk is.'

Max nodded his agreement. Yet there was something that

20

Seifert was not quite saying. He followed his boss through to the main office where he pointed to a desk in the far corner looking out over the street. Max stared at it keenly, sensing the challenge ahead, unnerved and excited in equal measure.

It was evening as Max strolled up in the direction of the Brandenburger Tor. He stopped outside the Adlon Hotel and watched a bevy of giggling women scuttle towards a tram stop. Taxis were ferrying passengers into the centre. A Rolls Royce drew up outside the Adlon. Men in dinner jackets and women in furs and luminous satin gowns were ushered inside. Money enough in there, he thought. A newspaper vendor was yelling at the street corner.

A black Mercedes sped up the street and drew to a halt outside the hotel. A chauffeur stepped out and opened the back door. Two men in leather jackets headed into the hotel. The doorman greeted them. A third man, stouter than the others, got down from the vehicle and followed them. Max thought he recognised Hermann Göring but before he had time to take a closer look the three men had merged into the opulence of the Adlon.

Three

Max had a sister, but it was a fact he would rather forget. This puzzled Rhiannon. Not that he didn't love Inge, he tried to explain, not that she hadn't been there for him when they had had to grow up quickly when their mother died – he'd been only twelve – it was just, well, complicated. The more reticent he became the more Rhiannon had the urge to press him. She was curious to know what his early life had been like and why he was the way he was. She had met Inge only twice and then on formal family occasions in Travemünde.

In Britain there was little need for Max to involve Rhiannon in his family, but in Berlin it was a different matter. Inge had offered – more out of a sense of duty than affection, Max remarked sardonically – to put them up until they found somewhere to stay. Rhiannon was eager to take up the invitation. He was not. As a compromise they agreed to pay Inge and her husband a visit.

They lived in Neukölln, a working-class area in the southwest of the city. At Rathaus Neukölln Max and Rhiannon got down in a square of decaying neo-Gothic facades. A gaggle of ill-fed, bedraggled children were playing in the gutter. Rhiannon noticed that some of them were not wearing shoes. Two trams creaked and rattled past each other over intermeshing tracks. They crossed into Spatzenstrasse. The apartment was on the third floor of a concrete block of flats.

'It's you!' exclaimed Inge when she opened the door to them. Surprise mingled with confusion on her face. 'Why didn't you call to let me know you were coming?'

'I sent a card from London.'

'That was days ago. You didn't call.'

'Well, here we are. Are you going to invite us in?'

Rhiannon was shocked by the sharpness of the exchange. Weren't they at least pleased to see each other? She said nothing but followed Inge as she ushered them into the sitting room where husband Hans grunted a greeting from behind his copy of *der Angriff*, a Nazi paper. He put the newspaper to one side and shook hands with them, as civility demanded. He, too, seemed taken aback by their presence.

'It's good you came now,' Inge altered her tone. 'Anna is having an afternoon nap. That gives us a bit of time.'

Rhiannon glanced around. The rooms were crammed with furniture and spotlessly clean, the Dresden dolls and rococo ornaments lined up on the sideboard while on another dresser photos of Hans Fichte and his kinsfolk stared back, stiff and unsmiling. A photo of Anna had been added. With a plait above her head and a plump, open little face, she was just like her mother. Rhiannon bent over the picture. 'What a lovely photo! You must be so proud of her.'

Inge gave a little smile. She tidied her already tidy bun and invited them to sit at the table before going off to the kitchen to make coffee.

Since the funeral of Max's father Rhiannon had made an effort to keep up with Inge, but Inge did not answer her letters. She claimed, in a cursive note inside her Christmas card, to be too caught up with Anna, who was a toddler now. Until recently Hans had refused to have a telephone installed. When Max had told Rhiannon not to bother writing she carried on anyway, her habit of sociability hard to break.

Hans joined them at the table. He didn't speak, instead he looked ahead as if lost in thought. She could hear a clock ticking away in an adjoining room. She glanced surreptitiously at Max. He seemed on edge. She recalled

23

being on a duty call to a distant aunt and made to suffer in silence in a well-dusted but seldom-used front parlour. At length Max and Hans managed to exchange pleasantries. Inge returned with a laden tray and placed a cheesecake and gold-rimmed cups and saucers onto the table.

Hans looked leaner and more muscular than the last time Rhiannon had seen him. 'And so, Max, you return to Berlin,' he said suddenly. 'You will not find it so easy, *weisst du?* Things are not as they were.'

Before Max had a chance to reply Inge cut in: 'Did you know Hans was promoted again? He's in charge of a branch of the Reichsbank.'

Max nodded. He had told her that since the *Katastrophen* of the previous decade people had become wary of banks and financial institutions, yet brother-in-law Hans was still scrambling up the career ladder, convincing enough people to put their money into deposit accounts instead of stuffing it behind their tiled stoves. 'My paper called me here. They need more staff on the ground,' replied Max evenly.

'I hope you will not fall under the sway of the Jewish Press.'

'*Die Tatsache* has been around for a century.'

Hans raised his voice as if addressing a meeting: 'They peddle filth in their attempt to destroy the national morale.'

Max shifted his chair back, making Rhiannon wonder what was coming next. She recalled Hans at their wedding. After too many beers he'd pontificated on the ills of the Weimar Republic. The Fatherland was benighted and only drastic action by right-thinking men could save it. Afterwards Max had told her that he'd had to move away to stop himself taking him on.

She flashed Max a warning frown.

Hans looked ready to spar. From the other side of the table Inge looked tense, but he carried on. 'Do you have any idea what's happening in this country now? Do you?' He jabbed the air with his finger. Despite his swagger, his receding chin gave him an air of hesitancy. He reminded Rhiannon of a lad in the village back home, who was always picked on to run errands.

'I'm here to find out more,' Max said.

'Then what would you do about it? These elections, for example, how will you vote?'

'Have some more cake, won't you?' Inge turned to Max with a fixed smile and for a moment Rhiannon saw the older sister attempting to put her younger sibling in his place. 'You won't have heard our latest news. We have something to tell you.' Her face was suffused with unusual ardour. 'Anna is to have a little brother or sister.'

'Oh, congratulations!' said Rhiannon. 'What wonderful news!' She smiled at the others. 'When is the baby due?'

'Mid April.'

'You must be delighted,'

'Hans,' commanded Inge. 'It is time for Sekt. To celebrate.'

Hans frowned, then sensing his moment had passed, went off to fetch a bottle of Sekt from the cold store in the basement of the apartment block.

'Max, I am afraid it would not be a good idea for you to stay here, after all,' said Inge when Hans had left the room. 'It just wouldn't work. People have started complaining about the Communists.'

'I'm not a Communist—'

'We just came to visit—' began Rhiannon.

'I know.'

'Inge, you wrote inviting us to stay,' said Max.

Inge reddened. 'Hans and I talked it over. We believe it wouldn't be for the best. There's Anna to consider. He has his standing at the bank to think about. And there's that trouble you got into with the police. People remember.'

'Your neighbours here hardly know me!'

Inge glared at Max. Rhiannon thought she looked weary, weighed down.

'Right, well we won't disturb you any longer,' said Max.

Rhiannon looked from brother to sister. Seeing them side-by-side she recognised at a glance their connectedness, and also realised how very different they were. Where Max was tall and lean, Inge was short and curvy. She had a plump round face and blue eyes, a face which wanted to please, to conform, to reassure. Max, on the other hand, had inherited the dark hair and penetrating eyes of the mother's side of the family. It lay even deeper than that: Max looked like trouble. But here, between brother and sister another dimension was struggling to assert itself. Within the family Inge would always insist on being the older, wiser one.

Rhiannon broke in. 'Inge – I brought something for Anna. In my bag here.'

Already Max had got up and was standing in the doorway.

'Just a minute,' she pleaded.

'We need to go,' said Max, frowning at her.

To cover her bemusement she adjusted the strap of her shoulder bag just as Hans reappeared clutching a bottle of Sekt and four glasses.

'*Was denn?*' asked Hans. 'What's up?'

'We won't keep you,' replied Max.

'*Kommt doch.* Let's talk things over.'

'What is there to say?' said Max.

Hans hovered, unsure what to do or say next. Max brushed past him and out of the apartment. He stood waiting for Rhiannon at the main stairwell. She shook hands with Inge and Hans and muttered excuses before hurrying after him.

'Max? You really embarrassed me.'

'Now perhaps you understand?'

'Not really.'

'It's a long story.'

'I'm listening.'

'We have other things we need to be getting on with.'

'As you wish.' She bit back her anger, now was not the time.

Four

They found somewhere to live. Rhiannon traipsed up and down the central districts, viewing and ticking off likely rooms and apartments culled from the *Berliner Anzeige*. She had been on the point of despair when she spotted the *Zimmer zu vermieten* sign in a shop window near the Zoo.

The apartment was at the top of a gabled, four-storey, ivy-clad house just off Steinplatz in Savignystrasse. The house had a faded grandeur about it. The jowled landlord was a cobbler. He lived on the ground floor with a cramped workshop overflowing with boots, lathes and straps of leather. She caught a whiff of old leather and beeswax as they passed it.

As soon as she entered the sunlit rooms her heart lifted. She could breathe freely again. A plane tree threw patterns against the windows of the sitting room and the bedroom was tucked under a sloping roof with a view of the Kaiser Wilhelm Memorial church. She feared it would cost more than Max was willing to pay, but for her the search was over.

'There must be other places,' said Max when they next saw each other.

'Must there? Well, you show me Max.'

He ran his hand lightly over hers. 'All right, all right, I'll come and take a look.'

The landlord showed them round.

'Could we have a moment alone?' Max requested after they had viewed the place. The man nodded curtly and went downstairs.

'The rooms are light and airy. As you say it's conveniently located. It's just the money…'

'I could make a home here.' She threw her arms round his waist, nuzzling into him.

He kissed the top of her head.

The landlord explained they would be sharing a bathroom with other tenants, who lived on the same floor, and then asked if they had the key money.

'I would prefer a written contract,' said Max. He had already told her that Berlin landlords could play hard and fast. The man's mouth dropped open.

'*Selbstverständlich*, of course, *mein Herr*, and you have someone to vouch for you – a bank reference?'

'We have been living in London. The bank there will give guarantees for us.'

'London?' bristled the other. There was a frisson of mutual suspicion between the two men.

'Tomorrow, we'd like to move in tomorrow.' Max reached for his wallet and unfolded several crisp Reichsmark.

'I can see no objection,' replied the man, pocketing the money.

A week later they were having a drink at Café Stein. Its cluster of candlelit round tables and its weatherworn awnings gave it an easy, casual air, making it a popular haunt of students from the nearby Technical University and Centre of Fine Arts.

'So how's your work going?' she asked.

'I've been making observations – just impressions.'

'Can I read them?'

'Not yet.'

She drew back, startled at his abruptness.

'I need more thinking time, that's all.'

She took a sip of coffee and looked round the café. 'We need more money. There are still things I need to buy.'

'We can't afford anything else right now.'

'So when will we be able to?'

'Can we just wait?' In London they had been used to eating out when it suited them. Here they would need to watch every pfennig, he said. The resettlement sum he'd finally wrested from his boss had already been swallowed up.

'How long will that be?' she asked.

'Until we get our finances in order.'

'Max, you couldn't wait to get back here and now you seem… lost.'

'It's not that simple.'

'What isn't?'

'You don't understand.'

'I believe we can make a life for ourselves here. I just hate it when you clam up and say nothing.'

Her face was in shadows from the trees in the square. She looked downcast. He knew he was being curt, unfair even, yet he did not know what to say to her. He hardly understood himself what was going on inside him. Being back in Berlin was releasing all sorts of unresolved questions. His body was taut. He wanted to get up and run, hit a punch bag.

He ordered another beer while she lingered over her white wine. Out on the street occasional cars rumbled by, dark sleek shapes, people with money going somewhere. After a moment he took her hand and intertwined his fingers with hers. 'Sorry I snapped at you. I know you're not quite at home here yet. But these things take time.'

She shrugged. 'I want to go home.'

'Let's go then.'

They walked the short distance in silence. At the entrance to the house he stopped: 'I have a couple of things to do.' She seemed on the point of protesting but he stood his ground. 'I won't be long. We'll eat in an hour, say?'

'But the food will be ready now. I've cooked a casserole.'

'It can wait, can't it, unless you're ravenous? Have a rest. You said you were tired.'

She turned and climbed the steps alone.

Five

Max strode away from the house, relieved to be alone. The impressions of the city he'd garnered so far perturbed him. Worst of all were the men hanging round street corners, kicking their heels, exuding rejection, despondency, helplessness. He had not noticed so many on his last trip. Many said the world was sliding into an even deeper depression. In Berlin the desperation was so much nearer the surface. It broke out here and there like boils in a plague. You only had to look at the boarded-up shops and dilapidated trams to see it.

Seifert had informed him that Kurt Stein had taken all his sources with him. Max had phoned him but the erstwhile colleague refused to meet, claiming new loyalties. For days Max had been going round the bars suggested by Seifert, but no one was willing to talk to him. He discovered that most of his former friends had vanished into the ether. He had become a stranger in the city of his birth.

He boarded a tram, changed on to another at Nollendorfplatz and then paced the pavement. Walking had ever been his method of confronting himself, of working things through; the mechanical one foot pounding the ground after another both cure of confusion and spur to action. He found himself in Kreuzberg. From an open window a violin was scraping. Elsewhere two people were arguing. On some window ledges flapped the Hammer and Sickle, on others the Swastika, fluttering in unison in the early evening wind. Graffiti of the *Rote Front* was scrawled next to the *Juden 'raus,* 'Jews Out.' The Nazi daubings sickened him. Many of his friends were Jews, as was his grandfather.

Bernard Schulz, his best friend at the Gymnasium, had often dragged him here to rub shoulders with 'true proletariats'. Max used to laugh at the pretension, but went anyway for the hell of it and to spite his father. The beer had also been cheaper here. The district attracted the disaffected elements of the capital, the extremes. Now opposing symbols mixed and shrieked against each other, while everywhere in the back courtyards poverty lurked.

The tenements evoked the revolution of 1918. Max was just a boy at the time, barely fifteen and still at school, but his mother had already been dead three years. He was totally caught up in the spirit of the times; it was in the air, he had breathed it in. The Spartacist Uprising lasted for nine days in January 1919 after workers seized the editorial office of a Berlin newspaper.

After the Armistice soldiers had started appearing at railway stations, looking grey and broken. Zombies in bandages, Max had thought, watching from the shadows. His teachers had warned him and his fellow pupils to steer clear of any trouble, but he was drawn despite them. The eyes of the returning troops were dead, they looked straight through you. Was it what they had been forced to do and witness? Or was it the shame from when their army was routed, and their Kaiser and leader was forced to flee to Holland? His father refused to speak about it, turning away in bitterness. Too old to serve he had watched the battles from afar, angry at his redundancy. He was a conservative, an old member of the Imperial Guard.

Though still living under his father's roof, Max had sided with the Spartacists and Karl Liebknecht when he declared a Free Socialist Republic from the balcony of Kaiser's Stadtschloss. This meant a new beginning, a passionate engagement. In Russia they'd ousted the Tsar after centuries of oppression. There the revolution was holding fast. Certainties of empire and capital were being destroyed. You only had to seize the moment. Believe in what you were doing. Max had been jubilant. Inspired. Convinced. Overnight he'd found a purpose. Artists returning from France depicted soldiers crucified and made mad by war. One, Georg Grosz, pranced around the Ku'damm with a death head on, shouting an end to the State. Yes, echoed Max: wanting an end to hierarchy at school and his father's rule. Inge, three years his senior and forever in charge, tried to talk sense into him, urging him back to his studies, but he slid away from her influence.

He and Bernard had crept closer to the fray. They were out there on the streets, watching, waiting. Until then their only escapade had been to skip school to go swimming in the Wannsee. Max had joined the Young Communists. The leftist leaders, Karl Liebknecht and Rosa Luxemburg, were captured and thrown into prison. There was outrage. Again the streets had filled up. Stones and gunshot flew through the air. There were cries of determination, shouts for freedom. The fledgling republic, only a few months in power, was in danger. So Chancellor Ebert unleashed the thuggish *Freikorps* against the insurgents, and the leaders, Liebknecht and Luxemburg, were murdered, 'while trying to escape.'

Max and Bernard were huddled with their Communist comrades, while the *Freikorps*, bigger and beefier than they were, marched towards them, steps crunching in rhythm on the pavement, guns cocked in readiness. Max was counting their steps, watching and waiting. *Eins-zwei-drei.* There was an explosion of gunfire, bullets whistling all around them through the air, hitting walls, ricocheting round their heads. Without warning Bernard slumped to the ground. A black trickle dribbled from his forehead, his limbs went floppy as a doll's. Max could not believe what he was seeing.

Hundreds had died over the nine days. But for Max the numbers meant nothing.

He coughed, his throat smarting. The familiar place names were triggering a crack in his wall of defence, leaking fears and feelings he thought were long since over. He walked faster, forcing himself back to the present.

If he needed to know what was happening in Berlin, if he wanted the true inside story, who else but his Communist friends would help him? Without making a conscious choice he found himself moving in the direction of the Communist Party branch office in Schöneberg. The editor's warning to steer clear of the Communists flashed through his mind, only to be dismissed. After all, he'd thrown away his card and had no intention of rejoining the Party.

He wandered down a crumbling alleyway and into a square with several thrift shops and a pawnbroker's on the corner. He rang the third bell on the board. Only his erratic pulse warned him he was entering a danger zone. This office had been a safe house, never busted in purges. In the meantime the Party had vacated it and a few years moved back in again. Still it stood, as innocuous-looking as ever. Impatience blotted out fear as he buzzed again.

Dieter Hartman opened the door. Dieter was a well-built man with a broad, strong face and open expression. He had lost his boyish roundness and his features were starting to sharpen. His mouth turned down in puzzlement. Max waited, astonished that Dieter was taking so long to recognise him.

'You?' said Dieter at last and gave a hearty laugh. 'I thought you were dead.' He clasped Max by the shoulders in a rough hug. '*Bist du wirklich da? Is it really you?*' They clapped each other on the back. Max felt a surge of gratitude that Dieter at least was still around. They went back to the time shortly after

Bernard had been killed. They'd attended the same school though Dieter was two years his senior.

They were in the hallway of the small office. Behind them newspapers were strewn on the floor. Sheaves of paper were piled so high they seemed to be propping up the desks with Remingtons on them. A small printing press stood in one corner. In another, metal typesetting letters were stacked in trays.

'So, what are you up to these days, *Genosse*?' asked Dieter.

'Just come from London.'

'And?'

'Got a job with *Die Tatsache*.'

'Is that so? You're looking good.'

'It's been a few years. I've got a wife.'

'Not Tanya back from the land of the Soviets?'

Max laughed. 'You've got a long memory.'

Dieter hit Max on the back. 'It's good to see you again. I thought we'd seen the last of you. A *pater familias*, eh?'

'You could say.'

Dieter fetched a bottle of beer from a cupboard. 'This is worth celebrating. Times such as these.' He poured the beer, holding a mug for Max and clinking. 'Do you want to work for us?'

'I have a job.'

'You sure?'

'I'd be in trouble if my boss found out.'

'Need he?' asked Dieter. In the past no one had had Dieter's knack of knowing what was going on, or his ability to draw out who was in whose pocket and who could be trusted. Max smiled then shook his head.

'Well, think about it.'

'Besides, I would want you to pay me.'

'There is precious little money about right now,' said Dieter with resignation. 'We're scraping groschen to make ends meet even though our circulation has gone up a bit.'

Max looked around, taking it all in. There were more machines than there used to be, but the whole place worked shabbier than before. 'So how are you, *Genosse?*'

Dieter stared at him levelly across the table. 'Why did you leave the Party?' A note of steel had crept into his voice.

Max gave a shrug, hoping that would suffice. 'I wanted to survive, make a living.'

'Don't we all? Another beer?' They laughed but their laughter was tinged with past events and dead comrades.

'I need to know what's going on in Berlin, behind the scenes, the stuff that doesn't make it to the dailies —'

There was a banging at the door. 'Dieter, Dieter, I've got the report to show you.'

Dieter swung it open to reveal a ruddy-faced man in check trousers and a worn pullover. 'I could have anyone in here with me. Don't they teach you anything these days?'

The man hesitated, shamefaced, in front of them.

'Okay Werner, *schon gut*, he's a friend.'

Werner handed Dieter a wad of typed sheets. Dieter motioned with his head. 'From the Youth Brigade, he covers the south of Berlin.' He turned to Werner. 'Wait out there? We're nearly finished.'

When the door closed behind him Dieter turned to Max, eyeing him for a moment without speaking. 'It's great to see you again.' He paused. 'You know, I could use you. If you were to consider writing something for us and I might consider telling you what's going on.'

Max had to laugh as he recognised the deal-broker of old. 'So much for friendship!'

Dieter grinned back at him. 'It is good to see you, but think about it.' He stood up, signalling an end to the meeting.

Six

Rhiannon was at the table, arms propped over a newspaper when a dishevelled Max arrived back home and threw himself onto the sofa.' So you decided to come home at last!'

'Wait till I tell you what happened,' he said.

'You've been gone two hours.'

'I met somebody from the past.'

She got up and served the food. An aroma of beef, red wine and vegetables permeated the room. 'This looks less appetising than it did an hour ago but I hold you responsible for that.'

'It looks good enough to me.' He kissed her arm as she leaned over with a plate.

'Max!' She swatted him away and then brushed a strand of hair from her face. 'Be serious now. What's going on?'

'You know I was once involved with the Communists?'

'I thought that that was years ago.'

'It was. I haven't had much to do with them in a long, long time.'

'So why are you bringing it up now?' She began to feel unsure of the ground between them. With Max she often had the disconcerting sense of something held in reserve.

He inhaled sharply, as if struggling to stay in control. 'There is so much about me you don't know. I wanted to start afresh.' The shadow of many possibilities played round his eyes even as a smile touched his lips. 'The paper wants stories about the Nazis. So far I've drawn a blank. Nobody wants to talk to me. It's beginning to rile me. I can't do my job properly.'

She watched him. He seemed ill-at-ease and was avoiding eye contact.

'I looked up an old comrade.'

'But Max you said yourself you want no truck with extreme…'

'Just listen, will you.'

'Go on, then.'

'It's like this. He wants me to work for him – just the odd article – in exchange he'd introduce me to a few people. He wouldn't pay much, but there again something is better than nothing.'

'But a Communist, Max?' She quashed a rising panic. In her mind Communists equated with radical rabble-rousers. Such men drew rabid disapproval from her relatives.

He leaned back and laughed, a little strained, she thought. 'Rhiannon, they're not a different species.'

'But they're extremists. They are against private property and the family.'

'Some of them may be, but not all of them. I wasn't thinking of joining up or anything like that. Besides, I told my boss I used to be one. When we were talking about political issues. He told me to steer clear of them.'

'You don't want to lose your job.'

'It's not just about expediency.'

'What are you trying to tell me, Max?'

'From what I've observed in the last few days it's only the Communists who have the courage to stand up to the Nazis. Many of them are Internationalists. Some of them are Jews. They, at least, stand for something. There are things they want to achieve. Everyone else just wants to stay in power.'

Embers of an old, dark fire glowed in him.

'You'd be venturing into an area where I can't follow you, Max. You do realise that, don't you?' She pushed away her half-finished dinner. 'Your job is to report, not to get involved in all that stuff.'

He snorted with frustration. 'You understand so little about it and yet you are ready to condemn.'

'Don't talk down to me like that. I've read—'

'—There comes a time when you have no choice but to get involved.'

'You can't throw your lot in with a political party! You said yourself that's not the way for you. You would do far more good being a conscientious journalist.'

'Have you been out there, trying to make sense of what's going on? Have you walked the streets hunting for a story, any tatter to hang on to?' Max turned away from the table.

'Of course I haven't. But that's not the point.' She hesitated. It would be so easy to acquiesce and go along with him without protest, yet she knew he was treading a dangerous line. 'Max, listen to me. You would be better to keep your own counsel, to stay away,' she paused, glanced across at him. 'Max, are you even listening to me?'

'I need to sleep on it,' he said quietly.

'Well sleep on it… but remember there are two of us here.'

Seven

'Does my presence distract you?' asked Rhiannon. Max had been working non-stop since first light.

'What? Not at all.' He ripped another sheet from the typewriter, screwing it into a ball and thrusting it at the wastepaper basket.

'You've hardly said a word all morning. I might as well not be here.'

'What?' He seemed surprised at her words. 'I'm working, what do you expect?'

Rhiannon considered the growing pile of crunched paper in the corner. About to tidy it away she stopped herself. Max, when he worked, existed in a world of his own. The last thing he worried about was keeping order. Besides she was not his housekeeper. She suppressed a surge of irritation, as much with herself as with him. No more had been said about his Communist contact. He said he had ideas flooding through his head and he wanted to capture them.

She did not argue. In the first days he'd proudly showed her sights, such as the Ku'damm, the Nicolaikirche and the Reichstag. With this he felt he'd done his bit. 'You're on your own now,' he'd joked on the third day. 'I'll be out a job if I'm seen to be enjoying myself too much!'

'I think I'll go for a walk.' She directed her words to his back, curved in total absorption over the desk.

'What? Yes, fine. You do that.'

'Are you here for lunch?'

'I have a meeting in an hour.'

She put on a coat, as it had become chilly, and headed

towards the Tiergarten. Usually with its buzz of activity round the cafés and ponds it reminded her of Hyde Park, but today it was deserted, apart from two children shrieking and laughing in the playground. She found a bench and sat down. Shrivelled leaves brushed her feet as wind gusted through the park. The sky was metallic with the threat of rain. She felt a tinge of sadness. She was beginning to lose heart; with Max so intent on his work, she was at a loss what to do.

The evening before in one of Max's former haunts, *Die Schnecke*, they'd bumped into an old university friend of his. While the men stacked up litres of Franziskaner beer and spent time laughing and swapping anecdotes, she'd struggled to keep up with the colloquial German. She'd asked herself if she would *ever* master the language. With its long, commemorative avenues, cellars which were bars and a strange zoo at its core, Berlin would surely test her. The winters would be severe, with snow on the ground for months at a time as icy winds blasted in from Siberia. Would she be able to settle here at all? The question goaded her. While Max was working, her hours stretched long and unfilled before her.

She had made more trips to KadeWe, eking out what she could from the few marks remaining to her. The rooms sang with splashes of red, yellow and orange in a bright array of cushions and frippery. She'd tied back the beige curtains with cheap satin, put runners on the tables and covers on the fading easy chairs. She was pleased that despite her dubious domestic skills she'd managed to turn the place into a cosy if somewhat Bohemian nest.

Yet she was bored. The walls stared back at her plain and unyielding, and outside the days grew duller. The thrills of the Museuminsel and Schloss Charlottenburg began to pall. There would be other, even greyer, days to view gilded rococo furniture.

In the meantime there was Max. There was no more talk of Dieter and the Communists. Once they'd sworn never to have secrets from each other, yet Berlin was changing him. In London a swirl of packing and terminating leases had left her no time for doubt. She began to wonder whether she'd gone along with Max's enthusiasm too readily. She had succumbed to the prospect of change, welcomed it even. Yet Berlin was more challenging than she had expected.

Was it one step too far?

She walked through trees that were swiftly shedding leaves.

Just get on with it, she told herself. It was a bright, cold day with clouds scattering before a high wind. She headed towards through the Tiergarten towards Charlottenburger Chaussee where she perched on the stone rim of Bismarck's memorial. Pigeons came pecking round her feet and she shooed them away. The fresh air cleared her head and buoyed her up. She thought of Inge with her baking and sewing. Such unswerving dedication to home and hearth were laudable, but not for her.

She carried on until she reached the British embassy, situated near the Brandenburg Gate. She would see if they had a schedule of events. The impressive three-storey stone edifice with its columns and pristine Union flag fitted perfectly into the august Wilhelmstrasse. A dapper young man in a pinstriped suit was tidying papers at the reception desk.

'Good morning. I was wondering what sort of cultural functions – talks and the like – you have on offer. I am going to be staying in the city for some time.' The man selected a couple of leaflets and slid them towards her over the counter. She flicked through what he had given her. He turned away and carried on sorting files into a cabinet. He seemed unwilling even to pass the time of day with her. She would have made a far better job of it. This gave her a flash of insight. Work. That's what she needed. Why else had she been studying English and History? And, of course, there was the Pitman's Diploma, which her uncle had insisted on.

'Sir, I have recently moved to Berlin and I was wondering what vacancies…?'

'*Vacancies*, you say?' He stared at her without smiling.

'Or agencies to find work? My German is good and improving by the day. I have a diploma in history. I have secretarial skills.'

'We are not an employment agency.'

'I realise that. I… Mr…?'

'Johnson.'

'Mr Johnson, is there anyone else I could speak to – in connection with employment? Someone in a position to tell me what situations might be open to a British subject?'

He paused, frowned, clearly piqued at the intrusion into his routine, then motioned her to sit down and grudgingly lifted the phone. It crossed her mind that she had not discussed any of this with Max. They'd had an understanding that she would concentrate on improving her German and enrol at the university. Later she might look for work.

After a few minutes a gaunt woman appeared, introduced herself as Miss Stonebridge, chief secretary, and led Rhiannon to a small side office where she drilled her about secretarial school and the university courses she'd taken. 'Quite fortuitous you calling by,' the woman eyed Rhiannon over her half-moon spectacles. 'We lost two stenographers last week. They both returned to Great Britain to get married. The sooner you can start the better. You will need to bring in your Pitman's proficiency certificate and your English and History diplomas.'

'Of course.'

'That is all for now.' Miss Stonebridge shook Rhiannon's hand and walked briskly away.

'A job at the embassy! Couldn't be better,' beamed Max. At Café Stein the awnings were flapping so hard in the wind that she and Max were driven inside where they sat at a table with a flickering candle, which oozed wax onto a saucer. 'We can do with the money. It will be good for your German too.' He motioned to the waiter for more beer. 'So when do you start?'

'Monday. I have a week's induction and then a probationary period. Bit of a dragon, she is. Two girls left to get married and you'd think from the face of her that they'd committed some crime.'

'Wedded to her work, no doubt.' The waiter banged down two steins of beer in front of them.

'I'm thankful to have found something.'

Max said nothing, just sipped his beer.

Eight

'The Reichspropaganda division has moved to Berlin. From here we can set the election campaign more thoroughly into motion. This time it will be difficult as the party coffers are empty… The clear and visionary organisation of the propaganda machine puts us in good stead. We can work with this…

Joseph Goebbels' Diary: 16 September 1932

'… journalists don't understand that at election time the main thing is the propaganda effect of the newspapers. Most are too thorough or more suited to science than the Black Arts. Our propagandists are much better. Day and night they are in constant touch with the wide masses… The best orators Germany has ever produced are in our camp…'

Joseph Goebbels' Diary: 1st October 1932

Hans Fichte was going to be late home again. He went over in his mind the excuses he would give to Inge. When she fixed him with that look of hers it made it difficult for him to stand his ground and stick to whatever version of the truth he was choosing to present her with. It was three weeks now since he had handed in his notice at the bank and joined the honourable ranks of party workers. She hadn't a clue. She still packed his second breakfast, rye bread with ham and gherkin, as neatly as ever, and gave him a peck on the cheek, wishing him a good day. She still welcomed him home with a thick pea soup with sausage and made the apartment as clean and sparkling as before.

It was worth the deceit. It would not be forever. In the end she would thank him for it. Dr Goebbels said they were entering a critical stage in the fight for the Fatherland. All hands and hearts were needed. What was it that Bismarck, the Iron Chancellor and true son of Germany, had said: Blood sweat and tears for the Fatherland? Or was it some other patriot? At any rate, who was he, Hans Fichte, to give less of himself than others were willing to give?

This evening's regional meeting had fired Hans with resolve. Dr Goebbels was of the opinion that they must not let things slide. The Nazi vote had surged in the summer but there was a danger of it tailing off. The impetus towards electoral victory must be sustained. As Doctor Goebbels rightly said, they must be firm and above all, stick together. Every party member mattered. Every action mattered. You won a tug of war by pulling together at the same time in the same direction. Those who saw things otherwise could only harm the true forward movement Germany must now take.

As Gauleiter of Berlin Dr Joseph Goebbels had responsibility for organising the election campaign. Hans was now clearer about this: it was vital to keep an eye on the information and arguments that were put before the public. It was also of utmost importance to keep a close eye on all the newspapers: regional, national and international. The sphere of influence of the Nazi Party was not to be underestimated. One always had to have a wider, deeper, grander vision than the regular Party hack. Loyalty alone did not suffice. Acute analysis of the ills facing Germany did not suffice. These were essential of course, but what mattered equally, if not more, was the art of taking the people where they needed to go, of making up their minds for them. The average man in the street was good-natured, but malleable and easily led astray by false doctrines and promises.

Once the Party had assumed office, and thereby its rightful

place in German life, Dr Goebbels hinted that there would be an immediate centralisation of all communications. With that would come complete control of everything that was written and spoken. It had to be. People were too gullible and too many lies were being broadcast about the Movement.

Hans took the steps of the apartment two at a time, energised in a way that was never the case when he'd worked as a clerk in the bank. He banged on the sides of the wall in a surfeit of joy. Things were going his way. Life had never seemed more positive. The Party was giving him enough to cover the rent – just – and some housekeeping money. Thank goodness Inge had always been a careful manager of funds. She was frugal and hard-working, and not adverse to a bit of mending and stitching like modern women were.

The main thing was that he had been spotted, selected and drawn out from the rough herd. Dr Goebbels' assistant had offered him a position in the Election Campaign office. His job was to scan with care all Berlin newspapers – and there were several hundred it seemed to him – and then to circle in red any article which might be relevant to the Gauleiter in his monumental work.

He composed his face before opening the front door. Inge should not see him looking too gleeful, after all, he had to affect the air of having worked overtime at the bank. He had to play the injured party: his employers took the liberty of asking him to stay behind to go through certain ledgers when they knew beyond the shadow of a doubt what a punctilious administrator and book-keeper he was.

Nine

It was evening and Max was wandering home from the office. He tarried by the Adlon, wondering who or what he might see tonight. As always a slew of taxis and chauffeur-driven cars came and went. Several Adler motorbikes thundered by. Still others flanked a black Mercedes, which drew to an abrupt halt outside the hotel. Several men emerged. Wearing trilbies and with their collars turned up they resembled characters from an American B film. It was then that Max recognised the diminuitive, limping Goebbels, and next to him, Adolf Hitler.

Max watched them go, baffled and curious, unable to move. This was the leader of the Nazi Party, the saviour of the people and guardian of the German spirit. The man looked more like a minor gangster. Max tried to bluff his way past the doorman but was told in no uncertain terms to quit the premises.

Over the following hours he pondered the chance meeting, wondering how to turn it to good account. The next day he was back on the streets, searching for stories.

Above all he was struck by the plight of the unemployed and their vulnerability. There must be something he could do to highlight what they were going through. He saw them shuffling about, pasty with lack of food. They turned up in the Westend outside big hotels to pipe out a tune on a tin whistle for a few groschen. He watched them shining shoes at stations and selling matches on street corners. Sometimes a spat broke out when they growled and snapped before retreating to their corners. Mostly they loitered, sharing jokes, betting tips and dog ends, and waiting. Always waiting.

The country had never been in such a parlous state. Hitler and his followers were blaming the Jews with their internationalist plots to throttle Germany, the Communists were blaming the Capitalists for their exploitative ways. Both were seeking simple explanations where none existed.

Agitated, he read *Das Berliner Tageblatt* over a mocha in a corner café. The leader article claimed the centre was splintering as Nazis and Communists gained ground. He chewed the corner of his thumbnail and watched the bartender clearing debris from the next table.

Should he write on the dangers of extremism? Pen a parody on the social utopia of Marx pitted against the wonderland of a Teutonic past where blonde maidens welcome home Wotan-like males who'd been on the chest expanders? He smiled to himself. *Schall und Rauch*, the essence of cabaret, that demi-monde of jazz and dubious sex, got so much closer to the bone than he ever could.

Dieter had recommended exploring the murky lives of these listless, unemployed men. He said a good place to start would be a labour exchange. Theories were two a penny, but encountering one of the great unwashed would paint a truer picture. Max decided to follow his advice.

In Wedding he made for the labour exchange. The squat, concrete building was situated at the end of a square. Outside hovered the usual pack of men, smoking and gaping at passers-by. They hunched together, their clothes patched and their faces drawn. On a nearby bench, Max awaited his moment. The men dispersed, one man shoved another in jest, others wandered towards a Gasthaus and two headed back into the labour exchange. One man remained behind, a stray from the pack. Max ambled over and offered him a smoke. 'How long have you been out of work?'

'A year.' The man was short and sturdy with an anaemic face.

'What line of work are you in?'

'You ask a lot of questions – you work for the police or something?' 'I'm a journalist.'

'*Ach so.*' The man seemed restless to be away, doing things, doing nothing.

'I am writing about what it is like to be unemployed.'

'So who gives a fuck about us?' The man drew deep on his cigarette.

'You don't think the government cares?'

The man guffawed, showing yellow, gap-ridden teeth. 'You must be joking.'

'What about the bosses? The union leaders?'

'When you don't have a job, you don't count. That's what. You're an embarrassment. Look at these.' He held out his hands, white and broad, shaking with emotion. 'I was trained as a locksmith, then took up cobbling, but who cares if I go hungry?'

'How many in your family?'

A look of dismay and suspicion passed over the man's stubbled face. 'What's it to you?'

'Just interested.' Because it matters, Max had the urge to say, but feared the reaction he might get. 'There've been so many problems. Bad economy. War reparations...'

The man glared at Max: 'So what's the solution, Herr Journalist?'

Max started; he was not here to reveal his own analysis. 'We have lost our trust,' he said, playing for time. 'Most no longer believe what politicians say. They claim to be for the workers but turn against them at the first sign of trouble.'

'*Verdammt noch mal.* What's to be done? Nobody wants the Communists. Nobody trusts them. The other day the Nazis were round collecting in our square. Now they seem to be getting something together. Giving us back a pride in being German.' His voice trembled with self-righteous indignation. His hand made a fist. 'Teach us how to be men again! Now there's party I would vote for.'

Inside Max shrivelled. Men needed more than bread and a critique of capitalism. They needed a sense of purpose. Years ago he'd forced himself to read the turgid and ranting pages of *Mein Kampf.* Talk about struggle, he'd had to grit his teeth to finish it. It struck him as grandiose and cut off from reality. Yet he could not deny it was pierced through with a certain perverted passion. Men such as the one before him were the perfect prey. Denigrated and redundant, they rumbled on and nobody seemed to care or be able to do a thing about them. He, and thousands like him, were burning with an unquenchable fury.

Max made his excuses and moved away.

'This is good.' Wolfgang Seifert leafed through Max's article. 'Makes chilling reading. You haven't wasted much time getting a feel of the place.'

Max and his boss were sitting in the Wilhelmstrasse office late in the afternoon. Most of the other reporters were out on assignments. In the back offices the secretaries were tapping away. With another two days before the paper was put to bed there was a relative lull before the tempest. Seifert leaned back in his chair and cupping his chin in his hand appraised Max. 'It's a good beginning. You've got to get a sense of what's happening here before you can proceed.'

Max was thoughtful. With his keen description of the forced idleness of a worker he'd scraped the tip of a treacherous and jagged iceberg. But it was not for this that he had been summoned, summarily, back to the capital.

'Yet we need to do more if we want to come through. There's a Reichstag election in the offing.'

'I'm not sure I'm following you.'

'You know all about Dr Goebbels? He's a shrewd number. They say he knows the art of persuasion and image better than anyone. He was to become a priest but then stopped believing in God. So now National Socialism is his religion. I guess you could say Adolf Hitler is his saviour. It's against the likes of him that we have to do battle.'

In London Max had read about Goebbels' tactics and the countless rallies he'd conjured up to bring the charismatic Austrian misfit to every corner of the republic.

'You're not alone in this.' Seifert leaned forward. 'We have to give the lie to this adulation that's building. Disprove that the Nazis are the party of law and order, the party of the people. We've got to enlighten people. Get some stories that prove, absolutely prove, that these men are a pack of thugs. Not fit to be deputies in the Reichstag, let alone lead the country. You need to get in there and find out what you can. Infiltrate them if you like. Find out more about their private lives. Whip the masks away, so people see them for what they are.'

'Is that all?'

'Yes, that's all,' replied Seifert missing the irony in Max's voice. 'I've been a newspaper man for too long to sit by and see the free press ripped to shreds by a bunch of cretins.'

'I saw the man himself, last evening.'

'Goebbels or Hitler?'

'Well, both of them, actually.'

'You never know when they're in town. They come and go all the time.'

53

'They arrived in a great big Mercedes at the Adlon and were dining in style, I'd say.'

Seifert sighed: 'You see what I mean about getting in with the Establishment? Who else can afford to dine in the Adlon? And they've made the Kaiserhof Hotel their unofficial headquarters in Berlin. You often see them there.'

'The doorman barred me when I tried to bluff my way in.'

Two secretaries emerged clutching sheets of paper for the editor to go through. Seifert looked up. 'I'd better get on with this. Come to me if you have any more questions.'

'Will do.' Max considered the editor for a moment. The connection he'd rekindled with Dieter flashed through his mind.

Ten

Max took once more to the streets. As the Reichstag Election approached, parties were vying with each other for pillar space. The streets became scratchy with contention, most prominent were the posters and scrawled graffiti of the Communists and Nazis. Posters shouted at him. Heroic Nazis with resolute jaws and bulging muscles thrashed effeminate parliamentarians and the Red Peril, while almost bursting out of their posters the equally virile Communist Workers demanded *Brot und Freiheit (bread and freedom)*. In more restrained tones, as though they already knew the game was up, the Social Democrats urged support of the republic and warned against extremism. Humourless the lot of them, Max grunted to himself. On one column was a faded and tattered advert for Kurt Weill's jazzy opera, *The Rise and Fall of the City of Mahoganny*. Its silhouetted, slinky figures spoke of the modern, zany era, promising pleasure and diversion.

As Max stood amid the traffic, catching the whiff of petrol and flattened horse dung, he watched a Brown Shirt ripping down a Communist poster and plastering a Nazi one over the gap. Fifteen minutes later, passing the same spot, he spotted another Communist poster stuck, skew-whiff, over the Nazi one. In London he'd known of these clashes, but seeing them acted out like this had an almost slapstick effect.

One thing, above all, was clear: most viewed the ruling Social Democrats as Public Enemy Number One. All other parties were thirsty for their blood. The Social Democrats were blamed for everything, especially the shakiness of the economy. At meetings he'd heard people rail against them for the miserable Versailles settlement, which ceded Silesia, the Ruhr, Saarland and much else. Throw in the scuttling of the navy and the army reduced to a handful of soldiers, yelled the Nationalists, and there you had it. The Social Democrats were traitors. Both Communist and Nazi posters caricatured them as ineffectual officials in frock coats, driven out by hefty workers who heralded a new future.

Max had agreed to meet Dieter in Neukölln. He got to the meeting point early. While he waited he found a café and scribbled notes. He described the poster war, the boarded-up shops and the old women who grumbled as they formed endless queues. He thought of his meeting with the editor. Snapshots of the city on its heels were all very well, but where was he meant to find those hard-nosed, concrete stories about the evils of the Nazi Party? He had to find a way of getting closer.

'There are rumours of a strike against the State transport system,' Dieter said when he showed up, half an hour late, harried and unkempt. Max reflected that his old friend seemed to be letting himself go. Sigi, his former partner had cleared off for Hamburg months before.

They walked until they came to a bench in front of an abandoned playground. 'What's it about then?'

'Not sure. I've been too taken up with the paper to go to any meetings.'

'You must have some idea?'

Dieter puffed up his cheeks and expelled air from them. 'It's down to general dissatisfaction. It's a way of getting back at the State. Strangest of all, now there's talk of Nazis and Communists joining forces to picket outside the U-Bahn stations. Some say Papen will declare martial law. But nobody seems to care.'

'What! You must be joking. They're sworn enemies.'

'You shouldn't be surprised. The government has lost all control. Everyone is just doing deals. It's getting desperate. The *Zentrum* party has approached the Nazi High Command to see if they can form a coalition. As for the Nazis and our lot, one minute they're beating the shit out of each other, the next they're up there, shoulder-to-shoulder in bogus solidarity, just to bring down the government.'

'But how could they?'

'It's Realpolitik.'

'I thought at least your lot had ideals.'

'The end sometimes justifies the means, don't forget.'

'Don't give me clichés, Dieter. Have you forgotten what they stand for?' Appalled, Max was the apostate who, despite himself, held the icons dear.

'Both parties happen to be in agreement on this matter. That's all. It's tactics, pure and simple. Welcome to Berlin. It's not so stupid. It's a temporary manoeuvre. By the way, do you have anything for me? We're going to press tomorrow.'

'I haven't even agreed to writing for you yet. I said we'd see. I'm still working my way in. Besides, you haven't given me any decent links— So where do you stand on this strike?'

Dieter sniffed and lifted his left shoulder a little. 'Chickenfeed. I don't think it will achieve anything. But let's wait and see. Max, when will you have something for me?'

'Not at the moment.'

Dieter kicked at the ground with impatience. 'You can't sit on the fence forever. Anyway, I better go. Do you want to meet the others?'

'Not now.'

'See you then. Look out for the SA, the *Sturmabteilung*. They've become the bullyboys of the Nazi Party. And they've really got it in for us – and the Jews, of course. Nobody would have taken any notice of them a few years ago.'

He watched Dieter retreat to a nearby *Gasthof* where his comrades awaited him. Max was keeping his distance from the Communists, but Dieter was another matter. He was an old friend, someone he couldn't help but trust. His eyes watered in the wind and he wrapped his coat closer. Two mothers with a bunch of scruffy offspring between them wandered into the play area. The children broke loose and ran around shrieking and pulling at each other. A bus trundled by, half full.

There was a time when Max would have given all for the Cause. As he made his way back to the U-Bahn station shadows of that past fell round him. There was there a taste of blood in his mouth, the stench of cordite in his nostrils.

After Bernard died he was determined more than ever to fight. The forces of the state were reactionary, tied up with protecting the interests of those who had wealth, status and power. He yearned to throw in his lot with the Communists. Only they would yank out the rotten roots of society and supplant them with something new. They had structure, authority and a common purpose. At the university there was a cadre of groups yet he held back from becoming a member of the Party, awaiting his moment.

Tanya Goldberg had a Russian mother and a German-Jewish father; her parents had met when the father visited Moscow as part of a trade delegation when the czars still held sway. Her mother, a daughter of peasants, had been at a market with her father when the delegation visited.

Tanya had flaming red hair and a temper to match. Max had never known anyone like her. She was a force of nature, who came blasting into his life and led him a merry *sema*. Until Tanya, his Communist leanings had fired the brain alone, but she caught the longings of the angry student and flung them back at him magnified. From the moment they met there was an unending flurry of argument, love-making and crashing through limits. Max moved out from home against the protests of his father and Inge, and took up with Tanya in her shabby attic atelier in Oranienstrasse. Father cut off his allowance. Max grew his hair long and started skipping lectures. Tanya painted, sometimes smoked opium and had her arms tattooed.

Max shared her apartment and the chaotic intensity of her life. Through her colours became keener, sorrows deeper. Faces were lit from within, words had layered meanings. Every dawn was an event. Painting was arduous and she was tired of being poor, but there was no other way. She had to do it. Her canvases were live beings inhabiting their space, whispering to him by day, disconcerting him in the early hours. At times, to distract herself, she resumed her studies of English, but not for long.

One day Tanya received a letter. Darkness suddenly encompassed her, shutting out all other concerns. At the time he was uncertain how to react, for he'd learnt that just as she blew hot as a desert wind she also carried within her the gloom and despair of a tundra winter.

As she'd fingered the crushed letter with stamps from the new Soviet regime he sensed it augured something momentous, her very silence portended ill. In Russia her grandmother was sick and asking for her. Collectivisation was afoot, and her grandmother's land had been earmarked by the government. The Supreme Soviet had decreed that this was the best way forward, the *only* way, in fact, to see that the country was fed after the harsh oppression of the czars. Tanya went along in principle with the policy: it was rational, it was good for the future. But her grandmother was suffering and needed her. She had to go to her – her own mother suffered from bouts of extreme nausea, which made it unwise for her to travel, her father had died the year before from a premature heart attack. Tanya was the only one who *could* go.

Max had insisted on joining her. She managed to get him a travel permit as by now he had signed up with the German Communist Party. Together they undertook the journey to Moscow and from there they travelled by train and horse trap to the village, which lay over two hundred *verst* further south.

The countryside was in upheaval. Everyone was on the move. The Communists had declared war on the rural population, which for the most part had remained unaffected by the Bolshevik coup. Brigades and komissars from the big town soviets were surging into the rural regions to seize grain. Everywhere Max looked he saw chaos, dereliction and dismay. *Kulaks*, the richer peasants, were being forced to give up their grain. Some were accused of hoarding and summarily executed. Shortly after the October Revolution Vladimir Lenin had described the *kulaks* as 'bloodsuckers, vampires, plunderers of the people…' and ordered a hundred *kulaks* to be publicly hanged as an example.

When they arrived at Kolya Tanya presented their credentials to the local komissar, who granted them permission to proceed. Tanya's grandmother was on the point of collapse. They entered her *izba*, her wooden dwelling, which was squat, sunken into the ground and modest by any standard despite its ornate carved lintels. The old lady was hovering in a darkened room where formerly she would have lit a candle before an icon. Now only the stove glowed darkly.

'She's so shrunken,' whispered Tanya, visibly in shock. 'She was always so strong. Did the work of a man in the fields…'

The old woman tottered to the stove, making them a gruel, which tasted more of salt than meat. Then the two women sat at table, lost in talk. Tanya kept watching the door. It was the first time Max had seen fear in her face. Later she'd explained how her grandmother had been accused of being a greedy *kulak* for the few cows and hectares she owned and how she had worked together with her husband until he died. They were all she had. Now the brigade from Moscow had carted off the grain and vegetables she'd produced. Unlike many others she had not had the foresight to hide them. Tanya did not know how her grandmother would see out the winter.

Max caught his lover's anguish and anger. It made him nervous. He had never experienced her so unsettled. 'It's part of the Five Year Plan,' she muttered with irony. 'I thought I was a revolutionary until I saw this.' He knew there would be no stopping her. Already she was on a collision course with destiny, much as he decried the term. Just as clearly he knew the komissars would brook no resistance; they had just appropriated hectares of peasant land, as they saw fit. Their attitude was hardening.

Tanya begged an audience with the kommisar; she would use her powers of persuasion to see her grandmother safe, to stave off the worst of the brigade's reforming zeal. She argued and grew red in the face while Max sat by, helpless, wishing he could speak Russian. They made pledges, the old lady would not be harmed. Her neighbours would take care of her. The new social order was for everybody. There would be an equitable redistribution for the good of all. Tanya was not convinced but there was little, for now, that she could do about it. She was admonished to return to Berlin like a good student and to bring credit and new skills to the Soviet fatherland when she came back, as they hoped she would.

Back in Berlin she became the worst of the Furies, organising, protesting, taking meetings by the scruff of the neck and shaking participants awake. A reckoning was coming. There would be a famine. Starvation. People would die in their thousands. The politicos in the cities did not know the peasantry. They did not love them. Already the civil war between Reds and Whites had seared through the country, but more terror was to come, they had not seen the worst of it. The German Communist party should stand up against the Politburo. But the more she railed, the more her German comrades sidelined her and wrote her off as a half-crazed artist.

That winter she returned to Russia. Max had been in Hamburg on a writing project. She left a note for him in the Oranienstrasse atelier; she had gone to see her grandmother, knowing the severity of the season, the lack of food. She had gone to see her, knowing it might well be the last time. She said he was not to follow her. The Cheka, the soviet secret police were taking over where the Okhrana of the czars had left off. Neighbour was spying on neighbor. The villages were being destroyed. She had sources of information, a few friends who could still be trusted. On no account was he to follow her.

Max caught a train eastbound but when he tried to enter Russia he was turned back at the frontier. He tried three times. It was futile to argue. His German Communist card no longer saw him through. Weeks later he received a letter from Tanya's mother. As a former citizen she had written time and again to the Soviet authorities and demanded an explanation for her daughter's disappearance. In time an official, standard letter arrived: it informed her that Tanya and her grandmother had been relocated and were fine. The good lady should now cease her communications as the People's office had other, far more important, matters to attend to, the fate of two individuals could not be expected to take up more of their precious, revolutionary time. The mother came and took all Tanya's paintings. Max was too grief-stricken to try and stop her.

He made one last assault on the ever-growing Soviet bureaucracy but was blocked. His search had become futile. From another source he learnt that peasants from Kolya were seen to be troublesome and had been herded northwards. Months later he received a smuggled letter from Tanya. Her grandmother was dead. She herself had joined a revolutionary cadre and had married a comrade.

At first he only half believed it, though the handwriting was unmistakably hers. Bitterness alternated with depression: the only woman he had ever loved had deserted him. In the end he accepted it. Tanya was a creature of imagination, always on the wing. She could not be constrained. In disgust with her, with himself, with the lumbering, callous machinery of Revolution he tore up his Party card and made arrangements to visit Britain.

Eleven

Miss Stonebridge handed Rhiannon a wad of papers. In the gloomy cubicle of an office assigned to her, Rhiannon flicked through the pile. This was not quite what her studies in London led her to expect, but it was a start. At first her fingers were clumsy. She had to pull out several sheets and start again, but after a while she fell into a rhythm and her fingers flew over the keys. When she checked what she had done, she was delighted to discover only two errors. Miss Stonebridge muttered a considered approval. By lunchtime Rhiannon's arms and back were aching. Miss Stonebridge emerged from her office and declared it was lunchtime.

With its long tables and rows of functional chairs the canteen reminded Rhiannon of her old school refectory. 'We keep ourselves to ourselves here,' Miss Stonebridge told her when they had taken their food and placed themselves at one of the empty tables. A controller if ever there was one, thought Rhiannon. A few minutes later Miss Stonebridge got to her feet and tidied her blouse though it was perfectly in order. 'I need to speak to someone. I'll see you back in the office.'

Rhiannon considered what remained of her burnt braised beef and dry carrots. She pushed the plate to one side and propped her elbows on the table wishing, fleetingly, that she'd taken up smoking. She could do with something right now. Certainly she had survived her first morning in the embassy, but if the job had no more to offer than a dingy pigeon-hole of an office and a crow of a boss, it would be hard to sustain.

She was on the point of quitting the canteen when two men

walked in. One was tall and thin. He had a slight stoop and a deep laugh which seemed to fill the space around him. He was leaning over a younger man, who with dark skin, lively brown eyes and a yellow cravat, appeared to be Indian. There was a looseness and freedom about the men, which were at odds with the austere surroundings. She found herself drawn to them. And they had noticed her.

'May we join you?' asked the shorter of the two. 'My name is Sid Khan, and this is Robert Denning, cultural attaché at the embassy. At your service, Madam.' Unsure whether they were being facetious or playful, Rhiannon nodded. 'You're new here, aren't you?' asked Sid Khan.

'Yes. I'm on trial – I mean probation.' She smiled her confusion as she shook his hand. 'Under Miss Stonebridge.'

'Ah, the clock-watcher,' said Robert Denning. 'A good egg, but she doesn't like her girls to mix with the likes of us.'

'And you? What is your work here?'

'We're just passing through, on secondment.'

'To do what?' she asked, emboldened by their friendly manner.

'To increase mutual understanding between the two cultures.'

'Ah, I see. And what does that involve – exactly?'

'We organise talks, concerts and other worthy items of cultural exchange,' he replied with such insouciance that she burst out laughing.

'Sounds wonderful. Do tell me more. How do you find out about these things? I haven't seen any notices.'

'No you won't have. Next month's meetings are about to be put up. Look tomorrow on the staff noticeboard in the corridor. Something for every taste.'

'You must know Berlin well?' replied Rhiannon.

'So – so. And you?'

'We've only been here a few weeks. I'm trying to get to know the city better.'

'If you really want to find out what's going on in this place you should go to a nightclub.'

She glanced at her watch.

Noticing, Robert Denning smiled. 'It wouldn't do to be late back late from lunch on your first day, not with the punctilious Miss Stonebridge!'

'And your name?' asked Sid Khan.

'Rhiannon Dienst.'

'Dienst?'

'I'm married to a German.'

'I see,' said Khan.

She felt herself blushing. Robert Denning got to his feet. 'A pleasure to meet you,' he said and walked away.

'So your husband is a journalist?' asked Khan. 'I'd like to meet him. What does he write about?'

Rhiannon, who'd spent the morning wading through countless menus and seating plans, was grateful for the diversion. She looked at Khan for a moment, trying to assess him. 'So far he's been doing feature articles, stuff on unemployment.'

'Is that so? And what did he do before?'

'In London he was a foreign correspondent.'

'Writing up the English? That must have been a lark.'

'It was. He loved it.'

'Now he's back in Berlin he'll presumably need to link up with as many people here as he can.'

'That's what he says. But I don't think he's finding it easy.'

'Oh, and why is that?'

She hesitated, wary of saying more. 'Better ask him yourself, Mr Khan.'

'Would you like to go to a cabaret with Denning and myself? The two of you, I mean.'

She laughed, taken aback at the suddenness of the invitation. 'Sounds fun. I'd better check with Max. If he has time, I'm sure he'd like to.'

'What paper does he write for?'

Just then one of the kitchen staff clattered away with a trolley of dirty plates, startling her. She looked up at the canteen clock. 'Sorry! I better go. I don't want to give the wrong impression…'

'No, mustn't let that happen,' he said.

She scooped up her things and scurried out of the canteen while Khan turned to watch her go.

Twelve

The Troika, hidden down a dim side street off the Ku'damm, was not easy to find, but Max knew it from the past. He had spent many carefree, rousing evenings at the cabaret with Tanya or with Dieter and the old crowd. What songs they had sung, what talks they had had, what fights! Now as they drew near to it he wondered how the place might have fared in the meantime.

They descended wrought-iron steps into a basement bar, eerily lit by blue lights. On the walls curled the familiar, worn posters of cabarets in Paris, Budapest and Vienna, handwritten menus, signed programmes and manifestos of long-gone political meetings. He smiled to himself, glad to be in a Berlin milieu he recognised.

Inside, spotlight beams collided on the podium where a woman in a Reichsbanner uniform and another in Nazi garb were ranting that someone had stolen their cat. 'It was the Gypsies!' shouted one. 'No, the Catholics!' shouted the other. 'No, the Jews!' yelled the first. 'Yes. Yes,' agreed the other. A man in a prayer shawl and a yarmulke wandered on with a cat. 'Does this belong to you?' he asked. In response they set about cudgelling him while others sang, 'Always blame the other, never yourself. Always the other.' The Nazi goose-stepped wildly until collapsing onto her backside to delighted roars. A woman in a sleek black jacket sidled in and wailed in a deep Blues voice about the need to follow your heart and not your fear.

Smoke spiralled and thickened towards the ceiling. People huddled round tables under low-hanging lights, waiters and waitresses in zebra suits wove in and out with beer and champagne. The men were smooth-faced and heavily made up while the women wore their hair cropped and had severe expressions.

Rhiannon spotted her embassy colleagues, ensconced in a corner with heads bent in talk. The smaller of the two got up to greet them. 'Sid Khan.' Khan extended his hand. The other man remained seated, waiting to be introduced. As they settled round the table Max was aware of Khan sizing him up. His colleague, Denning, stretched out his legs with such apparent nonchalance that Max was convinced he was doing it for pure effect. He smiled to himself; English upper-class *sang froid* no longer fazed him. Khan ordered more Sekt. Max asked how long they had been in Berlin. Denning's response, detailing their length of stay and respective roles, struck him as rehearsed. These men would be all things to all men. 'So what does a cultural attaché do – exactly? Apart from come to venues like this?' he asked.

'We set up opportunities for mutual exchange between the host country and Britain.'

It all sounded so anodyne – boy scouts and concerts – it made Max want to probe further. 'Do you? Is that all?'

'It's enough,' said Denning.

'Relations are at a pivotal stage right now,' added Sid Khan.

'Because of the Reichstag elections, you mean?' said Rhiannon, puzzled. Max glanced across at her. She seemed nervous, troubled even as she swirled the wine in her glass. Though part of her longed to better the lot of the poor the cabals of party politics set her on edge.

'Most people in Britain couldn't care less about the elections here,' he said.

'Is that so?' countered Denning. 'I am not sure I am of the same opinion.'

'That was my experience.'

'Actually, my aunt Vicky meets a lot of politicians,' offered Rhiannon hopefully. 'She says people are watching Germany with concern.' The men looked at her and said nothing. The waiter arrived with another bottle.

'Rhiannon says you're a journalist?' Denning broke the silence.

'Yes, that's right.'

'You work for one of the party organs?' asked Khan.

'Independent,' he said.

'No such thing!' exclaimed Khan. 'You have to come down one side or the other.'

'*Das Berliner Tageblatt* is the nearest thing to an objective voice around here,' Khan stated, waving his hand in the air. 'I've been following the independents. Not afraid to stick their necks out.'

'We are not yet under censorship,' said Max.

'Another glass?' Khan poured more wine.

A spotlight picked out a figure hidden in the shadows. *'Der Geist der beängstigt,'* said a placard above it: the spirit that instils fear – a play on Goethe's Mephisto. This figure, all in white, with plastered face and hair spiked up with cream, went round with a white stick ready to batter people over the head. Other figures appeared. 'I just came to see how my neighbour was,' said one, and straightaway the white ghost struck him dumb. 'I have an idea for a free society,' said another and towards him the ghost was brutal, hammering his head until he shrieked. Two figures were jigging around. 'We deal in fear, we live, breathe, eat it,' they chanted, chasing each other and screaming. In the audience strained laughter gave way to sudden talk and coughing.

'What was all that about?' asked Rhiannon. 'It gave me the creeps.'

'The further you get into cabaret the bolder the critique' said Khan. 'There are things going on in this city that people should know about. Another cabaret we could take you to not far from here.' He leaned in towards them. 'If you wanted to…'

'Steady on, old boy,' Denning broke in in mock joviality. 'Don't want to put the frighteners on people.'

'We're fine here,' replied Max. Though he sounded calm he was disturbed by the tenor of the place. The atmosphere was distinctly jittery. A year ago it had been more convivial.

Gradually the frenzy of the cabaret mellowed into muted conversation as people began to leave. The lights were turned down. Smoke continued to curl up from candles and cigarettes, creating a cloud, but thinner now than it was before. The gleam of satin evening gowns grew rare as the fast set moved on.

'So how is it writing for *Die Tatsache?*' Khan extracted the bottle of Sekt from an ice pail and proceeded to pour. 'You did say you wrote for *Die Tatsache*? Or was it *Die Rote Front?*'

'I didn't say,' Max sipped. 'A good vintage.' He paused. 'But I do work for *Die Tatsache.*'

'What do you write about?' asked Khan.

'In Berlin how many topics can there be? The money market, art reviews, who's bashing whom in the back streets.'

A fanfare and flash of lights interrupted them. A row of scantily clad, well-built women filed onto the stage, each with the right hand on the shoulder of the one in front. The drum beat. They swivelled in unison and confronted the audience. Only at second glance did Max realise they were transvestites, their chins and legs smooth as a girl's. They did the Can-Can, kicking long legs in the air and revealing red bulging panties. Max turned back towards Khan and Denning. 'So how do you penetrate the heart of Berlin – gauge the lie of the land, as you British put it?'

Khan lit a cheroot, offering the box to the others. 'Easy. You just have to stay around long enough.'

'And what is your analysis?' asked Max while Denning, deep in thought, examined the bottom of his glass.

'The Germans are searching a solution to their dire economic and social stress,' said Denning. 'So far they've not come up with anything.'

'That is evident.'

Before he could pursue the matter Khan chipped in. 'So, do you specialise, Herr Dienst?'

'I comment on what I see, report what I hear from reliable sources.'

'Do you know what fascinates me most about this country?' Khan paused, looking round the table, a touch of the showman about him, 'Right now it's a cauldron of possibilities.'

'You could have fooled me,' replied Max.

'A time of need, yes. There's unrest, yes. But out of necessity come great things. The break-up of certainties can be good. It can usher in new ideas through a process of fermentation. New structures arise. The collapse of the medieval worldview gave way to the Renaissance, don't forget.' Khan was warming to his subject.

'Look at India... the Empire is moribund, but we still have the structures. Gandhi will win in the end. No doubt about it... by sheer force of numbers and because – the Empire is a dinosaur. Wonderful in its way – for the British, at least – but an anachronism, more for the last century than this one.'

The Sekt was loosening his tongue. Max could scarcely imagine him spouting such stuff before the ambassador. With his broad flat face and quick eyes Khan had an animation and intelligence about him that drew one in. Denning, on the other hand, struck him as canny, what Rhiannon might describe as a dark horse. His steely eyes under bristling black eyebrows penetrated without giving much away.

Talk drifted onto the illegal transport strike, which was still in the offing. Then they veered back to the forthcoming Reichstag election. Khan spoke of things reaching fever pitch, of the lack of resolution. Max could see that Rhiannon was tired. It was late, by now she must be longing for bed. Yet something urged him to hang on.

'At heart,' said Khan. 'If I can trade with someone, I do. No desire to be superior or over-acquisitive. We get to hear a lot – about people – what they're up to, that sort of stuff… A journalist like you would need fresh copy, different angles. A chance to move beyond cant and left-wing rhetoric.'

Something in Max lifted. 'Facts are what I need,' he said as calmly as he could. 'Stories. People want to know what's happening.'

Khan added slyly: 'Who is in whose pay. Who's leaning on whom. Who's corrupt and who isn't. As you know, everyone has their price.'

'Not necessarily.'

'In the end it comes down to how hungry you are,' said Khan.

Max decided to grasp the moment. 'You know lots of people, do you – of every persuasion?'

Khan was immediately cagey. 'How do you mean?'

'People from across the political spectrum, from left to right. I'm looking for background stuff, about political leaders.' Max's head was growing muzzy from the Sekt. It was time to back out and reflect on what had passed between them. *Reculer pour mieux sauter,* as the French said. 'It's been a pleasure to meet you gentlemen. Now if you will excuse us, I think we'll take our leave.'

'We do meet all sorts,' said Khan slowly. 'Some might

interest you. You need to find out more about right-wing extremists in Berlin, I believe?'

Max threw a quick glance at Rhiannon, wondering what on earth she'd been saying at work. Rhiannon got up and excused herself, heading towards the Ladies. Khan continued. 'We might be able to give you a few introductions, a few leads.'

'And why would you do that for me?'

'There are stories which need to be told,' interjected Denning, suddenly solemn: 'for the public good. Nobody dares speak their mind.' He locked his arms across his chest. 'Somebody has to. We get to know things but can't broadcast them, whereas as a journalist you are well placed. But it's difficult to meet publicly.'

'Why?'

'We can't be seen to cavort with German investigative journalists. But maybe through Rhiannon…'

'I can't put my wife at risk.'

'Of course not, but you'll think about it at least?'

'I am open to suggestions,' Max replied slowly. His mind was still scanning the possibilities when Rhiannon reappeared with her jacket.

'Time to go!' she said brightly. 'Most of us have to work tomorrow.'

Max grimaced at her. She was right. It was high time. They took their leave and gained the dark streets.

It had been raining. The surfaces were glistening with moisture. Not wanting to slip in her heeled shoes Rhiannon linked her arm through Max's and looked down at the uneven flagstones as they walked. Scenes from the cabaret went flashing through her mind. The sight of those emotionless women in uniform and those silk-cheeked, pretty boys made her feel provincial. Then there was all that had passed, spoken and unspoken, between Max and the other two. 'What did you make of them?' she asked, impatient to probe his impressions.

He carried on as though he had not heard.

'Max, are you listening?'

'I heard you,' he said quietly.

'Then?'

'What did you say to them about my work?'

'Not a lot. Why – what's the problem?'

'He seemed more than curious. Did you mention I'd been asked to do stories on the Nazis?'

'Not specifically.'

'He seemed to know so much.'

'I may have said something. I can't remember exactly?'

'I have to know who I can and can't trust. Don't you understand that?'

'They work for the British embassy for goodness' sake.'

'Within the British embassy there are those who favour the Nazis. Those who think it is in Germany and Britain's interests to support the fascists.'

'Max, you are seeing dangers where none exist.'

'And you are being incredibly naïve.'

Angered, she pulled away from him, releasing her hand from the crook of his arm. For a moment she teetered before regaining control. They wandered on for a few yards in silence. A trumpet blared in a nearby café, its neon lights flickered, silhouetting his profile. He looked more focussed and graver than usual. 'And what's going through that head of yours now?' she asked with mock bravura.

'I don't like the way things are going.'

'Max, you were really strange in there.'

'Uncertainty is getting to people. Cabaret used to be about

75

entertainment. Now it's saying things people are afraid to express…'

'So?'

As they turned into Savignystrasse he rifled in his pocket for the house key. She followed him up the stairs. When they reached their rooms, before even switching on the lights, he took off her jacket and held her close. He brushed her cheek with his lips and kissed her forehead. She sensed tension in his body, the slightest tremoring. 'You need to understand that I don't want you to get dragged into anything,' he almost whispered. 'You don't know… I'm not sure about the future here.'

'No one knows the future,' she said. 'What's the point of worrying…'

He kissed her roughly on the mouth, taking her breath away, his clasp almost harsh. Then he sighed and pulled back, started stroking the top of her head. 'Berlin is not what it was. I no longer know how safe it is here.'

'Oh Max, it's all right. It's going to be all right.' She broke free from his grip. 'Look at me.'

She reached up and turned his face towards her. He stared down at her then buried his face in her hair. For a moment they clutched each other without speaking.

'Come on,' he murmured. 'It's late. Let's get to bed.'

They made love, hungrily, hastily, with an air of desperation. She sensed herself drawn along on a dark, storm-riven flood. They dozed, woke and made love again, this time more slowly and tenderly. She lay in his arms, murmuring whatever came into her head, aware she was hardly making sense, aware he was hardly listening. She traced a finger along his clavicle. He began to snore lightly and she pulled away. She closed her eyes and moved over to her side of the bed. Voices came in from the street, a drunkard singing incoherently into the night. For a while she tried to decipher what he was singing about. Max's words floated above her, disembodied. However hard she attempted to push them away they pursued her. Her heart throbbed against her rib cage. Eventually, exhausted, she drifted into a fitful sleep.

Thirteen

'...This year we have not been clear of election campaigns. And everyday we have to contend with upsets in the organisation, with financial concerns, and personal frictions... The longing for 6th November and an end to the election battle is indescribable...'
Joseph Goebbels' Diary: November 1st 1932 Kaiserhof

'We have put large posters on the pillars stating our position to the strike. They have made a mad proposal: anyone who fails to appear for work is dismissed on the spot. Of course no one turns up. Berlin has become a dead city...'
Joseph Goebbels' Diary: 4th November 1932

'It's happening after all,' said Max one morning when they were both preparing to leave for work. He was cramming his various notebooks into an old satchel while Rhiannon twisted round and looked over her shoulder to ensure that the seams on her stockings were straight. She hoped her bright red dress would not be too much for Miss Stonebridge; today she felt like jazzing herself up a bit.

'What is?'

'The strike against the state transport system.'

'Oh that! Damn. I'd forgotten all about it.' She turned to the small bedroom mirror, balanced among books and a jewellery box on the chest-of-drawers, and started dabbing her mouth with lipstick. She pulled a face at herself then glanced at Max, who was hovering by the threshold, restless to be on his way.

He fastened the buckle on his bag. 'These days there's always some industrial action going on. But it's the

Communists and Nazis together on the picket line that bothers me. Talk about shaking hands with the devil... '

'Max, to my mind they're both as bad as each other. I don't see the Communists as morally superior.' Her voice sounded brittle with conviction but he was in no mood to argue.

'I don't have time to talk about it now. I'll see you later.'

'Aren't we going in the same direction?'

'Are you ready then?'

'I'll have to change my shoes if I'm walking to work.' She hurried to find a pair without heels.

Outside in the greyness of a dull, overcast day Max was barely able to quell his annoyance, not with Rhiannon for her views, not with the picketers, but with the cynical opportunism that had brought the two camps together. The strike was about further weakening a government clutching onto the last vestige of political dignity.

They parted at the corner of Hardenbergstrasse and Tauentienzstrasse. He wandered down towards Bahnhof Zoo. Outside the station members of the two factions had already taken up their positions. They stared in glum defiance at the bewildered folk who tentatively approached the entrances in hope of transport. The Nazi and Communist picketers were refusing point blank to acknowledge each other. That, at least, was reassuring. Almost comical they were, as they stood stolid and unsmiling in their rigidity.

He walked down the Ku'damm. Outside an U-Bahn station he spotted a bunch of Nazis and Communists separated by several metres as they jeered at the black legs, who had turned up to work. Later he learnt that one or two trams had struggled through. These had policemen posted on them to keep order. Elsewhere he watched a tram being jammed to a halt by protesters, who smashed the windows with stones and forced the nervous-looking passengers to get down and walk. He watched and walked. At one junction in Kreuzberg a tram was hemmed in by raucous strikers. Missiles flew through the air: stones, bricks, chunks of masonry. A large stone whistled by his ear. He ducked just in time. It shattered on the pavement beside him. Brakes squealed and several policemen piled out of a car, wielding batons. The mob dispersed like rainwater down a gutter. The strike-breakers, though vindicated by the arrival of the police, seemed cowed. In other streets the people tramping to work seemed dejected rather than militant.

Nobody wanted to talk to him about the strike. People were just bent on getting to where they needed to be. At another U-Bahn station Max asked a Communist picketer why he was sharing a platform with Nazis. *'Heraus! Abhauen!'* The sickly-looking youth yelled at him to clear off. It started drizzling. Everything was blanketed in a patina of grime. Wherever he looked he saw muted chaos. No one seemed to know what to do next.

Over the next day or so there was little change, though Max sensed the action was petering out. On the third day of the strike he met Rhiannon at the Tiergarten after work. The evenings were drawing in. The first bite of winter was in the air, giving an edge, a sense of last, snatched moments. Soon the cafés would be too chilly to sit out in and people would be fleeing to the fug of the city pubs.

'You look down in the dumps,' she said.

'Dumps?'

'You know, fed up, depressed, dispirited…' She didn't look too bright herself.

'Frustrated, more like,' he replied.

She leaned her head to one side in that sceptical, enquiring way she had. He gave a deep sigh and folded his arms.

'I'm still not catching enough of the stories I need. The

Reichstag election is coming up. The editor says he wants something stronger…'

'And Dieter – you've seen Dieter?' Her quick, intelligent eyes searching his betrayed a mounting anxiety.

'Not lately, I haven't. He's caught up in the strike. Why do you ask?'

'I'm nervous…'

Max said nothing. Over recent days he'd thought more than once about dropping his reservations and working for Dieter. After all, that might provide the sort of ammunition he was after. Yet always, at the last moment, he'd pulled back, mindful of Rhiannon, mindful of his own ambivalence to the Party. Even in the few weeks they'd been there he'd noticed a distinct shift: people were closing ranks, drawing back into coteries. In pubs free talk had shrivelled in favour of solid drinking.

'Anyway, what about you – how is the embassy?'

'Sid Khan invited me to put together material for a couple of lectures. I complained the list they had was too dull. We could do with some female writers for a start. Less politics, more humour and life stories.'

'I didn't know women writers *had* humour.' He grinned at her shocked expression. 'Name me one.'

'Dorothy Parker? Besides, you don't know any because you don't read—'

'Okay you win. Let's go home. It's getting late.'

Fourteen

Sid Khan had other things on his mind besides devising the cultural programme for the British embassy. The transport strike did not bother him unduly either, for it gave him more reason for staying indoors or calling on associates, both licit and illicit. Among these was Tilda Dublovsky, the wife of a White Russian who ran the Kuka nightclub in the Westend. Tilda ran another sort of business unbeknown to her stout spouse. This she did from their villa in Grüneberg, at least she ran the organisational side of it from there.

Khan decided to pay her an impromptu visit. There were a couple of Canadians who had called into the embassy and wanted to be shown a little of Berlin's 'nightlife' and asked, a little too slyly, what it had to offer. Their awkward manner betrayed their inadmissible wishes. Would Khan be able to help in this? He would, he said. Apart from the pleasure of Tilda's company, he was keen to see if she had any up-to-date information about the Nazi Party and its shenanigans.

Khan would not have described her as a madam, and visually she did not fit that particular bill at all, for she was always well turned out and her pert face and open vivacity gave no hint of sleaziness. She possessed the remarkable and innate knack of bringing men and women together for the purpose of pleasure. That money exchanged hands in the process went without saying. But it was not a coarse business. As far as she was concerned she was merely providing a social service.

After doing his stint at the embassy Khan caught a cab to her house. Tilda looked inordinately pleased to see him. 'So, so, stranger. I thought you had left Berlin altogether. I haven't seen you for ages!'

'Are you busy? I don't want to intrude.'

'I have to go out in a while, but not just yet. You'll stay for coffee at least?' She led him through to a sitting room overlooking a lawn and apple trees, coated with frost. Seeing her again, relaxed and smiling in her own home, he could not suppress a glimmer of affection mingled with lust. Again and again he'd told himself he should distance himself from this sort of work, acting as go-between and procurer was surely beneath his dignity. Yet here he was, business as usual. And Tilda looked as enticing as ever. Her lightly made up, elfin face was glowing, her slender body was boyish beneath the loose, vaguely transparent pantaloons.

He had missed her. For a moment he wondered about her relationship with her husband. Boris Dublovsky was such an obsequious, pompous and self-serving creature. How on earth did she put up with him? It grew ever harder to picture her alongside the man. Where Dublovsky was sycophantic and slippery, Tilda was honest. With her sense of enterprise and her fascination with individuals, she looked to the heart of a person and weighed what she saw. The Nazis were a case in point. She despised their politics and their self-righteousness. Trade with them she might, but she remained lucid.

'*Wie geht's?* How's it going?' he asked, watching her move between the chairs in her diaphanous garments.

'Just let me make the coffee. Have a cigarette. There are some in the drawer.' He helped himself. In a box of the marquetry table she kept dark Turkish cigarettes with a tang like Havana cigars. He picked one out, lit it and inhaled deeply, closing his eyes in appreciation as the rich smoke entered his throat and lungs. From the kitchen he heard her clattering and filling pots with water. She emerged minutes later.

Over coffee they discussed the Canadians. She made a phone call and a rendezvous was arranged. Closer he noticed she looked strained. There were dark blue shadows about her eyes. 'Everything fine with you?' he asked.

'Yes yes,' she said dismissively.

'And business?'

'Busy as ever.'

'Anyone of interest?'

She leaned back, squinted slightly and made a sound halfway between laughter and a groan of exasperation. 'You never give up, do you, Sid Khan? What are you after?'

'*Qui – moi?*' he said in mock offense.

'You're like a spider, weaving all these webs around you. You thrive on other people's stories.'

'Do I? I wouldn't want to cast doubt on your professional integrity but...'

'What are you after?'

'Your friends, the ones that like marching around and saluting – what have they got up their sleeve?'

This time she let out an unrestrained burst of merriment. 'Firstly, they are not my friends. And secondly, men don't come to me to discuss their political strategies.' She leaned forward and lit a cigarette, holding it loft in a silver cigarette holder.

'You must have heard something. You see enough of them.'

'Not really.'

'No dazzling parades, no back street battles, no new alliances with the Bolshies, no under the counter deals between Hindenburg and Goebbels, or Schleicher?'

'You know as much as I do. All I can say is that they're not as cocky as they were. They're talking about: "It's now or

84

never," "seizing the moment" and all that heroic stuff. And of course, Goebbels has this drive to make people think the way he wants them to.'

'His press office has become pretty fierce.'

She looked thoughtful, watching the blue smoke she'd exhaled spiralling upwards. 'Now you mention it, I did hear talk of raids on the press, mainly the small boys.'

'Any idea when this is meant to happen?'

She eyed him warily and flicked ash into a shell-shaped ashtray. 'Soon, I think.'

The next day Khan made a foray towards Max. He sent him a scrawled note on plain paper and without a signature via Rhiannon. The Nazi *Sturmabteilung* (SA), or storm troopers, were planning a raid on small but as yet unnamed newspapers. 'Nothing drastic,' ran the note. 'Just enough to scare them till after the election.' The strike and joint picketing had barely finished and already the Communists and Nazis were falling back into former battle lines.

Max called in at the *Immer Freiheit* office. Dieter scowled as Max imparted the warning. 'That's nothing new. They're always threatening. But it's probably time we moved anyway.' He ordered Werner, who was lolling in a corner looking vacant, to start packing files into boxes. 'No time like the present.'

'And you? Anything useful to pass on?' asked Max hopefully. Dieter shook his head slowly. 'Too tied up with the strike.'

'Last time we met you didn't know a thing about it,' he said.

Dieter shrugged. 'I got pulled in, inevitably. So what are you after?'

'Anything. I only managed to speak to a couple of people. Most didn't want to oblige.'

'They probably didn't know much themselves,' replied Dieter.

'The strike didn't achieve a lot.'

'It weakened the Social Democrats.'

'But that's about all.'

'It was people getting into clinches, pow-wowing. Anyone with half a brain is afraid of the way things are going. I took a few notes at the meetings. I was about to bin them. But they might help you come to grips with the various groupings, pick up a few handy names.' He put them together in a manila envelope and passed them over.

Later, in his office, Max pored over them. Though they contained the usual dose of circular arguments and posturing, they gave a strong sense of the current thinking of the Communists. They convinced him that come what may the Party was bent on improving its share of the vote in the Reichstag.

When he mentioned the threatened Nazi press bashing to his boss, Seifert did not seem unduly perturbed. He reminded Max that *Die Tatsache*, ensconced as it was in the newspaper quarter round Wilhelmstrasse, was too large and far too well known to come under such crude attack. For now, Hitler was staying his hand. The man was eager to woo the wavering *Mittelstand*. With the Reichstag election pending, it would not do to alienate the masses: the National Socialists were to be the party of the people, the party of Law and Order. Max felt he'd done his duty and said no more about it.

The days went by and the raids did not materialise.

Fifteen

Boris Dublovsky, the conférencier and husband of Tilda, turned up at the embassy literary talk on *The influence of Dostoyevsky on the English novel*. Rhiannon had stayed on after work to do her bit and chat to the attendees. Though she'd found the man unctuous and not someone she would usually choose to spend time with, she had made the effort and engaged him in conversation. After a just few minutes she knew this was someone Max ought to meet, if only for his wealth of contacts. When she mentioned his name, Sid Khan said he knew the man and would take Max to his club.

Now Max and Khan were sitting at a prime table in the Kuka cabaret. On the podium marionette-like actors were jerking stiff arms and legs in the parody of a dance. Max lit a cheroot and blew out a stream of smoke. 'What do you know about Dublovsky?' he asked Khan.

'White Russian émigré, been here for best part of a decade now. Studied philosophy at Moscow and ran foul of the Bolsheviks on account of his revisionism. Set up this troupe two or three years ago. Has some links into right-wing groups.'

'Is he married?'

'Yes. His wife Tilda…' Khan came to a halt. Max could tell that Khan was reluctant to continue and wondered, idly, whether Khan entertained unofficial and dubious dealings with her. It would not surprise him. In the world of cabaret and diplomacy everyone seemed to be doing something under the counter.

'We'll have to go carefully,' said Khan. 'Nowadays people are changing hats so quickly it's hard to keep up with them.'

'Quite,' said Max.

During the interval, when customers were encouraged to order more drinks, Boris Dublovsky wandered over to their table and made an exaggerated bow of the head. 'You permit?' He drew out a chair.

He was a rotund, bloated individual with quick, piggy eyes. Max was curious. In an expansive gesture Boris Dublovsky beckoned for vodka. The waiter poured the ice-cold spirit into frosted glasses.

'Thank you for the invitation. You said you were keen to develop links?' said Khan clicking open his cigarette case. Dublovsky declined the offer and seemed bemused. 'At the embassy, remember?'

'Ah yes, as a matter of sociability...' replied Dublovsky. He coughed then sipped his drink. 'I did enjoy the talk. It made me realise how much in common our two cultures have – or had rather. So, how do you like the show?'

'Tip top,' said Khan.

Dublovsky went to say something then stopped, searching for words. 'How do you say... I am widening my circle of... acquaintances.'

'I see,' said Khan.

Dublovsky lowered his voice. 'The Nazis have been round here demanding protection money. Tin on the door, collecting. Sitting in that corner there, smoking, watching, muttering – solemn and sour as curdled milk. Just wondered if you'd heard anything – at your embassy?'

'What about?'

'How the election might go... any more deals between parties to form a government, that sort of thing.'

'No, we haven't heard anything. Nothing to enlighten you on that score anyway,' said Khan.

'Berlin,' stated Dublovsky, 'is a cat being mauled by dogs.

Not only are the Germans at each other's throats, but the Russians are too.' Again he almost choked on his vodka. He banged his chest to clear it. 'Now the Soviets have made it their main base abroad. So what are we White Russians supposed to do? It's impossible to know who to trust.'

Max nodded in sympathy, wondering just what the man wanted from them. 'And they say cabaret clubs are under threat. Do you think that's true?'

'Ridicule is subversive,' offered Max, observing the Russian more closely. A bead of sweat had formed on his nose. He exuded anxiety. 'It stands to reason it would make extremists nervous. They prefer the direct approach.'

'What do you mean?'

'Oh, you know, torch-lit processions, drum rolls, rousing speeches. Making people sit up and take notice.'

Dublovsky continued to look somewhat befuddled. No wonder, Max thought. Doesn't know where he stands or whose turn will be next. Only the day before he'd read of a cabaret owner battered within an inch of his life because he looked like an *Ostjude*, an eastern Jew. Passers-by watched, appalled, then melted away.

Leaning towards the conférencier Khan uttered: 'We are willing to cooperate…'

'On what?'

'Our mutual interests…'

When Dublovsky continued to look baffled Khan continued. 'We need to know as much as we can about certain people – your clientele, for instance. Who comes by, what they talk about, who leaves with whom, who is spreading sexual favours. You know the sort of thing?' The conférencier's small eyes shifted from Khan to Max, quick as a snake. Khan sucked on his cheroot for a moment. 'We cannot exactly offer you His Majesty's protection, but we can offer a certain diplomatic favouring.'

A slow smile spread across Dublovsky's face. 'Anyone in particular you wanted to know about?'

'We are looking for stories on people in the Nazi Party, especially the leadership,' said Max.

Over the following weeks Boris Dublovsky delighted in imparting what he could about all who passed through the club. He observed the habits of his clientele and reeled them off to Max whenever he called by. Dublovsky listed who came and when, who was addicted to cocaine, who had a weakness for transvestites and who blabbered like a baby when drunk. Several high-ranking Nazis asked for call girls and he spluttered his outrage, telling them to look elsewhere. No need to look too far, muttered Khan to Max, when they met.

Gossip proliferated. Though the Russian club did not run prostitutes and the performers were for the main part impoverished intellectuals eking out a living, a whiff of scandal was always in the air, part and parcel of the human trade in need and satisfaction.

One night Dublovsky pulled Max to one side. 'A strange one we had in the other night. Claimed he was in the Hitler camp, some sort of dogs-body. Said he had all sorts of stories to tell.'

'And?' Max flickered with interest.

'Thought you might be interested, that's all.'

'Did he say anything out of the ordinary?'

'No, but one of the actors said he's seen him in one of the dives off Nollendorfplatz. You know the sort?' Dublovsky sniggered. The area was a well-known haunt for homosexuals. Many of the SA surreptitiously visited the establishments there. 'Don't know what he was doing here really. Not his kind of place. I may be wrong but I thought he called himself Drosch.'

'Drosch?'

'Drosch, or maybe Frosch? I'm not sure. He'd been drinking. His speech was slurred.'

Sixteen

Crammed into a corner seat on the crowded tram or *Elektrische* on the way to work, Rhiannon folded away the letter from her aunt. She had no idea about Christmas. It was still only November for goodness sake. She thought fleetingly of the Valleys, mentioned in the letter. She could picture the bleakness in the hill villages as winter neared.

Not so different from here. Round the Ku'damm it was easy to be taken in by the fancy shops and neon lights, but a few hundred yards down the side streets people had started breaking down fences for fuel. One day she saw a woman pushing a pram. Something about the woman struck her as furtive. When she looked closer she discovered the pram contained not an infant, but broken planks of wood. So many were at it that the police had given up trying to stop them. Soup kitchens had started up. She passed a new one on the way back from work. The Nazis offered *Winterhilfe*, winter help, to dole out blankets and soup. Cynics claimed it was just about gaining votes.

As for her, she brushed off the growing scarcity of every day staples, like meat and coffee, and adopted a cheery air to offset Max, who was burrowing ever deeper into the crisis. Now her aunt's letter burned in her mind, accusing her of pettiness. The day before Sid Khan had been urging her to set up another meeting with Max, preferably at their flat. So far she'd demurred, unsure of the diplomats' motivation. By lunchtime the letter had made her so restless that she approached Khan in the canteen and invited him and Denning over to Savignystrasse that very evening.

When she returned home Max was standing in the doorway, looking pleased with himself. He took her coat from her and declared he has just finished *the* definitive article on the Zentrum party.

'We're going to have visitors,' she announced, throwing herself down onto the sofa. She pulled off her blue cloche hat and shook out her hair so it tumbled round her face. It was good to be home, in the warm, and to see Max for once satisfied with his work. 'Sid Khan and Robert Denning.'

He didn't seem surprised. He opened a bottle of Moselle and put it on the table. She looked at the label. 'Can we afford that?' she asked.

He smiled as he poured her a glass.

'Khan's been dropping hints all over the place. Yesterday he came right out and asked whether he could come round. I kept putting him off.'

'But why, Rhiannon? What have you got against them?'

'I've heard he moves in unsavoury circles. I don't want you get mixed up in all that.'

'Let me be the judge…'

'Anyway now they're coming, both of them. By the way, aunt Vicky asked about Christmas again.'

Before he'd had a chance to respond, a drum beat loudly in the square below. 'God, not those boy scouts again!' He strode over to the window and yanked back the curtain in annoyance. She moved alongside him. Brown Shirts were swarming around in the square. A portly young man had his mouth to a megaphone.

'Citizens of Berlin. The time has come. Germany awake.'

In the adjacent block of flats a man thrust open a window. 'May be, *Junge,* but there's people here want a bit of peace and quiet!' Before the man uttered another word a woman's arm dragged him away and banged the window shut.

'Citizens of Berlin, the time has come.' More drum rolls, another blast of the trumpet. From another house two or three people drifted down and joined those gathering on the outskirts of the square. 'Germany is awake,' repeated the fat one. 'Support the Nazi Party!'

Somebody opened a window and poured slops down into the street so they splattered loudly and caused an outbreak of mirth at the far end where several girls were walking away from the Ku'damm. A Brown Shirt rushed across to the offending apartment block. 'Someone's in for it!' said Max. The square-shouldered young man hammered on the door. No one answered. The lights in the building went out.

There was a loud banging at their street door below. He started.

'It's probably Khan and Denning.' Rhiannon rushed down the stairs before he could stop her. He followed. In the twilight of the threshold the men were swathed in shadows. It took a second to make them out.

'Cosy place,' Khan remarked as he and Denning entered the glow of the sitting-room, with its autumnal hues it was a haven from the grim weather outside. Khan asked if they'd seen the rally.

'How could we not? Bunch of halfwits!' said Max. 'So gentlemen, a pleasure to see you…'

Rhiannon went off to the kitchen to fetch more glasses. She was a little taken aback by his formality. She noticed Denning glancing at Max's notes spread out on the desk.

'And what does Whitehall have to say about the shifts in power here?' asked Max, eyeing the diplomats. 'Are they even aware of them?'

'They know the Centre is losing ground,' said Denning and tipped back his glass. 'And that does bother them.'

Max refilled it. 'Falling apart more like.'

'As far as the Foreign Office is concerned they've lost credibility. The Zentrum party is now doing deals with the Nazis for goodness' sake!' Denning sounded exasperated.

'So who is keeping the government stable?' Rhiannon asked.

'What government?' snapped Max. 'This is not Great Britain you know. We're being ruled by presidential decree. The Reichstag is empty these days. Empty. Only the Fascists want it because it makes them legal.'

She felt like she had been struck across the face. What a short fuse he was on! Moments before he'd been smiling and pouring her Moselle. He turned away from her and raised his glass. '*Prosit*,' he said, tipping his glass towards the others. 'Your health, gentlemen.'

'Your health!' they chorused.

'Sorry I spoke,' she muttered. She placed her glass with deliberation on the table. 'I'll get some nuts.'

Max glanced across at her.

She went into the kitchen. There were no peanuts. She rummaged in the cupboard but found only a half finished packet of cheese biscuits, which she spaced out on a plate. Through the half open door she heard the men mumbling.

'Hitler is courting the people,' she heard Denning start. '… curbing his henchmen. People want an end to the street violence. If they don't win now, they're finished. That makes them dangerous.'

'Do you have something new to tell me?' Max sounded weary, wary.

'He must be discredited. But, well, let's just say our hands are tied.'

When she came back in Max looked tense, like a cornered fox. He was facing her colleagues, his shoulders raised. 'How? Do you have any bright ideas?'

Denning pushed his head forward. 'We have.'

'Which would be?'

'We believe you have a lead, through Dublovsky. Is that correct? Someone who worked in the Hitler camp..?'

Max paused by the edge of the table. 'I haven't found him yet—'

'If we could discredit Hitler... It's worth a try, isn't it?' urged Khan.

'Why should that interest anyone?' asked Max. 'It would be gossip. Tall tales.'

For a moment Denning looked outmanoeuvred.

'There are all sorts of stories circulating about him,' said Khan.

'Like what?'

'People he has had killed...'

'Everyone knows their methods are ruthless...'

The shuttlecock flew back and forth. Rhiannon found herself growing so agitated that she burst out: 'To write about that now would be madness. You must realise that?'

'Leave this to me,' said Max.

'She needs to have her say,' replied Denning calmly.

'All right, this person you're talking about – this camp defector or whatever you want to call him – you know him, do you?' he asked.

'You haven't flushed him out yet?' asked Khan.

Max stared at him.

'We have a few more pieces of the jigsaw you may be interested in,' said Robert Denning.

'Like what?' Max said, frowning at them.

Rhiannon glanced at Max. It was hard to read his closed expression. It crossed her mind that he might not want her here now, that her presence was inhibiting him. In London they had led separate lives. That had suited them both. Here, of necessity, they were thrown together.

'Articles. About the growth of militarism, people putting by arms…'

Max fetched the bottle of Bordeaux Wolfgang Seifert had given him.

'Our ambassador is in the know,' continued Denning in a low voice as if others might be eavesdropping: 'but people don't always want to hear.'

Max opened the bottle and put the cork to his nose. The old, oaky wine was redolent of cool winter evenings by the fire: times of ease he had little knowledge of. She thought about the two men she had brought into their home. They knew so little about Max, but they would use him if they could.

'A good year,' Denning commented. 'Where did you get hold of this?'

'My boss gave it as a welcome to Berlin gift. Now where were we? By the way, I thought you were meant to steer clear of German domestic politics?'

Denning muttered: 'That's true.'

In the office Rhiannon had heard about the Third Party Rule, which stated that diplomats should not engage in any form of espionage or political interference.

'We want to tip the balance,' Sid Khan cut in.

Max responded: 'Simplistic. They'd target the liberal press.'

'You could act as a conduit. You wouldn't need to sign your name…' said Denning.

'Such activity could be pivotal,' added Khan.

'I doubt it.' Max was standing his ground.

'Is that greater than the risk of the Nazis winning more votes?'

Rhiannon felt unutterably tired. She wanted to leave the room, shut out the cabals and compromises her colleagues were bringing into their home. She smiled and got to her feet. 'If you'll excuse me…'

As she closed the bedroom door she heard Max say. 'I want Rhiannon left out of this.' Fat chance, she thought. Whatever they were concocting her knowledge of it could wait. 'Till tomorrow, then.' Max opened the door for them to leave. He wandered into the bedroom. He caressed her head, stroking the hair back from her face. She flicked open her eyes then turned away. She was floating, her mind too blurred to engage. Max went back into the other room, not yet ready to sleep.

Seventeen

'Last attack! Desperate drive of the Party against defeat. The press campaign rages with every means possible. We succeed in getting 10, 000 Marks at the last minute. This will be thrown into the campaign Saturday afternoon. We have done everything that was to be done. Now let Fate decided.'
Joseph Goebbel's diary: 5 November 1932

Settled at a window table in Café Mozart, Max was skimming through his notepad. He pondered his encounter with Khan and Denning. They talked of hitting below the belt, of discrediting corrupt politicians who feigned respectability. He and Rhiannon had not yet spoken about their visit; that morning they'd both been in too much of a hurry. The more he thought about it the stronger grew his conviction that Berlin was becoming too perilous for her. He could see it disturbed her. She was more overwrought than he had ever known her and often she was pale with strain, though she never tired of telling him that she was tough as nails. He hated the way he was growing so short tempered; his anger seemed to erupt out of nowhere and more often than not she was the butt of it. He should get her to leave. Any fool could see she would be better off out of it, at least for the time being. Khan could surely be relied upon to ease her passage back to London.

As for him, it was out of the question to quit what he was doing.

Just then he saw Khan swinging through the smoked glass door. Should he broach the subject with him now? He rejected the notion as soon as it entered his head. Rhiannon would be furious if he talked about her behind her back.

Khan was sporting a lime green waistcoat that was just too bright. His hair was slicked back with Brylcreem, displaying his wide forehead. His eyes lit up when he spotted Max. He pushed by the other tables and chairs and shook Max firmly by the hand. 'Hope you haven't been waiting long.'

Max beckoned to the waitress. 'I always have stuff to catch up on.'

'I know the feeling.' Khan gave one of his winning smiles. True, what Rhiannon said about him: he could charm the bark off a tree. Only that waistcoat gave him away. It spoke of an irrepressible flamboyance not even the strictures of the diplomatic corps could curb. Max was determined to find out more about him, but when he asked what had brought him to Berlin, Khan's mouth twisted in surprise. 'It's a long story,' he said evasively.

'I'm not in a hurry,' countered Max.

Annoyance flickered across Khan's face. Max pressed his advantage. 'If we are to work together I need to know more about you.' Khan pulled out a cheroot, tapped it on the table, then thought better of it and put it away. He seemed uncomfortable, yet started up in a low voice.

'I had just won my spurs at Oxford and was waiting to hear from certain people about work. But I wasn't optimistic.' Max grunted assent. It went without saying that despite his academic achievement, Khan would meet obstacles. The jovial connivances of the British Old Boys' Network would win out every time.

'I was in a pub in Broad Street. I was approaching the bar when a tall fellow in flannels hurtled back into me. 'Sorry old boy!' It was Denning. He grasped me by the arm. 'What'll it be? Just to prove I'm not always such an oaf.' He lined up the drinks. When the others had gone and Denning was pretty tight, he told me he was born in India. His pa had run a tea plantation up in the hills. Assam. Did I know the place? He wouldn't let me go. Kept on about the glory of the days before the wretched memsahibs took over. How he would have given his eyeteeth to be out there then.

'Then he told me about his posting to Berlin... out of the blue he asked if I'd care to join him. I thought he was joking. He spun some yarn about needing a loyal assistant. I said I'd think about it. He seemed no worse than most. I mulled it over then next morning, during a reluctant round of golf, I said yes.' Khan paused. 'So there you have it,' he said, keen to move on.

'You didn't want to return to India?' asked Max.

Khan bent to sip his coffee. 'I wasn't ready to.'

Max sensed there were cross-currents in the man that he himself was hardly aware of. Yet, for the time being, that would have to do. He needed to pursue the claim that certain sections of the British press were being gagged. This news had taken him aback. In London he knew reporters who worked for *The Times* and he had never caught any whiff of suppression. He even wondered whether this was a fabrication by the British diplomats just to draw him in.

As if reading his mind Khan handed him a buff envelope.

Max turned it over, as if weighing it. 'What's this?'

'A couple of English press contacts, names which might be useful.' Khan shrugged. 'It's worth a try. A friendly reminder – don't wear your heart on your sleeve. And just so you know, in the Nazi camp there's Putzi Hanfstaengl and Joseph Goebbels. Putzi is smitten with Adolf Hitler. And Hitler loves to sit and listen to Putzi playing the piano. Putzi is upper crust. He comes from a publishing family. He's become a sort of press officer for the Nazis. He helped Hitler get his autobiography published. He has a lot of links with the right-wing press in Munich. But Goebbels has been given Berlin. He is the one to watch here. And he's as clever as they come.'

'So what's in it for them?' Seifert seemed more puzzled than enthusiastic.

Sitting opposite his editor, it struck Max he should have had this meeting before. When it came to gauging sources Seifert was hard to beat. The office was deserted as everyone else had left for the weekend. Heaped ashtrays and overflowing wastepaper baskets signalled the ongoing industry of his colleagues.

'They say they want to discredit right-wing groups,' replied Max.

'Why should they do that?'

'To tip the balance away from the Nazis, I suppose.'

'Do you think it's that simple?'

Max shrugged. 'The British government abhors extremes, whether of the left or right.'

The other grunted and lit a cigarette. 'I know people in the embassy. In general they are reluctant to commit themselves in any direction. Mostly they just want to cover themselves.'

When Max said nothing Seifert continued. 'That's the official line. But British Intelligence is a many-headed Hydra. It's possible no one but the ambassador knows what they're up to.'

'Are you of the opinion that I should steer clear of them then?'

'No, it sounds promising. Just remember the number one rule in journalism: people always have vested interests. Intelligence services use who and what they can. It's like mating with a snake.' His voice glided over the words as though he had uttered them before. 'You'd have to go through several filters to get to anyone in the know. They'll be watching you like a hawk. This Frosch contact is more what I had in mind. Tonight would be an excellent time to wander around Nollendorf and see what you can pick up.'

'I haven't had much luck finding him so far. I've been to all the usual places.'

'Keep trying. He's bound to turn up sooner or later.'

'Will you run what I come up with?'

'It depends. Just go and get your story and we'll see.'

Impatience undercut Seifert's voice as he spoke. Max noticed his gold cufflinks gleaming. His skin had a slight fullness, redolent of good living. Max knew not to be fooled by appearances. Journalists lived close to the edge if they were any good. He could ill afford to be sloppy. They were not there to judge but to report, insisted Seifert, pinning him with a shrewd look before they parted.

Eighteen

Rhiannon looked up as the door to the flat opened. 'So, there you are. You decided to come home at last!' She was curled in a ball on the sofa, reading a book. Max squinted at the title.

'Bit heavy going, isn't it? *Die Leiden des jungen Werthers? The Sorrows of the Young Werther.* Sparked a wave of suicides when it first came out.'

'I'm enjoying it in a lurid sort of way. Reminds me of my adolescence – feelings so intense they could set off a bomb.'

'So, what's changed?'

'I met you.'

'You mean I dowsed your untrammelled spirit?'

She laughed and pulled him down towards her, kissing him quickly on the mouth. 'It takes one to recognise one, as the saying goes. I picked the book up at the Goethe Institute. I don't understand every word but I get the gist.' She put the tome to one side and stretched in a sinuous movement, elongating herself like a cat. 'So what shall we do tonight?'

Max brushed her mouth with his lips, cupped her cheek in his hand. 'That's just it. I have to go out again tonight.'

'Max! It *is* Friday night, don't forget.' She turned to face him. 'Max, look at me. What's going on? You haven't even told me the whole story about Khan and Denning. They put me on edge those two.'

'I'm sorry, darling. It can't be helped.'

'What can't be helped?'

'Friday night is good for going on the prowl.'

'You sound like a feral cat.'

'It's a lead I have to follow up. It can't wait. Look, I tell you what. We'll eat on the Ku'damm – and then I'll shove off for an hour or two.'

'Max, we can't afford to eat out.'

'I know this isn't... It's not what we imagined. But it won't be for long.'

'I hope not.' Realising there was little point in arguing once his mind was made up, Rhiannon got up without another word and went to change. She made an effort with her appearance, putting on a soft grey frock, which clung to her gentle curves. She sighed as she crinkled her hair so it framed her face. It was rare nowadays that they spent an undisturbed evening together.

They went to a French bistro not far from the giant hoardings by the Zoo station at the start of the Ku'damm. They ordered thick onion soup, which arrived immediately. Max devoured his as though he hadn't eaten for a week. She lingered over hers, looking thoughtful. 'I think I'll go and see Inge tomorrow,' she said.

'Inge? But why?'

'Why not? She's your sister, after all.'

'I would have thought you have very little in common.'

'That's not the point. She's concerned about you. I can tell.' He winced, tore at the bread to avoid looking at her.

'I would keep away from Inge if I were you.'

'I don't understand why my efforts at contact irk you.'

'It's less her than that idiot of a man she's married to.'

'Granted he hasn't got your power of analysis but he means well enough...'

'Rhiannon, you don't know him. You don't know the circles he moves in. He's not evil, he's gullible. And sometimes that's just as bad.'

'Max, why are you so – so...'

'So what?'

'Nervous. Aggressive.'

He leaned back, pushed the empty soup bowl away and stretched out his legs. 'Sorry. It's not intentional. My boss is leaning on me. He is keen for me to track down this Gert Frosch guy. He thinks Friday night is a good night to find him.'

'I see.' She looked at her watch. 'Do you want more to eat?'

'I'm fine. I need to get going, I think.'

She gave a little shrug. 'I suppose you had. I'll see you back at home.'

Rhiannon caught a tram home while Max made once more for the Nollendorfplatz. He'd found out a few bits and pieces about the *Bierkeller* putsch in Munich and pulled out other articles about the Nazi Party, its followers and history of clashes with the law. Nowhere was there any mention of Gert Frosch. But then why should there be? He was a camp follower, a nobody: one of the many drawn in and mesmerised by the charismatic leader.

Though he'd told Rhiannon not to wait up for him, he knew she probably would. She couldn't stop worrying on his behalf. Politically-motivated murders were growing and though he avoided talking about it – not wanting to alarm – she would be only too aware of that. Warnings had even gone out from her embassy to be extra circumspect. In his office there were constant rumblings about imminent press raids.

He ambled round the square where tramlines crossed under low and noisy railway bridges. Coloured advertisements hung on shop hoardings, blue and green neon lights blinked on four-storey buildings. In one corner glowed the *Erotischer Zirkus*, the garish red of a large ugly building dedicated to the pleasures and pains of the flesh.

Where should he start? Nollendorf was rife with clubs. Off every back street a wrought iron basement stairway led to another dubious dive; the epitome of Weimar degeneracy, complained some, while others welcomed it as a new, kinder world of acceptance. He looked around. Khan said there was no end of places Frosch, this putative valet person, might frequent. He could be anywhere: under the railway arches, off the main square, along any of the side streets. Did the man even exist, or was he just spun out of Dublovsky's over-rich imagination to string them along?

After hours of trawling bars, asking for the man by name, getting shrugged shoulders or lascivious invitations to try something else, Max decided to call it a night. The last place he entered was by the taxi stand. The chrome-plated facade gave way to a mauve interior with a glass-fronted bar. It was virtually empty. He was about to order a coffee when a man sidled up to him. Max, the man insisted, was looking sombre and in need of a little 'uplift'.

'I believe you have been looking for me…'

Max, by then weary from his endless search, became alert. 'You are?'

'My name is Gert Frosch.'

This was too good to be true. Max suspected the man had overheard him speaking to one of the barmen. 'Really?' He sounded a little disdainful.

'Here you can ch-check my papers. I've here…' The man fished into his pocket and brought out a scrap of dirty paper with stamp marks and an official-looking seal. The name on the pass was indeed Gert Frosch. Max moved closer, studied his face. He made an odd impression, this bar-hugger: his eyes were shifty and his upper lip was sweaty. He seemed a little nervous and quite drunk.

Max ordered them two vodka cocktails. He engaged him

in small talk, then asked how long he'd been long in the city and whether he had travelled up from Munich and why he had left the place. Gert Frosch's face clouded over. He propped his elbow on the side and it slipped. He lurched forward.

When Max went on to ask if he was involved in the Nazi Party, Frosch stabbed an uncoordinated finger in the air. 'Was! Was! No more.'

'And why's that?'

'I was one of them.'

'Was? Why did you leave?'

Gert Frosch looked suddenly wary and cast about him as though he realised he might say too much. 'I'm not saying another word.'

'I don't believe you were a Party member.'

'Of course I was. New morality, my eye,' he spluttered and swilled back the vodka. He leered at Max, ogled a passing waiter with smoothed back hair and then leant in towards the bar. 'I smelled a rat. And now – well, it's all cleaned up and nobody ever says a word.'

'What are you talking about?' interjected Max above his incoherence.

'The new hope of Germany. P-peace and prosperity. It's all lies. Just think what happened to Geli…'

'Geli?'

'Geli Raubal. You know, Hitler's niece?'

The man slouched over the table and within seconds was snoring indecorously into the ashtray. Max shook his arm, gently then roughly, but Gert Frosch would not budge. Max called the barman over. 'Do you know where he lives? He's *besoffen,* blotto. Need to get him out of here.'

'Round the corner. 8 Kleiststrasse. The keys are in his pocket. You'd be doing us all a favour.' The barman moved off, collecting empties. Max downed the remains of his cocktail and tipped some coins onto the counter. He hoisted Frosch up and half-dragged, half-walked him across the bar and up the steps to the street. It had been raining again and the roadway glistened black and silver. Two men were sauntering by, arm-in-arm. Max staggered beneath the weight while Gert's head drooped onto his shoulder. He belched. Tittered at nothing, slumped like a sack. Max attempted to step between puddles and came to a clumsy halt outside number eight. He had to negotiate more steps down. He propped Frosch up against the railing, sidled down and took the key from his pocket. Something shifted further along. Rats. A dustbin lid clattered in the wind. A shadow flickered, oscillated, a light went on above the alleyway. *'Rote Front!'* shouted someone from a window.

The door opened onto a corridor of let rooms. Worn linoleum covered the floor and a smell of damp pervaded the building. Frosch's room was the second along. It was piled high with boxes as though he'd just shifted in. Max pulled him onto the bed and went off in search of water. When he came back Frosch had rolled over onto his back and with his mouth wide open was snoring like a saw. Max found a space on a chair and watched him.

He waited. He sprinkled his face with water but drew no reaction. He tugged at his feet. He spoke close to his ear. All in vain, Gert Frosch was out for the count. Max decided to cut his losses and return home. At least he knew where the man lived.

Nineteen

The next day, while Max was at work Rhiannon went for a walk in the Tiergarten. Here she caught snatches of laughter and loud talk from clustered tables. Shrieking in high spirits children ran amok in the nearby bushes. Further over a little girl was wandering alone by the water. No one seemed to be with her. Concerned, Rhiannon approached. The child's thin face was dirty with tears and she was growing more distressed by the minute. She was hungry, she said. Rhiannon took her by the hand and asked someone where the nearest police station was.

She took her there and then carried on walking, soaking in the weak autumn sun. The little girl's plight jarred: she was just one of many, too many. Rhiannon began to wish she could do something to help on a practical level. She needed to engage, but also she needed to strike out on her own away from Max. His absorption in his work was finally getting to her.

In Wales she had worked with Aunt Vicky and the benefit clubs in the coal valleys during the General Strike. Before that she had worked with the church Goodwill Group doling out food parcels. There was never a time when she had not been involved in some project. In London her studies had occupied her and her life with Max has superseded all else. Now she felt increasingly pushed back onto herself. She headed towards the Technical University. As she entered the building her steps echoed in the empty corridor. She saw a board spattered with notices offering anything from Rooms to Let to Spanish courses. In one corner was a fading, hand-written note: 'Nationalism? Bolshevism? There must be another way. Saturday meetings. Room 171. Women only.' She hesitated, daunted by the grandeur of the place, then set off to find room 171.

At times she found the world of men enervating. She thought fondly of her friends back home. Women were pragmatic, they sniffed what was below their noses. In times of war and peace they put food on the table, scraping coupons and foraging if need be. In female company she could let her hair down.

Murmuring voices hushed at a stroke as she knocked on the door. A tall woman opened to her. Rhiannon peered in. Tables had been drawn together and heaped with papers. A handful of women were gathered in a circle, some smoking, others with elbows propped. Most seemed younger than her, in their early twenties. All had an air of intensity. They seem disgruntled at the intrusion. 'Is this the Socialist Women's Group?' she asked.

'This is not an open meeting,' said the gatekeeper.

'Then why put up a notice about it?'

'It's an old notice.'

'But why haven't you taken it down?' She smiled, though rattled at the woman's curtness. Two or three of the others exchanged glances.

The gatekeeper asked: 'You want to join the group?'

'I don't know anything about you, but I have an interest in – in Socialism.' This was the easiest explanation – and not so very far from the truth – though uttered there, on the threshold of their meeting room, it sounded trite. She could hardly admit to a longing for female company.

'You may come in,' said another woman, who seemed to be in charge. 'I'm Hannah Feder.' Rhiannon sat down across the table from them.

111

'So what brings you to Berlin?' asked one, cued by her accent.

Rhiannon demurred, unsure what she should and should not divulge, then reflecting that it was no secret where Max was working, told them.

They plied her with more questions, in particular why she felt motivated to join them.

'I was active in the mining villages in south Wales. During the strikes.'

Hannah, the rangy leader with blonde flyaway hair said. *'Na gut.* And you, do you want to ask us anything else?'

'What are your objectives?'

The gatekeeper frowned. 'How do we know we can trust what she says?'

'As I said, in Wales I helped miners' families during the General Strike. I…' Her mouth grew dry. She glanced from the wary women to the blank walls of the lecture room.

Hannah was more conciliatory. 'We concern ourselves with women's issues. On paper the republic has done a lot for equality, in reality it's quite different— Nowadays we just try and stop people going hungry.'

The secretary looked at her watch and reminded them how much of the agenda they still had to get through. 'On to the soup kitchen. Liese says she can't do the Neukölln stint. That leaves us a helper short today. Can anybody else?'

'I could,' Rhiannon blurted out. The women gaped at her. She too, was startled at the suddenness of her offer, which had slipped out involuntarily.

'We need all the help we can get,' said Hannah. 'I vote we accept the offer and see how it works out. All those in favour?'

Baffled, the women looked at each other then towards Hannah before slowly raising their hands. After more talk on practicalities they gave Rhiannon a sheet with instructions on the soup kitchen. Then they handed her a copy of the pamphlet they had just put together. She scanned it, struggling with some of the language. Hannah explained how they wanted to influence deputies in the Reichstag. The others nodded. From their set expressions Rhiannon guessed they had stopped thinking about it. She left the meeting soon after.

Still craving female company she decided to call on Inge. Max could say what he liked, and he had, but for her family was family and worth preserving. By now the transport strike had petered out and trams were running to schedule. Reaching the block in Spatzenstrasse she hurried to the third floor before she could change her mind.

'*Ach so*, it's you.' Inge's mouth twisted. Her hair was tied back and her hands were covered in flour. 'I am baking.' Her small, blue-green eyes were blank. 'I was not expecting you...'

'Can I come in a moment?'

They were standing in the dimly lit hall. 'The other day... I felt it couldn't be left like that... with your father gone...' Though her German was getting stronger, now her words faltered. 'Besides, I wanted to see Anna. I haven't clapped eyes on her since your father's funeral.'

She followed Inge to the kitchen where Anna was standing on a chair. 'Anna!' The little girl had a tiny pinafore on and her face was smeared with flour. Her chubby legs and arms poked out from her winter dress. Rhiannon gave her a hug. The child giggled and hugged her back. '*Tante Rhiannon*,' said Inge. '*Sag Guten Tag.*'

The range was rattling with saucepans of sweet-smelling sauce and stewed apples. The aroma caught Rhiannon by the throat. It reminded her of childhood, of a kitchen swathed in forgetting, of a mother in an apron – long since dead. Brushing aside a wave of sadness, she sat down and engaged with Anna, asking how she was helping her mother. Anna chattered away, explaining how she was getting rid of the *Klumpen* in the flour mix.

'Is there anything I can do to help, Inge? I don't want to get in your way…'

'I am baking for the week. Tuesdays I always bake.' Inge dusted down her *Kittel*, her voluminous overall, and submerged her pink hands into the bowl of dough. She gave Anna a wooden spoon and told her to move it round. *'Apfelstrudel,'* she explained to Rhiannon. 'Do you want to know how I do it? In Britain you have no such thing, *nicht wahr?'* She emptied the dough onto a board, cut off a section and began to roll it into long thin strips. Beside her Anna had a board and little rolling pin of her own. Rhiannon watched mother and daughter, side by side, and swallowed a taste of envy.

Inge's strong practical hands were kneading. She turned to the dresser to fetch a bag of flour. She carried on patting down the dough and applying more flour as though Rhiannon had not spoken. 'You have to get the right mixture. Too much fat and it won't gel, too little and it spoils the taste.'

Rhiannon took in the gleaming pots hanging from a rack, the scrubbed linoleum now wearing thin; the lace curtains, frayed and mended, but clean, so clean, no doubt a legacy from the days when the couple were still scrimping to make ends meet. Inge was concentrating on rolling strips while keeping an eye on Anna. Next she put on the lightly stewed apple and sprinkled it with cinnamon. Rhiannon had the impression she would repulse what she was not comfortable with, including her brother.

Rhiannon could not resist driving the point home. 'Inge, Max was hurt. I know you have your reasons. I know Hans is concerned about his job. But I hate to see brother and sister fight.'

114

Inge continued kneading and rolling and then she fetched a large dish from a cupboard and started greasing it, squeezing the strip of larded paper into the corners. Anna ran after her and pulled at her skirt. Inge lifted her up and whispered something into her ear after which Anna ran off into her bedroom and fetched a floppy doll, which she placed on the table near the tray of *Apfelstrudel*.

'I thought you might come round for tea – now we have a place,' offered Rhiannon.

Inge shot her a fierce look. 'Did Max send you here?'

'No.'

'Does he know you're here?'

'I just came just to talk. We live in the same town, why not visit?'

Inge started spooning in more apple and added raisins.

'Inge, sometimes we women have more sense than men.'

'*Ja*, that is true,' Inge conceded, deftly fingering the pastry into place.

'How often do you make *Strudel*?'

'There is a tree out back, we take what falls. This year there has been a good crop. You can have some if you want.' Inge's voice softened as she spoke of specifics. She glanced up suddenly. 'There is much about Max you don't know. Facts I will not go into. I know you mean well. But things are best left the way they are.'

'But why? If I had a brother I wouldn't want to lose him like that.' Even as she spoke Rhiannon knew a door had closed between them.

'You come by all means. Come like now, when the men are busy.'

'I'm doing a soup kitchen by the town hall in a couple of hours' time.'

'A soup kitchen, you said? You're not with the *Winterhilfe*, surely?' Inge looked alarmed, piqued even, at the news. In the cramped kitchen, clothes for mending were piled in one corner and knitting patterns and spools of wool in another. Inge bristled with disapproval as Rhiannon told her about the university group. 'You don't want to get involved with that lot, Rhiannon.'

'They want to help the needy. What can possibly be wrong with that?'

'Nothing on the face of it, but Hans says the Social Democrats are finished. It is time for something new.'

'Everybody's saying that – the only difference is *what?*' Rhiannon retorted with more vehemence than she intended.

'Hans says we need a new order. We need to do away with all this giving in to foreign powers, away with the decadence of the artists and cabarets, away with…'

'Oh stop it, Inge!'

Inge's lips tightened. 'Max and I are very different. He is putting himself in danger by writing what he does. And now you – who quite frankly have no idea what you're letting yourself in for – go and join some radical suffragettes at the Technical University.'

'What's wrong, Inge, with wanting to help people?'

'You don't understand – but then why should you?'

Rhiannon bit back her resentment. Inge could be so condescending. She tried another tack. 'Have you ever read one of Max's articles?'

'Hans has seen them. He recognises the tone. He knows the paper he works for. Max and Hans are total opposites and well, I am married to Hans, and that is that.'

'Max is trying…'

'He is a dreamer. Intellectuals are dangerous. They undermine belief in the Fatherland.' She stopped, her mouth almost disappearing in anger. They sat for a moment in silence before Inge started up again 'You don't find it easy to make friends here?'

'What makes you say that?'

Inge gave a little shrug of uncertainty. 'Don't take offense. I don't mean it unkindly. I just wasn't expecting you to visit again. I guessed it must be because you are lonely.'

Unused to such directness Rhiannon coughed in embarrassment. 'It's work, and then home, or the odd drink with a friend of Max... I wasn't wanting to importune you, Inge.'

'It's not that. I know it can't be easy in a different culture.'

'That's true. Anyway how are you? How is the pregnancy?'

Inge touched her bulge and smiled. 'As one would expect, everything is in order.'

'And how many weeks are you now?'

'About twenty four.'

'They say the middle trimester is the easiest.'

'And that's been true with me. I was very sick at the start. Now I can feel it kicking.'

'Really?'

'Just a flutter in the stomach, but it's reassuring. And yourself – what is your news?'

'I'm working at the embassy now... I've started arranging cultural events.'

Inge was hardly listening. She was fingering a piece of apple in distraction. 'You need to tell Max not to get embroiled with the Communists.'

'Max is not a Communist.'

'He needs to know. There's going to be a crackdown.'

'There were warnings before. Then the Communists and Nazis joined together on the picket line. How is one supposed to read that?'

'Pure expediency,' Inge said, as if from rote. 'It suited both parties and the state transport system needed to be taught a lesson.'

'What do you know about this so-called crackdown?' asked Rhiannon.

'Only that it is coming. And that it will be severe.'

'Has Hans joined the Nazi Party?'

Inge nodded. Somehow Rhiannon already knew this, just as she knew that neither of them had read a single word Max had written. She also knew that despite all, brother and sister could not help but love each other. It was inconvenient. It was not what they might choose, but it was an unalterable fact. She sensed by the sinking in her stomach that she would be better advised to get up and go. 'Inge, you remind me of Max sometimes.'

Inge looked taken aback. 'In what way?'

'You're both stubborn. I have no siblings, no parents, only uncles and aunts. It hurts me… to see how you carry your anger, the two of you.' Inge looked blank. Rhiannon's stab at deeper connection was clumsy and ill considered. 'I'd better be on my way. I see you have a lot to do.' She hesitated. 'Is there really nothing more you can tell me about this?'

'Just tell Max to be careful. Above all he should stay away from the Communists.'

Rhiannon eyed the snaking, queue of people in front of Neukölln Town Hall. Some of the children were scratching themselves, no doubt with fleas or scabies. She'd seen it before in south Wales. She could get a stench of stale clothes and old sweat from some of them. She sniffed and turned away, suppressing revulsion. Hot water and soap came at a price. Rhiannon tucked her hair under the cap they've given her and hefted a large pot onto the table from the brazier. She ran the ladle through the stew, dislodging vegetables from the bottom. It, too, smelled awful but looked substantial enough. Hannah was sifting through the potatoes, prodding and sorting by size. People in the square were stamping their feet to ward off the cold. Despite the bright start the weather had turned bitter and the sky was now hung with low, threatening clouds.

'Good to see you,' said Hannah. 'I wasn't sure you'd turn up.'

'Get a move on,' someone shouted to the person in front. 'I am freezing. My shoes have got holes in them.'

'So's your mouth!' Laughter rippled down the line.

Another woman arrived with a pile of enamel mugs. Rhiannon began ladling the soup and people surged forward. Two women pushed to the front. 'Get into line, you two,' yelled the policeman detailed to keep order. Rhiannon's hands were raw and tingling. She hopped from one foot to the other to keep warm.

'It's bad now but it was worse after the war,' muttered an older woman who appeared with more potatoes. 'During the blockade there was no meat. Not much of anything. But we came through.' Rhiannon took the pot from her. 'People are growing tired again. There just isn't the work.'

'Better than war,' said another.

'There'll be more of that, too,' declared the older woman, 'if the Nazis get their way.'

'Shhsh. *Halt's Maul*. Keep your trap shut!' hissed the policeman. 'Just get on with it. We don't want to hear your leftish ideas.' The woman threw him a black look and went back to fetch more potatoes.

'When's the beef coming?'

'Meat, my eye. When did you last see a knuckle of pork?'

'What I'd give for a piece of stewing steak.'

Rhiannon was reaching the bottom of the pan. People

continued to shuffle by, holding out their mugs. She fetched another pot from the brazier and carried on ladling. As the queue grew it turned unruly with people shoving and grumbling. The policeman ordered stragglers back into line. Rhiannon's feet were numb and her face chapped with cold. At last they reached the end of the queue. Hannah was going early to attend a meeting elsewhere, but as she left she invited Rhiannon to call round to her apartment later. Rhiannon stayed on and helped the other women clean and sort utensils.

It was growing dark as she found her way to Hannah's apartment in Zehlendorf. She lived in a well-kept, turreted, four-storey block. Its elegant stuccowork, lit by the lamppost, was redolent of genteel affluence. Rhiannon had guessed Hannah would live in such a place. Everything about her declared a social confidence. Inside, the rooms were lit with candles and warmed by a wood-burning stove.

Hannah poured Rhiannon a glass of Alsace wine. 'So, how did you find the soup kitchen – not too hard, I hope?'

'I enjoyed it – in a funny sort of way. Back home I used to deliver parcels to the poor.'

'A ministering angel, I see.' Hannah laughed, her sharp eyes trained on Rhiannon, who in turn kept wondering what to make of her. 'So how have your first weeks in Berlin been?'

Overcome by sudden emotion Rhiannon coughed, then gulped her wine. The night before she'd hardly slept. Max had not come home till four and then he'd left while she was still sleeping. Hannah topped up Rhiannon's glass and she found the wine was going to her head.

'It's a time of change. There a lot of upheaval.' said Hannah.

'The National Socialists talk about destiny, a plan unfolding through history, a mission…' Rhiannon was struggling to find

words. 'It bothers me. These – these – people so convinced…
They really believe in what they say.'

'They do, yes.'

'While I can no longer say why I believe in…'

'In what?'

She gave a shrug. 'The existence of a benign order, perhaps?'

Hannah switched on a sidelight, illuminating bookshelves and a boar's head above the door lintel. The décor was odd. Disparate items were jumbled with apparent carelessness together: a bust of Lenin was propped next to a Venus de Milo statuette, severe *Neue Sachlichkeit* lamps were juxtaposed with a traditional, heavily carved dresser. 'One might say you were brave, coming here at a time like the present.'

'My husband is from Berlin.'

'I know, but all the same… Karl Marx would say, when things start breaking down we're ripe for Revolution.'

'Crucifixion comes before resurrection.'

'Are you a Christian, then?'

'Well, yes.' At home Rhiannon had taken such things for granted. What she'd imbibed was an unspoken liberalism, a Christian-based belief in everyday decency and compassion where manifestos were unnecessary. 'At bottom we have only our conscience to go by,' she said quietly.

'I agree with you there,' said Hannah. 'Personally, I go by a simple rule. Follow your own conscience and not somebody else's.'

'But isn't the conscience formed by others, by social influences?' Rhiannon wondered aloud.

'There are all sorts of ideas flying around. You have to sift and discriminate.'

'We went to the Troika the other night. The men were dressed like girls and the women looked like soldiers. The songs had a bite to them. Everything was so upside down it made me feel ill.'

Hannah gave a wry smile. 'You don't have Cabaret in London?'

'Not really.'

'It's a powerful form of expression. We'd be the poorer without it.'

The candle, steady and bright, threw onto the dark wood a ring of soft light. It was getting late. Rhiannon feared if she drank any more her anxiety would spill out. 'I should be on my way.' Yet she lingered, not quite ready to leave. 'I grew up without parents from a young age,' she blurted out.

'How sad,' said Hannah. 'There's one thing worse than a family and that's not having one. Mine drive me wild sometimes. My sister is a teacher in Munich.' She lit a cigarette. 'Tell me more about yourself. How you met your husband – Max isn't it?'

'Yes. We met in Wales. He was doing some research, on the trade union movement. I think he just wanted to get away from his father…'

Hannah laughed. 'I know the feeling. My father is a bit of a tyrant. I think it's that generation. Duty before pleasure, order before beauty. They can't understand us children of the Weimar era who just want to have a good time. He thinks I'm decadent just because… well, I'm not domesticated. I prefer dancing to studying. Now I'm involved in a women's group, I'm way beyond the pale.'

Rhiannon's eyes were beginning to droop. The cold of the streets and then the warmth of Hannah's room, jumbled impressions of soup tureens and Inge's kitchen, the hours awake listening for Max's footfall on the stair – all washed over her.

She woke to Hannah's gentle touch. 'Rhiannon, it's getting late, perhaps you'd better…'

Startled, Rhiannon jerked forward. 'What time is it? Yes, yes I had better go. Sorry. I was so tired.'

Hannah smiled at her. 'You be all right, will you, getting home? You could always stay here.'

Twenty

As Rhiannon turned the key in the lock Max looked up from the sofa where he was attempting to read. He felt a rush of relief. Her dark, unruly hair was backlit like a halo against the hall light. Her face was animated, her cheeks flushed. Her coat was open. In that moment he wanted to gather her up and crush her against his body. She was exuding that blend of fire, vulnerability and resilience he'd seen in no other woman. Carelessly she pulled off her scarf and let it drop to the ground. 'Ah,' she sighed. 'I'm exhausted.'

'Rhiannon, where have you been all this time?' He sounded fiercer than he intended.

Her chin tilted towards him in mock confrontation. 'Now you know how it feels when you keep *me* waiting.' She shook back her hair and gave a little laugh. Annoyance mingled in him with desire. 'Where *were* you?'

'I had a drink at Hannah's, after the soup kitchen.'

'Hannah?'

'From the women's group.'

'What women's group?'

'I joined a group at the Technical University. They run a couple of soup kitchens.' She laughed. 'Max, you look very – solemn.'

'You've been doling out food?'

'At Neukölln.'

'Rhiannon, you do know it's not safe there at night.'

'I did – did the soup kitchen there then I went to Zehlendorf. I was invited for a drink by the woman who organises it.'

He said nothing, gathering his thoughts. The stirring of tenderness he'd felt was blotted out with amazement at her naivety. 'Rhiannon, you're not in Kensington, you know.'

She gave a nonchalant twitch of her shoulder and, stretching up, kissed him lightly on the mouth. He caught the faint tang of wine. Aroused, he pulled her towards him. 'Rhiannon, you don't realise…'

She broke away from his grasp. 'Last night… where *were* you? Three o'clock it was when you got back. I'm away for a while and you fret. You assume you can just come and go. There's one rule for you and another for me… it can't go on like this. You must understand.'

'*What* must I understand?' His voice grew tight.

'You must consider me – my feelings. There are murders here, every day of the week. You give no thought to what might be going through my mind.'

'It's my job, Rhiannon. I'm a journalist, not an office clerk. The work's unpredictable. You know that. You have always known that. Nothing has changed in that respect.'

'This place is not safe. Inge says there is going to be a crackdown against Communists. And they should know. Hans has joined the Nazi Party.' She had an air of defiance, yet her voice when she spoke next sounded small and faraway. 'These men, Max, what will they do to you?'

'What men are you talking about?'

'The crackdown men.'

'I told you to keep away from Inge.'

'But she's your sister, Max. The only family you have here.'

He sighed. 'I can't stand her husband. He's contaminated her with his loathsome ideas.'

'I was lonely, Max,' she said simply.

He felt a stab of guilt. With her work at the embassy he'd assumed she was slowly building a network of friends.

'I do worry about you,' she went on. 'I think you should heed what she says.'

'When I came back to Germany I vowed to stay and see things through.'

'What things?'

He gasped in exasperation, at himself, at her. This was not a discussion he wanted to get into, now least of all now.

'What things?' She was growing distressed. He stroked her back but he could sense her agitation. Again he said nothing, wanting to let the matter rest.

'Max, answer me.'

'You must see the state things are in?' he said quietly. 'What chance do we have if no one stays to fight for what's right?'

'But why *you*?'

'This is the place I grew up in. I need to make a stand. Besides, I have a contract.'

'But Max. What about us?'

'Rhiannon, I have a job of work to do. I can't just quit.'

'Can't you ask to be transferred back to London? There's plenty to do there.'

'Most reporters here have become too used to what's going on. Can't see straight. People are swinging between extremes. It's vital to show them. And now I've been given some good leads. There are people waiting in the wings,' he murmured, as if to himself. 'Ludendorff is one of them. An officer, but he doesn't want the army to serve the people, only subdue them. The army serves the interests of big money, companies like Krupp and Siemens. The people are nothing to them. I'm telling you. Nothing. Men like that need to be exposed. But I've got to get at the facts...' Even as the words left his mouth he knew they would misfire.

Rhiannon drew further away from him. 'I don't want to hear any more. Keep your rhetoric for your work.'

126

He regarded her with bemusement then linked his fingers through hers and pulled her towards the sofa.

'Calm down.'

'Max, do you really think we should stay here?'

'I've made a commitment. I can't just break that. The Nazis are good at spreading fear. Make people scared enough and you need hardly lift a finger…'

Spent, Rhiannon would argue no further. 'I'm going to lie down for a while.' She went through to the bedroom and shut the door firmly behind her.

He wished it had not come to this.

Later, they ate their supper in silence, each too preoccupied to indulge in small talk and afterwards, in bed, they had little use for words either. At first Rhiannon turned her back on him. He stroked the back of her head, murmuring into her hair. When she moved to face him he saw her face was streaked with tears. 'Rhiannon,' he whispered, drawing her close. He stroked the side of her head until she allowed him to hold her. 'Rhiannon.' They clung to each other. Then the holding became a clasping, as in panic they sought to rip away the difference, fear whipping and whetting and finally bringing them together. Afterwards they folded into each other as though their bodies knew a deeper truth than their overtaxed minds.

Twenty one

Max was in the hushed reference hall of the Prussian state library, sifting through old newspapers. Before him, faded and curled, lay a picture of Geli Raubal. She had a fresh-faced peasant air with guileless eyes, and a ready smile. With her chubby cheeks she looked barely sixteen, although she had been twenty-three at the time of her death, just fifteen months before.

He worked through the pile of newspapers in front of him. Geli, daughter of Angela, Adolf Hitler's half-sister, was nineteen years younger than her uncle. Max read how mother and daughter kept house for him in Berchtesgaden, and how Geli later went to live in his flat in Munich. An article in *Die Münchene Post* from September 21st 1931, entitled 'A mysterious affair: Suicide of Hitler's niece' repeated the rumour that Geli wanted to go to Vienna to become engaged. The reporter went on to write of quarrels between Hitler and his niece. According to unnamed neighbours, there had been loud and frequent disputes between the two just before she died. Max scribbled notes.

Out of the window it was grey and bleak, the temperature dropping, icy drizzle glistening on the lime trees in Unter den Linden. As he leafed through his jottings he found them difficult to summarise. There were too many gaps to piece together a story. The man's life spoke of an untrammelled desire for power, coupled with a messianic sense of mission. But how did these sit with his strange relationship with Geli?

It was said she was the only woman he had ever loved. It was said that Hitler himself was a mere mouthpiece of the Party, that he had been spotted in a Bierkeller and noted for his oratory. Some spoke of the hypnotic effect he had, others of his unstable, erratic nature, his yearning to be recognised as a painter, his rejection by Munich art school.

What did it all amount to?

-Was Hitler the 'something new' that many said the *'Volk'* was itching for? Max perused the last lines of Hitler's defense at the *Bierkeller* putsch trial six years before. *'The army we have formed is growing from day to day. The hour will come when these rough companies will grow to battalions, the battalions to regiments, the regiments to divisions, that old cockade will be taken from the mud, that old flag will wave again, then there will be reconciliation at the last great divine judgement which we are now prepared to face…'*

Product of a deluded mind they might be, but the words uttered a belief in fate compelling in its power. Hitler had gone on to serve only six months of a five-year sentence of treason at Landsberg prison. During this time he'd written *Mein Kampf*.

Max attempted to pull these findings together. In their last meeting Khan told him of secret meetings up and down the country between Hitler and captains of industry, deals in lonely forest glades, whisperings with Emil Kirdorf, the union-hating coal baron, or with Fritz Thyssen, the head for the steel trust or Georg von Schnitzler of IG Farben. The man was winning support and funds from all quarters. No longer just armed conflicts and the SA, he was slipping his way into the Establishment. Yet firm facts were hard to come by. He returned the reference material to the shelves.

'This is a bit thin, Max,' said Seifert over his expansive desk. 'Not exactly conclusive, is it, a few bits and pieces from last year's press, and the late night ramblings of a drunk? Did you at least interview Frosch again when he was sober?'

'He wasn't in when I called back.'

'We have to do better than this if you want to assert that his niece was murdered.'

Max heard the clear words of his boss while in his mind he was picturing Frosch's bloated body surfacing in the *Landwehrkanal*. 'What do you suggest?'

'A coroner's report, witnesses, somebody willing to come forward and swear to it. Not just innuendo and the say-so of a dubious Nollendorfer type. There are still laws of libel in the country.'

Max nodded. He knew all this. He was just testing the water. He watched the editor leafing through the notes he'd just given him. His hands were broad and solid; these were hands that liked tangible facts. Material proof. Not just the love of a compelling narrative. From the back office Max heard the steady, feverish clatter and ping of a typewriter as one of his colleagues completed a last minute report.

'I recall the incident. You might not remember, but the papers were full of it. I remember discussing it with a journalist in Munich.' Seifert seemed uneasy. 'It was big news at the time. That's why I got excited when you first mentioned it. Kurt looked into it I seem to recall… '

'Why didn't you mention that Kurt Stein would be unwilling to meet me? He's blanked me completely and now he's gone. Left Berlin.'

'I said before he got poached by one of our competitors. He's not going to be exactly cooperative now, is he? You have to make your own story. We have to deal with established fact.'

'There was never a post mortem. No photographs were taken.'

The editor looked thoughtful, anxious even, and ran the paper knife over a page as though erasing something. 'Where did you find this out?'

'Old newspaper reports.'

The editor paused. 'It would be risky resurrecting that story.'

'I thought you actually *wanted* something on the edge, not just tired thinking.' Max tapped the sheets in exasperation. 'He has had other people murdered. We know that. But this is different. People excuse political expediency and scraps between warring sides. This was family – his niece.'

Seifert's face grew tense.

'He was infatuated with her. At first she was flattered by the attention but afterwards less so. He wanted to control her. And then there was this story with his bodyguard, Emil Maurice. He fell in love with her, too. Hitler couldn't tolerate it.'

'Is that hearsay, too?'

'The story was that she killed herself because of frustrated ambition. She wanted to sing but she didn't have the talent and so she shot herself. Using Hitler's pistol, no less. That's what the Nazi press maintained. But I don't believe it.'

'How come?'

'There were inconsistencies. Criminal Commissioner Gläser objected to the hastiness of the judgement. He urged an inquest but he was overruled.'

'They're not going to exhume the body now.'

'That's not what I am after.'

'What then? You want to expose Hitler as a common murderer?'

'It would help.'

'Help what? There is still a judicial system in this country,' said Seifert testily.

'We have a duty to uncover lies being sold to the public?'

'Verify the facts. Don't get carried away. Let our readership do their own thinking.'

'So, about this article…'

Seifert snorted with impatience. 'I am telling you to get more professional about it. Find the women who laid out the corpse or something like that. Interview Frosch again. Otherwise it's too flimsy. For God's sake get on with it. Stop messing about. Now I have to go.' He strode out of the office and before Max had a chance to respond he let the door swing shut behind him.

Twenty two

Khan was on his way for a 'Treff' or Intelligence meeting, which Denning had fixed with a man known as Contact B. Khan walked briskly, staring at leafless trees within metal holders along the street. As he rounded a corner a gust of wind buffeted him, making him pull his coat in tighter.

He came in sight of the modest café where he and Denning had arranged to meet. Denning was already there. Seated at a table brimming with glasses, he appeared bored and was smoking furiously. Opposite him sat Bert Fingal, who ran a cheap restaurant in Wilmersdorf. Bert was fiddling with a packet of cigarettes. Denning was asking him about his family.

'My father died in the trenches in 1915. My mother never got over it. Blamed the Kaiser. Blamed the French. Blamed everybody I think.' They had heard all this the last time they met. With his sagging shoulders and narrow nose, Bert Fingal cut a pathetic and helpless figure. The more Denning encouraged Bert to talk about himself, the more he seemed locked in a circle.

Whitehall needed more on right-wing civilian groups, stated the latest missive to Denning. Who were stashing away arms, what sort and where? Who were the leaders? What alliances were being formed? In the mesh of militias and para-military organisations one could easily get lost. They needed more and better information.

The tentacles of the Intelligence service reached everywhere, but Bert Fingal seemed a curious choice. Denning was growing restive. He fired the odd question, his tone terse, but he was becoming detached. His manner was off-putting. Khan leaned forward and offered Fingal another drink before the man clammed up all together.

'Bert, we're trying to build up a bit of a picture. We think you might be able to help us. For instance, we'd like to know how much people are shifting their allegiances. Last time you said you know something about one of the unions.'

Bert leaned back and sipped the beer. He faced Khan, looking more relaxed. 'A cousin of my wife works for the Transport Union. I'll see what he knows. I do know people are switching when it suits them. Before, if you were a Social Democrat you belonged to the Social Democratic trade union, went on their holiday camp, drank in their pubs. You talked the same talk. If you wanted to, you could live in a Social Democrat bubble. But it's changing. Even Social Democrats are buying arms. Until now people didn't break out. Today some are switching sides. I'll find out about membership numbers.'

'That would be helpful,' said Khan.

'Hard to know what will happen next.' Bert shook his head. 'I guess people are frustrated at not having jobs when they're willing to work.' The man finished his drink, nodded goodnight and shuffled off into the evening.

'That's the last time we call on him,' snarled Denning later. 'Why can't they give us someone who knows what's going on?'

'Maybe they expect us to find out,' quipped Khan.

They were now in a *Gasthaus* further down the same street. Peals of laughter broke at another table. Near to the centre, the pub was neither Communist nor fascist, just somewhere you went in order to drink. It was a relief to be on neutral territory. The diplomatic memos that Khan had been

134

permitted to glimpse suggested that Germany was at last finding its feet. These emanated not from the ambassador, who was shrewder than most, but from others. These others spoke of the dynamic optimism that the Nationalists, especially the Nazis, offered ailing Germany. In Britain Khan had detected similiar leanings among certain members of the aristocracy.

More than once Khan had come across lackeys of Hermann Göring or Joseph Goebbels yelling on street corners. Some passers-by jeered. Others looked on with the glitter of hope in their eyes. 'Anything rather than the corruption of Weimar,' they muttered. Still others pleaded: 'Order, we need a new order.' Equally eager, though less organised, the Communists heralded World Revolution. They were a bunch of loudmouths, wanting to scrap private property and the structure of state.

Where would it all end? And more to the point, where did he and Denning stand in relation to the whole caboodle? Often he had the sensation of being one step behind Denning. There were those trunk calls to Whitehall that he made. Increasingly he was left in the dark about them. Berlin, ever a meeting place of East and West, was becoming a fulcrum of tensions. Jostling amongst the foreigners were displaced Junkers, irascible soldiers and the quick-witted Berlin underclass, which scolded, scrapped and scraped a living. With his knowledge of East and West, establishment and dissent, he had the sharper insight.

Their intelligence work was unknown to the rest of their colleagues at the embassy. Only the ambassador, the clear-sighted Sir Horace Rumbold, was in the know. They never spoke about it: the last thing anyone wanted to do was to compromise him. The rules governing foreign embassies and espionage were clear and had to be seen to be followed to the letter.

'Well, say something,' grumbled Denning.

'He confirmed what we already know, the basic pattern of instability.'

They were coming up with fewer and fewer ideas. After a few moments Denning said: 'You could do worse than get in there and find out more about Mihir Basu and his cronies. See what they're up to.'

Khan said nothing, cradling his arms and looking across at his boss. The man's vexation was growing by the day. It was as if he was blaming Khan for their lack of progress. As for Khan himself, he avoided acknowledging just why he was holding back from linking up with the leader of Indian nationalist movement. He preferred to distract himself, when he could, at soirées in elegant, chandeliered rooms. These harkened back to their first days in Berlin, though as the depression bit harder these were growing few and far between.

He would have to brace himself and look up Mihir Basu.

'You should put all other activities on hold.' Denning, suddenly cheered up.

'If you think so,' replied Khan.

Later they went to the Kuka club to see Boris Dublovsky. It was a wet, miserable evening. Everywhere there were gaps and empty tables. Khan and Denning joined Dublovsky. The man looked drained. He was droning trivia as if no serious topic could be grasped. Khan grew tetchy. No sooner sipping Sekt than he wanted to leave. He had things to see to. Earlier he'd agreed to find partners for two visiting diplomats from a Swedish trade delegation. 'If you will excuse me gentlemen, I need to go,' said Khan.

'Must you?' Dublovsky sounded at once childish and petulant. 'There's something I wanted to discuss with you.'

'And that would be?' asked Denning.

Dublovsky looked uneasy. 'What you said about diplomatic favouring...'

'Oh that,' said Denning. 'That's Herr Khan's department.'

'Another time, Herr Dublovsky. Forgive me but I need to be on my way.'

Twenty three

While Max was researching Geli in the state library that Saturday, Rhiannon was clearing up at home. She opened the windows to let in some fresh air, and shook out the bedding. They had agreed to meet for lunch, and she wanted the rooms in order before she left. Papers had piled up and when she switched on the side lamps the light showed dust lurking on too many surfaces. Outside, on the landing, she heard shuffling and light knocking sounds. She swung open the door and greeted Uschi Ruderstein from the adjacent flat.

'*Ach so*.' Uschi looked up in surprise. Red-faced from exertion, she put her hands on her hips. 'I thought it was time I had a go at the landing...'

'I thought it was our turn to do that,' said Rhiannon.

'Next week.'

Rhiannon smiled at her. On nodding terms with most of the other tenants, she and Max had more to do with the Rudersteins, not least because they shared a bathroom. Something about the intimacy of that arrangement made you either shun or befriend your co tenants. So though it could have entailed an irritable and embarrassing clash, it didn't, not least because Max and Bernard Ruderstein kept unusual working hours and the two women were easy-going.

More than once the women had had coffee together. Uschi had taken courses in English and was keen to nurture the contact. 'Time for a break?' she suggested.

'I've only just begun.'

'Just a quick one?'

Rhiannon laughed. 'There was I, being a good German *Hausfrau...*'

Over a hurriedly made coffee in a hastily tidied room Uschi lit a cigarette and affected her usual light-hearted, no-nonsense manner. Rhiannon sensed something was up. 'Is Bernard rehearsing?' she asked.

'Yes. They've got a new production coming up.'

'How's it going?'

'It'll be fine. They're doing *die Zauberflöte*. He's done it before and they have a great conductor.'

'Who is it?'

'Erich Kleiber.'

'Are you all right, Uschi?'

Uschi sighed. 'It's – I'm worried if you must know.'

'What about?'

'This coming election. Frankly, these Nazis scare me out of my wits. I keep telling myself people have got too much common sense to back that lot. But yesterday something happened. I can't get it out of my mind.'

'To you, you mean?'

'Not directly. I was walking back from work quite late, down the Tautentzienstrasse. Ahead of me, I saw people bunched outside a shop. There was a lot of shouting and screaming. This man was sprawled on the pavement, bleeding. I helped the shopkeeper get him to his feet and take him inside. He gave him a glass of water and a towel to wipe his face. Luckily, he wasn't badly hurt, so I carried on.'

'A street brawl? Was he drunk?'

'No, he wasn't. He was petrified. He could hardly speak German. He was an *Ostjude,* a Jew from Rumania. He was trying to sell bootlaces or something. They just picked on him – these louts – and laid into him. They weren't wearing brown shirts or anything. They just picked on him.'

'I can see why that upset you.'

'Can you?'

Rhiannon was taken aback by the sudden sharpening of tone. She noticed Uschi's eyes watering and said: 'It must have been horrible to see that.'

'Do you know what it's like to be hated – just because…?'

'In times of need people are always wary of the outsider, the stranger.'

'The Jews have been here over three hundred years,' broke in Uschi. 'They were invited here from less tolerant places – like England. Can you imagine that?' Uschi paused and finished off her coffee. 'Sorry, I didn't mean to get so upset. Bernard says we have no need to worry. We have good jobs. And don't exactly live in the ghetto.'

'I didn't even know you were Jewish.'

'We're the liberal, fully-integrated type, more German than the Germans. But then yesterday, when I saw this man – he was shabby and poor and had a straggly beard and smelled a bit – when I looked into his eyes, I was terrified.'

'That's not going to happen to you,' said Rhiannon.

'Bernard says I have too much imagination.' Uschi leaned back. 'I better let you go. Thanks for the coffee.'

An hour later, muffled in scarf, gloves and her old green coat, Rhiannon was rushing along, head bent against a smattering of sleet becoming snow, when she bumped into Max by his office.

'Hey, watch where you're going!'

Laughing she settled herself against him, her breath steaming by his cheeks. They headed in the direction of the Brandenburg Gate, towards the Reichstag.

'There is a little café down here. Not too far away. They do wonderful goulash,' he said. The sky was a dark yellow-grey behind the trees, signalling further snow. 'It's good to see you.'

She felt the warmth of his body as they walked by the Reichstag, a domed building dedicated to the German people. Inside, the rooms were in darkness. In the Tiergarten they approached a small, squat building half hidden by trees. Max led her into a cabin lit by oil lamps with a tiled stove in one corner.

'Used to be a watchman's hut. Not many people know about it. The owner only opens when he feels like it.'

The café had rough wooden tables and chairs. On the walls were old prints from Hungary. They caught a whiff of burning wood mingled with the aroma of beef casserole as they made their way to a bench by the stove, where they discarded their coats and warmed their hands. When Max noticed her looking round for a menu he said: 'There's no choice. What's in the pot is what we get.'

The dark-haired, be-stubbled owner ladled stew into two bowls and cut slices from a dark rye loaf. Max tucked into his food with relish while Rhiannon watched. 'You look as though you haven't eaten in a week.'

'It's the cold,' he muttered between gulps.

'I just had coffee with Uschi. She was really upset.'

'What about?'

'She saw someone being attacked. She says she's worried about the way things are going.'

'She's not the only one.'

'I didn't know she was Jewish. Did you?'

'I guessed it from the name.'

'You think she's right to be worried?'

Max tore into another crust. 'Depends what happens next. Anyone who has read *Mein Kampf* can be under no illusion.'

'*Mein* what?'

141

'Hitler's autobiography.'

'But that wouldn't affect the likes of Uschi and Bernard, would it? Surely no one takes all that stuff seriously?'

At the nearest table three men were deep in animated talk of their own, oblivious of their surroundings. Max pushed his chair back, let out a long sigh. 'People here are not easy with themselves. That's why upstarts with no culture are able to sway so many to their way of thinking.'

'You're losing me.'

'I was just thinking how Germans differ from other nationalities.'

'I'm not sure they do. I don't believe in national character.'

'Nor me, but there *are* cultural differences. Germans like philosophy, the next big idea, whether it's Fate, Communism, a proletariat dictatorship, history carving its way out of human sacrifice... You name it. The vision always has to be grand and set in the future.'

'How did your meeting go?'

'Which one?'

'With Wolfgang Seifert.'

'Okay.'

'What did he say?'

'Do you really want to know?' he asked. 'Fine. Well, not exactly. He says I need more – facts.'

'Does he? I suppose he's right.'

'Don't *you* start.'

'You're touchy today. And you forgot to shave.'

He looked towards the crackling wood-burner then back towards her, his face softening into a smile. 'Thanks for coming.'

'It's the only way I get to see you. You've been so...'

'I know. I'm sorry. There's just a lot to be getting on with. And sometimes... well, it gets to me. I forget I'm not writing a book, just an article or two.'

'So, I've noticed.'

'I'm going to be out late again. Either tomorrow night or the night after.'

'What are you working on?'

'I won't bore you with the details. It's connected with Hitler's niece.' He stared at her. 'To be honest right now I would rather just sit and look at you. Hole up here for a week, a month even. Let it all go hang.'

She laughed. 'I don't believe you for a minute. At the best of times I have a job dragging you away from your typewriter.'

'Only because it's my job.'

'So you say.'

He stared at the bowl he'd cleaned out with a crust of bread and beckoned to the owner for another helping: that was still one of the deals here. He dipped his spoon into his refilled bowl and ate. The owner came over, opened the oven door and thrust a couple of thick logs into it. They crackled and spat, sending out flames. Outside the light was fading.

Twenty four

Max returned to see Frosch. When he opened the street door in Kleiststrasse, Frosch looked puzzled and pale. 'What do you want?' he mumbled but let Max enter. He looked around. He guessed the man lived from hand to mouth: beside a bed and table there was no furniture to speak of, and the cupboards were bare. Frosch would not have a job, nor would he be organised enough to get himself to a soup kitchen. Though he seemed to have only the vaguest recollection of who Max was, it was not hard to persuade him to go for a drink.

Café Motz was a well-known haunt of writers and artists, where you could drink a decent wine at a decent price. Its décor was dingy brown from layers of nicotine, human sweat and grease. The place was half full. As they made their way to an empty table Max nodded to one or two people he knew.

When Max suggested food Frosch hesitated.

'The bean soup is good here. Let me get you a bowl. *Herr Ober!*' Max called over his shoulder to a passing waiter and placed an order. 'You don't remember much of the other night, do you?'

When Frosch shook his head, Max laughed.

'You consumed a lot of alcohol. My fault, I was stacking up the vodka cocktails.'

When the bowl of steaming soup arrived Frosch attacked it. The bones on his neck stuck out as he ate. Poor sod, thought Max, doesn't know me from Adam but has to get something down him. He leaned back, unwilling to mar Frosch's enjoyment. The man was licking his lips, cleaning out the bowl with a crust. 'Thank you,' he muttered without looking up.

'You enjoyed the soup?'

'What do you want?' Frosch threw him a sidelong glance, bordering on hostility.

'Nowadays it's hard to trust anyone. But the other night you knew I was looking for you...'

Frosch frowned. 'The barman told me. I've stopped drinking so much. It gets me into trouble.'

'I know the feeling.' He paused. 'So you won't have a beer?'

Frosch looked at him suspiciously. 'Who did you say you were?'

'My name is Max Dienst. I'm a journalist. I'm going to have one. Sure you won't join me?'

'All right then.'

Max picked up the hand-written menu. 'Would you like something else to eat? Pork dumplings, perhaps – they're very good here?'

Frosch's eyes glinted.

'*Herr Ober!*' Max called before Frosch could change his mind.

When he had downed the dumplings and a glass of beer, Frosch leaned back in his chair and rubbed his stomach with satisfaction. He nodded his gratitude, quashing a belch.

'You began to tell me you worked for the Nazi Party.'

Frosch smiled but did not answer.

'You worked in the Brown House, in Munich?'

Frosch nodded. A look of anxiety crept over his face. 'What's it to you?'

'Why did you leave?'

'That's my affair.' He shifted in his seat, looked over his shoulder.

Max thought better of pressing him for an answer. He tried

another slant. 'I'm interested in finding out about the Party. Why people are attracted to it.'

Frosch gulped at his beer, wiped his mouth.

'I've spoken to other Party members. Each has a different tale to…'

'I went to hear Adolf Hitler speak in one of the *Bierkeller*. They were all shouting and joking, and then he started. Worked himself up, good and proper. Said we were all sold down the river. We should have carried the day in Verdun. By the end you could hear yourself breathe. He had every one sitting there, afraid to move. We didn't know whether to clap or get the hell out of there.'

'That's how it started?'

'I went back the next day. He was talking in a school hall. But he got banned from there, and it was back to the beer hall. I started watching out for him. They began sticking up posters around the place. I used to go and hear him whenever I could. I felt he was talking to me. I just followed – from a distance.'

The more he spoke, the more confident Frosch grew. It was as though he were no longer with Max, but talking to himself. He went on to tell about his recruitment, how after a talk in a *Bierkeller* one of Hitler's companions was signing people up.

'I hadn't fought in the trenches,' said Frosch. 'I didn't have no grudges. No enemies. Not me. I just liked the sound of it – what they stood for. It was something new, especially for the likes of me. Then they asked if I would help out, addressing envelopes and that.' His voice grew louder. 'They must have thought I was a good worker because after a month they paid me. I was a runner. I was their first choice. They knew I wouldn't mess up…' Max could hear the small man puffing himself up. He was bandying around the names of the Nazi High Command, as if he was one of them.

'When Rudolf Hess needed anything doing he came to find me…'

'Did you know Geli Raubal?'

Frosch frowned. 'She was around a lot.'

'In the Brown House?'

'Not, not there, but on social occasions she was often seen with her uncle.'

He paused; the boastful tone had left his voice.

'What happened to her?'

Frosch glanced around the room to see who was within earshot. He took another deep draught from the beer, emptying the glass.

'Another beer?'

Frosch nodded.

'Nobody dares speak of her,' said Max.

Frosch shrugged. 'Then you can't expect me to either.' The man was staring into space, lost in the past.

'You believed in the Party but it let you down.'

Anxiety shot across Frosch's face.

'Before, the Party was there to look after you but now…'

'I didn't do anything wrong. I didn't.'

'I'm sure you didn't. But you went away.'

'So?'

'So, if they come across you again they might ask questions. About why you no longer work for them – why you left…' If Max felt guilt, goading a man who was vulnerable, he ignored it. It was essential to get as much of the story as he could. 'I have connections. If you ever needed to get away – leave the country even – I am in a position to help you.'

Bewildered, Frosch looked across at him.

'Whatever you tell me is safe. I'm a journalist. We never disclose the identity of people who tell us things…'

'I don't understand what you mean.'

'Something happened. This Party is your new hope. You are fascinated by the Leader, then all of a sudden, you no longer want to be around them.'

Frosch watched Max's mouth, as if he feared what he would say next. Max lowered his voice and moved in slightly towards him. 'Last time we met you said there had been a cover-up,' he said.

'You don't know these men,' answered Frosch, almost in a whisper. 'They are ruthless. Cold-blooded.' Frosch looked down at the table and spoke slowly to himself.

'She used to make him smile.' He paused. 'I wasn't around when it happened.' Frosch's head was bowed, gazing down in a stupor. Max was taken aback to see a tear wander down his face. He started to speak, almost inaudibly. 'She was like a spring day. She laughed and danced and sang. They say she wanted to go to Vienna to sing. She had a music teacher lined up. That may well be true… she hardly went out.' He hesitated as if weighing up whether to continue. He sniffed, the memory suddenly too strong to resist. 'I stopped believing in them after that.'

'After what?'

Frosch clenched his fists on the table. 'She made her uncle human. And they didn't want that. They wanted a machine to stand up there and rattle off… They said she could get round him. That she even teased him when – when he got carried away… She liked to go to the Viktualienmarkt. She liked to browse the stalls and walk by the river when the sun was out. I think she met friends there.'

'Anyone in particular?'

'She never said.'

'So where were you? Not in the flat on Prinzregentenstrasse?'

'We weren't allowed there. Only the odd time when a file was needed, or something had to be fetched for Herr Hitler.

I bumped into Geli on her way out. She was all smiles, happier than I'd seen her in a long while. That was the last time I saw her.'

He clenched his fists and got suddenly to his feet. 'Leave me alone!' he shouted. 'Leave me alone!'

People at adjacent tables stopped to see what was causing the din. Before Max was able to stop him Frosch had gone crashing out towards the exit. By the time Max reached the street Frosch had merged into the passing throng.

Twenty five

When Max called on Dieter the next day his old friend was sitting at an untidy desk, looking vague. Ashtrays were toppling over with dog ends, unwashed mugs littered the windowsills and the waste bin was crammed with empty beer bottles.

'You had a party, I see.'

'You could say.' Dieter's skin looked blotchy as though he had not been eating properly.

'*So, was gibt's?*'

'People shouting on street corners…'

'So what's new?'

Dieter looked across and laughed. 'A beer?'

'It's too early in the day for me. You look a mess by the way.'

'Thanks.' Dieter pointed to a pile of newspapers; *'Street violence rocketing,'* read one; *'Beware the wolf in sheep's clothing,'* another. 'Busy, that's all. Haven't seen you for days.' Dieter cleared a space between the heaps of paper on the table and eyeballed Max.

'I thought you were moving?'

'We are – in two days' time. I got word that the raids were not going to happen after all. But we're still going. I needed to get something sorted out.'

Max scratched the top of his leg. 'It's cat and mouse, isn't it? I had the impression no one had the upper hand in Berlin. That your lot and the Nazis were evenly balanced.'

Dieter winced. 'What do you mean?'

'If they see you take these threats seriously they'll think they're winning the battle. It's the politics of fear.'

'I don't think they're that clever.'

'You said before they're getting more systematic.'

Dieter stubbed out his cigarette. 'So you're going ahead with the Geli Raubal article?'

'Seifert is hedging. Wants more detail. He fears repercussions, I think.'

'So you want us to run it – is that it?'

'It's not your style.'

'Can I have a look?'

Max reached into his inside pocket and passed over his notes. Dieter spread on the desk and scanned them, grunting as he did so. He rubbed his chin, shuffled through the papers, stopping here and there to mull over a point, his face taut.

'You're right. It's not our house style. But we could use bits of it.'

'Haven't you got enough of your own material?' Max prodded a copy of the latest edition of *Immer Freiheit*.

'Most of that is familiar. But this is – well, incendiary. The Raubal story could make people stop and think? Show them that Hitler is not the man they think he is? The odious man attracts attention wherever he goes. He has something that draws people in and disarms them. All this adulation coupled with the razzmatazz is spawning something that looks suspiciously like religion.'

'Dieter, I know all that. But we have to be pragmatic.'

'Meaning?'

'There are certain journalistic standards to be kept up, as my boss is only too keen to remind me. You have to play the game.'

Dieter looked thoughtful for a moment, took up the notes and flapped them gently in his hand. 'Better if you put this out as a flyer. So they can't identify where it's come from.'

'I can't do that. I'm not some hothead…'

'No, but *we* could. Not *Immer Freiheit* per se. But we could take out salient bits and run it off.' Dieter eyed his friend and smirked. 'Berlin getting to you, is it? No stomach for a fight?'

Still out of his depth in the barbed interplay of factions, Max wanted to stride out of the room and tear up the sheets in frustration. But another, colder part of his mind was taking in Dieter's idea. Putting it out as a flyer would be like sniper fire. The Nazis would look all round, hungry for revenge, but be unable to pinpoint anyone. Seifert need never know. As it was, Goebbel's attacks against liberals and Communists in the ubiquitous copies of *der Angriff* were growing daily more vitriolic. Add to that the recent quasi beatification of the Hitler youth killed in a fight with Communists and it was evident the Nazis were pulling ahead in the propaganda war.

'You say you could run something off – anonymously?'

'Probably.'

Max cast round unable to stay still, a pent-up energy taking hold of him. 'A few leaflets on street corners are not going to change the course of history. There's already much too much bad journalism flying around the place.'

Dieter allowed the silence to surround them then said: 'You need not be involved. We'd just draw on a few things from your notes. We'd distribute at night. Use unknown runners and fly-posters. We don't want the SA to come round and give us a thrashing. Believe me. I have been in this city a lot longer than you have,' he paused. 'A few hundred copies showered around the place and you'd be up and away.'

Max's jaw worked in anxiety. 'I still don't think it will have much impact. The story was covered extensively when it broke.'

'People forget. People are by and large stupid. They only see what's under their nose. You're right, it's not going to change the world or bring about the Revolution, but it's better than doing nothing, isn't it? Better to chuck a stone against an enemy than pretend they don't exist. You've got to give it a try at least. I'm not asking you to do anything. Just let me use some of it. And if you feel like it you can help put them out…'

Max got to his feet. 'I'll think about it.'

'Well don't think too long. We don't have a lot of time. You let us take bits from your notes and then we'll just call it quits, shall we?' Max stood by the door, wavering. 'D'you need these?' Dieter waved the sheets in the air.

'That's a copy.' He eyed his friend who had turned out his palms in a gesture of pleading.

'You've got nothing to lose.'

'All right then.'

'I'll let you know about distribution,' said Dieter.

In the Konditorei Jaedicke Sid Khan was browsing over a copy of *Die Vössische Zeitung*. With its encrusted wooden floors, spiral staircase, brown leather seats, animated exchanges and clouds of smoke, the café had long been the haunt of journalists of every ilk. They gravitated here to swap tips, insults and to argue. It was the hub of the newspaper quarter. Not too crowded at this hour, it was a good place to retreat into a corner over coffee and a spread of the latest news editions. This had obviously been Khan's intention, as he appeared mildly disgruntled as Max headed towards him.

'I thought I might catch you here at this time. Where's Denning?' A sense of urgency blotted out social niceties. Khan gave him a wry smile.

'Getting a few reports together. He's going to London in a couple of days.'

'And you?'

'I'm staying put.'

'So he is to be debriefed, as they say?' Max beckoned the waiter.

'Something like that.'

'You don't mind if I join you? Would you like another coffee?'

'I've had enough.' Khan rolled the newspaper up and put it on the seat beside him. 'I hear you managed to track down Gert Frosch?'

Max was taken aback at the speed at which things were moving. Rhiannon must have talked about it to the diplomat. He'd have to have words with her.

Khan laughed, 'Don't look so alarmed. That's all she said.'

'I don't want her getting drawn in.'

'Have you written it up yet?'

'I've made notes.'

'So when's it going to press?'

'It's not. My editor refuses to print it until I unearth more facts.'

'He has a point, I suppose. Things are getting fractious.'

'I agree. People seem more cautious than they were even three weeks ago.'

'It's a small world here. Word would have got about that *Die Tatsache* has a new hack. People in some quarters might be keeping an eye on you. But don't take it to heart, old chap. They'll get used to you and then ignore you. That's how it goes.' His voice sounded suave, unconcerned. All very well, thought Max, for this Indian in his pinstriped diplomatic immunity to make such comments.

'How is Rhiannon enjoying her new role?'

'Very much, I think.'

'Do you have anything we might be able to use?'

Max hesitated. He wanted to get something out there, now, when it might have effect. Dieter's flyer would scarcely suffice.

Yet Rhiannon said she was still wary of Khan. As for him, he was reluctant to become a pawn in the greater game plan of the British embassy. But the election was imminent. There was no time to take a train to Munich and get more coverage on the story.

'What did you have in mind?' he said.

'Background information for the British public. Character a —'

' — Assassination?'

'I was going to say analysis.'

Max stretched out his legs under the table. He was growing weary with the complexity of it. He was a journalist for God's sake, not a wily diplomat trying to pull strings.

'Can I have a look at what you've done so far?'

Max hesitated. 'It's work in progress…' He passed over the second copy of his draft article and watched with curiosity as the diplomat went through them.

Khan looked up suddenly. 'How much of it is true?'

'The fact of a cover-up is evident. My gut instinct tells me it wasn't suicide, as everyone claims. But proving otherwise is tricky. Who did it? Impossible to say. My bet would be her uncle. He was the only one with a motive.'

Khan whistled through his teeth. He reflected for a moment, his face impassive. 'I have a few more bits you might be able to use. I'll send them through Rhiannon. Old press cuttings and an embassy report.'

'That would be useful.'

'So – would you consider filing this for one of the British papers?'

'You have people there? Contacts you could use?'

'As a matter of fact we do. On the quiet, of course. If the Nazis get in Germany will be heading for war. That's the last thing His Majesty's Government wants. It would be an unmitigated disaster.'

'They're not armed or ready for war.'

'The mind set is there. Armaments follow soon after.' Khan gave a slow smile, beckoned to the waiter for coffee. 'I'd give it serious consideration.'

Max nodded, his mind alight with possibilities.

Twenty six

The flyer was distributed before the Reichstag election. *Was Geli Raubal murdered by Adolf Hitler*? It shrieked, devoid of subtlety. Dieter opted for a sharp statement of the facts. How the Nazi Party was undermining the Justice system. How Hitler was implicated in the untimely death of his niece. No post mortem took place. Witnesses were intimidated. Was this man fit to run a political party, it asked. In a few, punchy sentences he laid out the challenge.

Max stared at the bold typeset and went cold. This was the worst sort of journalism. This was sensationalism, pure and simple. Yet part of him could not help applauding the boldness of the attack and the clarity of the vision, which avowed that Hitler and his party must be stopped at all costs.

Dieter got volunteers to go fly-posting in the early hours. Khan had taken a couple of hundred to throw around Wilhelmstrasse. The distributors ran up and down the streets, plastering columns and hoardings. They covered the Technical University and the Tiergarten cafés, going as far as the Brandenburg Gate and beyond, down Unter den Linden. Other associates saw to it that most of the restaurants and cabarets around the Ku'damm were leafleted. In the end they took to depositing bundles in the toilets and by the exits.

The fly-posting was swift and haphazard, the perpetrators with one eye over their shoulder and one on the target, always hurried, always nervous. Some flyers were glued to posts and walls, where they flapped and curled like strange black and white insects. Others were thrust onto the pavement, by café and cinema entrances.

Max kept watch. It was the least he could do. He had not written the flyer, but he could not stand by and see these men set upon by Nazis or hauled away by the police. Positioned with a good view up and down the Ku'damm he gave a loud whistle when he saw any threat to them. The others scurried up and down until their bags were empty. Max parted company with Dieter when the streets were deserted and he could he see no other fly-posters.

Halfway down Tauentzienstrasse two men stepped out of the shadows and blocked his path. 'What have you been up to?' asked one gruffly.

Max studied the earnest, pinched face beneath the streetlight before saying: 'What's it to you?'

'You wouldn't be handing out these would you?' said the other, his rancid breath assaulting Max's nostrils. The man's face was a tight mask as he waved a flyer.

Just then a car trundled behind them. As the two men half turned to watch it pass, Max thrust between them and ran. He clung to the shadows. Fifty metres further along he dived down a narrow passage, which wound between houses into an inner courtyard. The men gave chase, blundering and shouting, one of them waving a torch, which zigzagged light across the ground.

'*Komm' her,*' they yelled.

Max was breathless but back now on the main street. He strolled among the dwindling strollers of the Ku'damm, avoiding dark corners and alleys. He made his way home. About to slip the key into his front door he sensed the familiar bulk of the two men emerging from the blackness.

'So and what have we here?' leered one.

'A fly-poster, I believe,' said the other. 'Who would have thought it? Max Dienst, I believe?' He brought down a cosh on the side of Max's face. Max yelped in pain. The other moved quickly behind Max and caught hold of his arms, restraining him. In vain Max struggled to free himself. The man with the cosh kneed him in the groin. 'A warning,' he grunted and added emphatically. 'Max Dienst!'

The front door thrust open. It was Rhiannon. She shrieked. The two men turned. One jerked his thumb over his shoulder, signalling to his accomplice get out of there as fast as they could. Other lights glared throughout the house.

'*So was*,' muttered a neighbour, who peered out from a window. He saw the conflicting shadows and hastily retreated. Rhiannon rushed towards Max. He staggered into the hall. The right side of his face was pouring blood. 'Max!' she gasped, pulling him away from the door. 'Quick! Quick!' She half-dragged him upstairs and knocked on the Rudersteins' door, then remembered they were away for the weekend. Inside the apartment she searched for a towel and water. With shaking hands she attempted to clean the wound. 'Oh, Max.'

'It's all right. It's all right.'

'It's not! Look at you. Oh, Max. What happened?'

'Just a couple of thugs…' He pressed the towel to his face.

It was then she noticed a leaflet stuffed into his pocket. 'What's this?' She pulled it out. Max winced at the pain searing the left side of his face. He closed his eyes.

'Let me see.' Rhiannon removed the towel and dabbed the skin. The blunt instrument had caused bruising and swelling. He felt Rhiannon's light fingers on his face. Only now as the blood was staunched, did it sink in what had happened. Rhiannon settled him onto the sofa and went off to the kitchen to brew some strong tea with sugar in it, her remedy for shock.

He watched her light the gas stove. The blue flame licked up round the base of the saucepan, above it her face was pale as milk. He shut his eyes. He began to realise that every article he wrote, whether signed or unsigned, would push him closer to the edge. Collapsed on the sofa, he breathed deep and fingered his left eye, which was disappearing into folds of broken, swelling flesh.

'Do you think they'll come back?' she whispered, setting down the mugs.

Eyes still closed, Max said nothing.

'Did they know you?'

He muttered incoherently.

'Max, did they know you?'

'I doubt it. Just some thugs.'

'Do you want some schnapps or brandy. I think we have some left.' He mumbled assent and she returned to the kitchen, fumbling at the back of the cupboard until she unearthed some. She tipped up the flat, transparent bottle, emptying its content and tilted the glass towards his mouth. 'Sip, don't gulp.' She held the back of his head.

'They must have seen me with the others.'

'What others? What are you talking about?'

He slouched back against the sofa, his head lolling against the cushion.

'Journalists,' he muttered.

Rhiannon gulped down some of the schnapps, coughing as it coursed through her throat. She was shivering.

'It's all right. I'm all right,' he mumbled.

Rhiannon covered his hand with hers. 'Max, what are we going to do? It's too risky living here.'

'I can't stop now.' His voice was weary, little more than a whisper.

Twenty seven

Despite her pleas, Rhiannon was unable to stop Max leaving early the next day. At the embassy it took all her concentration to type three simple letters. The words jumped around the page and she made twice the number of errors than usual. Miss Stonebridge, covering a meeting between the ambassador and a French trade delegation, was not there to observe her agitation.

At lunchtime she slipped out of the building and called round to Hannah's office. Hannah worked as an administrator in a legal firm in Friedrichstrasse. The two women sat in the dark interior of Café Lindt on Unter den Linden. Rhiannontold her what had happened.

'It was three before I got to sleep. I lay awake, listening to Max snoring, to the wind, to my own heartbeat. At any moment I was sure these men would come back.'

'So what's he been working on?' asked Hannah.

'A story about Adolf Hitler's niece.'

'Geli Raubal?'

Hannah leaned back, appraising Rhiannon. 'Do you know who it was?'

Rhiannon pulled from her bag the leaflet she'd found stuffed into Max's pocket, and flattened it on the table between them. '*Down with the decadent Jewish press,*' it ran. '*Clean Germany from Jewish rabble. Away with back stabbers and profiteers. Make Germany a land to be proud of.*' It depicted a virile Aryan male sweeping aside a bent-up Jew with glasses.

'I didn't get the full story.'

Hannah lit a cigarette and emitted a long, lazy stream. 'Looks like the work of the SA.'

'What's that?'

'Haven't you heard of them? They're the storm troopers of the Nazi Party.'

'Max is out and about all hours. I am on edge the whole time he's away.'

'I would not have thought he's an obvious target. He's unknown.'

'He has no sense of self-protection.'

'He'll be more cautious now.' She paused. 'You might have to move house. I don't know how safe you'll be where you are now. Did they know who he was?'

'I asked him that and he said no, but I'm not sure I believe him.'

'They followed me home, Dieter. That's personal, no?'

'Maybe, maybe not. Calm down.'

Max and Dieter were sitting over beer in *die Schnecke*. Max's swollen face and reddened jaw were half–hidden by a scarf.

'All very well for you to say that. You weren't the one got beaten up. Do you think they had a tip-off? I couldn't see anyone when I left you. The street was empty.'

Even as he was saying this Max was wondering who might have leaked his address, pointed him out as a man who asked too many questions and probed where he shouldn't, a man who should be followed.

'Where's Werner these days?'

'Gone to stay with relatives in Hamburg.'

'And you trust him?'

Dieter laughed. 'His father was an old comrade.'

'That means nothing. You know that as well as me.' It could have been any one who had tipped off the SA. It could have been another reporter in Jaedecker or a waiter in Stein café with flapping ears.

'Want another beer?'

'Why not? Not going anywhere in a hurry. Don't want Seifert to see me like this.'

Dieter took another look at Max's face. 'That'll go down in a day or two. You need to put ice on it.'

'Ice is not so easy to come by.'

'Then a brisk walk in the cool air will have to do. On second thoughts it might not be such a bad idea for you to disappear for a few days. Same applies to all of us involved with the flyer. There will have been witnesses. Too many ready to go and tell tales to the nearest Nazi Party office.'

Twenty eight

The Communists had been fly-posting all over the Westend and up as far as Unter den Linden. In the Nazi central campaign office there were stern expressions and banging of fists on tables. Hans caught sight of Doctor Goebbels, face stiff with cold fury, berating the press officers because they had not seen it coming. Yes, scurrilous leaflets and emblazoned headlines were two-a-penny, the common currency in any election run-up. All sides indulged in such mud-slinging.

But Hans could tell by the solemn faces that this last attack had bitten deeper. It was like acid thrown into the face, a direct insult to the integrity of the Leader. The tatty rag accused Hitler of incest, it accused him of depravity and of breaking the most sacred bonds of family and kinship. It accused him of murdering his beloved niece.

It was not to be tolerated.

Hans was uneasy. One of his new colleagues had been on the case. He spoke of identifying the fly-posters, of knowing who they were and where they worked. He advocated setting the SA onto them while Doctor Goebbels stalled and demanded more information in order to be able to hit the target harder and with accuracy. The key task, he averred, was to sniff out all that sort of thing, to trail the scum reporters into their smoke-ridden lairs and to eavesdrop on them. Then they could be dealt with in the appropriate manner.

It should not be too difficult. They had their informants. People had switched from the Communists. They knew the faces. They knew the names. They knew where to look, where the offices and hideouts were.

Hans should have rejoiced in this. In theory he did. It was just that he could not rid himself of the uncomfortable feeling that things were creeping ever nearer to his own family and that idiot of a brother-in-law would land them all into trouble.

Twenty nine

It was late afternoon when Max made his way back to Savignystrasse. He found a hastily scrawled note in his postbox. Inge had called and would come back at four. He looked at his watch. That could be at any moment. What did she want, and more to the point how could he evade her? Their doorbell pinged. When he opened the door Inge looked tired and out-of-sorts.

'An unexpected visit,' he said.

She peered at him without smiling. 'What have you done to yourself?'

'Are you coming in?' He walked up the stairs and she followed, slow and heavy-footed. Inside she glanced at papers scattered on his desk, old newspapers and unwashed coffee cups. He could see she was itching to tidy up.

'What can I offer you?' They sat down opposite each other at the table. Max brushed his papers to one side.

She ignored his offer and folded her hands primly. 'I've come to warn you.'

'Not again.'

'This time you've gone too far.'

Max looked at her podgy, self-righteous face. There was something pathetic in the way she continued to pontificate where she was most ignorant. She had developed a nervous tic over the left eye. That was new. He found himself watching and waiting for the flicker. It echoed his own edginess.

'You were seen, you know.'

The blood drained from his head as the tic over Inge's eye grew fiercer.

'I know. How do you think I got this?'

'I heard about it last night. I came this morning, and again earlier this afternoon. Though I'm beginning to wish I hadn't.' Her manner softened and for a moment he regretted his brusqueness. 'Hans told me to wash my hands of you. You ignore warnings. He says you'll get what's coming to you.'

'But you came…?'

'Yes, I came. I thought of my little brother.' He said nothing, aware of sounds in Hardenbergstrasse, cars tooting and a tram clattering by. She slapped a flyer onto the table. 'What do you mean by stirring things up.'

'I didn't write it.'

'You were there. You were involved. You were causing trouble.'

'Trouble?'

'For you, for me, for the Party.'

'You seem to forget I am not one of yours. Never have been. Besides as I said I didn't write that. Not directly.'

'You need to disappear. You didn't even take the precaution of hiding your face.'

Max ironed out the sheet with his palms. 'What's written there is true. Hitler murdered his own niece, or one of his entourage did.'

Inge repulsed the flyer. '*Unsinn!* Rubbish! It's all lies and malicious gossip. You've been abroad too long. You don't know what's been going on here.'

'You think it's made up?'

Her face hardened, colour draining from it as altering emotions pulsated through her. 'You don't have much time. The order has gone out. Hans told me…'

He turned away, struck by a blazing urge to sever the ties between them. This woman so much like other women, in the market place, on the street, waiting for her saviour.

'What do you suggest? That I move out. Dive under. Abscond. Go to another city. Get a fake ID. Grow a beard.' He laughed.

'Max, this is serious. They could shoot you.'

'And still you support these bullyboys?'

'I told you, you've gone too far. Undermining belief in the leadership. They'll not stand for it. For the last time, give up what you are doing.'

'And if I don't?'

'The Party is unified now. They are getting stronger – you must know that—?'

He felt a surge of hatred. Did she really understand nothing about him? Her face had no hint of doubt in it. 'Tea or coffee?' He moved towards the kitchen.

She reddened. 'I'm not staying.'

He looked at her, wondering how long ago she had been won round by the Nazis' arguments. There was no point in blaming her; ideas were drunk in like wine. 'So how have you been keeping?' He indicated her bump.

'Me? I am well.'

He made a pot of coffee. She didn't get up to leave.

She let her shoulders drop and despite herself took hold of the cup. She had dark circles under her eyes and an air of exhaustion. By the tightening of her mouth and her clenched hands he could tell she was under stress. She lowered her voice. 'I'm not heartless, despite what you think.'

'I know.'

'The Party wants to let go of the past, all the shame of it, the squabbling between people.' She touched his hand. Her voice adopted a parental tone. 'I know you want the best, but you don't always make the right choices.'

Again he was the schoolboy fetched from the police station, with Inge scowling as their father vouched for him. Or he was the unruly student, brought to heel. She had had no original ideas then, and had none now. Yet rarely had he seen her so animated.

'Hans says things are going to get stricter. We mustn't let lies be spread about us.'

'What lies?' For a moment he tried to recall when the friction between them first arose. He remembered her shrieking into the night when their mother died, then never crying again, not one more tear. She'd buttoned herself up overnight, and was still doing it.

'Herr Hitler promises us peace and prosperity. He is encouraging women to have children, which is good. It will strengthen the home and make us a stable land once again.'

'Is that so?' said Max, but she missed the irony and sadness in his voice.

'Now inflation is over we can start to bring back what is ours. Only troublemakers and people who do not fit in will be excluded.'

For a moment he glimpsed the world through his sister's eyes. Oh, how she longed for a new order. She was aglow with the hope of it. Together with Hans she had discovered a new life purpose. He swallowed hard and looked into her eyes. 'I prefer the rule of law.'

'The Nazis believe in law too.'

'Do they?'

'Max, you are impossible. Though Hans tells me it's stupid, I do worry about you.'

He got up again and went to the kitchen to open a bottle of wine. 'Will you join me?'

She shook her head. 'Max, you must feel it. It is in the air. Something is waiting to be born. The Nazis will sweep away the divide between factory owners and workers. We can construct and develop. We can manufacture and produce.

And we can do it all in peace, as one nation. Together.' He wondered how many speeches she'd listened to in order to be able to reel off one of her own. She was beginning to sound like Hans.

'Really? What about the Jews, then? Or the Communists?'

The cold glitter of conviction had not left her eyes. 'People will never tolerate the Communists.'

'I'm not a Communist.'

'That's where your sympathies lie.'

'Sometimes you get pushed into a corner.'

'They're unpatriotic…'

'Have you forgotten you're a quarter Jewish? Grosspapa Mendel. A Jew, Inge. A Jew. Do you just want to brush that aside? Pretend your grandfather didn't exist?'

'Max, that's not relevant.'

'Isn't it? Have you even read *Mein Kampf*? The man hates Jews. Don't just take my word for it. Read the damn thing.'

She turned away. 'I'm going. I can see I'm wasting my time… You're as stubborn as ever you were. But a parting word of warning – the landlord's a Party member. You're known as a Communist sympathiser. Leaving aside the flyer, you're not safe here.'

'So much for your party of unity and peace.'

'There's no other way. No other party or leader has stepped forward.'

Max reflected that in this at least she was right.

'I see Hans is in the know. He must be pretty high up by now,' he said flippantly.

'Group leader in a regional bloc. And main representative in the bank.'

'He always did know how to look after himself.'

She averted her face.

He considered that this might be the last time they met. 'I

170

appreciate you coming to see me,' he said quietly. Now he wished her gone.

'Max, what are you going to do?'

He could see the argument circling in on itself.

'I'll do what I need to do.'

She was leaning against the table, her bump quite pronounced. He noticed her movements were becoming awkward and felt a stab of tenderness. They walked downstairs together. By the front door she hesitated. 'Where will I be able to find you?' she asked, stray strands of hair wisping away from the tight bun she'd scraped her hair into.

'Don't worry. I'll fend for myself. Call you if necessary.'

'But Max…?'

'Let me see you to the station,' he offered.

'I am safer alone,' she countered and strode away down the street. He watched her until she had turned the corner.

Thirty

'Now what?' Rhiannon was scrubbing potatoes at the kitchen sink. She gouged out the eyes with the sharp end of a knife and sliced them in half before plopping them into a pot of boiling water. She watched the bubbles subside then rise again to the surface. In silence Max laid the table before retreating behind the pages of a newspaper.

'At least two people have said we should shift from here. What does Seifert have to say about it?' she asked.

'Did you have to queue long for the meat?'

'No, I was lucky.'

He continued leafing through his copy of *der Tagesspiegel*.

'So does Seifert think we should move?'

'What's it got to do with Seifert?'

Her face was flushed from the steaming pot. She stood above him and stared down. 'Will you put that damn paper down and talk to me properly.'

'Calm down.' He pulled on her hand.

She went back and lowered the flame on the stove then joined him at table, folding her hands in front of her in a gesture of determination. 'I'm listening.' Her hair was wild about her face. Max took a strand in his fingers. She shrugged him off.

'You're looking very fierce.'

'I'm nervous of what you're going to say.'

'It's like this.' He paused. 'It's hard to know where to start… Seifert brought me back to write stories about the leaders of the Nazi Party.'

'I know that.'

'He wants to discredit them. But when I wanted to write up the Geli Raubal story he told me not to.'

'You said he thought you needed more facts.'

'I didn't have time to get down to Munich and get something together before the election. And I thought it was essential to get something out…'

'So what did you do, Max?'

'Dieter put a flyer together. I was sceptical about the effect it would have. But he wanted me to let him use some of the material. I didn't put my name to it. I didn't distribute. But I felt the least I could do was keep an eye out for them.'

'And of course you were seen.'

'I hate what these people stand for. Even my own sister has been corrupted.' He stared at her with such intensity that she was momentarily silenced.

'So what now?' she almost whispered.

He unravelled her hands and clasped them. She leaned back, unsmiling, disconcerting him with the blankness of her expression. 'I think I'll go down to Munich and get the rest of the story. Once I get what I need I'll come back.'

That night she lay awake listening to the rise and fall of his breath, stroking the curve of his shoulder. She turned from side to side, unable to settle. He was on his back, snoring lightly. She felt angry, afraid, unable to still the babble in her head. She went over his words. The last thing he said was that he could not falter now, he had reached a crucial stage. What did he expect from her? She wanted to shake him awake, drag the answers out of him. The conflict in the country was running clean through him, a fault-line of desperation enough to unhinge the sanest mind. It was exhausting to struggle against it, against him, against the black storm approaching land.

The Reichstag election on November 6th pushed all else into oblivion. For a while even the fighting factions had a truce. Max put off his trip to Munich for a day or two, grateful for the temporary reprieve. Along with millions of others, he cast his vote. He demurred at the ballot box, which was housed in a shabby, barely used municipal office not far from the Zoo. He felt caught between backing the Communists, the party he considered most likely to stand up to the National Socialists, and the Social Democrats, who though massively flawed still represented the Republic and a stab at democracy. In the end he opted for the Social Democrats, though with misgivings.

After weeks of frenzy and uncertainty the Reichstag election results took the Nazis by surprise. Overall they lost thirty-four seats and two million votes. The Communist vote leapt to six million; they gained three quarters of a million votes – the same number as the Social Democrats lost. The Communist seats rose from eighty nine to one hundred, while the Socialist Democrats dropped from one hundred and thirty three to one hundred and twenty one.

Instant jubilation burst out amongst Communist ranks – the Glorious Revolution was just around the corner. Speeches erupted in squares and fanfares exploded to rapturous applause in Nollendorfplatz. In districts such as Neukölln the Hammer and Sickle became ubiquitous.

Max watched, unnerved by the mania. Certainly the Communists had some cause to be optimistic, but to his mind their reaction was exaggerated. He went with Dieter to the other end of Wilhelmstrasse where the Communist leader, Bayer, had his office. Hundreds had the same idea. Everybody was in high spirits, shouting and greeting each other, singing and slapping each other on the back. Max could hardly hear himself think.

'The Nazis are done for!' shouted some.

And others: 'In six months Hitler will have no storm troops left!'

The building vibrated with the teeming mass of supporters coming and going, demanding that Bayer appear and make a speech. The man himself came to the top of the stairs, looking tousled and a little bemused. He waved, cleared his throat then uttered a few well chosen but jubilant sentences before disappearing back into his office. Max and Dieter managed to push their way through.

'What do you make of this victory – have we seen the end of the Nazis?' asked one of Bayer's followers.

'No, this is not the end of the matter,' replied Bayer. He looked grave. 'The bad state of the economy is in their favour. We have not seen the last of them.'

True enough, after the speeches of self-congratulation, confidence dwindled. For there were the unemployed, always the unemployed. Their number was waxing and no amount of talking could offset that fact. There had been six million of them at the last count and not the slightest sign of abatement.

Before long, the Nazis began claiming victory. In many ways they were right. Although they had lost votes, they still had twelve million voters behind them and over two hundred seats in the Reichstag. The Social Democrats had far fewer, while the Communists had fewer still. The Nazi drums rolled louder, the strutting was more cocksure and the good citizens of Berlin grew confused. No one party had an overall majority.

Max did his usual round of the cafés and pubs to glean what he could. There was whispered talk of the Communist party being outlawed. 'They wouldn't dare,' protested the Communist Party faithful, nervously stacking up beer in their crowded strongholds. Outside in the streets the '*Deutschland erwache*', Germany Awake, Nazi refrain became more strident, banged out in rhythm or glaring from the Nazi tabloids. Meanwhile, the cabinet under von Papen was teetering out of control: he was unable to form a viable government.

Max filed a report on the situation and sent it to the *Independent Chronicler*, with a copy to Khan. He mentioned the incident of being assaulted. He outlined the Geli story. The editor cabled back and told him the article would be run without amendment.

Thirty one

The atmosphere in the newspaper quarter grew distinctly nervous as once again the political parties drew up battle lines. Leaving Berlin regained its urgency for Max. He opted to travel incognito. In this Dieter said he was willing to help. He, too, had dived under and was staying out in allotment land. He was a man of parts: one of them, deriving from the fabulist in him, was to invent identities. With his myriad of acquaintances in Berlin he said he knew just the man and scribbled an address on a piece of paper.

Max made his way from the U-Bahn in a sharp wind towards a grey apartment block at the end of a long street. Dieter was in an expansive mood. 'Come in. Come in.' Max followed him into a dim room. Another man, dark and taciturn, was slumped in the corner. 'You better tell us just what you had in mind,' said Dieter.

'I need to go to Munich. For various reasons.'

'That so?' Dieter regarded him through narrowed eyes. 'You're still bent on unearthing stuff on Geli Raubal? It's beginning to obsess you, I think. And naturally Munich's the place. If I weren't so tied up with the paper I might have come with you.'

'You've already got me into enough trouble.' Max hesitated to say more. He knew Dieter would not give him away in the wrong quarters, but he might say too much to friends. The flyer had laid the groundwork, many would be hungry for more: hearing elements of a good story some zealot of a journalist might leap onto it.

By now Max was beginning to warm to the prospect of

going south. Munich was a jewel of a city, a Baroque beacon in rolling countryside beneath the Alps, a town renowned for its artists and good living, a place where a journalist might eat a knuckle of pork in a Bierkeller while keeping a sharp eye out. Easygoing as Munich was, it had, in its day, spawned coups, Soviets and failed putsches.

The man lounging in the corner, Anton Kontowski by name and Polish by nationality, was an arch forger. 'Anton,' said Dieter, 'has perfected his job as master of deceit in the city where you can be a career spy.'

'And what sort of person do you think to become?' Anton asked in a thick accent. Max was intrigued. On the low coffee table a dusty pot plant drooped over back copies of the Nazi rag, *Der Angriff,* lay scattered beside with the Communist *Die Rote Fahne.*

Dieter was keen to move things forward. 'You need to move around without arousing suspicion and gain access to press offices down there, The Brown House even.'

Max nodded.

Dieter studied his face. 'You'll have to pass as a member of the Nazis, the NSDAP. Are you prepared for that?'

'Hitler's rank and file! Are you mad?'

'It's one way to infiltrate. You'd need a registration number, ID papers – the lot. And you'd need to smarten up. Cut your hair. Make sure you're clean-shaven.'

Max's stomach was churning. Through his mind flashed images of Brown Shirts in the streets of Berlin. He heard their mindless bawling, read misplaced sincerity in their thuggish faces and smelled their desperation. At the same moment he pictured Rhiannon alone in their room, huddled by the window, putting on a brave face for the world.

'It's the best disguise,' urged Dieter. 'If you can carry it off.'

'Too risky I would have said.'

Dieter looked thoughtful. 'Or you could be a British journalist who wants to find out more about the Nazi Party. Yes. You work for a sympathetic paper – say *the Daily Mail*. You can bluff your way through that, can't you?'

'Sounds more plausible.'

Anton went into another room and came back, trailing photographic equipment. He set up his tripod by the window. In the meantime Dieter had gone to a cupboard and dug out passports, Nazi badges and insignia.

'What's it to be?'

'Where did you get this lot from?' asked Max.

Dieter grinned. 'A party member defected to our ranks. People are changing sides like they change socks. We've go to make you look the part. Best you widen your options. You can choose which identity to adopt when you're in Munich. Sit over there, will you.' To his alarm Dieter set about cutting Max's hair close to his head and giving him a good shave.

The back of the flat had been transformed into a dark room. Within hours the prints were ready. A stern Max stared in rigid expectation at the camera without the flicker of a smile or hint of doubt. They shocked him, though, these images, for they rendered him one of the herd. True, his hair was a little dark…

Before Max left Dieter gave him a Communist contact in Munich should he need to go to ground quickly.

When Max called in to the newspaper office later Seifert looked taken aback by his new shorn look. Max jumped in before the other could speak.

'I'm heeding your advice. I want to get more on the Geli Raubal story. So I intend to go to Munich for a couple of days, if you're in agreement.' Seifert folded his hands under his chin and gave Max a long cool stare. 'I intend to carry out more interviews with the journalists who covered the story.'

'From the *Die Münchene Abendpost?*'

'Amongst others.'

'When did you want to go?'

'As soon as possible.'

Seifert leaned back and sighed. 'You might as well I suppose. Don't go for long though. We need you here. Go and get a few more facts. But watch your back. Don't draw attention to yourself. There've been too many fights down there between journalists.'

Before Max could respond the phone rang. Seifert covered the mouthpiece. 'Look, I need to take this call.' He scribbled on a piece of paper. 'Here – take this. It's a contact on *Die Münchene Post.*'

That evening he told Rhiannon the arrangements for Munich had been finalised.

'I've never seen your hair so short. You remind me of a hedgehog.'

Max ran his hand over his scalp. 'It's not that bad, is it? I have to become somebody else.'

'Isn't that risky, Max?'

'Less dangerous than travelling under my own name.'

She leaned her head to one side, considering him. 'How will you get by, Max?' Her hand reached out to touch his cheek. He looked away. On the point of remarking that most foreign correspondents did not wear their hair long, he held back: how much should he give away? Need she know he intend inveigling his way into the Brown House? She would only worry herself sick.

'I'm travelling as a salesman,' he said hastily.

'What are you meant to be selling?'

'Does it matter?'

'Are you going to have a case with samples?'

180

'That comes next.' He demurred. She had a point of course. What would he be hawking if he were a salesman? 'Encyclopedias. I can hardly be expected to lug those around with me all the time.'

'You couldn't sell a dog a bone.'

He laughed. 'Thanks for the vote of confidence.'

'Samples, lists, catalogues. You'll get hold of some of those, I take it.'

He nodded. They had cleared away their dinner plates and were lingering at table, not yet ready for bed. She stared at him over the flickering candle. Her drawn face was full of disquiet; it was getting harder for her to maintain optimism. He suppressed a stirring of guilt. Yet he was not willing to say more about his trip; he hardly knew himself what the next step was. Years ago they swore they would never have secrets from each other – surely a misguided notion of what it meant to love someone? It was unwise to divulge everything.

'Then you don't mind me going away over the weekend myself?' Her question was in fact a statement.

'You? Where are you going?' He looked at her sharply.

'Hannah has invited some of the soup kitchen women to her family place in Brandenburg. I was going to say no, especially after what happened to you. But if you're not going to be here anyway, I might as well go.'

'You never told me…' He was jolted, disconcerted. He had not expected this. Her eyes were blazing at him, challenging him to dare call her to order or dictate what she should do. He lowered his gaze.

'The landlord glares at me every time I pass. We've already worn out our welcome here.'

'Let me get this trip over, then we'll sort something out.'

'Yes,' she said with an air of resignation. She got up to tidy away the glasses and water jug from the table.

'It's good that you're making friends in the city,' he said.

'Yes,' she repeated.

Bahnhof Zoo was noisy with an air of exhilaration and movement. Everyone seemed to be leaving Berlin. Suitcases were stacked on trolleys. Women sported pork pie hats, while men were wearing trilbies and long trench coats. Steam was blasting out adding to the cacophony of shunting, shouting and whistles.

Rhiannon felt her excitement bubbling up. In contrast, Max was subdued beside her. He'd insisted on coming to see her off. He'd insisted too that she travel First Class and had made sure that all her travel documents were in order. When it was time for her to board she was reluctant to draw her body away from his. Her apprehension was growing. 'You have an address I can write to?' she asked.

'Don't worry, I have the number in Brandenburg you gave me…'

'But still…'

As she mounted the metal step and the train started slowly forward he kept pace with it. 'I'm not sure where I'll be staying yet. But you – have a marvellous time!' As the train was gathering speed she took off her scarf and trailed it out of the window, waving it until Max was nothing but a distant blur on the platform. The train snaked away out through the allotments and apartment blocks of the city. She leaned back watching the suburbs and woods of Berlin slipping ever faster by.

'Max,' she murmured as the train bore relentlessly on, clacking and rattling her on a trajectory away from him.

Thirty two

In Munich there had been a heavy fall of early snow. Church spires and fir trees were coated white before a leaden sky. The *Hauptbahnhof,* lying in a seedy area on the western edge of the city, was quiet and its shunting yards were desolate. Walking out onto Luisenstrasse, Max pulled his collar up. It was even more bitter here than in Berlin. In the distance the Bavarian Alps were swallowed by low-lying cloud. The snow had a softening, silencing effect, vehicles glided along as if on air. Men were shovelling pavements clear and dark brown horse droppings steamed against the flattened white roadway. Trams ploughed through, slurping and whirring as they threw up banks on either side.

As he walked his shoes leaked, letting in the cold and the wet and after a while they seeped into his whole body. He stopped in a café to warm up then set off again. He found he'd forgotten most of the street names. Seifert had told him that of late the Nazis had been gaining ground here and that Hitler had singled it out as the heart of the Movement; it had also become an organising centre for Red activists. Yet Bavarians were a stubborn, conservative lot, keener on hectares of land than ideologies.

Finowstrasse, where he'd booked a cheap boarding house, turned out to be a small street of nineteenth century villas and apartments off Maximilianstrasse. The block he sought was set back behind a frieze of rigid bushes. After registering with the landlady he lay on the bed in the shabby room allotted to him and flicked through his notes. He needed to prepare himself as best he could. Seifert had given the details of the journalist who'd written up the story. He put through a call to his office and arranged a meeting in the *Englischer Garten* the next day.

In the morning he pulled on a rough serge jacket and trousers and took off for an amble around the city. Little remained of the medieval centre, yet the place was redolent of mad kings, intrigues and haughty bishops. Its onion-shaped churches looked to the Catholic south. Against all evidence to the contrary he hoped this link would offset the budding of nationalism.

He recalled his last visit here, a blurred student trip during the *Oktoberfest*, one long round of carousing, brawls and lechery. Schwabing, his favourite watering-hole, was a shabby, tolerant Bohemian sprawl of students and artists on the hunt for cheap rents and lively cafés. Today, after the snow, the place seemed sluggish and the streets were almost empty.

In the park the paths had been scraped clear and heaps of compacted snow lay like mini icebergs on either side. The wind knifed through the branches, knocking down clumps of snow. His contact, Otto Drost was waiting for him by the entrance. They shook hands.

'So, what brings you to Munich?'

'Didn't Seifert tell you?'

'Not in so many words, he just said you'd want to pick my brains.'

Max weighed up the man opposite. Otto was rangy and nervous with a ready smile, sharp eyes and quick, energetic movements. He had coffee stains on his shirt and scuffed shoes. Not a man to worry overmuch about appearances, then. Max gave him an outline of his project.

Otto shrugged. 'I've almost forgotten about that story. It was a while ago.'

184

'What *do* you recall?'

'The whole thing left a sour taste in the mouth.'

'How come?'

'Young girl, close to the leader of the Nazi Party dies in her prime. A lovely young woman by all accounts.' Otto paused, shuddered with cold and dug his hands deeper into his pockets. He drew on the last of a cigarette and flicked it in an arc amongst the frozen hydrangeas, where claw marks of a large bird trailed into the bushes. 'Our article stirred things up. The police were forced to investigate. But that didn't get very far.'

'What happened?'

'No one was bothered. Too many people were scared of upsetting friends in high places. In many circles the Nazis are despised. But they're also feared. People – that is the people who count round here – just gave in and said: "Well she's dead, nothing will bring her back."' He reached into his pocket and lit another cigarette. He was restive, keen to keep moving. He avoided looking at Max. 'Her mother was shattered.'

'You met the mother?'

'I was doing the follow-up. She fainted flat out when she saw her daughter laid out on the slab. But she could hardly admit to any suspicions about her death, could she? She went off to Austria for the funeral. She was a fully fledged member of the party by then.'

They paused by a pond where ice was thinning to water in floating sheets. A black swan paddled in a broken circle, ripples fanned out and buffeted the remaining ice, cracking it further. 'As for Geli,' continued Otto, looking suddenly reflective, wistful almost. 'He called her princess. At times he would not let her out of his sight. He controlled whom she saw and what she did. Brought her clothes even, and paid for her singing lessons.'

185

'Do you think he killed her?'

Otto raised a shoulder, emitted a sigh. 'He was hundreds of kilometres away at the time. But he *was* becoming obsessed with her. Others in the Movement did not like it. They tried to warn him. And, of course, he didn't take kindly being told what to do.' Otto moved from one foot to the other. 'Damn, the café's closed.' He pointed through the bushes to a shuttered and firmly locked little building. 'Let's keep going.'

'Were you able to substantiate any of this or was it just hearsay?' cut in Max. Behind the pond two boys were pelting each other with snowballs over a squat snowman.

'Hearsay and fact got pretty mixed up. There were several versions of the story.'

'Did you manage to put out the story as you saw it?'

'I've done my bit.'

'But it never got properly aired, did it?' Max felt he was venturing into a mist. Something continued to baffle, making it hard for him to let go. When Otto next spoke his voice was almost inaudible.

'I brought up the question of injuries to the face. They were not compatible with the verdict of suicide. I stressed the fact that no post mortem took place. Undue haste was shown in shifting the body across the border into Austria – where, incidentally, her uncle Adolf Hitler is still not permitted to go because of his part in the Bierkeller Putsch. When they found out who had written the report, I got a visit from two Brown Shirts. They were polite but direct. They said they regretted that I had been misinformed: I had been listening to unfortunate scandal. They would present me with the correct facts. I thanked them for their concern, and showed them the door. Then the editor put me onto another story.'

Max grunted. They walked on. 'So you think I'm wasting my time too?'

186

'I'm not sure how I can help you further.'

'I want to write as full a story as possible but I wasn't there. And from what you said there weren't any eyewitnesses willing to speak.'

Otto's thin face was taut, as memories stirred. 'I covered the story and moved on. That's what we do, don't we? You can't go mulling over every incident. Do you know how many homicides and suicides there are in the city these days? If we dealt with every one in detail we'd have no room for anything else.'

'*Na gut,* Otto. I understand …'

Otto drew up his shoulders. 'I'm getting cold here. I need to get back to the office.

'Maybe there are other people you think I should speak to – like the women who laid her out? One seems to have disappeared off the face of the earth, the other has moved out of town. I intend tracking her down.'

'Don't think you'll get far there. I interviewed both of them soon after the incident. They denied that there was any injury to the nose when I hadn't even asked about it. They spoke parrot fashion, rattling off the same sentence, word for word. I think they'd been briefed by the men from the Brown House. They were terrified.'

'They must know what they saw. After all, they got her ready, made her respectable enough to be looked at.'

'They are ordinary women with husbands and families. They don't want to live in fear of their lives.'

Max jumped as a lump of icy snow thudded down beside them. Despite the cold, it was thawing fast. He could hear the justifications being snapped out: necessity and purpose, to hold and pursue a worthy goal, giving all for the Fatherland, the weakness and gullibility of women, taking a stand, showing resolve, being a man, being a German. It was a

187

language devoid of connection. It was the mindset of the soldier, the politician. He could hear his own father's voice booming out, that old Prussian army officer and civil servant.

'I just remembered the name of the third laying-out woman. It was Helga Holst. Frau Helga Holst. She never gave evidence. She was still learning the trade. It might be worth a try.'

Helga Holst was in her late forties. She was stout, with strong arms, spatulate hands, and an expressionless face. For some reason Max pictured her coming from a long line of dairy farmers. It had proved easier than expected to find her, her name one of a dozen listed in the telephone directory. With a carefully worded set speech and much determination, Max managed to winkle her out from the others. He invited her to coffee and cake on the pretext of doing a survey on her 'art'.

He posed questions on the matter of coping with rigor mortis and asked about hygiene, preserving and embalming processes. The woman warmed to the subject and was speaking of her increasing experience over the previous year when Max pounced, homing in on the matter of Geli Raubal, surely the most famous corpse that she had ever had to lay out?

Frau Holst's mouth fell open. She suppressed a frown of suspicion and was off again, recalling the occasion, proud, it seemed, to have been part of the event: 'We got to the apartment at two or three in the afternoon with a pail, bar of soap and hand mitt. Frau Fischbauer washed Geli's body. I was helping her and Anna Kirmar. I was quite new to the trade and still had much to learn. The body came in a wooden coffin that three men from the east cemetery had hauled up the stairs…'

'Were there any signs of injury – beside the gunshot?'

She halted, her pale eyes flickering. She looked down at her hands in her lap, suddenly anxious. 'It was very messy. She shot herself through the heart, you know. But other signs – not especially, no.' She avoided his gaze, then averred: 'There were no injuries to any part of the nose.'

'Did you have many visitors afterwards?'

'Naturally there was a lot of concern. She was Herr Hitler's niece after all. People were keen to know what had happened.'

'And you had been instructed, of course?'

'Instructed? I don't know what you mean.'

'There was an official version, with all the discrepancies ironed out. The Nazi press office had a statement issued. Is that not so?' The woman began to look uncertain, unsure of her grasp of facts. He continued. 'Her mother was told it was suicide. But the reporter of *Die Münchene Post* wrote that the bridge of the nose was shattered, and there were other serious injuries to the body. I believe Angela Raubal fainted when she saw her daughter at the mortuary?'

Helga Holst gazed blankly out through the window of the café where they were sitting. A trap clattered by, the horses' hooves clinking on the scraped roadway. 'Frau Holst?'

The woman shot him an angry flash. 'Who are you? What paper did you say you worked for?'

'I work freelance. I am covering the history of the Movement. Would you like to see my credentials?' Max backtracked as he realised he was alienating her.

'I am a professional. I lay out corpses. There are always stories about the dead. It's not my business to get involved in all that. I have given my statement. I have seen many bodies in my time and this one…'

'Frau Holst, you said you were learning your trade then?'

'I had already been assisting for some time.' Her voice was

flat. 'They said she was unstable. She quarrelled with her uncle. She wanted to be a singer, but lacked the talent. These artistic types are all the same…' She was speaking quickly now, hands fidgeting beneath the marble-top table where she had left untouched her slice of *Schokoladetorte*.

'Do you have a clear memory of what you saw, Frau Holst?'

'I do the job I was trained to do. What do you want me to say? It was over a year ago. I have laid out a hundred bodies since then.'

He moved in closer, whispering: 'But perhaps this one was special? Perhaps there was an atmosphere surrounding it?'

She looked across at him, frightened, unable to speak. Her shoulders were coming up around her ears, as if to fend off further unpalatable truths.

'Frau Holst, I believe the body you laid out was a murder victim.'

She exhaled suddenly and looked at him, tears in her eyes. 'Who *are* you?' she demanded. Already she was gathering her belongings and dashing towards the door, drawing stares.

Outside on the street Max watched the trams coming and going. Neon signs advertising Schultheiss beer were winking among the mellow beams and facades of the old town. Slowly he walked back to the boarding house. As he went he kicked at the kerb. He recalled the articles he'd come across in the Prussian state library. In some it was rumoured that Hitler and Geli were lovers. Certainly, according to articles at the time there'd been loud and frequent disputes between them just before she died. It was hard to imagine Hitler as a lover. But then it was hard to imagine him as a soldier, yet in the 1914 war he'd reached the rank of corporal. 'The idol with feet of clay' he thought, then rejected the headline as hackneyed. That did not address the core of the problem: this enchantment that people craved, this desire to be led, taken over. Hitler's life spoke of an untrammelled desire for power coupled with a messianic sense of mission. How did these sit with his strange relationship with Geli?

In the tobacco-reeking room in Finowstrasse he sifted through his notes. This should have been an easy enough story to write up, but something kept sticking in his mind. It was the notion of Geli's invisibility: that she was disposable, an item to be used and discarded. Even *his* sense of her was still nebulous. Yet for him she was becoming more than herself. She foreshadowed what might befall others if her murderer went unchecked. He considered Otto's hypothesis: Hitler wanted to bend her will to his, then insecurity drove him to destroy that which he desired above all else. Apart, that is, from political power.

It struck him that he had to interview someone who could bring the young woman alive to him. In her last days she had had few friends, encircled as she became by Hitler's entourage. But before then, when she'd still had a life, there must have been people she associated with.

Thirty three

Rhiannon had been keen to visit Brandenburg. The place had a history. Brandenburg had seen bloody battles for supremacy amongst the German tribes. The first ruler was Albrecht the Bear, who gave Berlin its symbol. Eager to embrace the Reformation, the province had been laid waste in the Thirty Years War and took years to recover. In the 1700s Brandenburg had merged with the duchy of Prussia.

Yet for all her interest in history so far she had barely ventured out. Now she slipped off her shoes, stretched out on the sofa beside the ancient stove and gazed at the eighteenth century dames depicted on its tiles. The nearest village was Lebde, where the train had dropped her. She recalled the stop only vaguely, for driving sleet had blotted out the houses. She was picked up from the station in a trap. It was like going back in time. All around the undulating landscape of hill, wood and river was cut through with straight tree-lined avenues that stretched to the horizon.

Judging from the size of the estate and the rambling old mansion, Hannah was from minor gentry. Her parents were off in Paris, so the women had the 'freedom of the castle', with only a myopic housekeeper, Frau Schwarz, to cook for them. In the outbuildings the steward was busy mending farm equipment.

It was good cycling country, she mused. There were cycles outside in the shed. Yet at the moment she could no more get on a cycle than run a race. She was exhausted – delighted to be away from the frenzy of Berlin, glad to feel country air in her lungs, but tired into her bones. That morning she'd slept till almost noon. The others had gone off to get provisions in the village and she had been happy to be alone.

Suddenly, from outside she heard voices and shuffling feet. The women were back from the village. She got up and checked to see whether the stove needed replenishing.

'So,' said Hannah, throwing off her coat and warming her hands against the stove. 'I bumped into a school chum. She's getting a few of her friends to come over for tea. They're farmers' wives.'

The others came in from the lobby, loaded with bread and meat from the village shops. 'Whose turn is it to help Frau Schwarz with the cooking?' Outside it grew darker.

Later Rhiannon saw a cluster of well-wrapped women approaching over a sea of gloom. Clouds of vapour engulfed their faces in the biting cold. Voices travelled far in the still air. 'They're here!' she called out. 'They look frozen.' Hannah came through and glanced at the table, which one of the women had set with a cake and plates half an hour before. Coffee bubbled on the stove.

'Come in! Come in!' The Berlin women were crowding into the hall to greet the new arrivals, who stomped around, red-faced and glowing with the chill of open fields. They discarded their scarves and hats.

Rhiannon wondered how the two groups would get along. The Berlin women were committed to helping the needy, but they were ambitious. One of them was a trainee engineer; the others were trainee technicians. The Brandenburg women plied more traditional roles.

'So,' said Renate, who seemed to be the spokesperson for the visitors, 'the tea and cake have been splendid, not to speak of the schnapps to warm us through on a cold day, but if I know Hannah she has an ulterior motive.'

Hannah laughed. 'Can't a body just offer friendship and hospitality? Have another glass. It's my father's finest!'

'Does he know?'

Laughter rippled round the table. Hannah got up and refilled the glasses.

Renate moved her chubby, open face closer to her old school friend. 'You haven't told them how you tried to get a teacher sacked – just because she gave us too much homework.'

'I was only eight.'

'Nine, I thought.'

'What's that got to do with anything?'

Renate emptied her glass. 'I wanted to bring things out into the open. Last time we met you wanted us to sign a petition on equal pay for women…'

'That's all gone by the board. Now we're just scraping food together. In Berlin it's getting desperate. At least no one's going to starve round here.'

'Depends what the authorities decide to requisition,' said Gretchen. With her slight figure and long legs she looked more like a ballerina than a farmer's wife.

'Requisition? They don't have the power to do that,' retorted Hannah.

'Not yet, they don't,' said Gretchen. 'But who knows what's coming?'

'Bread and soup are the same, whoever gives them to you,' interjected another.

'No, they're not,' snapped Gisela, the Berlin secretary.

There was an outburst of excited chatter around the table, everyone striving to get their opinion heard, the alcohol and conviviality exerting an effect. The din showed no sign of abating. Hannah rapped on the table. The women fell slowly silent, deferring to their hostess.

'Renate is right. This isn't just social. I wanted to see if there are ways – ways we might work together.'

'We're not necessarily of the same mind as regards how things should be done,' Renate protested.

'Or which party to support, for that matter. Socialism is not the be-all-and-end-all of everything. A lot of good is being done through the Churches.' The speaker, dark-haired Laura, had not uttered a word till then.

'*And* by the National Socialists. At least they're getting organised,' protested Gretchen.

'You must be joking!' Gisela almost shouted.

'What makes you say that? Just because I disagree with you!'

The women broke into clusters and raised their voices as each pushed her opinion. No one was listening to anyone else. 'The point is — the point is —'

Hannah tapped a glass. They ignored her. She kept tapping until the hubbub subsided.

'We are not here to preach or convert. It goes without saying different organisations are offering help. But it lies close to my heart to bring us a bit more together. I've sat through debates, invariably led by men, and heard people scrapping over doctrine. I've seen a person torn to shreds for daring to oppose another. We don't need to get like that – if we stay grounded. If we see what needs to be done and get on with it…'

'Well said.'

'So you've given up ideas about changing the world, Hannah?'

'In a way, yes. I want to tell you something I read yesterday. Forget Socialism. Forget Nationalism. It's about Russia before the Revolution. On the last Sunday of February in 1917 Russian women began a strike for "bread and peace" in response to the death over two million Russian soldiers in the war. In this they were opposed by every single political leader. But they continued. Four days later the Czar was forced to abdicate. The provisional government granted women the right to vote.'

'What's that, if it's not socialist propaganda?'

'Shh. Let her finish the story!'

'My point is – not that they were fighting for Socialism, but that they got together and held to their purpose. Men ignore us. They treat us as though we don't have a brain between us.'

'Russia is Russia. That would never work here.'

'Who says so?'

Rhiannon could sense the tension building. Once politics entered the arena any hope of cooperation evaporated. 'If I may say something,' she began. For a moment the others stopped wrangling, curious to see what the *Engländerin* might bring. 'You might vote for different parties… I'm struck by your passion to do what you think is best. But it bothers me to think your good will might come to nothing because of…'

'That's life, isn't it?' piped up one of the countrywomen. 'That's why the country's in such a mess. No one can agree on a solution.'

There was another outburst, some agreeing with her, others loudly affirming their take on the economy. Rhiannon had the sudden image of Aunt Vicky chairing a WI meeting that threatened to break apart. Vicky was rapping a glass, 'Ladies! Ladies!' and in her most powerful voice quoted the constitution, which proscribed the espousal on any political party or creed.

'Surely,' asserted Rhiannon, cutting through the babble,

'surely it makes more sense to put aside differences. We need to think about the poverty facing families. Poverty means hunger... children with grey faces... women old before their time. I have seen hunger in the south Wales valleys, and I see it here. We all know what hunger does. If we, as women can do anything, anything at all, to prevent this happening, then we should.'

She sat down, perturbed. The group was silent.

'Brava,' said Hannah after a moment. 'There we have it. We need to move beyond squabbling. We need to take stock and do what we can. Do you agree?'

The women muttered to themselves.

Later, in her room, Rhiannon felt dejected. Outside a wind had sprung up. It rattled the windows and whistled down the chimneys. The room was chilly. It had high ceilings and a lukewarm pipe from the antiquated heating system, which knocked and gurgled. Outside she heard the intermittent screeching of owls and the yapping of farm dogs. From Max she had heard nothing. At first she'd hovered by the phone in the entrance lobby, but soon gave up. She felt hollowed out, unsure of the way ahead. She had spoken out, said her truth, but she was a stranger among women who knew how to read each other. She sat on the edge of the bed, drained but too agitated to sleep. What of Max? What scrapes would he be getting himself into? She sighed, unsettled by misgivings. Max was a law unto himself. She could no more restrain him than he could her.

The women were growing restive. They needed to return to Berlin. All the signs were there: the sporadic curtness of response, restlessness at being corralled together and an underlying impatience when things could not be resolved. The encounter with the country cousins had been fraught and conciliatory in turns. They reminded Rhiannon of the Women's Institute. They were bent on remaining practical, while the townies enjoyed intellectualising. Hannah, as undisputed leader, had suggested a final get-together. The very thought wearied Rhiannon.

She kicked off her shoes and lay back, shivering. The temperature was dropping. Immediately she sat up. Somebody was at the door. She shuffled into her shoes and crossed the worn floorboards. At the threshold stood Hannah, a blanket across her arm. Her figure was thrown into relief by a paraffin lamp behind her. Her hair wisped away from her face, her eyes glittered like a cat's in the half-light.

'I brought you this,' she said. 'This room faces north. I thought you might be cold.' She lay the blanket on a chair near the door.

'How kind!' said Rhiannon. Hannah moved forward and looked at her.

'I was wondering how you were... Sometimes you seem very quiet, anxious even.' Rhiannon gave a little laugh. Hannah showed no signs of wanting to leave. She sat on the bed and gently pulled Rhiannon down next to her. Her hand softly over the eiderdown as if stroking a pet. 'I realise it must be difficult for you here... among so many strangers, in a different culture.'

'I'm used to it by now,' said Rhiannon.

'Your husband is away so often.'

'It's his job.'

'Sometimes I don't think men understand.'

'That's true enough.'

Hannah gently clasped Rhiannon's hand. 'I'd like to see you relax a little more...'

'I'm grateful for your friendship.'

Hannah began to stroke Rhiannon's arm, her touch so light

Rhiannon thought she was imagining it until she glanced down and saw the white fingers travelling over her elbow. Hannah touched her cheek. 'You seem so vulnerable here. I feel I want to protect you...'

Rhiannon shifted slightly, looked at Hannah's glimmering eyes. There was a fragility about them, an unasked question. The fine nostrils flared, the mouth pursed. Hannah lay her hand gently above Rhiannon's breasts, moved her face towards hers. With a shock Rhiannon saw the mouth come towards hers, the lips were on hers, the hand was moving down towards her breasts. *Mein Schatz,*' said Hannah. 'My treasure, my dear little English woman.'

Rhiannon pulled back.

'It's all right,' Hannah whispered. 'I mean no harm. You are so beautiful. Like a doe. A frightened doe...' She bent her head to kiss the breast.

Rhiannon inhaled sharply, pulled back.

Hannah gave a little laugh. 'There are many sorts of love,' she said. 'Don't be afraid.' She touched Rhiannon's arms, looked steadily into her eyes. There was a smile of tenderness on her face. 'The first time I saw you... I knew there was something. Your husband doesn't have the measure of you. Doesn't appreciate you. Why else would he leave you so often?'

'Hannah, no. That's not the way it is.'

'He may well have another... men are like that.' Her eyes glinted in the darkness. 'Take my word for it. I know all about men.'

'But you don't know Max.'

'But this could be something different.' She caught Rhiannon's hand. 'A deeper friendship.'

'Hannah, please. I'm tired. I want to be on my own.' She lowered her voice, shifted away from her. 'Please.'

Hannah frowned, got to her feet, and then walked towards the door. 'Here!' She picked up the blanket from the back of a chair and laid it across the end of the bed. 'These are difficult times, my naïve one. Best to take love where you find it.' Her eyes lingered on Rhiannon's as if awaiting a response. Rhiannon glanced away.

Thirty four

Max found the *Bierstube* where he'd arranged another meeting with Otto. With its wooden surfaces, dark walls adorned with folksy sayings, beer steins, and Dutch interior paintings, the place had a cosy familiarity about it. He ordered a Franziskaner. Within minutes Otto walked into the muggy atmosphere, looking, in his dull brown jersey and serge trousers, like a worker. Max ordered him a beer. 'Munich's falling into line, I see.' Max tilted his head to a group of Brown Shirts marching by.

'On the surface, yes.' Otto shrugged. 'The average Bavarian is happy to leave all that to the elementary school teachers.' They stared for a while at their drinks. 'How's it going? Do you have enough to go on?'

'Could always do with more. But I have another question.'

'Carry on.'

'Did you interview Heinrich Himmler?'

Otto's look sharpened. 'No, why?'

'He seems the most lethal of the henchmen.'

Otto shook his head. 'They drew a wall around themselves. Still do. In fact, he was one of the two who came to warn me off.'

'Do you think he would agree to be interviewed now?'

'Not a hope in hell. He was totally buttoned up then and I see no reason why that should have changed. Besides, he's out of town right now.'

Max ordered another beer for Otto and then asked 'Do you know what frightens me most?'

'What?'

'Behind all the flag-waving and heel-clicking, is the sheer seductiveness of it; all this pulling together. Duty. Discipline. You don't have to take responsibility for yourself. You assume your superior knows what's best. Could there be anything simpler? When you see chaos all around you there is someone setting matters right.'

Otto nodded. 'Depressing thought for those who believe in independence of spirit.'

Max looked at his watch, restless to be on his way. He needed to send off a preliminary dispatch to his editor. 'I wanted to talk to one of her university associates. You mentioned someone called Charlotte Blau.'

Otto looked thoughtful. 'I can give you Charlotte's address. She's a legal secretary. She used to work in the Kaiserstrasse. She's better known as Lotte.'

Otto and Max left the glow of the *Bierstube* and parted at the street corner. Otto was glancing over his shoulder as if he feared surveillance; fear gets to everybody in the end, thought Max.

At the three-storeyed mock Gothic house in Frauenstrasse near the Viktualienmarkt a disgruntled, pepper-haired woman answered the door. She turned out to be Lotte's aunt. She told Max, in no uncertain terms, that he was wasting his time: Lotte was now engaged, and he, along with all the other hopeless suitors, could go sling his hook. Max smiled to himself, quite a girl then, this Lotte. She no longer lived at this address and there was no way, insisted the aunt, that she was going to supply him with her niece's address. Nor was he going to wheedle out of her where Lotte worked.

There was nothing for it but a trawl of the legal practices on Kaiserstrasse. This he did, and after hours enquiring after her, he was on the point of giving up when he came across the young woman herself, acting as receptionist for *Loftus und Blick*.

As Lotte Blau sat opposite Max in the Carlton Tea Room, she seemed as flattered as she was puzzled. Her soft brown hair parted on the side and held back by silver slides, gave her a girlish look. She kept throwing Max sly glances as she drew on her Gaulloise. Her eyebrows, plucked thin like Marlene Dietrich's, were raised in an expression of constant surprise. For a woman who'd once circulated within Hitler's orbit she was wearing rather too much make-up. He noticed she was wearing silk stockings. He flashed open his lighter to ignite her third cigarette.

'You a journalist, then?' Her cornflower blue eyes challenged him. 'You keep asking about Geli – but she's dead and buried.' Lotte's neck grew pink as she spoke. She blew out a stream of smoke.

'I read the reports,' he said. 'As you say everything has moved on.'

'So?'

'I just want to build up a picture of her.'

'What's it to you, Herr…'

Max hesitated, momentarily unsure who he was supposed to be. He sensed subterfuge would be futile with Lotte for despite her air of worldliness she spoke with a marked directness. His eyes lingered on her as he assessed how much he could trust her. 'Dienst,' he said. 'Your aunt wanted to send me away. She said you were engaged and I was wasting my time.'

'Oh, don't mind her. She doesn't like the idea of women having male friends. I grew up with her. She thinks I should be married off by now. You know the sort? Was against me going to university but I thought otherwise.'

'That's where you met Geli?'

'We were in the same English class.'

'What was she like?'

'Geli?' Lotte stared hard at the parquet floor then up at the counter where an array of cakes, jellies and *Sachertorten* tempted the chattering afternoon tea drinkers. 'Mostly I try not to think about her.'

'You were close?'

'For a while we were, when she first came to Munich. Afterwards, it was different.'

'How?'

She looked at him warily. 'You're not from there, are you?'

'Do I look as though I am?'

She gave a little laugh and rearranged her packet of Gaulloises on the glass-topped table. 'She was afraid of no one. Not even him. At first he enjoyed that. We often went shopping together. He'd come with us, and sit nearby while she pranced in and out trying on dresses and hats. She'd make him wait. He even carried the boxes for her.' She paused, tipping the ash from her cigarette. Her voice grew softer as she remembered.

'She used to tease him, flirt with him even. After a morning class we'd wander over to Café Heck and he'd be holding forth at his *Stammtisch*, his favourite table, surrounded by leery types who lapped up everything he was saying. His face would light up when he saw her. Then we'd go off and let them get on with it.'

'But things changed?'

Lotte looked at him warily. 'Who did you say you wrote for?'

'I didn't, but it's a paper in Berlin. We're covering the story.'

'I don't understand why. It was over a year ago.'

'You were saying – you were telling me about your friendship.'

'There's not much more to say. But yes, things did change.

He got more taken up with his – you know – politics and speechifying. He was gathering people round him, in church halls and beer cellars. She got bored. I don't blame her. He went on for hours sometimes.'

'And Emil?'

'You know about that?' She sipped her tea. 'There's been a lot of gossip but I saw it at first hand. They obviously had eyes for each other. Geli was such fun. Everybody loved her. She knew how to enjoy herself. Well, while Uncle Adolf was tied up with all his meetings, she and Emil started going out, nothing much – to the cinema, strolling by the Isar, coming here. At first it wasn't a problem. But you could tell they were attracted to each other. Her uncle couldn't stand it. He was jealous as anything. He forbade it. Said he was acting *in loco parentis*.'

'I bet she didn't like that.'

'She hated it. Free as a bird she was. In fact she kept canaries and let them fly round in her room. Herr Maurice was put in his place and Geli stopped going to lectures.'

'What was she doing instead?'

Lotte shrugged. 'Singing lessons. Partying. You know, Nazi functions and the like. We started moving in different circles.'

'Was she happy, do you think?'

'Hard to tell, but I doubt it. To look at she never lost her *joie de vivre*. Except at the very end.'

'Do you think she committed suicide?'

Lotte stabbed her cigarette into the ashtray. 'How should I know?'

'When was the last time you saw her?'

'A few weeks before she died. She looked miserable as sin. By then she'd moved in to her uncle's flat in Prinzregentenplatz. He said she had to go there because he could no longer afford for her to live in a place of her own. But I think it was to have

205

her near him. He was obsessed with her. She gave up any attempt to study, which is what she'd come to Munich to do. She concentrated on singing.'

'How did that go?'

She looked across at him, her cheeks quite flushed by now.

'I heard she was intending to go back to Vienna to study music and voice. She even had a teacher. But it never came to pass.'

'What do you think happened?'

'I wasn't there, was I?'

'But you know her. She was your friend.'

Lotte finished off the remains of her tea. She was silent for a moment then looked up at him, her eyes moist. 'She was a caged bird – unable to fly. She loved the good things of life: men, champagne, music, singing…' Lotte tossed back her head, ran her hand through her hair. She looked reflective for a moment. 'Is it Oscar Wilde who says we always kill the thing we love? Whoever pulled the trigger, Geli's life no longer belonged to her…' She sighed. 'I don't even know who you are and you're making me say all these things.'

He said quietly. 'I want to tell her story. So people know.'

She examined her nails then continued in a low voice. 'If you want my opinion the Brown House lot wanted her out of the way. She could appeal to him and had a certain power over him. This made him insecure. So it wouldn't do.'

She sniffed loudly and got to her feet. 'It's getting late. I'm meeting my fiancé at seven.' With that, she adjusted the belt of her skirt, gave him a quick placatory smile and headed for the door. She half turned towards him by the exit to give a little wave. Max poured himself more tea.

The next day he wore the brown shirt and neatly pressed trousers provided by Dieter, peering at himself in the bathroom mirror as he clipped on the swastika badge. He could no longer put off gleaning what he could from the Nazi press machine, but after the flyer fiasco there was no way he could trade under his own handle. There was nothing for it but to pass himself off as a Nazi from Berlin, keen to aid the Movement. He looked at himself glumly. His dark eyes questioned and probed, his cheeks were a little sunken. Despite the shortness of his hair he looked more dissident than conformist. His grandfather's Jewish genes shone through, giving him a foreign, un-Germanic look. He would never be able to pull it off. A reporter from *The Daily Mail* it would have it be after all. He changed his clothes and fished out the relevant documents Dieter and Anton had forged for him.

Situated on Brienerstrasse the Brown House was the nerve centre of the Nazi Party in Munich. Just east of Königsplatz it had been dedicated in January 1931. Before then it had been a private villa, Barlow Palace, and had undergone extensive refurbishment to house the growing needs of the party. Max approached the place slowly, rehearsing his words of introduction, his legs stiff with fear.

The building had a great bronze door and was guarded by solemn sentries in black uniforms. He kept his face as neutral as he could. In his head he heard Hitler's renowned underling, Baldur von Schirach, the Nazi student leader, spouting: 'My church is no longer the altar of Christianity but the steps of the *Feldherrenhalle*, where the old combatants poured blood for our sake. Their spirit lives on in Adolf Hitler, our leader and hero… ' Max was assailed by panic, a bad liar at the best of times, the guard would surely spot him as an imposter.

In the event, a pale-faced man with a receding chin appeared and shouted: *Heil Hitler* while his arm flew up like a wind-up toy. Max hesitated then did likewise, uncertain how a putatively pro-Nazi British reporter would behave in the circumstances.

He proffered his documents. 'I have come to find out more about the Movement,' he explained. 'Many of our readers are following it with interest.' His voice sounded hollow. The guard hesitated, doubt darkening his face.

'*Moment bitte*,' he said and retreated into the building, emerging minutes later in the company of a round-faced, earnest man who introduced himself as Erich Haffner and demanded to see Max's papers. Max handed them over, hoping Anton had done a good job. 'Did you seek permission before coming here?'

'I have been reporting on recent events in Berlin for London,' Max spoke haltingly as if seeking the right words. 'In England we have many of the same problems as you have. We are interested in learning more about the Nazi Party.' He gave a weak smile, sensing the impact of the noble cliché. A glimmer of appreciation crossed Erich's face. He nodded.

'Follow me.'

Easy, thought Max: so the Movement was still hungry for approval. Erich said he would show him round.

Inside Max had an impression of bright chrome and efficiency. The floors were of gleaming marble, oak-panelled the walls and swastikas decorated the stucco ceiling and window glass. Their feet echoed over a marble floor. 'Here is the records office. We have five hundred thousand party members. When we reach a million we stop taking applications.' Erich beamed. 'And that won't be long.' Upstairs was the Hall of Senators, where high-ranking Party dignitaries sat at conference. Sixty chairs of red morocco leather were arranged in two horseshoes facing the seat of the leader of the party. Heroic busts of Otto von Bismarck, the iron chancellor, and Dietrich Eckhert, a martyr for the putsch, frowned down from pedestals. Beside them were plaques illustrating the Party's ten-year history, from its fledging days in beer cellars through its defeat at *Feldherrenhalle* to its glorious renewal after Hitler's release from Landsberg prison.

'Is this hall ever used?'

'At times,' he hesitated, as if unsure what to say. Max suspected the layout was too democratic for the Nazis, too much League of Nations or Reichstag. Wide doors opened onto an elegant first floor restaurant with soft lights above walls of herring-boned oak. Now this would be used. There were gold damask chairs and side shelves of marble. Waiters were putting out Dresden china and silverware, arranging blooms in crystal vases and vacuuming the plush red carpet. 'Bit luxurious for a workers' party,' he murmured before he could stop himself. This drew a cold stare from Erich, who shunted him on.

The offices of Rudolf Hess, Himmler, Goebbels, Schwarz and other party officials were on the upper floors. Each office had a desk, black telephone, writing pad and fountain pen, their Spartan simplicity contrasting with the opulence of the dining room. In every hallway hung an oil painting of Adolf Hitler. On one wall a map of Germany was pinned with black swastikas over the cities and towns.

The place sent a chill of apprehension through Max. This was a kingdom in the making. He gave a grave nod. Erich, still po-faced and by now quite impatient, brought him back to the start point where he showed him into a cubbyhole off the main records office. 'We are growing so fast…' He pointed to a pile of filing a metre deep: these were the latest applications. 'These have still to be sorted.'

Erich said there were more recruits in the north, many were clerks and teachers, even more were unemployed. Max stared at the bulk of paper and for a moment wished he could put a match to the lot of them.

'This is the press office,' said Erich as they moved further along the same corridor. It was a box room lined with filing cabinets. Max eyed the shelves stacked with folders, the desks piled high with articles. Erich looked at his watch, glanced over his shoulder as if eager to be getting on with something else.

'Don't let me detain you,' Max said. Erich hesitated. He peered at Max.

'I have appointment,' he said. 'You may be interested to look at back copies of our Nazi papers. I shall be back in fifteen minutes.' Max nodded solemnly. Erich strode away. Max waited until the steps faded before starting his search. He hunted through the previous year's press releases and articles, tentatively at first then ever more avidly. He found little on Geli Raubal, just a brief notice in *Der Völkische Beobachter*. He carried on rummaging through neat piles in the countless boxes. He glanced at his watch: Erich would be back shortly.

Lodged at the back of one cabinet, as if forgotten, were two cardboard cartons. He pulled them out. They contained crumpled manila envelopes. Inside one was a pile of yellowing photos, now sticking together. They were shots taken by Hoffman, Hitler's official photographer. They were so dog-eared that they must have been left there by mistake.

With mounting tension he rifled through them. It was an odd assortment of snaps of Hitler and his entourage, mostly caught in moments of relaxation, hiking, in Lederhosen, up in the Bavarian Alps, outside country inns. In one series Geli featured as the main attraction. There she was smiling over a clutch of puppies, eyes shining. In another she was sitting at Uncle Adolf's feet, in his shadow, looking vulnerable and staring up at him like a child. In yet another she was quite the woman, wading into water – which Max supposed was at Berchtesgaden – skirt hitched high over her thick thighs, giving a seductive, come-hither smile to the camera. Max leafed through them, summoning the spirit of the woman. He was struck by the transparency of her face, how it echoed without subterfuge her changing moods. He gazed at the images, shuffled through them.

So this was the Leader's vulnerability.

Erich was approaching. Hurriedly Max stashed away the photos. Erich entered, sniffed and glanced around with an air of solemnity. 'You had a look through our papers, I see.'

'Very interesting,' remarked Max and added: 'Does the leader still mourn his niece? I just came across an article on her death.' He was met by a frown, which barely hid disgust.

'We do not talk about her.'

'I see.'

In his research Max had read that on the anniversary of Geli's death Hitler kept vigil. He'd abstained from meat since she died. Some even said say it had turned his mind.

They moved out of the room towards the general typing pool. Max noticed a man in uniform eyeing him from across the way. He had the same glassy-eyed expression as Erich. The man walked up to them and nudged Erich to one side after muttering to him. Max caught the reference to identity papers. The man in uniform moved towards Max. 'You want to see my papers?' Max forestalled him, affecting surprise.

'I haven't seen you in here before. What's your name?'

'I thought your colleague explained.' Max paused. 'I'm

John Whiting, from *The Daily Mail.*'The other frowned as Max opened his identity card. The man scrutinised it. 'And yours – if I may ask? Name, I mean.'

'Helmbrecht Doberling.'

'Is there a problem?' Max's voice became sharp.

'Can you come this way, Herr Whiting ?'

Doberling walked down the corridor and opened a door onto a side office. Once inside he pointed to a bow-backed chair opposite the desk. As Max sat down the man's grave face, with its broad chin and thickset neck, was trained on him.

'You're from London, you say?' said Doberling.

'Via Berlin,' added Max.

'Why have you come to Munich?'

Max sensed the clichés he had used with Erich would no longer suffice. From his quizzical expression this man appeared to have the wily wit of the intuitive. Max felt his throat grow dry. He forced a response: 'I believe Munich is the epicentre of the Party – even more than Berlin. There the big battle has only just begun.'

The words sounded strained. Max looked past his interrogator to the wall.

'Say more.'

Max stared down, noticing how highly polished and dust-free the floorboards were. He took a deep breath, struggling to appear calm. 'Berlin is a cosmopolitan place, open to outside influence, the foreign press. It has seen skirmishes between Communists and Nationalist Socialists. A third of Germany's Jewry lives there. It will take an effort to persuade people… but Munich too has seen its share of putsches and soviets.'

Max's mouth was now quite dry. He suppressed the urge to clear his throat. He wondered how he had drawn attention to himself, whether he'd messed up some piece of protocol or whether the man doubted his identity papers. He wondered how often foreign correspondents came visiting the Brown House.

'I was once a student here,' he said. 'Doing German studies. I wanted to visit again and find out more about the Nazi Party at close quarters. There are many in Britain who admire the Movement. Many who want a way out of chaos.' He had attempted to lace his speech with a subtle English accent and sentence structure. His heart was racing. He stared past Doberling to a map of Germany on the wall. It was stuck with triumphant little swastikas.

'Who did you say your editor is at the moment?'

Pub signs and the offices of Fleet Street flashed through his mind. He couldn't for the life of him to retrieve the editor's name. 'Jarrow,' he said thinking of the northern hunger march. 'Henry Jarrow.' Doberling pulled out a ledger and started leafing through it.

'There is no one of that name listed here.'

'There wouldn't be, ' said Max hastily. 'He has just assumed office. In the temporary absence of …'

Doberling continued to regard him with intense curiosity. Max felt a knot in his stomach. Again he studied the floor. He looked up and noting the puzzlement of the other started reeling off a list of some of the newspaper men he knew in London. Doberling fixed him with a stare.

'*Na gut*', he said, getting to his feet. 'I like to see people who come as visitors here. It's important to keep an eye out. You can never be sure if people are really who they say they are.'

Once out of the room Max hurried down the corridor. He had to get out. At any moment Helmbrecht Doberling might reappear, ordering him back to his swastika-mapped office in order to step up the probing. He sauntered towards the main entrance, feigning an air of calmness. On the point of leaving the building he heard someone call:'Herr Whiting! Herr Whiting!'

He nodded to the iron-faced guard and scurried down the steps into Brienerstrasse. He walked faster, not daring to look back. He took a left turn at the base of the steps, heart pounding. Someone was clattering down the steps, and was now only metres away. At a tap on the back he swung round. It was Erich.

'Herr Whiting, you forgot this.' He looked into Erich's flushed face. He was holding out his identity papers, now duly stamped with the Nazi insignia. 'I passed by the recruitment office and saw it on the table. I was puzzled. One of the secretaries told me she saw you heading out of the building. You wouldn't get back inside it without proof of identity. You need to be more careful.'

'*Ach so*,' said Max. 'How careless of me.' He put the card in his inside jacket pocket while Erich stared at him, disconcerted. Max walked away through the icy streets.

Thirty five

A hint of St Bruno's pervaded the reading room at the British embassy. Khan sat, legs outstretched, in a wing chair under a glowing standard lamp. Not yet four in the afternoon yet dull outside, it was a good time to be indoors awaiting the tea and scones ordered from the canteen. *The Times* and *The Daily Telegraph* lay crumpled from a thorough perusal.

In London nobody seemed concerned about the parlous state of Germany. They had enough on their own plate: for the fourth day in a row there had been pitched battles between police and supporters of the hunger marches. In Trafalgar Square thousands protested against the government Means Test, ending in fourteen arrests and many bloody noses. Winston Churchill was urging Parliament to strengthen the army and navy while others, bent on disarmament, pointed to the magnificent work being done by the League of Nations. In *The Times* there was a reference to the Reichstag elections. One journalist struck a note of surprise that even before the election the Prussian parliament had been dissolved, and that nobody was doing anything about it.

Otherwise, it was business as usual. Austin had introduced a new model of car, the Austin Ten, and evening gowns were becoming backless. More women had taken up smoking. Khan was relieved to hear the rattle of the tea trolley. The turbaned tea lady fussed as she set out the crockery among the scattered papers.

After leaving the embassy he walked through the drizzle to the temporary residence of Mihir Basu in Charlottenburg.

He'd been given his address weeks before by an acquaintance from Calcutta. Before departing for London Denning had again insisted that he follow it up. British Intelligence would want to know what Basu was up to. He had caused more than his share of mayhem in Bengal. At first Khan demurred; the card in his pocket had started to shred. But right now he wanted to hear Indian voices. See a darker skin, smell or imagine he could smell the spices of Mother India. He was tired of playing the diplomat and go-between. He wanted to kick off his shoes and relax.

A minion ushered Khan into a salon, which was crammed with visitors, Indians and Europeans alike, sitting on sofas and floor cushions. They looked eager, waiting to receive *darshan* from the great man himself, the guru of militarism. Khan had met Basu once before in Calcutta and they had disagreed heartily over Independence; when it should come about, and how. Basu had come to Europe ostensibly on health grounds but a steady stream of supporters and would-be revolutionaries had been pouring towards him. Khan moved forward, gave the namasca sign.

'This is an unexpected visit. I am honoured.' Basu was not wearing the white dhoti and pyjamas of Bengal but army issue khaki, the garments fitting close to his body. 'We were about to have a meeting, but please come in.' Khan followed Basu into a smaller room, which grew silent as they entered.

'Don't let me stop you,' said Khan, knowing at once it was useless: nothing would carry on with him there. Of course they were too well bred to say so. He should leave at once. 'Just came to pay my respects,' he muttered. 'I get so tied up. I rarely get a chance to see my fellow countrymen.'

An amazed, sceptical silence greeted him. They were staring, more in surprise than hostility. Whatever was he doing here? A circle of men had gathered, not in dhotis, as he'd half expected, but in dark business suits. They frowned first at him then at Basu, as if to say: who is this *ferenghi* you've brought amongst us? Is he who we think he is?

'Don't let me stop you,' he said again. But how could they proceed with him in the room? These men might be hoping to do a deal between the New India Movement and the German Nationalists, maybe even with the Fascists. What they wanted was to cut out the very government and Empire he represented. No wonder they were staring.

He swallowed hard. 'I'll not be staying,' he said with a formal nod of the head. 'I see you have important matters to discuss.' Mihir Basu, too wily to betray his feelings, nodded likewise and moved with Khan back towards the door.

Later the meeting played on his mind. He would have to return. From afar, he had followed the Free India Movement. Denning had a point. While Mihir Basu was still in town it was worth another crack at penetrating it. Mihir Basu was not a man for compromise, unlike Mahatma Gandhi. For Gandhi combined political acumen – that tricky lawyer's mind of his – with spiritual vision. Some said Gandhi lacked Basu's ruthless drive.

So Khan returned to Charlottenburg the next day. Persistence might just pay. A manservant opened the door to him and showed Khan upstairs. Apart from Basu's wife, a lean, keen-eyed European woman in her thirties, and a deferential personal attendant, Basu was alone this time. He was wearing a *dhoti* and loose pyjamas. Khan looked around at the scattered cushions, burning candles and low divans. He drew in the aroma of patchouli. Had Basu been meditating? He was rumoured to have this mystical streak. Basu nodded politely. He invited Khan to sit down opposite him.

Basu looked tired. Months in prison in Calcutta and the constant warring, not only against the Raj but against many of his countrymen, was beginning to tell. He often suffered from illness. His wavering health had been the pretext for his early release from prison and this trip to Europe. Without warning, a quick warm smile lit Basu's face and threw Khan off guard. Cross-legged on a saffron cushion, he bent to sip his tea. He peered at Khan.

'Two visits in as many days, Herr Khan. To what do I owe the honour?'

'I was wondering – that is, if there might be ways we could help each other. I have been keeping an eye on your movement.'

The other stared at him and said nothing.

'There are many ways to achieve the same goal.'

Basu leaned back and appraised Khan. When he spoke it was with quiet deliberation. 'You have the look of someone who has done too much living of late and is not sure of the way ahead.'

Taken aback, Khan bowed his head. Basu raised his hand as if in a gesture of peace. 'We tread different paths and yet were we not bred in the same womb? Now our destinies force us to meet.'

Khan looked askance at his jowled compatriot whose bulky form had an odd grace and refinement. He did not trust the man's gestures of gentility, Mihir Basu would have the imperialists out of Mother India at any cost. In India, particularly Bengal, he had a fierce reputation.

'I might say your arrival is timely, Sri Khan.'

Khan waited for clarification. When none came he tried another tack. 'And your health, Sri Basu? I heard your health was … giving cause for concern.'

'Health is nothing. It is my mission that is giving cause for concern.'

218

'How has your – your mission been progressing?'

'I have seen through to the hollow core of their philosophy. The German Nationalists are more with the colonialists than against them. They consider the British natural allies and blood brothers,' said Basu.

Ah, thought Khan, so that was it. 'The Nazis are misguided men. I would have as little to do with them as possible,' Khan said.

'I admire their methods. Not, I stress, their goals. But to be made small by their doctrine of race! Only now do I realise they hate people of dark skin, as much as they hate Israelites.' Basu grabbed a fistful of channa and chomped on it. 'I'm hedged about... made to wait. A meeting, that's all I requested.' He smacked his palms together. 'Though they have granted me funds. That at least is something.'

Khan studied the trembling jowls and wavering hand as Mihir Basu put a teacup to his mouth. Years before he'd seen saw a photo of Basu soon after his release from jail in which he'd looked unwell. Today he had the same air of fragility.

'I've been seen as a hot head,' muttered Basu, 'when my only wish is for the liberation of *Bharat Mate*, Mother India. The English make us believe it is in *our* interest that they rule our land. They bring not only civilisation and Christianity, but also capitalism to our benighted shores. Those who question that are mere ingrates... mad men. But I tell you they have bent our minds. They make us doubt our ability to rule ourselves. The white man's burden? The most evolved of the species? The pinnacle of culture? What tosh! Do they know nothing of the Ganges valley culture and the Upanishads? Our swamis are wiser by far than their stiff-necked preachers who are a sop to British matrons – just so the Raj can continue to exploit us.'

For a moment, in full spate, the man's energy returned.

Khan had heard such talk before, at university and in the left-wing coffee houses of Calcutta. Basu smarted at being fobbed off by Hermann Göring or refused an audience with Adolf Hitler. Already he had heard talk of Basu wanting to draw support in Europe for a Free India. This would depend on connections and attracting sufficient force. Once the pivotal point was reached Britain's dominion over India would end.

His tirade over, Basu closed his eyes and appeared to be dozing. Khan waited. Basu emitted a snore. There seemed little point in hanging on. Khan got to his feet. 'Where do you think you're going?'

Basu's eyes snapped open.

'Sri Basu, I thought you were unwell.'

'That is nothing compared to the state of our motherland.' A man, Khan had heard, ruled more by passion than pragmatism. They were true then, these rumours of his resolve to set up a Fifth Column, a military wing supported by kindred nationalist parties in Europe. Khan said nothing, his mouth describing a gentle smile. Basu launched forth. 'You find me laid low by the inhospitable and overweening Germans…'

'You attempted to negotiate terms with the Nazi Party?'

'Yes,' Basu burst out. 'My love for India makes me lose caution. I say to you, the British in India can only be driven out by force. Arms. Guns. Ammunition and bombs. Words have not had the desired effect. Diplomacy is for the patient, those willing to wait another century for freedom. I say: those who oppress will be oppressed. Those who live by the sword will die by the sword. Has not their own Bible said so?'

'How do you intend to make this happen, Sri Basu?' asked Khan. At the same time he heard a rustling from behind the door.

'If you are in earnest – which to be frank I have severe

doubts about – you might see to getting me the names of a few good contacts – in the Nazi High Command, or in the Black Reichswehr, for instance. Then perhaps we might have something in common. Until then…' He looked towards the door. 'Forgive me, but I have matters to attend to.'

Khan was rankled at being dismissed like an underling, yet relieved too. After a cursory exchange with Basu's wife, he gained the street. He breathed deep, expelling the fetid air of intrigue.

A plane whined across the sky and vanished behind the rooftops in its descent to Tempelhof airport. His shoulders gave a slight judder. Mihir Basu was becoming rash in his ardour for India. Khan quickened his step. India, Britain, Germany: a conundrum, a tangle to be unpicked and put back together. He passed a *Lokal* where he'd stopped last time on his way to visit Basu. The tables were empty but he went in. He ordered beer and sausage with black bread. The waiter was wearing a dirty, torn apron and was unshaven. The sight of him disgusted Khan. People were letting themselves go.

The sausage arrived curled on the plate with a gherkin, a squirt of bright yellow mustard and a slice of heavy black bread. He chewed on the gherkin, relishing the snap as vinegar and cucumber flesh tingled his palate. He scooped the stub of it through the mustard and cut into the sausage. His standards were slipping, too. German sausages were gristle and flesh of the pig. His relatives would have been appalled.

A couple entered the café. The young woman reminded him of Rhiannon. She flicked back the hair from her face. It fell about her shoulders, long, brown and shiny. She smiled toward her companion, a sweet, uncomplicated smile. Khan suppressed a surge of longing.

221

Later he picked up the latest copy of *The Independent Chronicler*. Max's article leapt out at him. *'Germany's descent into chaos.'* Different in tone from all other reports and editorials, it had the sharp veracity, observation and fire of an eyewitness account. As he read it he took in the sweep of it. He blew out air through his teeth.

There were statements about the demise of Hitler's niece, as in the flyer, only couched in cautious, reputation-guarding terms. There was the analysis of the current Berlin atmosphere: the thoughts, feelings and fears of the people, the topplings of politicians, the murders and the casual brutality. The article caught at his throat like a vice. Max had had the audacity to do it after all. The piece would not go unnoticed.

Thirty six

Goebbels sought to have the best possible intelligence: especially near the *Hackescher Markt*. He wanted ears and eyes everywhere. A centralised office might lead to lazy thinking. The room where Hans Fichte found himself was dingy and in need of decoration. It smelt of damp. It smelt of feet and unaired bedding. Despite the cold Hans opened the window and gazed down the street.

Nearby was the pomp and glitter of the New Synagogue, the renowned centre of Jewish learning and a hub of liberal Judaism. It was always busy with students, worshippers, businessmen and artisans coming and going. Jews owned many of the dwellings in the courtyards beyond in the *Hackesches Viertel*. It was the nearest Berlin had to a thriving Jewish quarter. There were also the cramped tenements round the Ostbahnhof, where ragged arrivals from the East dredged up. He sniffed with displeasure. Dr Goebbels was right. The Jews were a problem. The immigrants were a problem. As if there wasn't a scarcity of work and resources already, as if Germany did not have problems enough without this influx of debris from elsewhere.

He surveyed the papers on his desk. Amongst them was the most recent Communist flyer. Hundreds had been gathered up and stashed here. He picked one up. It was muddy and torn. The sight of it filled him with loathing but he forced himself to read it. The headline, hot on the accusation that the Leader had murdered his niece, was demanding that her body be exhumed and her murderer be brought to justice. It was an outrage! What sickened him most was the knowledge that the public might be taken in. What perturbed him in a different way was the suspicion that his renegade brother-in-law might well have had a hand in it. An ex-worker from the Communist *Immer Freiheit* was certain that the flyer emanated from there. Max had been seen visiting their premises, he often drank with the editor. Hans thrust the leaflet aside. He shoved the jumble of flyers together and heaped them all into the wastepaper basket.

Later, Hans was alerted by a colleague who kept an eye on the foreign press: the latest report in *The Independent Chronicler* not only covered the lead-up to the Reichstag election but resurrected the rumours around Geli Raubal's death. Not one of the others was able to identify the writer. They were hindered by the fact the article was in English. The scurrilous, badly-printed leaflets of the Communists were one thing, but a major attack against the Nazi Party in the foreign press was another. For months now Gauleiter Goebbels had made it his business to broadcast a better, more reasonable face of the Party to the wider world. He nurtured beneficial contacts where he could and scrutinised all reports concerning Germany. He was particularly sensitive to any mention of the Nazi Party abroad.

Goebbels, though he spoke no English himself, was furious when he found out. It could not be allowed to continue. There was no question about it: the perpetrator must be found. Hans scanned the article, ringed in red. Though his English was rudimentary, he could tell it was inflammatory.

Thirty seven

As the Munich train drew into Berlin, Max looked out over the frost-layered rooftops and steeples of the city. It was a clear day, the sky blue, and buildings sharp in the morning air. It was still early; he had time to write up his report before he saw Seifert. There were gaps in the Geli Raubal narrative he wanted to fill. He wanted to speak to Gert Frosch again, although he guessed he would not yet have surfaced. In the meantime he would call on Dieter out in allotment land.

At the S-Bahn station he passed a knot of men gathered round a brazier playing Skat. The allotments, barely discernible in the half-light, stretched over several hectares. He scanned the assortment of low buildings until he identified Dieter's hideaway; a wisp of blue-white smoke snaked up from a spindly chimney.

He knocked and pushed open the door. Inside, Dieter was mulling over a newspaper. Beside him on the table was a pile of potatoes. 'Hello stranger. *Was gibt's?*' said Max. Dieter stood up, surprised, staring at Max as if he had just pitched up from the Amazon. Max sank down onto an old sofa. 'Where do you get potatoes at this time of year?'

'Potatoes *are* becoming scarce. They're good for bartering.' Dieter pushed the door to; the wood, swollen by damp, barely fitted into the frame. He glanced at Max again. 'It's cold out there. Want a schnapps?'

'So early? That fire's dying. Let me get some more logs.' Max went foraging outside. Behind the shed he found a tumbled heap. He fed the fire, which began to crackle and spit as flames curled round the wood.

Dieter poured Max a decent slug of schnapps. 'So how was Munich?'

He took a gulp of the drink and told Dieter about the interviews. The logs in the stove shifted, sending up a shower of sparks, went dark and flared into life again. 'I wanted to interview Geli's mother but I didn't manage to track her down.'

'She'll want to put all that behind her. Her brother is the new hope of Germany, don't forget. I wouldn't go near her.'

'I suppose you're right. But I did penetrate the bowels of the monster.'

'What are you talking about?'

'The Brown House. Good name, you know: it *is* full of shit.'

'And?'

'I came across some fascinating photos. I couldn't go back though, the man in charge was getting suspicious.' They were quiet for a moment, watching the fire.

'Things are getting tighter.'

'What's been happening here?'

'I haven't been venturing out much. I've been lying low. Most of the others have too.'

'Was there any more backlash after the fly-posting?'

'Their press office was up in arms. They gathered up as many of the flyers as they could.'

'You've finally moved out?'

'No choice.'

'So where are you working from these days?'

'Out here.'

Max warmed his hands by the stove, lapsing into silence. After a while he said: 'I thought I knew what had happened but it turns out that I don't. I have a hunch Geli was murdered but I don't know who did it. I thought it was her uncle, but I'm no longer sure.'

'Max, listen to me. You can't do this alone. You've got to be more tactical.' Max felt a surge of irritation. It was all too easy for Dieter to criticise but from where he stood, Dieter and most of his own colleagues were ineffective.

'Strikes me, people in the know are not doing enough.'

'Have you even read our latest issue?'

'No.'

'Well you ought to. We've compiled eyewitness accounts of recent political murders in the city. Whereas you go digging up old stories…'

'You were happy enough to gain political capital out of them.'

Dieter laughed. 'True enough. Come on Max, you're looking tense. This Geli story's getting to you.'

'There's still Gert Frosch. He's sitting on something, I'm sure of it.' As Max spoke he had the image of circles within circles, arrows darting towards each other, missing, intersecting, cancelling each other out. He heard Nazi slogans drummed out: *'Moving in an orderly direction with impact,'* or *'Dynamism and optimism for the future,'* *'Sacrifice and pulling together.*

'So where exactly are you operating from?'

'Over there.' Dieter jerked his thumb over his shoulder. 'Did you notice a block of flats on your way here?'

'Vaguely.'

'Our office is on the top floor, in the attic space. I know someone who lives there. These potatoes are for him. Do you want to see it?'

'Why not?'

Dieter slowly uncurled himself and reached for a sack, which he promptly filled. The two men made their way across the allotments to the block of flats. They passed a scrawny woman scrabbling in a patch of hard ground. 'Batty as hell,' remarked Dieter. 'Her only child got killed in a road accident. She's a permanent fixture here.'

The caretaker of the flats nodded when Dieter told him he wanted to see Gerhard. They knocked on Gerhard's door. In singlet and braces, he was only just getting started on his day. '*Alles in Ordnung?*' he asked if everything was in order. Dieter handed him the sack of potatoes and said he needed to get to his office.

They walked up the concrete back stairs and Dieter unlocked the metal door to the attic. They stepped into a vast, echoing space. To one side stood printing presses and to the other trays of type. Three tables were piled high with paper and two other desks had typewriters and telephones on them. Behind these stood a couple of battered filing cabinets. Max whistled. 'You're well set up here! Roll on the Revolution, eh?'

'Doesn't do to be too visible nowadays.'

'What about your neighbours – don't they suspect anything?'

'The flat below is Gerhard's. The one alongside is empty most of the time. They're business people from Hamburg who use it as a pied-á-terre.' He indicated the black telephone on one of the desks. 'Everything we need to stay in touch.'

Max picked up an art nouveau lamp, a ceramic svelte dancer.

'She's been with me since I was a student,' said Dieter. 'My muse, you might say.'

Max gazed out of the skylight over treetops and factory chimneys. He looked around. 'Can I make a call?' He tried to connect with *Die Tatsache*, but nobody was answering.

He decided to head back towards Frosch's place in Nollendorf. Hopefully the man would be at home or in the neighbourhood. Max guessed that he whiled away hours in cheap cafés over a solitary coffee to keep warm. The streets were busier now with trams trundling to and fro and a flurry of housewives and workers going about their business. He was relieved to note the absence of eager-eyed youths, peddling propaganda. When he arrived at Kleiststrasse Frosch opened the door to him. He looked bleary-eyed, as though he'd indulged in a bout of drinking. His hands were tremoring.

They found a café, nestled under the S-Bahn flyover. Max ordered coffee and ham rolls, and when they arrived Frosch's eyes widened in appreciation. He guarded his coffee like a wary bear. On the edge, thought Max, part of the city's human flotsam: an unwitting pawn. He felt a surge of compassion towards him.

After a while he said: 'I went to Munich. I interviewed one of the laying-out women and journalists who covered the Geli Raubal story...'

Gert Frosch's look sharpened. He shifted away from Max and gazed at the table. He looked more gaunt and vulnerable than ever. One way or another his days were numbered. He started murmuring, almost inaudibly. 'I will never forget her.'

'She was living in the apartment on Prinzregentstrasse then?'

'Yes, yes. You know that. Why do you keep asking me the same questions?' His irritation flared. His foot tapped the ground in anxiety. 'I wish you'd leave me alone.' He fumbled in his pocket for a fragment of cigarette and lit up, then fiddled with the straying wisps of tobacco, head down. He sniffed. Max called the waiter over and ordered two more coffees. They sat for a while in silence. Only when he seemed reassured that Max was not going to keep firing questions at him did Gert Frosch start speaking again. 'Nobody knew, but she'd found someone, this man who worked with signals on the railway.'

'They were lovers?'

Frosch shrugged. 'She told me about him one day when she'd been out. She was in a rush. Her uncle was at a meeting. She asked if he was back yet. She said this new man loved music, too, and they laughed a lot.'

'What was his name? Did you find out?'

'I stopped believing in them after that.'

'After what?' Frosch seemed to be talking to himself.

'Like hawks they were, watching her the whole time... They thought she pulled Hitler away from his great...'

'Destiny?' added Max.

'She would sneak out to meet him and got people to cover for her, saying she had gone to see a girlfriend. But it got difficult.' Frosch's hands were shaking, cupped round the dwindling cigarette. He stubbed it out.

'Want another?' Max fished in his pocket and lit two cigarettes, handing one over. He leaned back and blew out a stream of smoke, giving Frosch a moment to settle. But the man was steeped in the past, unable to speak.

'Did they kill her?'

Frosch's foot tapped the ground like a pneumatic drill. He fell back into silence then gave a deep sigh, the energy seeping from his body. 'She knew how hard these men could be. She liked to walk by the river when the sun was out. I think she met her friend there.'

'This was the day she died?'

'If you're not one of them, you're nothing. I think she wanted this new – start. It gave her hope. She told me she'd be back by coffee time. Her uncle was away so she had more leeway.'

'Where were you?'

'Generally we weren't allowed there. But I'd been asked to drop something off. I bumped into Geli. She was on her way

230

out. She was all smiles. In love, all right – you could see it all over her face.'

'Do you know what happened?'

Frosch's head dropped towards his chest.

'Do you know what happened?'

Frosch started muttering so Max could barely hear what he was saying. 'Everyone had a soft spot for her, despite her moods. Sometimes she was like a cloud. You wouldn't want to cross her then. But when she was performing – singing I mean – she was all light.'

'What happened, Gert?' Max was finding it hard to breathe. He leaned forward to catch what Gert Frosch was mumbling. It was hard to catch the words.

'I was a bit drunk. They told me to come along, there was a job needed doing…' He halted staring at unseen spectres. 'I thought they were just bringing her back to the house. They tracked her down. She was on a tram or a bus – I can't remember which. She was in a bad way…' He came to an abrupt stop.

'And then?'

He sniffed, wiped his face with the cuff of his sleeve. 'They would stop at nothing. She made him human. And they didn't want that. They wanted a machine to stand up there and rattle off…'

'How many were there?'

'My mind went blank…'

'Who was there?'

'I can't…'

'You must remember one of them at least.'

'It all blurred together. Himmler, yes, Himmler was there.'

'What happened next?'

'The housekeeper had the day off. Herr Hitler was away. The housekeeper's elderly mother was there, but she was deaf. They carried her upstairs. Later everyone said it was suicide.'

Max sat back, let out a deep breath. 'And the gun shot? She died from a bullet.'

'She knew about guns. She had shooting lessons. The bullet didn't pierce her heart. It went through the lung.' Frosch said coldly, calmer now he had told the story.

'Did you hear the shot?'

'No.'

'What happened next?'

'I don't know.'

'Is that when you left?'

'It made me feel ill. I made an excuse and went.'

'It was that easy?'

'I— I told them my mother was sick and had no one to take care of her.'

'They didn't bother verifying?'

'What?'

'They didn't bother to see if it was true?'

'They were too busy. Hitler was terrible. He refused to eat. Refused to leave her room. Just stared into the darkness. They were afraid he was going mad. Afraid he would kill himself. They had to stand guard over him. I think he loved Geli as much as he ever loved anyone. He was a changed man. You could see it in his face.'

Max had read this elsewhere. He had also read that Hitler had been beaten when he was growing up, then abandoned. Angela, his sister, and Geli were the only family he wanted to have anything to do with. There were others. But he was ashamed of them because of their deformities.

Max sat back. The matter was far from clear. It was evident there had been a cover-up. Not enough questions were put. No thorough investigation occurred. From Frosch's account there was a distinct whiff of foul play. Yet the man was too broken to recall the events clearly. Max's eyes watered: a visceral, instinctive recognition of truth that bypassed his intellect. Frosch looked dejected. He was still shaking. His eyes had a faraway, lost look. The memories stirred emotions he was incapable of dealing with.

'You're not going to say I told you anything?' he whispered.

'I said before, journalists protect their sources.'

Frosch continued to gaze at the stained floor of the café. When Max spoke again, he ignored him. He got up and without saying another word walked unsteadily towards the door. Max knew he would never see him again.

Thirty eight

Max arrived in Friedrichstrasse mid morning and walked the short distance to the newspaper office. On the street corner a youth was selling *der Stürmer*. He bought a copy to see what the Nazis were up to. On the cover was a piece by Julius Streicher. A cartoon showed two evil-looking Jews, knives in hands, scooping blood from the severed throats of angelic blond children. The article shrieked how since time immemorial Jews had sacrificed Christian children. Max screwed the paper into a ball and booted it into the gutter. A gust of wind lifted it and sent it scooting along into the path of an oncoming car.

Wolfgang Seifert was nowhere to be seen. Max decided to file his reports before his boss got back. People were coming and going behind him, he wandered over to the kitchen area and poured lukewarm coffee from the pot. He hunted for biscuits in the cupboard and found some stale ones, which he munched on. Then the hunger became too great. He had not eaten properly in days and could not think straight while his intestines were grumbling. Pushing his papers together, he grabbed his notebook and went down into the street.

He walked down the wide avenue of Unter den Linden, which stretched ahead up to the Lustgarten and Humboldt University. The trees were bare now, the branches scratchy and twisted against a sky that was becoming overcast. In the central reservation mounted generals, cast in iron, strutted their pompous way. Fleetingly he recalled walking down here with Tanya when the linden trees were in bloom and giving off a sweet fragrance. He was tinged with regret. It was a different city then. Whatever had become of Tanya? He brushed away the question.

He found a modest café with a dark, cosy interior where he ordered pea soup with *Bockwurst.* He tucked in greedily. Involuntarily his mind reverted to Tanya. For months, years even, he had not allowed himself to think about her. From time to time she erupted into his dreams where she caused havoc, drawing him in and repulsing him at the same time. The longing Tanya set up in him would never die, though he knew she could never have been a long-term proposition: his nerves would never have survived her. Tanya remained entangled with the stirrings and aspirations of youth.

He rubbed the top of his head: he needed to get a move on. He skimmed through the pages, adding a note here and there. In between he thought of Rhiannon's imminent arrival and was assailed by concern about where they might stay. For the time being Savignystrssse would have to do, but with the material he was handling it was becoming imperative for them to shift elsewhere. He scribbled a few more lines, filled in more details from his last interview with Gert Frosch.

Back at the office he set to at the typewriter but was soon distracted from the job in hand. Cars were tooting down below, voices shouting and clashing in the street. He got up to find out what was going on. A car had run into another and the drivers were bawling at each other. Within minutes the police had arrived and broken up the warring parties. He went back to his report. He sipped the now cold coffee. It tasted like rust. An hour later he had completed the article. He put it in a folder on Wolfgang's desk while he left his notes in a heap on his own. He nipped back out into the street to fetch the latest editions of the midday papers. Most carried the same headlines: '*Hitler offered co-leadership of government by Franz von Papen*' They went on: '*Hitler will only agree to be head of government if they eliminate*

Social Democrats, Communists and Jews from leading positions. No deal.'

Wolfgang Seifert entered the office, looking sombre in a dark suit and tie. 'You look as though you have just been to a funeral,' said Max.

'I have,' replied Seifert. 'Kurt Stein was found shot dead in Neukölln.'

Max sidled past him to a seat. 'You're joking!'

'No, he had just returned to Berlin. He was investigating links between a cabaret club and some of the leaders in the Nazi Party. He was also on the brink of exposing Hermann Göring for corruption.'

'I thought that was a prerequisite for ascending the party ladder,' quipped Max.

'Kurt made a lot of enemies, one way or another — Look, we need to talk.'

'I have just got my latest report together.'

'We need to talk, I said. Go into my office, will you.' Seifert walked through to the typing pool to give some instructions to his secretary. As he did so, Max pondered Kurt Stein, the man he had replaced on *die Tatsache* but never met, the man now cold in a coffin, a nuisance casually removed, a man laid low by those who feared his pen.

Seifert returned. As he saw Max hunched in the chair opposite his desk, waiting, his face froze. 'I'm glad you're in one piece at least,' said Seifert, though he did not look at all relieved. A frown was darkening his face. He shut the door behind him and pulled out his leather chair. 'I'm pleased you're alive. Glad I don't have to attend another wretched funeral…'

'You have no idea about the scoop I've just landed. I've written it up. It's here, on your desk.' He pointed to it with a growing sense of achievement: even Seifert would be impressed with what he'd come up with.

'What on earth do you think you're up to?' Seifert started, wasting no time on preliminaries.

Max was taken aback. 'You know what I'm up to. Let me show you.' He reached for the report.

'Just hold on, will you…' Something in the gravity and determination in Seifert's expression made Max pause. The editor seized the word. 'This latest Munich escapade – you masquerading as a British reporter. You *do* know they are after you? The Nazis don't like to look stupid.'

Max stared at him. 'How did you find out?'

'By now it's common knowledge in some quarters.'

Seifert looked grimmer than Max had ever seen him. As his mind somersaulted through the last few days Max began to wonder just what his boss might know. In a place like Berlin you could not keep a secret for long.

'And who told you to get involved with flyers? Pure propaganda! Who told you to go writing for, or at least aiding and abetting some Communist rag? What got into you?'

'I thought…'

'You thought nothing. Thinking was not something you were doing. That is for sure.' Max shifted back. Seifert's vehemence was almost physical. The room had become an interrogation cell. 'I trusted you to stay objective.'

'You do know what we're up against?' snapped Max in reply.

'I know quite well what we're up against. You're the one who is naïve. I have no more use for you. You're fired!'

'What? You can't do that.'

'You heard me. This time you have gone too far. No sense of boundary.'

'But it's the truth.'

'What's the truth? That Hitler murdered his own niece when he was two hundred miles away? Listen, the German

237

state is on the brink of dissolution. The President is in a fix. Chancellors are changing like dance partners. That's what you should be writing about instead of getting yourself caught up with Communists and then blasting your way into the Brown House.'

'You knew I was going to Munich. I was hunting more facts. More interviews. Doing what you asked me to do.'

'I didn't know then about your other activities.'

'You gave me the freedom to write. You told me to dig up stories about the Nazis…'

'I can't trust you any more. You have to stick to the facts.'

'I did. I had sources. Eyewitness accounts.'

'What in God's name made you get involved in putting out incendiary flyers like some student?'

'I didn't write them.'

'But you were involved. I know that for a fact. I have my sources, too. And you were seen.'

He threw Seifert an angry and uncomprehending look. 'Just why did you recall me to Berlin?'

'We've been over that enough times. It hasn't worked out. Let's just leave it at that.'

But Max was unable to. 'We have a contract, don't forget.'

'Yes, we have a contract. But I don't want to see you around. I don't want you to have anything more to do with the paper.'

'Read what I've written at least.'

'No, Max, it's no good. Sue the paper if you like. But I don't think you'll do that. You haven't exactly kept your side of the bargain, have you? I'll make sure you get a fair settlement. That's the best I can do.' He fidgeted with a paperweight, impatient now to get on with other things, impatient to rid himself of this maverick in front of him. He pushed Max's report away from him as though it were contaminated.

'Is that all?'

Seifert looked at him coldly. 'It's dangerous for you now in Berlin. You need to get out. God knows, I might be joining you myself any day.'

Max exhaled sharply. What more was there to say?

Max wandered down a side street in the newspaper quarter. His throat smarted. He needed to digest the meeting. Seifert felt betrayed by what he saw as duplicity. He was within his rights. No two ways about it, Max had fallen into a trap of his own making. Self doubt bit at him like acid, bile rising through his gullet.

Reluctant to retreat home, he slipped into a journalists' pub on the rim of the newspaper quarter. He searched for a familiar face in the cloud of smoke and overwarm air. The din was even louder than usual. 'As I see it,' Peter Ulm, a journalist from the *Berliner Tagesspiegel* was holding forth in a pompous air. 'Hindenburg is on the ropes. What's more he knows it…'

Another journalist, half-collapsed over a stein of beer at the other end of the bar, called out. 'What about the meetings between von Papen and Hitler – what's cooking there?'

Max ordered a beer.

Another hack took up the theme: 'Not one of them gives a monkey's about democracy, let alone the Republic…'

Arms were reaching for mugs, slopping beer on the floor, as a hefty waitress pushed between, clearing empties. Max nudged his way back to the counter, impatient to hear more.

'This takes the biscuit…'

'Hitler demands…'

A man elbowed Max in the back.

'Over here!' another was shouting. 'Over my dead body…'

'What are you talking about?'

Ulm gave Max a supercilious stare. 'Where've you been for the last couple of days?'

'Obviously not here,' said Max.

Ulm raised his voice: 'Hitler demands to be made Chancellor. Hindenburg won't have it. So he leaks a statement to us lot. As if the press can do anything. He can't make Hitler Chancellor, he claims, because such a cabinet would develop into a party dictatorship…He does not want to take the responsibility. Did you ever hear such piffle?'

'At least he believes public opinion counts.'

'Don't believe a word of it. It's just tactics,' quipped another reporter sitting alongside.

Max leaned over the counter, head pounding, and asked for another beer. 'I just got fired,' he said.

Ulm stared at him. 'You work for *die Tatsache,* don't you? What happened?'

'Never mind. I'm looking for work. If you hear of anything…' he scribbled his details on a scrap of paper. He wanted to quit the bar with its Babel tower of tongues and stories, hearsay, fact, fiction, its noise, and all these journalists better informed, with jobs, with inroads into cabinet secrets and sources of influence… He was tired. Overwrought. He needed to get out. He needed fresh air. He needed… he was no longer sure what he needed. If senile Hindenburg symbolised the state in free-fall, this bar, rowdy with banter and confusion was like the inside of his head. He downed the beer in one and lurched towards the street.

He headed towards Café Mozart, hoping to catch Khan there. Café Mozart was only half full, and there was no sign of Khan. A waiter was removing debris from the tables. Max stopped at a post office to put through a call to the British embassy where he was told Khan was out on business.

Most likely he was doing the rounds of the cafés. Max

caught a tram to the Zoo and wandered into the Römer café where, not unexpectedly, he found Khan ensconced behind a copy of *Die Vössische Zeitung.* He was sporting the familiar slicked down hair and a bright cravat and was busily imbibing wine, reading and dispensing aphorisms to all who had a mind to listen to him. His voice carried across the tables.

'It's only a question of time before it starts going up again...' It could have been the price of pork he was talking about, or the Centre Party in the Reichstag. He exuded the same levity whatever the topic. 'And now look who comes here...' Khan cast the paper to one side. 'My dear Max, how good to see you. Take a seat, there's a good chap. What'll it be? Coffee or something stronger? I haven't seen you in a while.'

Max nodded a greeting to one or two journalists and sat down beside Khan. He was keen to sound him out. Dieter moved in left-wing circles, and Seifert in liberal ones. Even together they seemed to have less access to the networks Khan enjoyed. 'Seifert has just given me my marching orders.'

'What!'

'The damn flyer – amongst other things.' He gave Khan a resume of events then said: 'I need to find a job and fast. Any ideas?'

Khan studied his face. 'Not the best time to...'

'Don't I know it. I'm putting out feelers. You seem to know lot of people...'

'I'll keep my ears pricked.'

Max leaned back and signalled to the waiter for coffee. 'Have you picked up much in the way of reactions to the Geli Raubal story being resurrected?'

'It's stirred a lot of mud,' said Khan. 'Goebbels' office is on full alert.'

'What does that mean?'

'It means… Hell knows what that means. Sometimes they're organised, sometimes they're too busy squabbling amongst themselves…'

'I interviewed Frosch again. Dynamite.'

'That so?'

'Can't talk about here.' He glanced around.

Khan lowered his voice. 'The Nazis were furious about the flyers. They sent out sleuths to determine the provenance. But couldn't point a finger. A few distributors were seen from a distance. Your disappearance down south was timely, to say the least. But then,' he looked Max up and down, 'you changed your appearance. You've gone very Prussian-looking.'

Max sipped his coffee. 'You know they followed me before? Beat me up.'

'I heard about that. You all right now?'

'I'm still here, I guess.

'Did you get paid yet for *The Independent Chronicler* article?'

'Yes.'

'Now that *really* ruffled feathers. Goebbels has been courting the foreign press. Will you file another report for them?'

Max considered the round, marble top table. 'I have one ready to go as a matter of fact – now I'm a free agent.'

'They'd be very keen, I'm sure.'

'I'd need to translate it. It's in German.'

'How long would that take?'

'A couple of hours.'

'Will you do that?'

'I could get something together pretty quickly. But are you able to influence opinion at the embassy?'

Khan regarded him quizzically. 'That's a tall order.'

'I thought you knew everyone – where and how to gain leverage?'

'You flatter me. If I knew what the ambassadorial top brass was thinking at any given time it would help. There's the official line and then there's reality.'

'But you could bring stuff to the attention of those who count within your diplomatic circles?'

'I would be only too happy to oblige,' said Khan.

'Now I've lost *Die Tatsache* I need to widen my contacts as much as possible.'

'Get it off as soon as you can. Thumbs are being screwed. The President was so adamant in his rejection of Hitler. But now they've discovered his Achilles' heel.'

Max grunted. Otto had been saying something similar. 'You mean the scandal involving his son?'

Khan nodded. 'The cabinet is falling over itself to back the man they despise. They see him as the means for controlling the masses and putting an end to all these strikes we've been having.'

Max turned back to Khan. 'And your colleague – is he back from London?'

'Denning? I haven't heard anything. Usually he cables before he comes.'

'What else have you been up to?' asked Max.

Khan shifted his seat closer. 'I went to see Mihir Basu. Now there's a story if you had a mind to write it. The man is wanting to throw off the British Empire by force of arms.'

Max gave a snort of laughter. 'In an unarmed land under occupation, he's either inspired or insane.'

'Both, probably, said Khan. 'There's a scoop in that for you.'

'I have to get this one sorted first. Then try and land another job.'

'How is Rhiannon, by the way? She's been off work.'

'I'm off to pick her up now.'

'Is that so?' Khan's eyes lit up. 'So where did she disappear to?'

'She's been away with her soup kitchen friends.'

Khan clapped him on the back. 'Ah, the suffragettes!'

'Not exactly.'

'Anyway, she's a great asset. Cheers the place up no end. Miss Stonebridge can be so dreary.'

The two men looked at each other, a guarded smile passing between them.

Max sauntered along the Ku'damm where neons signs blinked beneath a sky now metallic with the threat of snow. In this part of town little had changed: in Kempinski's the lights were glowing, further down the Ku'damm the furriers and elegant ball gowns glittered among de luxe cafés and Hungarian restaurants. The shopkeepers were still plump and doing a fine trade. Rock-bottom prices and reduced- to-clear sales were conveniently pushed out to the edges of the city. He approached Bahnhof Zoo.

With an hour to go before Rhiannon's arrival he sat by the end of the platform over coffee and watched the milling crowd. Around him a few listless men were looking to scrounge a few *groschen* by acting as unofficial porters, one was serving lemonade from a trolley in competition with the station canteen. Two Brown Shirts hovered by the exit, pushing their political rags. Max took care not to draw attention to himself. What Khan had said hit home. He knew only too well 'undesirables' were being knocked off without a second thought. He was forced to admit, despite himself, that the momentum behind the Nazis was building. The article he was carrying would be a clear death sentence if it were found on him. He folded it up and put it into a luggage locker in the station for safekeeping. Once he'd picked up

Rhiannon he could retrieve it and they'd catch a taxi home. There were far too many Nazis around not to be wary.

He returned to the café and drank more coffee. After a while he felt the urge to urinate. He walked briskly towards the Gents' lavatory. He had just finished relieving himself when he turned round and saw two Brown Shirts blocking the exit. 'What have we here?' said one, a thick-set man in his mid-twenties with a red face and no neck. He reminded Max of a second-rate boxer. His companion-in-arms was a thin youth whose clothes sagged on him. His chin jutted out as if to say: I may look young and callow but just you try me. Max moved to pass between the two of them. They refused to budge.

'Not so fast, *mein Herr*. There are people who wish to ask you a few questions. If I am not mistaken…' He glanced at a folded paper he'd been holding in his hand. 'I must say you fit the description perfectly. Right build. Right profile. Now sir,' he began sarcastically. 'Would you tell me your name. Or better still show me your ID card.'

Despite the shakiness of his knees Max stared hard at them. 'Why should I show you anything? You're not the police'.

'This is why,' said the tall one and kneed him in the groin. 'And this.' He gave a sharp punch to his kidneys. Max doubled up, clutching himself in pain. Just then another man walked into the lavatory. The two Brown Shirts shuffled to one side and made a quick exit. They had obviously been told not to cause a stir in a public place. The man glanced over at Max then continued to the urinal.

'Help me,' groaned Max. When he had finished the man came over and eased him off the ground. 'Will you walk out with me? They're unlikely to attack both of us.' The man, a rotund citizen in his fifties, looked away.

'Leave me out of this. I don't know what all that was about

and I don't want to know.' He stalked away and Max struggled to keep up with him. Soon he was lost in the mêlée. Max looked around. No sign of the bullyboys. He wandered into a dim bar at the other end of the station, rubbing his back.

Thirty nine

With minutes to go before the city, open fields and woods gave way to a huddle of villages. Here and there glittered ponds of black ice. Wilhelmine apartment blocks alternated with the mesh of railway tracks. The sky was gunmetal as snow scattered across the window.

As the train drew into the station people shifted towards the doors. Rhiannon was relieved to be back in Berlin. The last evening had been fraught. She'd attempted to be as natural with Hannah as possible but something had shifted between them. Hannah remained correct but was cold, bristling with efficiency as she went about organising lifts to the station and settling last minute details of the soup kitchen.

The women alighted and after farewell hugs dispersed in all directions. Rhiannon searched for Max among the sea of faces. On the concourse she looked again, but he was nowhere to be seen. Already the crowd was thinning. Her grip on her suitcase tightened as she moved forward. At the exit a brash young man thrust a copy of the Nazi *Der Stürmer* towards her. She brushed him aside. She decided to go to Max's office and took the first free taxi.

Lights were burning on the upper floors of the newspaper offices. She had only ever been here once before on a fleeting visit en route to an embassy function. The porter indicated where she should go. The lift cranked open at the second floor where she asked for Herr Seifert.

'Ah, Frau Dienst.' Puzzlement flickered across his face then he flushed as if embarrassed. 'Frau Dienst – how can I be of service? I presume it's about your husband?'

'As a matter of fact it is…'

He looked around then got up and shut the door behind them. 'Did he explain my position?'

'I am sorry. I don't understand.'

'Please, take a seat.' He indicated the empty chair opposite the wide desk. With a growing sense of alarm Rhiannon lowered herself and stared at Seifert, who was fiddling with a paper clip.

'I was wondering if you knew where he was. He was meant to meet me at the station but he didn't show up.'

'Ah, I see.' Seifert seemed to relax suddenly.

'Did you he say anything – about going to meet me?'

Seifert looked down at the desk. 'No, he did not.'

'When did you last see him, Herr Seifert?'

'Earlier today.'

'And was everything..?'

'It didn't come up in the conversation, Frau Dienst.' Something about Seifert's manner struck her as furtive.

'So what did come up?'

Seifert coughed. 'It was a professional matter,' he said gravely.

'I see. So – so you can't help me. You have no idea where he might be?'

'I am afraid not, Frau Dienst.'

'Do you think any of his colleagues might know?'

'I don't think so.'

He got to his feet. 'He is probably waiting for you at home.'

'Undoubtedly. ' She stood up and shook his hand.

When she returned to Savignystrasse, Max was still nowhere to be seen. She thought Uschi Ruderstein, her neighbour, might know something, but when she knocked on her door a short woman with sparse hair answered. 'I was looking for…'

'Frau Ruderstein no longer lives here.'

'But…'

'I live here now. If you want to find out more ask the landlord.'

Rhiannon had the sensation of stepping into a maze. She gazed for a moment at the placid face of the other. Something in the set of the woman's jaw made her feel uneasy: Uschi had said nothing about moving. Rhiannon explained who she was and asked if she had seen her husband by any chance. The woman shook her head and shut the door. Rhiannon nodded and retreated into their rooms. She looked around. All was pretty much as she had left it, yet the place had an air of abandonment. The pot plant was wilting. The rooms felt stuffy. As if for the first time she noticed the dull beige carpet was heavily stained.

Despite the outside temperature she thrust open the window to let in fresh air. In their bedroom she slid a drawer. She picked up one of Max's shirts and held it to her cheek, drawing in the smell and feel of him. 'Max,' she whispered, choking back a wave of fear. From outside came the chink of crockery as someone cooked.

'The Rudersteins no longer live here,' said the landlord curtly when she approached him: 'Did your husband not inform you?'

'But Frau Ruderstein didn't say they…'

'I have another tenant. Here – Frau Ruderstein left some things here. You can give them to her. This is her new address.' He thrust a shopping bag full of opera programmes towards Rhiannon. Without thinking she took the bag. He was about to walk away.

'Please Herr Schneider, have you – have you seen my husband this evening?'

'I can't be keeping track of all the comings and goings here.'

He grunted good evening and shut the door before she could say more.

She stood for a moment, wondering what to do. There was a phone in the lobby for the use of tenants. She considered calling Inge but decided against it. Instead she asked to be put through to Khan's apartment in Wilmersdorf.

'It's Rhiannon. I'm back. But Max – no sign of Max. He wasn't there to meet me at the station. Have you heard anything?' Khan told her he would come over. He asked if her train had been on time. 'Yes, it was. So where *is* he? Where *is* he?' She heard the pitch in her voice getting higher.

'I'm on my way,' said Khan and within half an hour he was waiting outside for her. He opened the door of a black BMW. 'I borrowed a friend's car,' he said. 'Thought it might make life easier. Don't worry about Max. I saw him a few hours ago. He couldn't wait to see you.'

She stared ahead. His attempt to reassure only fuelled her alarm. 'So where *is* he?'

They sped through the silent streets. 'Not many people about tonight, cold's driven them inside,' he said as they drew to a halt outside the Kuka club.

She fingered the strap of her handbag and pictured the smoky, frenzied interior of the nightclub.

'Would you like to wait here while I make enquires?'

She nodded.

He returned a few minutes later shaking his head. 'No one's seen him tonight.' They drove on without speaking, calling at one nightclub and cabaret after another. Everywhere they went it was the same story. They ended up in *Der Römer* café. All about them were high-spirited theatre-goers, loud in praise of Hauptmann's *Die Weber*. Khan laughed with them.

Later he said: 'I think we should call it a day. He was up at Dieter's a night or two ago. Dieter might know something, but he was not in his local and I don't have his address. I suggest you go back home and try and get some sleep.' He put his arm around her. 'Come now, it's not like you to worry.' She nodded and got to her feet, stumbling with tiredness.

They travelled back through the dark streets, her stomach knotting in anxiety. She tried to speak but the words refused to come. In Savignystrasse Khan accompanied her to the front door. His gaze searched hers. On impulse he drew her towards his chest. 'I'll call round tomorrow afternoon.' For a moment she rested there then pulled away and walked to the apartment door without looking back.

In her room she sank onto the bed. Before she could stop herself she was clutching the pillow and sobbing. Afterwards she washed her face and lay on her back. She pulled the eiderdown over her then cast it off, snuggled into a foetal position then kicked out her legs. She slumped into the old easy chair by the window. With the stove dead, the cold bit into her. She crawled under the bedclothes, head spinning, and fell into a fitful sleep.

As a grey dawn seeped into the room she got up, dressed and walked out into the misty air. She wandered in the direction of the Kurfürstendamm. Most of the shops were still closed, street cleaners were swabbing down the pavement. The sweet whiff of loaves just out of the oven made her stomach churn. One by one shopkeepers scrolled up metal guards and unlocked premises. A kiosk vendor was folding newspapers into a metal box. Sometimes he sold old copies of British papers. Knowing Max had recently sent something to London, she rushed over to buy a copy of *The Independent Chronicler*. An article leapt out at her. '*German Reichstag election*' and lower down a subheading: '*Geli Raubal: A story that refuses to die.*' Did Geli's very existence stand in the way of the Nazi Party, asked the reporter. The article concluded that the case should be re-opened.

Rhiannon could not prevent her hands from shaking. She folded up the paper into a small package as if to contain the chaos it could unleash. Fears breed in the dark hours, the sobriety of morning often dissolving them, but the cold light of this one cast a horrid glare over Max's disappearance. It was possible, she told herself, that Max had dived under until the furore passed. Possible. But was it probable? Most disturbing of all was Khan's avowal that Max had been on his way to meet her.

She looked at her watch. It was after eight. Khan had told her he would be over in the afternoon. Her head was buzzing, making it hard to focus. People were filtering out into the streets now: office-workers scuttling along in dark suits, housewives off early to the shops to beat the incessant queues. She stared down at her hands. She had painted her nails a vibrant red over the weekend. One of them was chipped. She breathed deep, trying to suppress the quivering that invaded her body.

The first step would be to report to the police. She found the nearest station not far from the entrance to the Zoo. She approached a counter clerk, who looked up at her in mild surprise. 'My husband,' she began. 'I want to report my husband missing.'

'Name?' asked the clerk.

'His or mine?'

'Yours first, then his.'

She was beginning to feel light headed. She was referred to a second clerk.

'Address?'

She fished in her bag for the rent book.

'Place and date of birth?'

'With all due respect, are all these questions necessary?'

He shot her a look of disdain. She lowered her head. 'I've just given most of these details to your colleague.'

'Place and date of birth?' repeated the officer.

'His or mine?'

'Yours, first. Then his.' She resigned herself to the thoroughness of the German state machinery. While she was responding, question by mundane question, a slow scream was building inside her. 'Your husband's occupation?'

'Why is that relevant?' She baulked at disclosing so much.

'Occupation?' snapped the other.

'Journalist,' she said quietly.

'Which paper?'

'*Die Tatsache*.' Did she notice a frown of disapproval or was she just imagining a reaction?

'And you, Frau Dienst, do you work?' As she replied he wrote in a slow, elaborate Gothic script. 'So – so what happens now?' she asked.

'We file the report. Your husband will go onto our missing persons' register.'

'Is that all?'

The clerk slammed the ledger shut and leaned over the counter towards her. 'Do you imagine we have nothing better to do than go chasing missing husbands?'

Caught between fury and humiliation, Rhiannon walked out letting the door bang to behind her. She did not know where to turn next. She felt too ill to go to work, too afraid to settle her mind to anything. She watched the passing cars, her mind in a blur. Her instinct would have been to seek out Hannah or Uschi, or perhaps Inge; yet Hannah felt barred to her, Uschi had vanished and Inge would only make her angry.

In the end she decided to put aside any unresolved awkwardness and to seek out Hannah, who was surely the most connected person she knew in Berlin. Hannah looked inordinately pleased to see her when she arrived at her office. 'So, to what do I owe the honour?'

'Can we talk somewhere – in private.' Hannah took her into a little side office, piled high with files.

'This is a surprise, I must say.'

When Rhiannon began to explain her mounting concerns, Hannah frowned. 'So you need my help?'

'I don't know where else to turn.'

'I see –' said Hannah.

Rhiannon paused. 'I know hardly anyone here, just in the embassy. Then Max's sister. But they are not on good terms. She's married to an up-and-coming Nazi. It might make matters worse if I tell her.'

Hannah leaned back and sighed. 'You complained he neglected you. You claim he put you both in danger and now...'

Rhiannon stared down at the floor: she could feel tears welling. She blinked angrily and began getting to her feet.

'Sit down. Sit down. Don't be so sensitive.' Hannah paused then went on. 'You assume the worst, but you have very little to go on, and no proof that they know who wrote the British article.'

'In every office there's someone with Nazi leanings. A secretary in the editorial section, for instance.'

'There again, one has many friends,' countered Hannah.

Hannah's boss poked his head round the door and told her she was needed for a meeting. Hannah lifted a placatory palm. For a moment she looked thoughtful. 'In your position I would ask around – at his paper, at the embassy. See what information they have. I would visit the sister. Speak to his brother-in-law. The more places you go to the more you'll pick up. Someone is bound to have heard something. Did he have a local he went to? A café like *der Römer*? This is not a city where people keep things quiet. If you like I could make some enquiries.' Her words were measured as she slowly got to her feet. 'I'd better go.'

Rhiannon watched Hannah pick up some files and swing out of the room, trailing a whiff of Chanel No 5. She battled a sense of helplessness. Minutes later she consulted her city map to see how to get from Frederichstrasse to Neukölln.

Inge was disconcerted to see her. 'I was just going to the shops with Anna,' she stated without preamble.

'There is something I need to tell you.' Alarm passed across Inge's face only to be replaced by a blank stare.

'Then you'd better come in.' She led her into the kitchen where Anna was giving her dolls a tea party on the table. 'Anna, clear your things away. Then go and play in your room. Mummy needs to talk. We'll go to the shops in a minute.'

Anna peered at Rhiannon in curiosity then began scooping up the tiny cups and saucers into a heap.

'Quickly now,' said Inge, dropping them into a bag.

Anna scowled, trailing a floppy doll as she disappeared into her room.

'It's Max,' Rhiannon chewed on her thumbnail as they sat either side of the table. 'I went to Brandenburg for a few days. When I arrived back Max was not at the station to meet me. A colleague saw him go and my train arrived on time…' Her voice faltered.

Inge's brow lined in confusion.

'Would Hans…' Rhiannon hesitated then pressed on, 'be aware if Max had been taken in by the SA? I know he works in this part of Berlin and Max works in another. I was wondering…'

255

'You do not understand these things,' stated Inge. Her voice was strident but her face had gone quite pale. 'These matters are organised region by region. Why should Hans know what is happening in another part of the city?'

'But he could find out, couldn't he? I thought his standing in the Party had risen?'

Inge flared into life. 'Of course he has some rank. He has not been working away all these months, years even, for nothing.'

'So?' Rhiannon was surprised how easy it was to flush out Inge's pride.

Inge laid her hands flat on the table, spreading her fingers, as if to iron away the disturbance of what she was hearing.

'Inge, this is Max we're talking about. He was due to meet me at the station but he never turned up.' She tapped the table in frustration.

'Then you must tell me what he has been up to that makes you think he has fallen foul of the Party.'

Rhiannon stared at the grain of the pine, tracing it with her fingernail, wondering how much to divulge. She raised her glance to Inge, whose eyes were looking unusually sharp. Inge abhors conflict, she thought: what she avows in public she wants to own in private. This is making that untenable. 'You know he's a journalist. He writes what he sees.'

'He is opposed to the Nazi Party and its aims.'

'He hates their anti-Semitism…' Rhiannon kept her voice steady.

'So why are you coming here to me when he is an enemy of all that we stand for?' Inge's eyes grew small with irritation.

'Wasn't one of your grandparents Jewish, Inge?'

Inge reddened. 'I am German through and through.'

'Max says…'

256

'Max doesn't know what he's talking about.'

'Max, your only brother…'

'My brother, yes. Yes yes yes! Ever since our mother died I have been clearing up after him. One mess after another he gets himself into. The unrealistic way he behaves. The way he flouts rules. The way he thinks he is above society. The way he thinks he can change the world. The way…'

'You know as well as I do that Max has intelligence and integrity. He wants the best for…'

'You come here from another country. You understand nothing of what it is to be German. The humiliation we've had to face, the lack of basics. We hardly have enough to feed ourselves so we tear ourselves apart. Like dogs scrapping over bones. Then when we have our chance – a Party to take us out of the mess – he and his comrades set out to destroy it. They would keep us in misery forever. You don't understand. You come from a different culture.'

Rhiannon grasped hold of Inge's hand, half in anger, half desperation. 'Inge, you know the methods of the SA. If anybody disagrees with them they beat them up. Or kill them. Is that what you want to happen to Max?'

Inge's eyes widened. 'It's not me who will be causing these things to happen, but Max himself.'

Rhiannon tightened her grip on Inge's wrist, her throat constricting. 'Inge, you've got to help me find him. Hans can find out who's been taken in and where they're being held.' She thrust Inge's hand away, swallowing hard. 'I know he's caused you pain…'

Inge rubbed her wrist, looked up at Rhiannon. 'You put me in an impossible position.'

'I don't like the way things are going. Day by day the climate here is changing. If you're not German you're considered inferior. I don't want to stay here any longer than I need to.'

Inge sighed. 'Then you haven't counted on Max's stubbornness. He won't leave Berlin in a hurry.'

Rhiannon leaned back, exhausted. 'Inge, think about it, will you? I'll telephone as soon as I hear anything.' Inge was looking uncomfortable. 'I'm sorry I raised my voice to you. I – I'm just very worried.'

Inge got to her feet and grasped Rhiannon's hand. '*Na, ist schon gut.* Never mind. Times like these.'

Outside on the street Rhiannon could not stop herself from shaking. She decided to call on the Pastor she had visited once before, when she first came to Berlin. At that time she'd been impressed by a sermon he gave in the *Gedächtniskirche* when he spoke out against what he called 'the enemies of morality.'

The Gothic villa was set back from the street. She rang the bell. A middle-aged woman in an overall asked Rhiannon to wait inside. At the back of the house a clock was ticking. Rhiannon heard the clanking of a tram, then heavy footsteps and a key turning in the lock. The pastor muttered a quick exchange with the housekeeper and entered.

Rhiannon began in German then switched to English, knowing the pastor had spent time in Scotland. 'I thought you might be able to advise me. It's my husband. He's disappeared. I went to the police this morning… I need…'

'Sit down Frau Dienst. Sit down. Tell me again what happened. You're speaking too fast.'

Rhiannon's mind could not stop racing as she vented her fear. 'I went to his sister but her husband's in the Nazi Party. But the police – do they do anything about missing persons or just take details?'

'The police play down wives reporting husbands missing. They assume it's just domestic strife.'

'I tried to explain. In the end they told me to come back in a day or two.' She slumped back in her chair. The pastor cleared his throat.

'Frau Dienst, my colleague is the prison chaplain in Tegel. I will find out what I can. Come again tomorrow. If he's been taken and charged by the police we shall hear about it.'

'And if he has been taken in by the SA?'

'Then I am afraid I will not be able to help you.'

Forty

Max was finishing off his bitter-tasting coffee in the dingy bar as he eyed the arrivals board. He recognised the two men from the Gents. One was leering at him in a quasi-comical way and urging him to step outside. Max gave a snort of derision and pushed him away, moving towards the counter. The other man thrust out his leg and Max sprawled onto the floor. He felt a boot in the small of his back. The bar quickly emptied. At the other end the waiter was clearing glasses, banging down ashtrays. Max heard the whistle of trains and the shuffling of feet. The boot held him fast. He turned and the next he knew was the flash of a knuckle-duster in his face, a blinding ray of light from the side and the warm trickle of blood into his mouth. He groaned. One arm was trapped beneath his body. He felt himself being dragged to his feet. A hat was thrown over one eye, masking the wound. Gruff voices were making excuses, joking that their friend had had one too many to drink and needed fresh air. Max let out a shout then felt a sharp jab to the kidneys. Another yell muffled as the two men pulled him through the doorway and out onto the concourse.

He struggled to break free but they tightened their hold and were joined by two more men. Max could only see their legs in brown, perfectly creased trousers. He gave another yell and broke their grip, spurting forward, but at once he was surrounded, arms and feet everywhere. They trampled him to the ground, struck him on the head. 'Degenerate ponce!' shouted one. 'Get him outta here!'

They formed a wall, blocking him from view. Nobody

seemed to be paying attention. Now he was being marched towards an exit, blood trickling down one cheek. He was bundled into a large car – a black Mercedes. He could smell seasoned leather and petrol. Another sharp prod in the ribs while a blindfold was tied round his eyes, smearing the blood and sweat. He flinched in pain. Rough fabric was stuffed into his mouth, he almost gagged and had to inhale sharply through his nose.

The car sped off. The men inside were braying in an excited, boyish way, jubilant at having captured and carted off their victim in broad daylight in a public place. The thought sickened him: how could he have let this happen?

He heard the tyres crunching over the uneven streets and caught the rattle of a tram, then music from a café. Every minute the streets were growing quieter, with fewer cars. He tried to gauge the direction they were taking him. He wondered if they had caught up with his article in *The Independent Chronicler* yet, and if they'd worked out the provenance. Once before they had warned him. They had known then where he lived and what he did. How come they knew so much about him? Dieter and Seifert walked about unscathed, whereas he became prey. His mind blurred. Why didn't they just shoot him down some back alley like Kurt Stein? Why go to all this trouble?

They had rammed him into one corner and now one of them bound his wrists so fast it threatened his circulation. He twisted and groaned in protest but to no avail. One jabbed him. '*Halt's Maul!* Shut your trap!' After a while they grew quiet.

He sensed the car turning off the road onto a track and lurching over a bumpy surface. Allotment land? Up by Wannsee? Out towards Potsdam? There was no way of telling. He wondered how long he'd have to stay trussed up.

By now he had given up struggling and attempted to settle as best he could, keeping his breathing low and steady. Eventually the car slowed and stopped. The men jumped out. He heard another door being opened and other voices, the crunch of feet over gravel. Then they were yanking him out of the car by his arms. 'Out you get, out of there…! Get to your feet…! No slouching!'

He stumbled, groping to either side for balance. They elbowed him forward, prevented him from falling. He caught a whiff of pine resin and through a chink in the blindfold glimpsed mud and tatters of grass under vestiges of snow. He guessed that they had travelled about ten kilometres from the Westend. Two men either side of him urged him up some steps. Slivers of light shot out from the interior of the house.

'So you got him?' The cool, crisp voice sounded more educated than the ruffians in the car. 'Take him to the back room.' The men, subdued in the presence of their superior, led Max through what he took to be a lobby to a confined space beyond. Once there, they brought a chair and commanded him to sit down. One of them pulled the cover from his eyes. Max blinked hard in the glare of electric light. They removed the rough cloth from his mouth. He took a few deep breaths. He took in his captors. The two assailants from the station were younger than he'd surmised. Now, in the new surroundings, they became brutish boys back home after a rowdy spree.

The room was like some giant cupboard or gunroom. A table was propped against one wall with a chair tucked beneath. Through the doorway he glimpsed a carpeted hall beneath a chandelier. It seemed he was in a well-appointed, private house. The Nazis did not own official barracks or quarters but improvised where they could; his contact with the Brown House taught him that they were fast gathering resources and business associates.

A man in military-style khaki came in. His hair was slicked back. Were it not for a fencing scar above his left eye, he would have been handsome. Max recognised the insignia of the *fechtende Burschenschaften,* the student fencing fraternities, where manhood was proved by not wearing a guard when they duelled. Until now it had been the hallmark of old, conservative families. So it was true what they were saying: the Nazi Party's appeal was permeating the universities.

The man was glaring at him. Max put his fingers to the outside of the eye. The bleeding had stopped but the skin was swelling. The man inclined his head and gave a sly smile. 'I apologise if the men were a bit enthusiastic. I told them to bring you in. They did not want to let me down.'

'Why am I here?' asked Max.

'Why? I think you can tell us better. The wonder is that the Movement has not brought you here sooner.' Movement, thought Max. Just when did the narrow outlook of a Party transmute itself into a Movement? The word suggested philosophy: the vision and brightness of a vivid, optimistic future. The man's eyes signalled all this, and more. Max tried to read them. They were intelligent and searching, but without warmth. The tight line of his mouth and the rigid jaw spoke of intolerance, cruelty even. 'Shall we begin again, Herr Dienst?'

Hearing his name Max suppressed a shudder. Gazing at the man's gaunt face, the arrogance of his youth – surely he was at least five years younger than he was – Max wondered what lengths the man would go to achieve satisfaction. They wanted information, that was evident, or why else this high-risk, roughhouse abduction?

'On whose authority am I here?'

The man's eyes flickered. 'Who are *you* to ask about authority?'

Max gave a faint smile. 'This is not a police station. You are not a police officer. I have not, as far as I am aware, infringed the law. So I repeat – on whose authority am I here?'

'On the authority of the Nazi High Command. You stand accused of crimes against the state.'

'And what might they be?' Max sounded considerably calmer than he felt.

'Sedition. Damage to national morale. Insulting the Fatherland,' barked the other, losing patience. Unpractised in the art of debate, the man seemed on the brink of losing face. That would insupportable for him. Already Max could see the man's jaw working. He should try another approach.

'As far as I am aware you are not a policeman or part of the judiciary. I was dragged away from a train station in broad daylight where I was waiting...'

'Yes, Herr Dienst, who were you waiting for?'

He hesitated, then carried on. 'For my wife, as a matter of fact.'

'Yes, I believe that is correct. You have a foreign wife, no?'

'My wife is British.'

'And works at the British embassy.' The man looked pleased with himself.

'That is also true, Herr...?'

'*Kreisleiter* Sturm,' snapped the other. 'And you work for *Die Tatsache* newspaper, do you not?'

Max was silent.

'What have you been writing, Herr Dienst? Can you tell me precisely what you have been writing?'

Max took a deep breath and gazed at the man's Adam's apple as it moved up and down his lean neck. He felt a rush of gratitude that at the last minute he had put his report in the station locker. If they'd found that in his possession he would not have stood a chance. 'I am a general reporter,' he stated. 'I only recently returned to Berlin...'

264

'You were a student here. According to our intelligence, you were a Communist.' The man's eyes narrowed. 'And you still have Communist sympathies. You have been seen in Communist haunts.' He spoke the words in a slow, menacing way.

'And what of that? Even you fellows make alliances with the Communists. The transport strike – remember? Even before that. Your High Command was in constant…'

'Enough! Keep your mouth shut.' Sturm got up from his seat and paced the room then came towards Max and bent his head so his eyes were level with his. 'You are under investigation not us.'

'I was just pointing out…'

'Well don't! *I* will point out. You listen.' His face pinched tighter. 'I want you to tell me who you are working for. I want you to tell me what brought you back to Berlin. I want you to tell me who authorised this!' He strode over to a table by the wall, which was piled high with papers and leaflets. He snatched a flyer in the top and waved it in Max's face.

'You are involved with Communist propaganda. You are a disgrace to your country!' He stared hard at Max.

Max glanced down at the flyer. It was a later one that he had no knowledge of. For a moment he was outside himself. Though his chest was heaving in anxiety, a sudden clarity detached him from the whole thing. He asked himself just what they might know. What they were hoping to find out? Above all, how he should handle himself? There was no point in denying involvement. But whom did he need to protect? *Immer Freiheit* was not an underground paper. *Die Tatsache* was part of the Centre-Left establishment. Both had been around for years.

It struck him that these papers expressed the very freedoms most at risk, they gave voice to a variety of opinions and sections of society. All this was becoming anathema to the Nazis who craved a universal credo, which would unite all. To lop off a few dissenting heads was a paltry price to pay. He looked at *Kreisleiter* Sturm then said slowly: 'I think you are wasting your time.'

The other got to his feet balled his hand to a fist and struck Max across the mouth. Max recoiled. The two men glared at each other.

Forty one

Khan was more concerned about Max than he cared to admit, even to himself. Unaccounted-for vanishings were becoming more commonplace by the day. In street fights the Communists were as vicious as the Nazis, but they were less prone to instigating random abductions.

Somewhere, in their collective pomp, the Nazis must know that ridicule was the fiercest weapon against them. With the bombast of their swelling ranks they took themselves very seriously. In London they would never have got away with it. They declaimed how much better and more evolved the Aryan Germans were: their heads were the right shape, their bodies were taller, stronger; they worked harder; they had better music; they were cleaner and more thrifty and upright. So did they not deserve more than they presently had? It was their civic duty to pull together to fight for it.

In England, there might exist an implicit belief that there was nothing under the sun quite like an English gentleman. Yet there was no need to shout about it or proclaim it as something new. Anyone reared under the Union Flag just knew it. How one fitted into the scheme of things was communicated by accent and subtle social sanctions.

He looked at his watch. He hurried down the embassy steps and mingled with the crowds on Unter den Linden. His work for the day over, now was an ideal time to find out what he could for Rhiannon. He was not as hopeful as he'd put across the evening before. His links into right-wing groups were shrivelling.

There had been just too many elections, cabinet reshuffles

and alliances made and then broken. Nobody trusted him anymore. People were being forced to take sides. This made them suspicious of an outsider. He was hard to classify at the best of times, but now an Indian in Berlin for goodness sake! And working for Britannia to boot, when all knew that India was pressing for Home Rule.

Some said another European war was brewing. Some days he was sceptical: the carnage of the last one was still too harsh in the mind, the League of Nations had been urging disarmament for over a decade. Other days he thought the Germans were so aggrieved that they were longing for a good old scrap. At the moment, though, they were ill prepared. At the moment they couldn't battle their way out of a circus tent.

But what about Max? All this deliberation was not solving *his* problem. Khan knew that expecting the police to help would probably be futile. By and large they favoured the Nationalists. To track down an errant leftish journalist would be their lowest priority: his file would have been lost.

Boris Dublovsky was a possibility. Dublovsky had gained in confidence as an informant and now listened in where he could at the Kuka cabaret. With its reputation for being non-political and the beauty of its dancers, it attracted the more affluent Nazi Party members. After a few glasses of Russian vodka, they grew uninhibited, talking freely. Perhaps Boris Dublovsky would have something to tell.

But first he should visit Bahnhof Zoo.

When he arrived there he demurred: where to start? He looked around. People were shifting up and down, hurrying to greet someone or catch a train. Every day it would be a different crowd. At the entrance were the usual Hitler types selling their wares. Inside a young man in a cloth cap was selling *Immer Freiheit*. Khan approached him. 'Excuse me, were you here yesterday?' The man eyed him warily. 'A strange question, I know. But I was meant to meet a friend and he didn't turn up. You didn't notice anything strange, did you?'

'I wasn't here,' snapped the man and moved away. Must think I'm nuts, mused Khan. People had become uncomfortable with strangers. A year ago it would not have been a problem.

The stationmaster was a small, wiry man, who reminded Khan of a weasel. Khan wondered how to frame his enquiry. 'Do you keep a log of incidents on the station, sir?' he began.

'I beg your pardon?' The official bristled.

'Have you had any fights or disturbances that have come to your attention?'

The stationmaster looked at him from head to toe: 'You are?'

'Herr Sid Khan, at your service,' Khan offered his hand and after a moment's hesitation the man took it. 'A friend of mine came here yesterday to meet his wife and he seems to have – well – disappeared. I just wondered whether anything untoward happened. Did your staff notice anything? Any signs of someone being…'

The man's eyes became unfriendly slits. 'Of being what, Herr Khan?'

'Taken away against their will.'

'We run an orderly station here. There have been no fights. No kidnappings. And now – if you will excuse me…'

'Of course. Thank you for your time.'

Khan was on the point of leaving the station when he passed a small bar. It crossed his mind that had Max had been waiting for Rhiannon this would be a likely spot to while away the time. Inside he approached a stout man wiping down tables. He explained what he was after. The man carried on wiping.

'We get all sorts in here: drunks, salesmen, people waiting, men trying to dodge their wives, lovers – if I took notice of everyone I'd never get any work done.'

'You don't remember a man yesterday? Dark hair. About six foot. Lean. He was wearing a brown jacket, I think.'

The man looked at Khan. 'That description fits about a hundred men who pass through the station every day.'

He put down his cloth and stared at Khan, his eyes lingering a little longer than was usual. 'Who are you? Do you work for the police?'

'No, I don't. I'm looking for a friend, that's all.'

'There were some rough types in here yesterday now you mention it. They looked like Brown Shirts. One of them fell flat on his face and the others hustled him out. I didn't pay much attention. When people get drunk they behave like that.'

'Where did they go?'

'Search me.'

'What time was it?'

'Afternoon. I don't remember exactly.'

'Can you remember what they looked like?'

'Youngish guys. Average looking. Then the other one, the drunk one, looked different from the others. At the time I just thought he was the worse for wear, but now you mention it, he didn't look too good. His face was bleeding.'

'Anything else?'

'No.' The man moved away towards the bar, signalling that the questioning was over.

Khan nodded and left the dark interior. He was cold with misgiving. Instinct told him that this man had unwittingly witnessed Max's abduction. People were growing skilful at minding their own business. Any signs of manhandling or fights were not their concern.

As Khan left the station he decided to seek out Dublovsky.

The front of the club was shuttered. Khan walked round to the side entrance in an alley alongside and rang the bell. Dublovsky greeted him with surprise and asked him in. 'To what do I owe the pleasure?' Khan still abhorred his unctuous manner. 'A vodka perhaps? Or something lighter? We haven't had you round the club for some time now.'

Khan took a chair opposite Dublovsky in the cramped kitchen-cum-office. A pile of unwashed glasses cluttered the sink, receipts and account books were stacked on the table. The room had a grubby feel. 'I won't take up too much of your time. It's Max Dienst. He's gone missing. I was wondering if you'd heard any talk of late – amongst our Nazi friends? Any plan to snatch journalists?'

Dublovsky's eyes widened. 'The one that went after Gert Frosch?'

'The very same.'

Dublovsky leaned back and whistled through his teeth. 'So, so. These are difficult times.'

'Yes,' said Khan, weary of hearing the same comments. 'So, what can you tell me? I know you keep a good eye out.'

Dublovsky laughed, shifting in his chair. His round eyes disappeared into folds of flesh. 'You made enquiries at his usual haunts?'

Khan shrugged. 'Done all that. But it's not straightforward. Fear is eating into people. They don't want to know.'

'Quite.'

Khan eyed Dublovsky, wondering just where his interests were most deeply entwined. Dublovsky said he despised the Nazis for their crude thinking, but they brought custom and increasingly, with their ambition and drive, a sense of the future; all of which appealed to his self-importance.

'So?'

'What can I say? They come in their hordes now, drinking

271

and taking up table space. Some are stern and idealistic. Behave very correctly. Others are loutish. One or two we had to show the door. But generally – well, they're just men after all. They like to relax. Ogle the women. Drink.'

'And what else? They talk, don't they?'

'They come to enjoy themselves, not plan the next revolution.' Boris Dublovsky's eyes shifted away. He became inordinately fascinated by something on the wall behind Khan's back. Khan felt sure he had shifted his allegiance towards the golden goose of the Nazi Party. He would be better off tapping Tilda, his wife.

'If you do hear of anything, give me a call. His wife is frantic.'

Forty two

Exhausted though she was from the day's efforts, Rhiannon paced up and down the bedroom in Savignystrasse. She was running over the responses of those she'd visited: Hannah had been offhand but in the end not unhelpful, the pastor was as sympathetic as he dared be and Inge was predictably angry that once again Max had put himself at odds with authority. A ring on the doorbell on the door broke her train of thought. Downstairs Khan stood by the front door looking earnest. She rushed up to him, searching his face for clues. He gave her a brief hug. 'Shall we go?' he said.

Out on the street she asked if he had any news. He started whistling, which made her think he was nervous. 'Tell me, what is it?'

'I went to Bahnhof Zoo.' They moved onto the broader thoroughfare of the Ku'damm where people thronged either side of them. 'Let's go in here, so we can get out of the cold and talk for a bit.' He pointed to the Sultan Ahmet with its array of brass pots and exotic carpets by the entrance. They found themselves a corner table.

'I need to know everything.'

Khan swirled the wine in his glass. He stared at the heavy velvet tablecloth and recounted what the barman had told him. He paused. 'Rhiannon, we have no way of knowing whether this involved Max.'

She inhaled deeply. 'But it sounds plausible, doesn't it?'

'I need to make more enquiries. I haven't managed to get hold of Dieter yet.'

'I haven't come up with anything myself.'

'Rhiannon…'

'Yes?'

'It's just…' His dark eyes grew moist. 'I'm concerned about you.'

She softened. 'I'm okay.'

'It's more than that. I feel responsible. I encouraged Max to write articles to stoke up the opposition, to write for the British press. And now you're here, alone in Berlin, when things aren't looking too clever.'

'Max is not someone you can push into anything. What he did he did of his own free will.' She paused. 'And I can take care of myself.'

He smiled. 'You are very resourceful. But there are the practicalities.'

'Do you think there's any point in going back to the police?'

'I wouldn't have thought so.'

'So, it's up to us, more or less?'

Khan seemed reluctant to agree with her. The temperature was falling. It was approaching midnight and the streets were deserted. Khan suggested they go back to his place in Wilmersdorf. Frozen and approaching desperation, Rhiannon agreed. She was not yet ready for her empty quarters.

His apartment was in an elegant stucco edifice in Wilmersdorf. The rooms were well lit and furnished with sofas and easy chairs covered in chintz. On the walls there were swirling prints by Matisse and in the hall a languid, glittering Klimt gave off an air of decadent refinement. The whole place worked an uncommon mix of comfort and modernity.

'What can I get you to drink?' He took her coat. She sank into an enfolding armchair and closed her eyes.

'Whatever you like.'

She started when Khan touched her arm, offering her a shot of schnapps. 'It's going to be all right,' he murmured.

She gave him a sharp look. 'What are you talking about? What's going to be all right?' Much as she fought against it, the emotion she'd been holding back broke through. She gave a loud sob. Khan sat on the side of the chair and attempted to put his arms around her.

'It's all right. It's all right.'

The more he spoke, the more upset she grew. Only when he said nothing but just held her did she become still. She leaned against him, allowing her tears to soak into his shirt, not wanting to move away. She allowed herself to absorb the comfort of his body against hers. He lifted her mouth towards his and he was pressing towards her, holding her. Her lips parted as he kissed her, gently at first, then with growing urgency. She felt a pull towards him, she was falling headlong. She wanted to fall. She wanted to forget. She wanted to shut out the darkness of her fears. So much she wanted to be swept away. He was pressing her back against the sofa, moving alongside her.

She gasped. 'No. No!'

She struggled to her feet and shook her head. 'I want to go home.'

His astonishment gave way to assent. He nodded.

Afterwards the incident remained a blur in Rhiannon's mind: she was unsure what she recalled and what she imagined. She only knew that had she allowed it, Khan would have kept her there all night. Awake on her bed, she traced zigzags of light thrown by passing cars. His concern for her was far from altruistic. This stirred her. It angered her. It filled her with misgiving and fascination. What did his feelings have to do with anything? Yet as she lay mulling it over, she knew it was a comfort as well as a disturbance. If nothing else, it took the edge off her alienation in the city. She drifted into the deepest sleep she had had for days.

She woke in a cold sweat. Outside in a back yard a dog was barking. She went to the bathroom and drank from the tap, swallowing in thirsty gulps. Her peace was broken. Fears circled like crows, pecking at her. She sat in the armchair, wrapped in a blanket, until the thin light of another winter morning broke in.

Forty three

Tilda Dublovsky could not disguise her surprise when Khan called at her villa. 'So, it's you. I thought you'd abandoned our friendship.' She gave a chuckle at his bemusement. 'Come in.' Khan did as he was bid, hanging back a little then following her into an airy sitting room, which looked out over a garden planted with evergreen shrubs.

'How are you?' he asked, then added: 'You're looking well. Last time I thought you looked, well, exhausted.'

She pushed her hair from her face. 'I was under strain. Boris and I had just separated. He found out what I was involved in – I suspect he knew all along. But that was not the problem – though he did yell at me and called me a madam and a whore. But that was just rhetoric. He didn't really care…'

'So what happened?'

'When we'd calmed down we admitted we no longer needed each other. It was hardly a love match to begin with. But when it came to it, it *was* a wrench. I've grown used to the old codger. He used to look after me. In other respects we were incompatible.' She wrinkled her nose. 'Silly, isn't it? Anyway, that was weeks ago.' She looked at him mischievously.

Khan clasped her hand. 'It's good to see you.' She intertwined her fingers with his and for a moment seemed at a loss. He moved closer to her.

'So what brings you here today?' she asked crisply, rescuing her hand.

'Who's being businesslike now then?'

'One of us has to be. No use sitting here gazing at each other. Something might happen.'

'And if it did?'

'It might get complicated.' Their eyes locked for a moment. Why not, thought Khan. She can look after herself, not like these young girls who want marriage and commitment. Tilda caught the glance of fervid appraisal. He noticed her neck was flushed, like a girl on her first date. 'You didn't come here to flirt with me. I know you better than that.'

Khan glanced down at the intricate swirls of the carpet and said quietly. 'You're a beautiful woman. Have I ever told you that?'

She smiled at him. 'Yes, the first time we met. I assumed it was part of the protocol.'

Khan felt nonplussed. He gave a little laugh. No wonder women never took him seriously. 'Tilda…'

'*Wie geht's?* How's it going?' she asked. He watched her move between the chairs in her purple, floating garment.

'So so,' he replied.

'Good. Just let me make coffee. I'll be right with you. Have a cigarette. You know where they are.' Khan helped himself to a Turkish cigarette.

When she came back with the coffee he laid his hand on her wrist.

'Tilda, you're…'

'What?' There was a look of surprised amusement on her face undercut by something more vulnerable. There were days when she must struggle, he thought, days when she must wonder who she was and where she would end up in the welter of Berlin. Her mouth had dropped open.

Before he knew it he had taken her in a passionate embrace. She gasped, returned the pressure. They clasped each other. She moved her body in towards his, moulding herself to him. He caught the scent of roses mixed with the slightest trace of nicotine. He kissed the top of her head, lifted her face towards

278

him. They shifted in silence towards her bedroom, towards her bed piled high with pillows and magazines. With a careless sweep of her hand she knocked them onto the floor, pushed aside the night-clothes she had left there.

They made love. They dozed a little. Made love again. Khan had not felt so good in weeks. He smoked another of her Turkish cigarettes, then glanced at the alarm clock on her bedside table. It was time to get on with things.

'Remember Max Dienst?' he murmured.

'Who?'

'You know – the journalist working at *Die Tatsache*? The one writing a story about Hitler and his niece?'

'Vaguely. What about him?'

'He's gone missing. Probably landed himself on a Nazi hit list.'

She sighed, settled herself back into the pillows. 'Not the first one that's happened to. And won't be the last.'

'I know.'

'So what's it to you?'

'I work with his wife.'

Tilda groaned slightly and looked towards him. 'So that's why you're here, is it?'

'No.'

'You can't fool me.'

'I'm not…' He ran his hand over the contour of her body, hidden now beneath the covers.

'It's all right, Sid. I don't fool myself…'

He pulled back the eiderdown and started to hunt around for his hastily discarded clothes. 'He was due to pick his wife up at Bahnhof Zoo yesterday. But he didn't turn up. I'd seen him a couple of hours before. I'm trying to find out what I can.'

'That's where I come in, is it?'

He came and sat beside her on the bed, nuzzled her shoulder. 'I know. I just thought… I know how shrewd you are.' He ran a finger over the sinew of her neck. 'You get people to relax. They tell you things. Like me…'

'Not any more,' she said briskly. She got up, pulled on a silken dressing gown and went through to the bathroom where she started running herself a bath. 'You're off are you?' she said as she came back in.

He nodded.

She sat at her dressing table and started brushing her hair in vigorous strokes. 'There's a swing away from the easy-going days. People are getting harder, demanding more but giving less. Numbers are falling in the nightclubs. If you ask me, it would be a good time to decamp to Paris or somewhere. There's not the money about. People are getting cautious.'

'But you still have dealings with our friends, the Brown Shirts?'

'Not the lower ranks, they're too poor. But higher up, yes. Needs must.'

'So?'

'Allegiances are shifting. Big businessmen are getting on board. Now that's where the money *does* flow. Some of the top echelons of the Party fancy the high life. They're happy to pay for sexual favours, but want it kept quiet.'

'Do you get to hear anything about their…?'

'*Komm doch.* They're not stupid. Why should they discuss any of that with the likes of me? They come to us to get away from all that.' A note of irritation had crept into her voice.

Khan paused. 'I guess we have a day or so to discover Max's whereabouts. My fear is they will just put a bullet in him. As long as they think he has something to tell them they'll keep him alive. Once they're done with him they will want him out of the way.'

Tilda put down the hairbrush and turned towards him, her face shadowed with sadness. 'You're probably right.'

He moved towards her. 'I encouraged Max to write for the British press. They know he was a foreign correspondent. That makes him a likely target. I want him to get out of this in one piece.'

She was thoughtful, looked at Khan from head to toe. 'One thing I *do* know. There are villas up by the Wannsee where they hold meetings and things. It's out of the way. Those houses have all sorts of outbuildings and cellars. The police are not going to go poking their noses around there, are they? Not in the house of some party chief, who to all intents and purposes is a perfectly respectable citizen…'

Khan watched a sliver of weak sunlight slanting across her face. She seemed softer and more vulnerable than he'd ever known her. 'Tilda,' he said. 'You're a gem. A true gem.' He strode across the room and lifted her to her feet. He gave her a sudden and passionate kiss on the mouth. 'Thank you for everything. I'll be in touch.' He made for the front door.

Forty four

Max was getting cramp in his legs where he'd been thrown into a corner of the cellar. He attempted to stretch but he was still bound. As well as the ligature around his hands they'd tied a cord round his feet he could barely move. The cold was biting into him. He shifted and a poker of pain shot up from his ankle up through his thigh. The dark, airless space stank of wine and stale beer. From upstairs he heard odd sounds: a door banging, shuffling, the sound of furniture being dragged across the floor, then silence, long hours of silence or an occasional shout.

It was a large house: a villa, he guessed, rather than any sort of institution. Now and then from above him at street level he heard the rumble of a car but no trams nor trains. When they'd arrived here an owl had hooted nearby and the air had smelt fresh. He guessed they must be at some distance from the city centre, in a place surrounded by trees.

He wondered if they were holding anyone else here. If past tactics were anything to go by, his abduction would not be an isolated event. There could well have been a round-up of all journalists the Nazi Party had taken exception to, but he'd heard nothing to indicate this. So far they'd given nothing away, apart from waving the flyer under his nose. He had no idea how long he'd been there or what time of the day or night it was, for despite his efforts to stay alert he'd dozed off, woken with a start, drifted off again until he became disoriented. At least they had left him alone for a while. Dieter told him Nazis often tormented victims by shining constant lights in their eyes.

Apart from the *Kreisleiter* his captors seemed new to the game, amateurish even. The Brown Shirts from the station became less convincing here as they waited on Sturm's orders, not knowing what to do until he instructed them. Such ignorance would make them dangerous.

He thought of Rhiannon. He pictured her arriving at the station, looking out for him. He must escape, the words drilled through his head. A second later came the sober realisation that this was impossible.

A bolt was drawn back and light flooded down the steps. 'So,' shouted a voice. '*Aufstehen!* Get up. There is work to be done.' He recognised the voice from the car, one of the fellows who had roughed him up and delivered him here: no doubt one of the city's army of unemployed now pressed into service by the Movement. He came clattering down the stairs. The light caught the side of his face. He had slightly bulging eyes and his hair was slicked back in the manner of *Kreisleiter* Sturm. There were freckles over his nose, which gave him a boyish, untried look.

'Slept well?' the youth jested. He pulled Max to his feet, released the cord round his ankles, then dragged him up the steps and through to a lavatory on the ground floor. He loosened the binding on his hands. Max stared at the lavatory bowl then up at the tiny slit of a window.

He was pushed along into the gunroom. *Kreisleiter* Sturm was already seated opposite behind the table. 'You have had time to reflect. I think today you will be more co-operative, no?' He was flicking through a dossier of notes, looking every bit the efficient civil servant. Max stared at the papers wondering what facts they had gathered and who had done the gathering. Sturm was fiddling with a pen, rolling it between his fingers.

'I am still no wiser as to why I am here,' began Max.

'Then let me enlighten you. You returned from London several weeks ago. You have been working for *Die Tatsache* and sometimes for *Immer Freiheit*. We have identified you as the author of several articles.' Sturm opened one of the files and pulled out several sheaves of paper, which he placed on the table between them. 'At first they were general, commenting on the state of the economy, on the massive queues for food, on the growing number of unemployed.'

'That's what I was asked to do.' Max kept his voice level.

'We have been watching the newspapers. Especially yours. *"Eyewitness snapshots after a period away"'* He mimicked and gave a supercilious smile. 'Communist rubbish! Once we come into power we will unify the newspapers. People must be made to understand...'

'*What* must they be made to understand?'

The man stuck out his chin. 'We need to inform people of how the country has been betrayed. We need to claim back what is ours.'

'I do not doubt your sincerity...' began Max.

The *Kreisleiter* jumped to his feet as though shot through with electricity. 'You are not to speak of sincerity,' he yelled. 'You are here to comply. You are here to give information.'

Someone rapped on the door. *'Herein,'* commanded Sturm.

From outside Max heard a door opening and closing, the sound of feet moving, other people about to enter the fray. In the event only one man entered carrying another folder. Max looked over the *Kreisleiter's* shoulder. What he saw made him freeze. Gaping at him, looking equally appalled and shocked, was none other than Hans Fichte, his brother-in-law.

Forty five

Khan had a rendezvous with Rhiannon in Café Mozart and was in no mood to receive any last-minute phone calls, so when a secretary poked her head round the door letting him know that there was someone on the line he waved a dismissive hand. When she added: 'Mr Denning' he said he'd take it.

Several clicks later he heard his boss's voice. 'So what have you been up to?' asked Robert Denning by way of introduction. The question irked. How was Khan supposed to sum up his activities, some of which which fell strictly outside the remit of his post? Nevertheless, he waded in.

'Max Dienst has been kidnapped, killed or gone astray. I'm helping his wife track him down.' He registered Robert's gasp of surprise, followed by a thoughtful pause before Denning responded.

'I would have thought the police are better equipped to do that.'

'One journalist is of no significance. The police themselves don't know who's giving the orders.'

'Khan, we need to talk.'

'Where are you?'

'At the airport.'

'You didn't tell me you were coming back.'

'I didn't know till yesterday. I couldn't get hold of you.'

'Are you coming to the embassy?'

'Can we meet first?' There was a note of urgency in his voice.

'I'm meeting Rhiannon Dienst at Café Mozart. Do you want

to come there? We will be about an hour or so. By the time you get there from Tempelhof, we'll be finished.'

Robert Denning grunted in response. Replacing the receiver Khan was puzzled. From London Denning had sent the briefest of memos, outlining his meetings. So what was he agitated about? Their intelligence operation was in danger of faltering, of that Khan was sure. For months they'd been feeding back what passed their way. From Whitehall they received muted response to their memos. What was the purpose in tracking the burgeoning of right-wing groups when nothing was being done about them? The only party seen to impact directly on the interests of the Crown was Mihir Basu and his followers in the Free India Movement.

It would be good to hear what was going on in London and how people back home viewed events in Berlin. What, for instance, they were making of the latest: the conservatives seeking to draw Hitler into the cabinet in order to tame him? Others were playing down the man's military goals and passing off the mass rallies as some grand floorshow. Khan was left unsettled. Mulling over the coming meeting, he tidied his desk and told the secretary not to expect him back that day.

When he arrived at Café Mozart Rhiannon was tucked away behind a column. Looking pale but self contained, she was leafing through a copy of *Das Berliner Tageblatt*. She glanced up. Her eyes held an unspoken question. He kissed her lightly on either cheek. 'Busy morning?' he asked, not knowing how else to broach their separate attempts to ferret out what they could about Max. He mentioned what Tilda had said about the villas in the Wannsee area. 'It's a long shot, mind.' He suppressed his doubt about finding anyone in that domain of privilege and privacy. 'I thought I might go up there and have a look,' he added.

'I'll come with you.'

'Now wait a minute. Do you think that wise?'

She looked annoyed. 'What else do you expect me to do? I can't just sit here and do nothing.'

His hand shot out and covered hers. 'Don't get me wrong. We – we must think about this.' He had the urge to step in and direct the operation. She drew back into her chair, folding her arms. For a moment she seemed lost, then she leaned forward.

'We must get to him as soon as possible.'

'I agree. But we have to have a plan.'

'I was not suggesting otherwise. I'm going to see Hannah. She seems well connected and well informed. I'll see what she has to say.'

'Rhiannon, do be careful what you divulge.' When she looked irritated by this remark he said: 'You never know quite whom you can trust.'

'I will be discreet.'

He nodded. 'You're sure about her, are you, this Hannah woman?'

'As sure as I am about you.' He winced. She gave him the faintest of smiles. 'As Max is always telling me: Berlin is crawling with spies.'

'Are you sure which side she's batting on?'

She snorted with laughter.

'What is it?'

She looked down at the table then finished her drink. 'Nothing. Nothing. Look, I need to go. There are a few things I need to see to.'

'I'll call round later.' They gave each other a swift embrace. He watched her moving with grace between the tables to the exit. His chest tightened with emotion, aware as ever of her strange blend of vulnerability and resilience.

When she had gone, he took out papers from his briefcase and began leafing through memos from the embassy. His boss would want to know what had been going on in recent days. It was another hour before Denning pushed through the glass doors. Looking mildly disgruntled, he wedged his travel bag into the cramped space where Khan was sitting. Khan got up and shook his hand. 'Good to have you back, old boy.' Denning pulled out a chair and ordered lemon tea. Khan filled Denning in on the latest cabinet events before outlining what he knew of the murderous in-fighting not only between political parties but within them. Denning grunted and threw a few questions at him. Khan watched discontent play across his boss's face.

'That's not all. As I mentioned on the phone we think Max Dienst might have been taken in by the Nazis.'

'Is that so?' Denning caught the attention of a waiter and ordered a large brandy. 'Want one?'

'No thanks. At Bahnhof Zoo, we think. And there's a possibility he might be holed up in a Wannsee villa.'

Khan looked across, disconcerted that Denning was guarding an air of careful neutrality as he sipped his brandy.

'I thought we might try and get him out.'

'What are you talking about?' Denning raised an eyebrow.

'We urged him to write for us. Remember?' With a sliver of apprehension, Khan recalled that Robert Denning was still in the dark about the pre-election flyer and the article for *The Independent Chronicler*. 'We were pushing him. Giving him tips,' he continued, with less certainty.

'He had a choice. He was keen to get more stories. We just helped.'

Khan gave Denning a sharp look. The man sniffed, folded his arms and looked away.

'So all of a sudden it's none of our business?'

'He's not a British subject. It's an internal German matter.'

Khan could barely believe what he was hearing. 'He's been hauled in by the Nazis. Doesn't that bother you?'

Denning brushed a speck of cotton from his trouser leg. 'It is something that happens.'

'And what is that supposed to mean?'

'Sometimes sacrifices have to be made.'

'And what about his wife, Rhiannon Dienst? Can't the embassy do something on her behalf? She still works for us. Can't we take it up with the Chief of Police? The Justice department?'

'What good do you think that will do?'

'We have to do something!'

'We can't be seen to be dabbling in internal German affairs.' Denning finished his brandy and put down the glass. 'I will have to think about it. Give me an hour or two back on German soil.'

Khan sighed. There was clearly something else on his mind: better to get that over and done with. 'So how's it going? Is anything up?'

Denning blew air out through his cheeks. 'Might as well come straight to the point: they're pulling the plug on us. That's what.'

'How do you mean?'

He glanced around to make sure no one was eavesdropping and shifted his chair a little closer. 'I had two meetings in Whitehall. The policy has changed. They're shifting even further towards reconciliation. At least some of them are. Opinions are divided. There is a lot of heated debate.'

'Yes I know.' Khan paused to reflect. 'So His Majesty's Government is no longer interested in the machinations of the right-wingers and their intention to re-arm?'

Denning gave a nonchalant shrug. 'As I said opinions are…'

'Does it no longer concern them the way things are going here…?'

'They're now talking about a posting to Delhi of all places.'

'What?'

Denning cleared his throat. 'That is, for me?'

Khan glared at Denning. He felt queasy. 'What are you telling me?' When Denning glanced away he said: 'Blood is thicker than water, eh? They don't believe they can trust me, is that it?'

'I argued on your behalf. Said they would be crazy to let you go – you being a native son and all that. But they would not see reason. They spoke of divided loyalties. Believe me, they're hard bargainers. The long and the short of it is they think it's got too messy here. They're saying that the Germans pose no threat to the Crown but what's stirring in India does. That of course was obvious from the outset. Only now they believe the ferment in India is something to be influenced. Subdued if you will.'

'And Mihir Basu? Surely it remains of utmost importance to keep a close eye on Mihir Basu and his cohorts? To stymie that investigation makes little sense.' When Denning said nothing Khan experienced an earth tremor of doubt: the man's intentions were as opaque as they were complex. What other secret talks had taken place on his recent trip to London?

Khan leaned back and lit a cheroot, not offering one to his colleague. 'I have sensed the change for some time now,' he said at length, blowing a long, lazy streak of smoke towards the ceiling. 'I am not so sure they meant business. Strikes me we were never dealing with professionals. The Crown has no stomach for confrontation and wishes to remain blind, is that it?'

'Could be,' replied Denning drily. 'Some believe the German state is about to implode.'

Khan called over the waitress and asked for another coffee. He eyed his boss. The man was avoiding committing himself. A wedge was driving itself between them as deep-seated loyalties rose to the surface. Perhaps their time together had just run out. In the end it was the unspoken rules of self-interest which would apply.

'So, they're giving me the boot?'

'Something like that.' Denning paused. 'They have given us another three months. They want nothing sudden or abrupt, in terms of departures. They don't want us to arouse suspicion.'

'Can you give me one good reason why I should go along with their wishes, considering they regard me as one hundred percent dispensable?'

'I reckon that choice is yours, old boy. I guess it always has been.'

'So how long has this been cooking?'

'They'll give you a good payoff.'

'Payoff be damned,' muttered Khan.

'Don't be slighted. It's the way they do things.'

There's an art to your deception, Khan wanted to say but held back. They understood each other well enough.

'I've been given the green light. Your work with Basu was most valuable as it happens.'

As it happens, what a cool way Denning had of expressing himself. So there he sat serving Khan notice, this mandarin who had picked him up in an Oxford pub and was about to drop him, just as unceremoniously, in a café in Berlin, his impassive expression giving nothing away.

Khan took his leave and started walking down Unter den Linden away from the embassy. He wanted time to think things through. His pending dismissal transformed recent conversations he'd had with Denning into a kaleidoscope of deceit. Khan hated to admit it, barely allowed himself to think it, but the truth was that Denning no longer trusted him. Now he wanted to get out. Was it as simple as that?

As he walked, he found anger building. For one who had always lived by his wits he was often slow to recognise his emotions. Yet now he tasted in full the bitterness of abandonment. He had tried to serve the Crown. He'd learnt to squash rising doubts, which told him Empire was merely another brand of self-interest. He'd seen the poverty in the north, when he toured Great Britain. Yet at some level he believed the English knew the better way. He may have spoken lightly of it, jested even with Denning, but he'd stood by the notion that the Home Country would lead India out of its confusion of peoples and religions to bring it more fully into the twentieth century.

Now he realised it was a chimera. Greed was greed, what ever cloak it wore, how ever fine the tongue, which gave it voice. And as for him, he had been duped.

Forty six

By the time Rhiannon reached Hannah's place in Zehlendorf a peculiar numbness had taken hold of her. Hannah answered the door. *'Sag' doch,* you look terrible!' Rhiannon laughed nervously and followed her through to the sitting room where two women from the group were at the table, scribbling notes. 'You remember Helga and Gisela from Brandenburg?'

'Am I interrupting something?'

'It's the newsletter – we're just finishing.' The three of them talked for another few minutes then in a flurry of coats and farewells, Helga and Gisela departed. Hannah came and sat opposite Rhiannon on the sofa, giving her a quick, brittle smile: very much the methodical group leader. 'I made enquiries,' she said. 'I talked to relatives and some of the university people I know, old acquaintances. The word is that they – the Nazi elite – are keen to widen their appeal. They are easing back on marches and things.'

Rhiannon felt deadened. She had heard all this before, from Max, from Khan and Denning. She watched as Hannah grew more animated. 'That's the general picture. But it's not going their way. People are still saying they're louts. So they're trying to convince them otherwise. Firing bullets into bodies is no longer seen as the way. Now they want to dig out the intellectuals. They're talking about rehabilitation. It sounds reasonable, but it's just a tactic. But here's the interesting bit – they have set up cells to pick off eminent public figures and bring them round to their way of thinking.'

'Where would Max fit in to all this?'

'Nobody could say. I was careful not to mention him by name, mind you. It seems these cells have waylaid strategic people and carted them off.'

Rhiannon was not convinced. Why would they trouble themselves to alter the thinking of a left-wing journalist when a bullet would do? 'Nothing specific then?'

'I haven't finished.' Hannah's lean face was pensive. 'I thought about Wannsee. I have an aunt up there. I contacted her. She and my uncle have a house by the lake. She mentioned that a nearby villa has been taken over, just a week or so ago. I spun her a yarn about property speculation and the economy – something my boss wanted me to look into – whether Wannsee villas were a good investment and whether they changed hands frequently…'

'Taken over by whom?' Rhiannon's pulse quickened.

'When I prompted her she said it wasn't a family. Cars come and go at all hours… I thought it sounded promising. Of course I couldn't push it too far or she'd get suspicious.'

'They're not Nazi sympathisers are they?'

Hannah looked at her askance. 'Not that I know of, but who can be certain nowadays? He was a member of the *Stahlhelm*.'

'What's that?'

'It's a right-wing paramilitary group of army types. But I'm sure by now he has hung up his sabre. He's getting too old for all that. They're conservative. Aunt Liese is one of these women who have nothing better to do than sit behind their net curtains and watch neighbours.' She gave a little laugh then looked at Rhiannon long and hard. 'All things considered you could do worse than go and have a look round.'

Forty seven

Kreisleiter Sturm, regional leader of north Berlin, was glaring at Max. 'So you see, we do not have a lot of time on our hands. There are certain facts we need to know. We believe you can provide that information. If you cooperate, we are willing to look leniently on you. We aim to re-educate where people have been misled.'

The voice sounded reasonable, measured, as though the man wanted to bring to the proceedings a sense of business and discipline. Max looked at his face and wondered what had been his story before he got mixed up in politics. Was he a law student, perhaps? Certainly he was not a scholar of philosophy or history, for the night before he'd snarled at any hint of debate.

Sturm leaned forward. 'Silence is not an option here.'

Max stared at the *Kreisleiter* anew. In the light of morning – a weak winter sun glimmering through from the hallway – his scar showed a livid white. Such a man would love to fight. He would have eagerly awaited for the call-to-arms. Younger than Max, he would have grown up on stories of the 1914 war and be itching to claw back the losses of that time.

The *Kreisleiter* folded his hands and leaned forward. 'We need to know certain things about your organisation. Who is your leader? What are your aims?' He paused, letting the words sink in. Max watched his face, searching for a speck of humanity, but Sturm was giving nothing away. 'Are you going to help us?' His eyes were grey-green, attractive in themselves, but glittering with an icy conviction of righteousness.

'It's no secret what paper I work for...'

'Not so simple, my friend. You are also an acquaintance of Dieter Hartman, are you not?'

'Yes, I am. Is that a crime?'

'He is a Communist and the editor of *Immer Freiheit*, is he not?'

'He is, yes,' answered Max with deliberation. He wondered what was coming next.

'When did you last see him?'

Max did a quick calculation. It was only two weeks since Dieter moved his office from Schöneberg. 'Three weeks. Perhaps longer.'

The *Kreisleiter* drummed the desk with his fingers. 'I see you are going to make it difficult. You are lying. You have been seen several times with this man. In *Die Schnecke*, just days ago. Do you know where this man is now?'

Max reddened. How long had they been tracking him down?

'And this. What do you know about this?' The *Kreisleiter* opened a drawer and brought out the flyer on Geli Raubal. 'Who wrote it? And who helped him do it?'

Max jerked involuntarily. This was moving too fast. Sturm who had been observing him closely gave a smirk. 'I see we are getting somewhere? Now are you going to help us or not? We can do this in a civilised way or we can find other means.'

He leaned back, pointing the leaflet towards Max so he could see every word. Max gazed down at the floor, sorting facts in his head. There was no doubting what the Nazis would do if they discovered Dieter and his attic office.

'I do not know where he is now,' he said slowly.

The other snorted. 'This is not your style, but you've been involved. We have it on good evidence a foreign journalist penetrated our headquarters in Munich, trying to dig up dirt. Who was it?'

Max shrugged. 'Who knows?'

The man leapt up from behind his desk. 'I want the truth!' he yelled. 'Who are you protecting?' Max bent his head, said nothing. 'So? What is your decision?'

The other's face knotted in frustration. 'Hans!' he yelled. 'Hans, *komm' mal her!*'

Hans's large frame filled the doorway, blocking the light. Max looked towards him. For a moment it crossed his mind that it was because of Hans that he was here in the first place, but then he recalled the look of stark disbelief on Hans's face as he'd walked into the room and seen him. Even now, there was an expression of extreme consternation on his face. He looked trapped. Hunted. His mouth clammed shut in fear.

'Our friend is telling us fairy stories. You will help him remember, no?'

Hans hung his head and avoided looking at Max. Sturm got up and tied Max's hands and feet to the chair with a rough cord. 'You know what to do.' Hans was about to say something, then looking at the stern face of his superior thought better of it. He nodded solemnly.

Max recalled that Hans had given no obvious sign of recognising him. Only the sudden jerkiness of his movements gave him away. Possibilities of escape through Hans flashed through his mind only to wilt under scrutiny. He knew him well enough to realise he could be vindictive. After Sturm had left the room the two men glared at each other, neither daring to speak. Max felt a needle of hatred: he longed to thrash out at Hans, this man who had ensnared his sister and was now sitting opposite as his jailer. 'So what are you doing here? Part of your bank work, is it?'

'Shut up,' snapped Hans. 'Remember who has the upper hand.'

'So what are you going to do: beat the shit out of me or put a bullet in my skull?'

Hans' mouth worked in anxiety. 'I heard the boys had picked up a dissident, someone spreading propaganda against the Movement. It crossed my mind it might be you. I hoped it wasn't.'

'Now you know.'

Hans had grown a world away from the naive Pathfinder he'd once been, the young man who'd adored outdoor life and running races for his local *Rennband*. Already his eyes were acquiring that glassy, mindless look Max had spotted in the men at the Brown House.

How much room remained for negotiation? There was always Inge, of course. In the end it always came back to Inge. 'What are you going to tell Inge tonight?' he said slowly, in a whisper almost.

'Inge will never know.'

'You will never be able to keep it from her.'

Hans stood up abruptly as if too many words were passing between them. The *Kreisleiter* would be growing impatient outside. 'Why not tell us what you know?'

'Like what?'

'Like the names of your friends and the players in the propaganda machine of the Communists.'

'The people I work with are journalists. All of them are in public life. There are no secrets there.'

'Dieter Hartman – where has he disappeared to?'

'I haven't a clue.'

Hans sighed. He looked ill at ease. Time was slipping by. His young boss was waiting in the other room, hungry for names and facts. Hans slapped the flat of his hand onto the table. 'Max, you must do this.'

'I don't have to do anything.'

Hans went red in the face, thumped the table with a balled fist. 'I warned Inge. I warned you. I tried to help you in the only way I knew. But you are stubborn. Can't you see the Left is finished?'

'Hans,' Max leaned forward and lowered his voice. 'You've fallen in with a bunch of fools. Blaming the Jews for Germany's troubles, International Zionist plots. It's all drivel.'

Hans got to his feet reached across the table and yanked Max forward. His eyes were bulging, his mouth opening and shutting like a fish gasping for air. 'You! You!' He lashed out, smashing his fist against Max's jaw. 'Shut up! Shut that big Communist mouth of yours!' Once started Hans was unable to stop. 'Just shut it!' he kept yelling as he pounded Max's face and neck.

Max recoiled, ducked his head, but with hands bound he was unable to stem the onslaught. He tasted the sickly metallic tang of blood. Heard a crack as his nose took another blow. He screamed. Pain went searing from forehead to chin.

Hans' face was tight and bright in the act of inflicting pain. 'I'll teach you to make fun of me. I'll teach you!' After a minute Hans inhaled deeply, as if coming to his senses.

Max slumped back against the chair. His left eye was disappearing into a puffiness of bloated skin. He bent his reeling head, blood dripping from his nose and mouth. He coughed. He squinted across at his brother-in-law who was looking down at the floor. Outside was a scuffle of boots. The *Kreisleiter* came back into the room.

'*Und?* And so – has he told you anything useful?'

Hans looked abashed. 'He will. We were just having a political discussion.' The *Kreisleiter* glanced at Max's bloodied face.

'Not on the face, Fichte. Didn't they tell you that at training camp?'

'He was being resistant.'

Max was astounded that the High Command or whoever had ordered his arrest, were not aware of the connection between them. If that was the case, there were still gaps in their intelligence. That, at least, was something.

The *Kreisleiter* nodded for Hans to retreat and find a cloth to wipe the blood now dripping down Max's neck onto his shirt. 'My colleague is overzealous,' he said. 'But you see we do need that information.'

It was after ten and Hans had not yet arrived back at the Neukölln apartment. Inge was waiting up for him. He had said he had Party business to attend to, but never before had he been quite so late. As she shifted between the settee and the window overlooking the courtyard, her last conversation with Rhiannon ran through her mind. Was it possible that Max had fallen foul of the Party and been abducted, as Rhiannon claimed? She watched shadows in the corner of the room thrown by the beaded lampshade.

The key turned in the lock. She jumped to her feet and rushed down the hall just as Hans came staggering into the apartment. Flushed in the face, he banged his fist against the wall. *'Wie geht's, Schätzchen?'* He started to roar a drinking song, remarkably still in key. 'So, my fair maiden of the Rhine, what's been happening? Why so sad?'

Inge gasped. While he was blabbering, she grasped hold of his clothing and shuffled backwards, until she was able to place him firmly on a seat. 'I'll fetch some water,' she said and hurried to the kitchen. She came back and pushed a glass towards him. 'Drink,' she said. His head drooped. He gave a loud belch. She smacked his hand. 'Drink,' she commanded. 'Then tell me what all this is about.'

He sipped the water and threw his head back. 'I couldn't help it, Inge.'

'Hans, what are you talking about?'

His eyes were closed now and his head kept lolling from side to side as if wanting to shrug something off. Her apprehension grew. She had not seen Hans in such a state since their early courtship. Then he would drink himself silly on a Friday night with his running club friends, but that was long before he'd joined the Movement. Since then he had become the model of sobriety.

'Was ist es, Hänsli?' she whispered, half curious, half afraid, certain his behaviour had a deeper root. To her astonishment he gave a loud sob.

'I had no choice, Inge. They would have suspected me.'

'Hans, what are you talking about?' She felt herself go cold. Her hands started shaking. He leaned back, closing his eyes, overcome by tiredness. A deep snore emitted from his throat, then he started. 'I said he would tell. I would make him tell… ' He nodded then started to doze off again.

'Hans, wake up! Wake up!' She spoke roughly, putting her mouth to his ear. She shook his arm. He sprawled, dishevelled and large, plumbing unconscious depths. She fetched a wet towel and dabbed his neck with it.

Images buzzed in her head. She pictured Max as she saw him the other week, stubborn and pale with intensity. If only Hans would tell her what was going on. She picked up the wet towel and tumbler and retreated to the kitchen. She scrubbed all the surfaces there. Her worst fears were balling themselves together. She went back into the living room and stayed for a while listening to Hans snoring and muttering. He had fallen into a deep slumber and hardly stirred. She retreated to their bedroom and slid into bed, sleeping in short spurts.

In the morning he walked past her to find fresh clothes in the wardrobe. 'Hans – tell me what's going on.' But Hans Fichte did not want to look at his wife. Her fecund, bulky shape moving about their kitchen was a reproach to him. In the Party things were simpler. Right now he longed to be away from her and this nest of domesticity. He wanted to be amongst his fellow Party members with their rough edge of masculine resolve where drunkenness and physical violence were not a problem.

They did not speak over breakfast. Bleary-eyed, Inge served him from the gilt-edged coffee set, her mouth a thin line of anxiety and determination. Anna looked from one parent to the other in bewilderment. Hans tore at his breakfast roll, smearing it with butter. Were it not for him there would be no butter on the table and no ham, but she took all that for granted, just as she took for granted the regular salary coming in from the bank. He left the kitchen without saying goodbye.

'Hans!' she called after him as he walked to the front door. 'Hans!' He did not turn round. He shrugged his shoulders and carried on walking. He hoped he had not said too much the night before. In fact he hoped he'd said nothing at all. But he could not be sure. The night was a blank in his mind, a glaring beer-induced blank.

For weeks now he'd been on the verge of telling her about his new position within the Party, the notice he'd served to the bank, but when it came to it he had found it was beyond him. Now was certainly not the time.

Forty eight

Khan found his way back to Mihir Basu's apartment. On the last occasion he'd been unnerved by the shakiness of the man. Basu's wife opened the door. She was wearing a beige woollen cardigan and beige skirt, which gave her a sallow look. She told him he was the first visitor in days. Khan assumed things were not going well for the leader. 'Come,' she said. 'The visit will do him good. He has not been allowing himself to see anyone.' They entered a room where the blinds had been pulled down as if to keep the city at bay. Basu gave the namaste sign and bowed his head.

'I have come to say goodbye,' said Khan. 'I am to leave His Majesty's Service.'

The jaw of the other tremored. 'What of our discussion?'

'There was no agreement,' said Khan.

'You change like the wind,' said Basu, suddenly animated. 'One moment you declare your loyalty to Mother India, the next you jettison all ties.' He laughed. 'You are a slippery one.'

Khan took a step back. 'My post here is to be ended. That is all.'

Mihir Basu moved backwards too then indicated two floor cushions. 'Tell me how it happened.' He sat down cross-legged like a saddhu. Khan slipped down and did likewise.

'Our contract here is over. My boss is to be posted to Delhi, but not myself.'

'Ah,' said Basu, awaiting clarification.

'I will be compromised, it seems,' he added, unable to quell his annoyance.

Basu let out a guffaw of laughter. 'The Empire has detected a dissident, no?'

Khan was in no mood for humour. Mihir Basu was known to be volatile: one never knew what was surface and what manipulation. Where did the true man lie? Perhaps there was no true man. The man was simply his mission: the liberation of Bharat from the imperial yoke. 'I did not want you to be waiting for information I would never bring. I did not want you to hope in vain.'

'Good, good,' said Basu, mind elsewhere. Then he pounced: 'You realise your redundancy as a go-between.' His eyes pinned Khan. His legs, wide of girth in their white pyjamas, were remarkably flexible. He rocked back and forth as in some weird ritual. Khan felt a tightening in his chest. 'Men use men,' murmured Basu. 'Just as women do.'

Khan thought momentarily of Rhiannon in torment over Max. He thought of Tilda carving a new path for herself after her rupture with Dublovsky, and of their recent encounter. 'I can be of no further use to you,' he said.

'In fact you have been of no use to us all along. And now His Majesty's Government knows of our intentions.'

'They were not exactly top secret,' he said calmly.

'What will you do?'

Khan shrugged and lifted his hands in the air. 'The world is my oyster.'

'Indeed. But where will you go?'

'Go? Nowhere. Not for the time being at least.'

Basu rubbed his hands together. 'So, you are footloose and fancy free.'

Khan stared at the cushion beneath Basu's bulk. Until that moment he had not projected himself into the future. 'I will finish my contract and then most likely return to London.'

Basu chortled. 'You're a charlatan, as I suspected.'

Khan got awkwardly to his feet. 'I wish you well in your mission,' he said. 'Despite myself, despite my better judgement, I admire your tenacity. You will never succeed, of course. The National Socialists in Germany do not take you seriously. England will crush you as it would an insect. But in the end India will free itself. It is just a question of time.'

He wanted to get out of the room, away from the fervour of the man. He could not throw in his lot with him as he'd half hoped he would. 'I must go now.'

Basu clasped his hand, unwilling to let him go. 'You came here with the purpose of joining us…'

Khan withdrew his hand. 'I came, as I stated earlier, to say goodbye.'

Basu's eyes lingered on his face. 'You are a son of India and she will not release you so easily.'

'Good day then,' said Khan.

'Do come again.'

As Khan walked towards the door he heard a rustle as Basu's wife moved away from the keyhole.

'You do not stay long today,' she said.

'Good day *meine Dame*.' Khan strode away from the apartment, more perturbed than he cared to admit.

In Café Mozart Rhiannon was poring over a town map when Khan turned up. She looked even paler than the last time he saw her. He kissed her lightly on the cheek. She seemed too preoccupied to respond. 'Look,' she said pointing to a spot on the map. 'Hannah's aunt and uncle live here.' She'd marked it with a cross. 'Her aunt said the next villa along changed hands recently. There's been a lot of activity there… I want to go and investigate.' There was a feverishness about her.. He touched her arm, attempting to calm her. She shrugged him off moving her hands in agitation. 'Today. We have to go today.'

'Yes, right. I've got the use of my friend's car again. It's parked round the corner. But wouldn't it be better if I went alone then report back what I find out.'

'We've been over this before. I'm coming. Besides two people – especially a man and a woman – will look less suspicious'

'Okay. Okay.' He smiled to himself: what point was there arguing with such a headstrong woman?

Cheerless city streets gave way, as they approached Wannsee, to avenues lined with plane trees, apartment blocks ceded to turreted villas behind hedgerows, where the wealthiest of Berliners had their homes. Although not yet dusk it was a dark day, the sun hidden behind a bank of cloud. Lights glimmered here and there through the thickness of shrubs. They skirted the shadowy gardens and dark water. Rhiannon struggled to make sense of the map as they wound around the perimeter on the narrowing road.

They came to a halt some way from the villa of Hannah's relatives. They got down from the car. In front of them, by the side of the villa, a garden sloped down to a small jetty and the shallows of the lake. The winter sun caught ripples on the lake in a silvery-grey light and a throng of starlings scattered over the few boats left afloat during the winter.

'This could be the wildest of goose chases,' said Khan, glancing around at the high fences, at the solid edifices of the moneyed classes. He was worried that Rhiannon would have set her hopes too high. There were several sprawling villas along the secluded lane. He looked at her. 'Are you okay?'

'It's all very quiet,' she said, moving forward.

'Did Hannah say which villa changed hands recently?'

'Further down, away from the jetty. That one there I think…
'She pointed and started pacing in the direction of the second

306

house along, barely visible through trees. He felt the urge to restrain her. Utmost care was called for. They should arouse no suspicion. He caught up with her and grasped her arm.

'Look, I think it would be better if you kept watch. Stay in the car and give a blast on the horn if you see anyone approaching. I'll go and have a mooch round. See what I can discover. Better still, give two blasts if you spot anything untoward.'

She stared at him for a moment then nodded. She got back in the car while he sauntered towards the villa. Overall the ground sloped gently to the lake. He slowed down as he drew parallel with the entrance. Shuttered and closed to the casual visitor, the place seemed deserted, but when he grew closer he noticed lights in the lower rooms.

The grounds were surrounded by a high wall, smothered in Virginia creeper and spiked with glass along the ridge. He looked up and down the road. Making sure he was not being observed he tucked his trousers into his socks and clambered up the lime tree, which leaned from the road over the garden. From this vantage point he spotted outhouses and a side alleyway, hemmed in by bushes. He lowered himself into the garden, pressing up against the wall, then squeezed through to the back, branches clawing at his clothes. One window on the side gave off light. He held his breath. There was activity inside. Voices. He could see shadows moving and was just able to make out deep, masculine voices. There seemed to be an altercation going on. There was a shuffle, a clatter, as though a chair had been thrust to the ground.

He crept closer. Between slats he made out a stark room with a table and desk. Inside were two or three men. Were they wearing uniform? It was hard to tell. Could the window be forced? A car hooted. He started, slid back against the wall. Was it Rhiannon?

He heard a man talking, muffled shouts, then excited voices. He breathed deep. This could well be the place. Max could be holed up here. But there again he might be miles away. He spotted a door leading down to a basement. He descended the slippery, overgrown steps, pulling aside trailing foliage. The door was bolted on the outside and had a large old-fashioned lock to close it from the inside. Across the walls he heard shuffling and yelling. Inside it sounded as if someone was approaching. He backed off. A door slammed. There more shouts and the sound of a man screaming in pain.

He ran back to the car, where Rhiannon was staring ahead, frozen in fear. 'Well?' she said.

'There's something going on there. I heard…'

'What, Khan?'

'Noises. Men's voices. Dogs barking as if they were keeping guard.'

'So it could be…?'

'Yes. I think so.'

'What did you find?'

'There is a door in the garden, half hidden and covered in ivy. It gives access to the cellar. It's bolted on the outside, which is not a problem, but I think it will also be locked from the inside. I need to find someone's who's handy with locks.' He paused and said slowly: 'I think this is the best chance we have.'

Her eyes were glittering in the streetlight like a cat's. They sat for a moment in silence. He clasped her hand. He felt her stiffening, pulling back into herself, as uncertainty and terror seized hold of her. 'We'll have to come back then,' she said in a clipped, determined voice.

'Yes. Tonight. It should be tonight.'

Forty nine

In the Wannsee villa *Kreisleiter* Sturm was frowning over an enamel mug, shifting papers on his desk, in a disgruntled, fault-finding fashion. He called Hans Fichte into his makeshift office.

'Sit down.' He pushed a copy of *The Independent Chronicler* towards him. 'Look at that,' he snapped.

'My English is poor,' said Hans, glancing at the article he had already tried to decipher.

'There,' said Sturm, pointing to a typed translation. *'Germany's descent into chaos.''*

Hans scanned the first paragraph. His heart beat faster. He had already seen this report and suspected the worst.

'So you see, Fichte. It is necessary to move things on.'

'Yes, Herr Kreisleiter.'

'We have every reason to believe this man is the author of this and other treacherous articles.'

'Is that so?' replied Hans nervously. He felt increasingly unsure of his position.

'The man did not act alone. We need to find out who he worked with. We need to find out the whereabouts of Dieter Hartman. You understand?'

'Yes, Herr *Kreisleiter.'*

'One more chance to extract what we need then a bullet in his head. He and others have continued to defame our leaders. This latest outrage goes too far. They are vilifying the Party abroad. But first we must find out what we can.'

Hans suppressed a gasp. He had not expected to reach this point so soon. The *Kreisleiter* eyed him then tapped his pencil on the table. 'I have a feeling you know more about this man than you have let on.' Eyes of steel locked onto Hans across the desk until he felt his stomach turn to water. A smirk twisted the *Kreisleiter's* lips. 'Come now, you can be honest with me.'

'There is nothing to say, Herr *Kreisleiter*.'

'Really?' Sturm tapped the pencil more insistently. Hans became incapable of swallowing. How stupid to have imagined these strands of his life would remain separate. He saw Inge's pale, panicked face superimposed over Sturm's.

In recent months he'd let the Party do his choosing for him. It presented him with a clear cohesion of thought and action, a beauty in itself. Never before had he felt so engaged and optimistic, never so drawn towards a gleaming horizon. And now this muddiness of blood ties which he would rather ignore. His days at the bank rolled before him: dutiful and unending. He'd been a reliable employee, a reliable part of the system; but the Party had changed everything.

The *Kreisleiter* spoke slowly. 'In fact, I have it on good authority that you are related. Is it possible you have been deceiving us?' Hans suppressed a gasp, his ribcage suddenly too tight. 'Mmm? What do you have to say?' Sturm's tone was cool, even, unfathomable. He leaned back in his chair.

'We party members must be prepared to make hard decisions. To take the actions we know to be best for the Fatherland. You will extract the information we require. Then you will dispose of him, once and for all. Is that understood?'

Hans stared blankly at his superior. 'Perfectly, Herr *Kreisleiter*,' he snapped back while his mind was tumbling: blood and Fatherland, weakness and strength, good and evil, brother-in-law and stranger. It was suddenly a court martial, the eyes of the *Kreisleiter* a searchlight searing his soul. '*Jawohl*, Herr *Kreisleiter*,' he repeated. 'You can rely on me. If the man is found to be a danger to the Movement he will be eliminated…'

The *Kreisleiter* paused. 'You misunderstand me. Our evidence is conclusive. He is implicated in sedition. He has written or aided others in the writing of articles, which vilify the Leader. He has consorted with Communists and other left-wing rabble. He has refused to cooperate. You think there remains any doubt as to his guilt?'

Picturing the pulped face of Max the evening before, Hans baulked. 'I thought…'

'Yes, what did you think?'

'That it was part of our – our creed to convert and rehabilitate.'

'Enough,' snapped the Kreisleiter. 'Such ambivalence does not serve the Party. The man is a menace and must be got rid of. There is a pistol in the top drawer. Do I make myself clear? You have till dawn to find out what you can.'

'Perfectly,' said Hans and gave the Nazi salute.

Max had no idea of the hour or day even. His stomach growled with hunger. They'd given him only stale bread and watered down onion soup. What were they planning to do to him?

Hans came down to the cellar and motioned Max to follow him. Hans' movements were awkward, his arm stiff as if fearing the contact. The *Kreisleiter* was waiting in the gunroom. He stepped closer to Max, peered at his face. 'I thought you might have broken his nose but you didn't.' Hans grunted. The *Kreisleiter* undid the rough cord binding Max's wrists and sat him down in the chair. 'You know what you have to do,' he said to Hans and left the room.

'Is there anyway out of here?' said Max.

'Do as you're told and you'll be out soon enough,' Hans muttered.

'Will you get a message through to Rhiannon? She will be desperate by now. Will you do that?'

Hans winced as if being prodded by a sharp object. 'Not possible No one knows where you are. And that's the way it's going to stay.'

'She doesn't need to know where I am but she needs to know that I am still alive. That much you could do for me.'

Hans leaned over and peered at Max's face, which was still bruised and swollen. 'I got carried away. But you'll heal. Nothing is broken.' He faltered. 'Sometimes strong medicine is the only way.'

'The only way for what?'

'The trouble with you, Max, is that you never stop asking questions.'

'And the trouble with you, Hans, is that you never start.'

'Enough. You've got to be realistic…'

'Meaning?'

'The only way out of here is for you to co-operate.'

Max stared sullenly at his brother-in-law. A bead of sweat was forming on his forehead. The man looked terrified. Max lowered his voice.

'What have they done to you, Hans?'

Again Hans winced. 'Where is Dieter Hartman?' he demanded.

'I don't know.'

'I don't believe you. You're associates. You've often been seen together. You worked together on the flyer. There were witnesses…'

'He's gone under cover for protection. I have no idea where.'

Hans banged the table. 'You're lying, damn you. Just give me a straight answer.'

Max was silent. He examined the grain of the wood in the

table and took a sly glance at Hans who was looking more desperate and morose by the minute. 'Do they know we're related by marriage?' he asked.

'Yes,' snarled the other.

'Not so good for your standing in the Party, eh? Do they know your wife is part Jewish?'

'Just answer the question.'

'I can't. I don't know…'

Again Hans thumped the table. His eyes were restless as he bent forward, speaking quietly. 'Look, you tell me where Hartman is and – and I might be able to help you. Otherwise there's no way out of here. I've had orders to shoot you…'

A chill ran through Max. The blood drained from his head. Hans was undoubtedly speaking the truth; he looked too disturbed to be fabricating. Already Max knew too much, had written too much. There was no way his captors would liberate him; they were just marking time. Hans was his only means of escape. He and Dieter were marked men.

Fifty

Khan called on Wolfgang Seifert in his Wilhelmstrasse office. Seifert was wearing a slate-grey suit and looking more preoccupied than usual. The ashtray beside him was high with dog ends and ash, betraying a bout of chain-smoking. Khan told him he had a fair idea where Max Dienst was being held.

Seifert gave him a stare of appraisal, his face tinged with anxiety. 'His wife was here looking for him. I knew he'd turn up sooner or later.'

'Did you?' said Khan flatly. 'Strange, if I might say so – with so many disappearing.' Seifert gave him a curious look as he continued. 'He's been taken by the Brown Shirts. We have a good idea where. But they run a tight outfit. Don't know how we're going to get him out of there. Locked cellars and though I didn't see any, they will have their quota of guards.'

'You do know he no longer works for this paper?' said Seifert.

'What? No, I didn't. What happened?'

'Look, it's a long story which I don't want to go into.'

'Can you help? I want to secure his release.'

'What did you have in mind?'

'A break-out party. We need to go and get him out. I'm pretty sure he's holed up in a villa…'

'The best we could do is send a reporter. You must realise we can't get involved in any direct political action. That's not our role.'

'Of course not.'

'Besides, you need to be sure. No point in kicking up dust until you are certain.'

Khan could tell by Seifert's brusqueness and the cold glint of his eyes that Max Dienst, investigative journalist and left-winger, was no longer an issue for him. Not unlike Denning, he was guarding a stance of careful and complete neutrality. Khan understood. It just left him feeling helpless, and more than ever an outsider.

He left the newspaper office deflated. Was no one willing to take a risk? There would be safety in numbers so he would need at least a couple of men to fall back on, preferably with weapons, and even then there might be casualties. He hurried down Unter den Linden towards *Die Schnecke*, hoping Dieter might be around. Entering the dim bar Khan peered around before spotting one of Dieter's comrades and drinking mates.

'It's Karl, isn't it?'

The man peered at him for a moment. 'Ah, Sid Khan! *Wie geht's?*' The man said he recognised him from the evening when they'd distributed the flyers. They chatted a while then Khan enquired where Dieter was. Karl looked hard at him as if weighing something in his mind.

'Dieter's been making himself scarce of late.'

Khan drew closer. 'So where will I find him?'

'You won't.' Smoke curled thick in the air. People were concentrating on backgammon, Skat and chess but not saying much. The heated debates common in public places just weeks before had given way to periods of broody silence. 'He's working his allotment,' said Karl finally. 'Why do you want to see him?'

'It's like this – I've got a friend in a spot of bother. I need help to – to extricate him from the situation.'

'Oh yes?'

'I have got to get hold of Dieter.'

'You are going to do this, are you? It's not just boy scout stuff?'

Khan turned on him. 'You think I'm doing this for the fun of it?'

The man clapped Khan on the back. 'You have a plan then?' Aware he had none, Khan bristled with irritation.

'So where's his allotment?

On the corner of Steinplatz Rhiannon came across a straggle of SA members, hectoring passers-by with large swastikas flapping round them. 'Get lost!' she yelled in English, drawing stares. Further on she saw a street brazier, glowing red, and caught a delicious whiff of charred chestnuts. The sight pierced her with anguish. She remembered it was Advent, with Christmas fast approaching. She thought of their first Christmas here, candles on the tree and the family in a circle singing 'O Tannenbaum.'

Never had it seemed less like Christmas.

She was feeling quite ill. The nausea and tiredness she had been experiencing in recent days had increased. One way or another she had to determine what was wrong. She had made an appointment to see their doctor. Now, in the surgery, her shoes squeaked over the shiny tiles as her number was called.

'Please sit down, Frau Dienst.' The portly doctor peered at her over his pince-nez. She felt a flutter of apprehension. Folding well-manicured hands on the desk he gave her the whisper of a smile. 'You'll be wanting to hear the result of the test, Frau Dienst.' He paused then looked her in the eye. 'You'll be pleased to hear it was positive.' The smile widened. Rhiannon searched his face. He looked bemused at her reaction. 'You are going to have a child, Frau Dienst.' She gasped. 'Now if you'd like to step behind the screen, I'd like to give you an internal examination.'

Something in her quickened. Of course! Why hadn't that occurred to her? She'd been so busy attributing her lack of bleeding to anxiety over Max, that she'd overlooked the obvious. She had ignored the weeks-long dragging sensation in the womb and her tendency to be tearful, her reluctance to cook or eat, and above all the bone weariness which made her want to sleep the whole time.

Behind the screen a white-clad nurse asked her to put her clothes on a chair. Up on the examining table the doctor asked her to 'open wider' as he fumbled between her legs. She lay back and closed her eyes as he probed into her with his speculum and rubber-clad hands. After she got to her feet, her fingers trembled as she fastened her skirt. 'About six weeks,' he pronounced.

She wandered back into Hardenbergstrasse in a state of shock. There were hours to go before she and Khan had agreed to meet. She would found it impossible to sit out the waiting time alone. Though she hated to admit it she knew she was in too heightened a state to devise a sound rescue plan; she hoped Khan would do better. For now she pushed the news of her pregnancy to one side. It could not have come at a worse time. It felt like everything was rushing in at her, leaving her dizzy and helpless. It was not a condition she was used to.

Though sceptical as to the outcome, she presented herself at the police station. Once again she breathed in the stuffiness of long-shelved dossiers and shut windows. Today another officer was on duty, a plump man with greased down hair. She explained why she was there. He retreated to another office, lugging back files, which he thumbed through until he reached the case. It surprised her that the form was there at all. The man peered at her over wire-framed glasses.

'Has any action been taken?' she asked.

'Do you have any idea how many people go missing in this town?'

317

'I was told that yesterday. But I have to ask.'

'Sit down, while I consult with my colleagues.' He reappeared minutes later shaking his head. 'Have you checked the hospitals?'

'No one of his name has been admitted.'

'I am afraid there is nothing else we can do.'

'You won't mount a search?' Even as the words left her throat she knew the request was in vain. The door opened and closed behind her. The officer looked over her shoulder towards the newcomer. 'Why don't you call by tomorrow, Frau Dienst? We will check the reports. See if anything has been reported in other stations.'

'But...'

'That is all we can do.' Impatience tinged his voice. He dismissed her with a nod.

Outside the air was cold on her cheeks. She found a café where she sipped black tea laced with lemon. A deep weariness invaded her but as she squeezed lemon into the infusion she told herself she must continue. She went on to the Prussian state library, further down the avenue, where Max had researched Geli Raubal. In the public rooms she leafed through journals. Like a widow searching out traces of the deceased, she peered around wondering which seat Max had sat on.

She decided to call on Pastor Neumann to see if he had heard anything through his network. Besides, she needed to renew her belief that good things could happen. The world was upside down, as Max would say. He had told her how this happened before, during the Hyperinflation, when values were shredded and people had nothing to hold on to.

The pastor invited her into his visitors' parlour. He offered her schnapps or tea to warm her up on the chilly December day. She declined. 'Have you any news of your husband, Frau

Dienst? I spoke to my colleague in Tegel. He is not being held there.'

'We believe the Nazis have captured Max.'

The pastor's face was grave.

'I am in danger of losing hope,' she said quietly. The pastor folded his hands and leaned forward. She noticed he had a squint in one eye. 'I am afraid, so afraid. I don't quite believe it works like that but will you pray for him?'

'Of course.'

She left soon after. For a moment, walking past Zoo station and hearing the clatter of trains, she was drawn back to Neukölln and Inge, longing to cling to any part of Max. But no, now was not the time. What if Hans were there and she revealed too much? No, no, no.

She returned home where she lay on the bed, staring up at criss-cross patterns thrown by streetlights. Exhausted, overwrought, she fell asleep. She was disturbed by a vivid dream where large insects with black eyes and metallic antennae were prodding her. She turned over and slept again only to be startled awake by someone banging on the door. 'Frau Dienst! Frau Dienst! You have a visitor.' Rhiannon sprang to her feet and opened it. There, focussed and ready for action, stood Khan.

Fifty one

Khan's eyes were gleaming with purpose. He paced the confines of her room, restless to get going. 'You will stay here and wait?'

'I'll keep watch again,' she said firmly.

He nodded and said: 'I couldn't get hold of Dieter. It's biting closer. In *die Schnecke* there were a few suspect types, hanging around, listening. But I found someone. Willi – used to be part of Berlin's lowlife – they say nobody's better at finding his way into barred premises. He joined the Communists. Now only does political jobs.'

'As long as he know what's he's doing…'

'Let's go. You'll need to wrap up. It's cold out there.'

As they got into the car she greeted Willi. She caught a whiff of tobacco and stale clothes. Scrunched up in the back of the car, he was buried in a scruffy black coat. He mumbled in an incomprehensible Berlin dialect.

They were soon speeding through the darkness. The car slewed across a patch of ice, righted itself, sped on. Eventually they arrived at the lake. It glimmered black under a high, bright moon. There were few clouds. Rhiannon stared ahead, taut as a spring. Khan grasped her hand to reassure her. They pulled up some distance from the house. Willi pulled out a bag from the boot. Rhiannon was to warn them by means of three blasts of the horn if she saw anyone approaching.

The house was still. They'd brought a length of rope and this they attached to the tree to escape later. Willi had his box of tricks with file, candle for smoking, jimmies and a set of keys.

The men crept along the lane, hauled themselves onto the tree, dropping quietly into the garden. Willi who was carrying a bit of extra weight cursed when his leg slipped and he skinned his shin.

For Rhiannon the minutes were passing snail-slow as she fought to control her fear and keep at bay blood-spattered images of Max shot 'while trying to escape'. She breathed deep, looked towards the house where the others had disappeared. It was black, no glimmer of light from where she was sitting. The garden was dark, too, with its jungle of bushes and trees. On the street two empty Daimler-Benz cars lurked like waiting panthers behind her.

In the garden the men were shifting forward, one behind the other. In the house lights were burning in several rooms. Khan heard the low hum of voices as he edged towards the house. He put his fingers to his lips, warning Willi to stay put. He found the darkest corner of the garden and told Willi to remain there. He had already ascertained there were no guard dogs or sentries; no doubt it was a temporary hideout rather than a prison. A house, he supposed, of a rich party supporter. The occupants would not be expecting to be tracked down here and were unlikely to have put in extra locks or security.

Then Willi circled the premises, checking windows, estimating distances and exploring other means of entry. 'Outside bolts. No external guards. Looks straightforward enough,' he said, adding that there was no telling what the inside was like. There could be any number of guards posted there with any number of guns.

At the ivy-grown outer door leading to the basement, Khan pulled back tangled skeins of greenery while Willi slid the heavy rusting bolt slowly across. He caught his thumb in it and cursed to himself. He carried on. It seemed to be taking forever. He examined the keyhole with his finger then unhooked an array of heavy cellar keys from his belt. Luckily there was no key the other side. He slid one of his in. It met resistance. He tried another, and then another. 'Ah,' he muttered and withdrew the key, lit a candle under his jacket then smoked the key and reinserted it into the lock. He took it out and examined it by the light of a match. It was shiny where it had met resistance. He took a small file from his inside jacket pocket and began to file the key. He slipped the key into the keyhole, withdrew it and repeated the process again. It refused to budge.

Suddenly a beam from a torch zigzagged across the bushes, the wall, the overgrown footpath. Two voices drifted across. Bushes rustled and there were loud grunts, A couple of men were thrusting into the garden along the passageway. One appeared drunk as he rolled from side to side. The other gave him a hefty shove and laughed. A dog barked. Its dark shape lumbered by, sniffing in excitement. It growled deep in his throat. It barked again. One of the men urinated into a hedge. Torchlight fanned the foliage. The man zipped up and turned back towards the house.

Khan and Willi fell back against the edge of the garden, tumbling away from the random torch beam. Willi hissed angrily. The two men from the house lumbered back along the path into the building. The dog, held on a leash, continued yelping and growling. '*Ist was?*' one of the men asked the dog if anything was the matter. The dog growled anew. The other man cuffed it and told it to shut up.

Motionless, hardly breathing, the rescuers waited.

Willi crept back out and put his shoulder to the door he'd been trying. In desperation he kicked against it. Slowly it creaked and gave way. He paused, let his eyes adjust to the deeper blackness, and groped his way down into the basement.

It reeked of wine and damp grain. He peered around. At first he could make out nothing but odd wine racks and lumpy sacks. Then in one corner he picked out a long soft mass sprawled on the ground. He tiptoed over, paused to get a better look, then retraced his steps. He beckoned to Khan to follow. Khan, not yet accustomed to the gloom, groped forward. Willi pointed to the supine shape.

'Is that him?' he whispered.

Khan stooped over, tried to focus his eyes. The sleeper rolled over, gave a low moan, jerked his legs though his movements were restricted. Khan nodded. Willi moved quickly, pulling a knife from his belt. Khan shook Max gently awake. Willi cut through the binding and signalled Max to follow. Groggy, Max was waking from a dream. He started to speak incoherently then stumbled to his feet. Willi moved towards the exit into the garden. Khan blundered after, banging against a shelf, which sent the wine rack jangling. A bottle smashed to the ground. The guard blasted in from upstairs, lights ablaze behind him.

It was Hans.

'I told you there was someone out there!' yelled another hoarse voice.

'Shut up! Get the gun!' yelled Hans. He turned to Max and whispered fiercely. 'Get out! It's your only chance. Get Out !'

Another guard leapt forward, cocked a rifle under his arm. Fired. It gave a loud report. Bullets ricocheted off the wall, thudded through the air. There were shouts and more shouts. Feet came thumping down the stairs. Hans shoved the man firing the gun, causing him to stumble. He grabbed hold of the gun. A third, seeing what he had done, turned his rifle on him. Took aim. Startled, unable to react in time, Hans screamed in pain and went hurtling down the steps. From the ground he took aim at his assailant. There was a scurrying of shapes in the half-light. Max heard the crunch of bone on the stone floor.

'Quick!' hissed Willi. 'Outta here!'

The men flitted through the shadows. In the rest of the house more lights glared. There was a rush of feet as more men jumped awake and threw themselves into the basement. Willi whistled, racing up the steps to the exit. The others followed. In the outer darkness they guided Max towards the rope dangling from the tree. Loud commands broke the night air. More bullets flew, falling into the shrubs. Dark forms swept with torches through the garden.

Rhiannon caught sight of figures rushing towards her. She looked back at the fleeing figures, heart wild with anticipation. Was Max with them – was he? Lights were flashing up and down the lane. People were running towards her like birds scattered by gunshot. The neighbours' lights suddenly glaring. The cold, cold night. Other houses now bathed in lights. Was Max with them? Was he? Her head was pounding. She was unable to move, body frozen in fear. Suddenly, as she made out Max in the mêlée, she cried out in relief.

The men jumped into the car, Willi into the driver's seat. The car leapt forward. 'Down here! This way!' yelled Khan indicating a narrow lane. She heard the roar of a motorbike being kicked into life. Now it was close behind them. It rounded a curve in the road and was gaining on them. Khan opened the window and thrust one of Willi's hammers into its path. Swerving to avoid it the bike careered out of control and skidded into a hedgerow. A car was speeding up the higher road, its headlights flashing crazily across the darkened woods. They heard the sound of gunshot. Rhiannon screamed.

'It's okay,' said Max. 'They've taken a wrong turning. They won't catch us.'

'Keep going!' yelled Khan. 'Down there!' They cut down a track and switched off the lights, crashing and crawling along the lakeside. 'They'll never come down here. It goes right round this part of the lake and comes out by a jetty.'

They continued to jerk along the twisting lane, watching out for potholes. At last they reached the jetty and came to a standstill. In the distance they heard the fading sound of the motorbike.

Khan said: 'We'll just wait it out then head towards my place.'

Khan's apartment was dim as they shuffled into it, shaken and unsteady on their feet. Khan switched on some lamps. Max blinked hard as he entered, the rooms and all they represented were from another lifetime. Khan offered whisky to steady the nerves. Willi looked bemused. He said he would be grateful for a blanket and a bit of floor space. Rhiannon and Max were relieved to retreat into the spare bedroom.

Here Rhiannon could not stop touching and looking at Max. He looked pale and drained from the ordeal. 'I can't believe you're here.' She could not stop shaking.

'I thought – I thought I might never see you again…' he said.

'Shush! It's alright. We're alright. You're here…'

Only much later, after holding each other, falling asleep, waking, did the terror bit-by-bit start to abate.

Fifty two

'*Another Martyr for the Cause*': the headline would be made to serve a purpose. *Kreisleiter* Sturm informed Dr Goebbels straight away of the Wannsee episode. Only later, under pressure, did the true story emerge. Goebbels pieced together the boldness of the break-out and the fiasco of a bungled interrogation. Two operatives had been killed.

He was livid.

So another wrong-headed reporter was again at liberty to carry on vilifying the Party. Hesitating, clearly discomfited, Sturm recounted how Hans Fichte and another guard had died from stray bullets. No one was clear what had happened. One, still breathing, had been transported to hospital, where he died. The other was already dead on the scene.

Martyrs for the Cause. It was essential to get the story out, the line of narrative clear. It was vital that this incident should not be written off as another spat between factions, another sign of the brutality surrounding the Nazi Party. Hans Fichte and his fellow guard would receive full honours as patriots, as Fighters for the Just Cause. Their widows would be cared for. The heroes would be granted a candlelit vigil and a place in the annals of Nazi history.

This was an ambush of innocent parties.

The arms were hidden. Any signs of imprisonment dismantled. It was an act of pure Communist aggression against loyal and Fatherland-loving men. The first issue of the Nazi papers would carry the story. Everyone should know what they were up against if the left held sway. The culprits should and would be brought to justice.

The matter would be turned, systematically and completely, to advantage. *Der völkische Beobachter* and *der Angriff* would seize the day.

Fifty three

Rhiannon surveyed the growing throng of people awaiting soup. How ever would they accommodate so many, even with the extra supplies from Lebde? The queue was longer than last time, half a mile at least as it twisted from the main square into one of the side streets. It was colder too, the air sharper as they approached the dead of winter. Flurries of snow swept down. She set about ordering the enamel mugs in rows. Once the rush started they'd be no time as the stream of need surged ever forward. The word had spread that this soup contained more meat than usual.

She had decided to go ahead with her shift at the soup kitchen as she'd agreed to do it long before the Wannsee episode. 'Rhiannon, fetch more mugs, will you?' called one of the women. She moved around, doing as she was told. In between, her mind reverted to Max, hoping he'd stay put in Khan's apartment as she'd advised him to. She started ladling the thick mix of potato, vegetables and tiny lumps of gristly pork into the mugs and handing them out. The mood of the crowd was restive as hunger bit. Concerned they might soon run out of supplies, Rhiannon cut the measure, which elicited grumbling. She said nothing, head down, concentrating on what she was doing.

Somewhere down the line, a man punched another. Before she knew it there was a full-blown free-for-all. A police whistle shrieked. Others panicked, banging into one of the trestle tables. With a loud clatter the table crashed to the ground, spattering the contents of a large cauldron onto the cobblestones amid gasps of anger and frustration. The police set to, wielding batons. The mob fell back into some sort of order and became subdued. Many, having had their fill, fled.

A gaggle of Brown Shirts was lurking on the street corner. Wary and rough like scar-worn street dogs, they watched the pandemonium, then picked off several people, known to be Communists, and laid into them.

'This is getting ugly,' said Hannah as more police poured out from a van. 'You better get going. Any excuse and they'll lock you up.'

Rhiannon did as she was bid. The cauldrons were virtually empty by then anyway. It gave her a heavy feeling though: every activity seemed bound up in political warfare.

She came back to an empty apartment in Wilmersdorf. So Max had gone out after all, despite all that had happened, despite the passion of her pleas. A shudder of terror passed through her. She had a pain in her womb, which made her cry out with its sharpness. Doubled up, clutching herself, she struggled to get herself into the bedroom. Oh no, she thought. The pain was dragging now, making her want to lie down and curl into a ball like a foetus. She sunk onto the bed, keen to lock herself away, keen to protect her womb. It pierced her through. This little being, this inconvenience, she was startled to discover, was exactly what she wanted.

When she woke the pain had subsided and she was ravenous. She searched the cupboards but found nothing. She pulled on her coat and went down into the street where she stopped at a corner café and hurriedly finished off a bowl of bean soup, and then another. She was wandering back to Khan's flat when she heard a Verdi aria wafting down from an upstairs window. It reminded her of Uschi, her friend from Savignystrasse. She had the sudden urge to see her, and took off in the direction of nearby Gertnerstrasse, the Rudersteins' new address.

Uschi registered no emotion as she opened the door to her and this flatness alerted Rhiannon to the change in Uschi's life. They sat down in her cluttered kitchen. Uschi was the tidiest of people, but the challenge of two rooms instead of four was telling. Rhiannon peered over Uschi's shoulders to the piles of music scores in the corner, the stashed family albums, everything from their life crammed hurriedly into these small rooms. She also noticed goods packed in boxes stacked along one wall.

'I had to come and see you,' she said.

'Nasty bit of work that Herr Schneider. Evicted us for no good reason. He's caught this Hitler virus like half the population.'

'You poor things! I knew something odd had happened. What rotten luck to have him for a landlord.'

'We have had to give away many things.'

'Not your lovely dresses?'

'I hardly think I'll be needing them now. Anyway, what's your news?'

Rhiannon hesitated. Her eyes were glazing over. 'I went to the doctor. I'm expecting. Six weeks.'

'Wonderful!' Uschi beamed at her.

Rhiannon went on to tell the story of Max's disappearance and rescue while Uschi sat open-eyed and solemn, taking it all in. 'I thought I was losing the baby. It happened this morning after I did the soup kitchen. I stayed in bed. I fell asleep. When I woke the pain had gone...'

'Here, I'll take those.' Uschi took a sheaf of music scores left on the chair. 'I've been going through them for Bernard, seeing what can be safely thrown away.' She dropped them onto the floor then looked across at Rhiannon. 'From all that you've just told me I think you should seriously consider leaving Berlin. Get out while the going's good.'

'That's what I want to do.'

'But not Max?'

Rhiannon drew her shoulders up and sighed. Her friend nodded in sympathy. 'You look tired. Let me make you some tea.' She fetched the tea things and a crumbly *Streuselkuchen* cake from a cold shelf in the larder. 'As for us, we're watching to see what happens,' she said. 'If Hitler becomes chancellor, we're off.' Uschi pursed her lips. 'I hate to think about it. But Bernard says we must – the way things are tending. We've been living out of boxes now for weeks.'

'But you have your work here. Bernard has his.'

'At the moment, yes. The musicians are fine. But there are others in the administration talking about ridding the arts of the Jewish influence, as if we could be weeded out like some – some bacteria or something. They are crazy some of them.'

'So where would you go if you left Berlin?'

'Paris, probably. We have cousins there and Bernard has some music colleagues.'

'I see.' Rhiannon spooned the cake into her mouth. It melted on her tongue with a tang of sugar and cinnamon. She discovered she was still hungry. She ate three slices.

Uschi's eyes brightened. 'Paris would not be a bad place for us. It's cosmopolitan. Quite a few artists are talking of shifting there. It could be a new beginning.'

'As you say, there are far worse places…' Rhiannon could not help admiring Uschi's resilience, though she sensed with sadness that their days of laughter and conviviality were over. It angered her the way their lives could be so easily torn apart.

They moved on to talk about other things, chatting until the light outside began to fade. She was reluctant to leave her friend. 'Anyway, now I know where you live I'll come by more often.' Even as she spoke the words she knew they were overly optimistic.

Fifty four

Max had not been idle. After retrieving his article from the station he headed towards the newspaper area. It was essential to get things moving as fast as he could. At *die Taverne* he hovered on the rim of an avid circle of newshounds, who were snapping at titbits of stories as usual. In front of him was the very man Khan had told him about – David Wilson was a stocky fellow with a sharp gaze. Even at first glance Max could discern in him a quiet focus and dynamism. Khan said he had links with all sorts of people, including government officials. Rumoured to be privy to cabinet secrets long before they broke, he disliked the Nazis and was distrustful of Hitler in particular.

When there was a lull and several of the others had left, Max introduced himself. 'Yes, I've heard of you,' said Wilson genially, shaking Max's hand.

'Not bad things, I hope.' The man laughed, regarded Max for a moment, saying nothing.

'You were on the Geli Raubal trail, I believe?'

Max took a deep breath and decided to take a gamble. 'I just got the sack.'

'Was there a reason?'

'People are keen for blood, but it has to be the right sort.'

'Say more.'

'What is there to say? If it were just a matter of impressing the public it would be easy. We just need to use the tools of our trade. But sometimes it's your own editor who becomes the enemy.'

'Strong words.'

'If not enemy, then the blockage.'

They eyed each other for a moment. Max did not intend railing against Seifert; after all, in his position he might well have done the same. Yet something about the receptivity he sensed in the man opposite him led him to vent his frustration. He told him about the editor's refusal to run his article.

Wilson had taken out a pipe and was slowly filling the bowl, tamping down stray tobacco. When he finished he puffed on it with such an air of leisure that Max sensed he was playing for time.

'Let me buy you a drink. What will it be?'

'I'll have another beer, thanks,' said Max. They took their glasses and sat down at one the tables that had become available. 'It's been a while since I was in London,' continued Max. 'Things are unsettled there, too, aren't they, what with hunger marches and the like? Do you think the real mood of Germany is being conveyed to the British public?'

Wilson raised a single eyebrow. 'Not always.'

'You write for *The Times,* don't you? Is your editor always open to what you write?'

Wilson looked abashed by the question. Max wondered at his own temerity in posing it. This was the great correspondent, the man who boasted acquaintance with the wielders of power. 'My editor wants us to stay friends with Germany, come what may. Nobody wants war,' the other replied slowly.

'Some say another European war is on the way.'

Wilson took another luxurious puff on his pipe. 'Opinions vary. I get to talk to a lot of people. If the Nazis start running the country it looks exceedingly likely...'

'Your paper is the most influential in Great Britain. You're here, on the spot. That gives you an authority those back

333

home don't have. Are you able to give your considered view free of editorial constraint?'

Wilson took a sip of beer. 'One is never a totally free agent. As you know yourself, the editor always has the last say.'

'Even with someone of your calibre?'

Wilson gave a smile of resignation. 'There are always macro politics and the slant a newspaper in its entirety chooses to adopt. When stories or facts are reported that don't sit well with those basic attitudes then – then you have to find another outlet for them.'

'And has that ever happened to you?'

'There are always ways and means. That's all I can say. You have to find your medium. But for now don't expect *The Times* to run any article criticising the German Nazi Movement. If you want to do that I'd try elsewhere.' He got abruptly to his feet and prepared to leave.

'Mr Wilson...' Max held out his hand. Wilson shook it.

'My advice to you would be – keep going. Presumably you're no longer bound by contract? Others have to be more circumspect – can't go giving scoops to rival papers.' He hesitated for a moment, screwed up his eyes as he considered Max through his eyebrows. He bent closer to him.

'Look, are you sure you got the whole story? I know someone who covered the proceedings in detail. There were all sorts of rumours at the time: about blackmail, orders to have her liquidated. Here...' he scribbled on a piece of paper. 'This is someone you could speak to.' And then he was gone, disappearing into the street trailing clouds of tobacco smoke, the unflappable, calm-faced Englishman. Max took out the chit Wilson had given him. He recognised the name from Otto's notes.

Franz Jacob was the editor of the anti-Nazi paper, *Die Zeiten,* which was housed apart from the newspaper district above a shoe shop in Schopenhauerstrasse. The office was small, lined with reference books and neat stacks of newsprint. Despite its modesty the place gave off an air of quiet efficiency and attention to detail. The editor, a slight, dark, Jewish man, was bent over a book when the anxious-looking secretary showed Max in.

Even after a full introduction the man seemed suspicious. Max found himself giving away more than he would have chosen to. Moved by a mounting sense of urgency he knew he had to gather what he could as fast as he could. The story might come together elsewhere, but the bones of it were to be found here. He spoke more about David Wilson and of how it was becoming impossible to get to the truth because of political fear.

'I remember the case well,' said the editor when Max got round to Geli Raubal. 'I was working at the *Münchene Neue Nachrichten* at the time.'

'But you left...?'

'That's another story. The whole thing – well, quite frankly, it stank.'

'But you gathered evidence?'

Franz Jacob pushed his spectacles further up his nose and gazed at Max, who was lost in thought. Franz cleared his throat and folded his hands in front of him. 'Who did you say you work for?'

'I don't. Not any more.'

So?' Franz Jacob opened his palms in a questioning gesture. 'You walk in here, unannounced, off the street. I don't know you. Yes, you say you know David Wilson. Or at least you come through him. He knows all and sundry, I might add.'

'Look,' Max leaned closer in. 'You see those bruises on my

face, the swelling round my nose? How do you think I got it – by falling over in the street or getting into a drunken brawl? Do you want to know what happened? The Nazis carted me off in broad daylight. Kept me in a Wannsee villa. They beat me up. I escaped by the skin of my teeth. I am still on their blacklist. I need to get out of Berlin. And fast.'

'So why not just clear out, Mr Dienst? I would.'

'I want to take as much of the story with me as I can. He said you were the one. You gathered more information than anyone else…' He leaned back, studied Jacob through his eyebrows. 'Look if it helps, I'm part Jewish. I hate what the Nazis stand for. They've ruined my sister's life. They'll ruin a lot more lives before they're through.'

Franz blinked hard, lined a fountain pen up with several sharpened pencils on his desk. After a minute he said: 'It's no secret that the paper I edit attacks the policies of the extreme right, the National Socialist German Workers Party but also the extreme left, the German Communist Party.' He spoke slowly, pedantically, like a schoolteacher. Max found himself growing impatient. 'I know. I've read several copies,' he said.

'We're not Socialists. We advocate the restoration of the monarchy under Crown Prince Rupprecht.'

'Quite frankly, I don't think there is a political solution right now. I only know…'

Franz Jacob cut him off. 'I know their leader. If Adolf Hitler gains power it will lead to enmity. Enmity with neighbouring countries, internal totalitarianism, civil war, international war, lies, hatred, fratricide and infinite trouble.' His voice was solemn, declamatory. It gave Max the sense that he had thought long and hard about the issues.

'Will you help me then?'

'To do what exactly?'

'To complete the Geli Raubal story. To get it out, if not here, than overseas. After analysing all the data and talking to a lot of people I am sure you came to certain conclusions.'

'Opinions are not facts.'

Max sighed. 'So what can you give me?'

The other took off his spectacles and leaned slowly forward – he seemed burdened by what he knew. 'You are asking me to take a huge risk.'

'I want to stop the plunge towards Nazism as much as you do…'

'How can I trust someone I have only just met?'

Max ran his hand over his hair. 'Maybe you need to follow your instinct in this. I worked for *die Tatsache*. I wrote the article for *The Independent Chronicler*. I've been sticking my neck out. Foolishly, some might say…'

Franz Jacob said nothing then rubbed his hands together as if he had come to a decision. 'As you will know if you have studied the reports, there are many versions to what happened.'

'And many of them have been suppressed.'

'One way or another they wanted her out of the way. She was a distraction, a dangerous blabbermouth.'

'The Nazi High Command, you mean.'

'Yes, yes. Heinrich Himmler, Rudolf Hess, Franz Schwarz and all the others around him.'

He got to his feet, went over to a filing cabinet which he unlocked and rifled through. When he spoke again it was in a deliberate, considered way. 'I have affidavits. Witness reports. According to Ernst Hanfstaengel, Franz Schwarz, the treasurer of the Nazi Party, was responsible for paying off blackmailers.'

He pushed the papers towards Max. Max shuffled through the notes, some handwritten, some transcripts of interviews. He read the top report, notes from a conversation with an assistant to Schwarz.

'One day in 1930 Schwarz admitted that he had to buy off someone who was trying to blackmail Hitler. The man had come into the possession of a folio of drawings. Hitler had made... They were intimate sketches of Geli Raubal.'

Max grunted in surprise while Franz Jacob continued. 'Hitler, who often changed his mind at the last minute, reversed his decision about letting her go to Vienna. It is my contention that the other Nazi leaders were putting pressure on him. They told him it was unsafe to set her free: she knew too much. They may have found out that she had confided in other men about Hitler's peculiar habits. Schwarz knew she had modelled for him. If she talked indiscreetly in Vienna, stories might get picked up by the liberal press.'

'And here, look at this. It's a copy of a state's attorney inquiry into the matter of Geli Raubal....'

'That's genuine, is it?' Max could barely breathe. Franz Jacob shrugged.

'There are further affidavits from Willi Schmidt, the critic Geli had consulted about teachers in Vienna. There are those who even question Hitler's alibi at the time of Geli's death. You'll find it all in there. It's from one of the police inspectors. This man – we do not know whether it was Sauer or Forster -- came to the conclusion that, instead of leaving for Nuremburg, Hitler postponed his trip.'

Max gulped, longing to peruse the material at length, to copy down what he could. As if reading his mind Franz pointed towards a small table in an alcove. 'You can go through them over there. And here,' He thrust a buff envelope towards him. 'Photos of Geli before they sanitised her face. They'd murder you for this.'

Max spread out the photos in front of him. They showed Geli's chubby face smeared with blood, her nose battered: clear evidence of a brutal assault.

Fifty five

When Khan set out on a foray of fact-finding Tilda was his first port of call. It was a sobering experience. She was poring over a thick ledger in the poky Kuka club office where she often helped out with the books. 'I believe you got your man.' She frowned at Khan through tinted reading glasses. 'Caused a storm in the process. Did you hear?'

'Hear what?'

'I picked it up at the nightclub last night. I heard some of them talking about the guards. Two were killed. One died on the spot. The other was wounded. When he didn't come round they rushed him to hospital. He never regained consciousness. Cerebral haemorrhage,' she paused. 'Two less Nazis to worry about, I suppose.' She sniffed and shrugged her shoulders with an air of carelessness but he was not convinced; this was all getting too close for comfort. She was looking more perturbed than he'd ever seen her.

He recalled Max telling him on the journey back that his guard had been none other than Hans Fichte, the husband of his precious, though estranged, sister. 'Good God,' he said grimly, 'they'll be after blood now.'

'The order has already gone out. If they don't get Max, they'll pull in a few liberal journalists to exact reprisal. They mean business.'

Before Khan could get any closer to Tilda, Boris Dublovsky came in. He nodded brusquely at Khan without smiling. With a new coldness he did not even offer him a drink as he would have done weeks before. Khan sensed the *conférencier* observing him intently. When Khan probed, Dublovsky said he had no news of any description to impart. After just five minutes he started bundling together the bills Tilda had gone through: 'I better get on. As you can see, I need to settle my accounts. If you'll excuse me…'

'You managed to spring him, after all?' Robert Denning said, but did not look gratified by the news. They were sitting in the library at the embassy, the remnants of a log smouldering in the woodburner.

'Delivered safe and sound,' replied Khan warily. 'How did you know?'

Denning put aside the newspaper he was reading. 'The word has got out that two men were shot.' He glared at Khan. 'And what if it gets out that a diplomatic representative of His Majesty's Government was mixed up in some sectarian squabble?'

'It was dark. No one would have recognised me…'

'In London a lot of people are betting things might swing in favour of Hitler.'

'Unlikely,' said Khan. 'Granted there are so many moves and countermoves going on that it's hard to tell. But the point is… we got him back. I guessed that's all I wanted in the short term.'

Denning grunted. He glanced at the corner clock. 'Let me know of any developments, will you?' His fractious tone was of no surprise.

Khan left the confines of the library soon after. He was becoming less sure of his ground by the day. His circle of trusted associates had shrunk to a handful. He could not compromise Tilda further, the last thing he wanted was for her to end up on some Nazi hit list. He needed to find a safe house for Max and Rhiannon. The more people he spoke to the more he realised that Max could not walk around freely.

He had not yet apprised him of the fact that Gert Frosch had shot up on the Nazis' hate agenda. This was according to Tilda, who had no reason to lie about it. They must have suspected his hand in the newspaper reports.

So who remained? Who could be trusted?

Mihir Basu was lounging on a sofa reading a newspaper when his wife ushered Khan into the room. The leader leapt to his feet. 'The prodigal son returns,' said Basu affably.

'Hardly.'

'I've had the fatted calf slaughtered.' Basu laughed.

Khan sat when invited to – Western-style on a chair on this occasion – and accepted the tea he was offered. 'My days here are…' began Khan.

'You said that last time. Sounds like you're in a bit of a fix?'

Khan winced. 'The elections have not pleased the Nazis,' he said slowly. 'Now there is even more speculation.'

'A good time to strike,' replied Basu.

'Strike?' asked Khan. 'Strike what?'

'To bring down the cabinet, of course. The system is fatally flawed. Look my good man, be honest about your intentions. Why are you here?'

'I need to ask a favour of you.' He put down his cup and saucer on the coffee table and let out a deep sigh. For all his bombast there was something about Basu that struck him as loyal. He did not deviate from his course, nor pretend to be what he wasn't. By contrast, Khan had had enough of British diplomacy with its umpteen shifts and nuances of meaning.

'It's like this: I want to get out of Germany and back to India. But before I do that I may need to help some friends out, should things take a turn for the worse.'

'That's where I come in is it?'

'There have been many… incidents. Political murders.'

'So what has your so-called friend done? Killed a key Nazi or something?'

Khan drew in a sharp breath. 'He was hauled in for interrogation. We got him out. Someone got shot in the process. One of them...'

Mihir Basu stared at him. 'I heard something about that. Not one but two. Yesterday, wasn't it – or the day before? Up in Wannsee?'

Khan was aghast at what he'd just done, realising too late that until that moment Basu had known nothing of his connections with Max. The situation was unnerving him, causing him to jettison caution. He nodded, realising the futility of denial. Khan wondered where on earth the man was getting his information from. There was a gleam of superiority in Basu's eyes.

When Khan was silent, staring at the floor, Basu continued. 'So you want me to offer him protection. Is that it? You want me to shelter a fugitive from the long arm of the Nazi Party? You want them to come here and stay perhaps?'

'I didn't say that.'

'You think I might have the privilege of diplomatic immunity?'

Khan got up. His head was pounding. He had taken a huge risk, unsure even now what had led him to contemplate putting confidence in his wily compatriot.

'I wouldn't rule out running such a risk,' said Basu, opening his palms in a gesture of negotiation. 'I might be willing. But it would need to be worth it. For example, I would dearly like you to fill me in on what is the current military and civil thinking of His Majesty's government in the Raj – in the face of all the civil unrest. Something specific, I mean.'

'I am not privy to that information. And never have been.'

'But you'd be in a better position than I am to find out. So far, with regard to Berlin you've given me nothing I haven't already gleaned from other sources. You come with bits of this and that. It won't wash, my dear friend.'

Khan was silent. With a growing sense of helplessness he was only too aware he now had few secrets to betray. Never before had he felt so poor. He bid Sri Basu farewell and said he would be in touch later.

Fifty six

'Max, what's up? You look – have you been drinking?'

Max slumped over the table, his movements uncoordinated. It was obvious he was struggling for control. 'Rhiannon, there's something I need to tell you…'

They were perched at Khan's table over the frugal supper of bread and cheese she had fetched on the way back from the Rudersteins.

'I have news, too…'

'Listen, this – this is important.'

She was nettled at his inebriation, nettled that he could push her concerns so readily aside. 'You're making me nervous. Why have you been drinking?'

'Hans is dead,' he blurted out.

'What!'

'It was an accident, we think.'

'Good God, what happened?'

'When they came to break me out there was a lot of commotion. Hans was one of the guards. He had a gun. But he didn't fire at us. In the end he tried to divert attention. I think one of the other guards saw…'

'Oh my God! Does Inge know?'

'I don't know. I didn't even know he was dead until today. Khan told me…'

'Poor Inge!'

'Yes, poor Inge.'

'Will you go and see her?'

Max sighed, said nothing.

'Max?'

'That will be difficult.'

'What a mess!' she paused. 'She's your sister,' she added softly.

'They'll have their – their spies out.'

'Do you want me to go?'

'No. Not there.'

'Then?'

'That's not all, there's something else…'

'Max, I don't believe this…'

He took a deep breath, looking across at her through his eyebrows, summoning whatever psychological resources he could. He gulped down a glass of water. 'I got fired!'

'But Max, whatever for?'

'Isn't it obvious?'

'No, it's not. Max, what is going on?'

'It happened before I was captured. Seifert thinks I overstepped the mark. He found out about the flyers.'

They sank into silence, Rhiannon too shocked to think with any coherence, pushed her own news from her mind.

'I'm going to meet with a few other correspondents… The bottom is falling out of the government… The work is there, it's a case of having the stomach for it. I have to get out there and find it…'

She was barely listening. Her head was swimming while her body felt as heavy as lead. She forced back the tumult that threatened, the useless tears pricking the back of her eyes, but the gathering emotion was too strong. 'Yes, you better had. You always knew better, didn't you? You swore you had a contract, which couldn't be broken. You swore you had to stay and see things through. And now look at you! Thinking getting drunk will solve the problem. Max, for God's sake – pull yourself together.' She thumped the table making the tumblers tremble. 'I don't want to hear anymore.' She grabbed her coat and strode out into the silent, dark streets of Wilmersdorf.

Her coat flapped open as she ran, the cold air cutting into her neck and chest. She stopped a moment to button it up and then continued. She was out of breath and the bitterness of the night caused her to cough. She dug her ungloved hands into her pockets. Pulling up the collar she continued at a stride. Her anger dispersed a little as she moved so she began to regret that she had yelled at Max, that she had flung out of the apartment in such a rage. Yet she could not help herself, she was unused to feeling quite so out of control, quite so overwhelmed. What on earth were they going to do now?

She went to cross the road. A car appearing from nowhere sped by, causing her to leap backwards. She looked up and down the street before she picked her way across in the meagre lamplight. The shadow of a cat streaked by her left side, startling her as it dived into bushes. She stopped again, her head aching. How much further was she going to go? And to what avail? She could not run away the whole night, away from Max, from herself, away from the impossibility of what she realised could and must be true.

Max had always had a tendency to be too direct, too obvious. Before, perhaps unfairly, she'd put this down to his being German, now she realised it was more a function of his temperament. Though was the situation entirely of his making? She began to walk again.

At the junction of two roads she didn't know she passed a café with a few people propped by the window. She walked on. She would keep going until she exhausted herself. Tears were useless, she was too cold to cry, too het up, too angry still. Even as she was thinking this she heard steps behind her. Someone was approaching, catching up with her however rapidly she moved. She half turned. The dark shape assumed form, familiarity. It was Max. She was not yet ready for Max. She moved faster. But he moved faster still, caught up with her as she was about to enter the green enclosure ahead of her.

'Rhiannon!' His voice was hoarse, concerned, passionate. 'Please don't run away from me.' He was standing by her, his arms about her, gathering her towards him. She wanted to lash out, fight him off. At the same time she felt his desperation, the pain searing through him. They moved forward, his arm around her. 'I am so so sorry,' he murmured. 'I would do anything *not* to hurt you. Anything.'

She found it impossible to speak. The warmth from his body was seeping into hers, a reassuring animal presence, a sense of home, of safety. Where else was there for her to go? She let herself be persuaded, led back home. Her face was raw now. She took off her coat and sank into the softest, most lush of Khan's sofas. Max went off to make her a warming drink. She took it without speaking. She glanced at him, not wanting prolonged eye contact. She saw that he had lost weight during his time away, that he was in anguish. His dark eyes flickered towards her. She would not look at him. She would not speak. She dared not speak. He moved around her as if she were a difficult child, an invalid. At last he sat down beside her on the sofa, touched her arms with his hands, stroked them from shoulder to wrist, without speaking.

She stared at the plumped up cushion, took small sips of her drink. Despite herself she was growing calmer, lulled by being near him. 'And now there are things I need to tell you.' She glanced around. He was looking at her intently. She reddened. 'Max, I'm expecting…' The words were out of her mouth before she could consider them. He started back as if recoiling, his eyes widening.

'You mean you're pregnant? Are you sure?'

She nodded, unwanted tears burning her eyes. She blinked hard. 'I went to the doctor. I hadn't even suspected. I was so fraught and felt so unwell I thought it was something else...'

'Well,' he said. Rhiannon hovered between defiance and fear. 'Well,' he repeated.

'Is that all you can say?'

'I'm shocked. That's all.'

'So you see,' she said at length, 'it is getting urgent to sort something out.'

They sat for a moment in silence. Max's hand slid across the table towards hers. He clasped it and pulled her closer.

'Rhiannon,' he said. There was warmth, tenderness in his voice but it could not offset the look of sheer panic she'd glimpsed in his face.

'In London I wanted us to start a family. You know that. But here it all changed... I'm tired, Max. Bone tired. I want to sleep for a week. I don't want to be worrying about men watching us from doorways. You getting into situations...'

'That's over.'

'Is it? I'm not convinced. I don't want to wonder if you are coming home. Whether you have work or if we have enough money for the rent...' She felt blank, angry, emptied out. There was no more in her to give. She was a tree toppled in a drought, uprooted and powerless.

She thought of Aunt Vicky: such tenacity and self-belief she always had she never let anything get her down or stand in her way. From where did Vicky get such strength? Max's eyes searched hers across the table.

'I'll take care of you,' he said.

You can't even take care of yourself, she wanted to say but swallowed the barb. 'I wasn't going to tell you,' she said.

'Why not?'

'So much going on...'

'I'm glad you did. How have you been then? You never said anything?'

'I've been sick a couple of times at work. Felt giddy in the mornings. I didn't take much notice.'

Max continued to look thoughtful.

'Your reaction – you don't seem exactly pleased,' she said.

He looked up sharply, gave a quick smile which went only some way to reassuring her. 'I need to sleep on it.'

She drew back into herself. The notion of this new life needed time to seep into their awareness, even as the cells were busy with a vitality of their own, multiplying by the million. 'What are we going to do, Max?' she whispered, her hands clenched so the knuckles stuck out, white and bony in her fist.

Fifty seven

In the early hours Max finished another report for the foreign press. He depicted the worsening labyrinth that was Berlin, outlining closet power deals between the President's son and his minister, Meissner, and between the Cabinet and the Nazis. He spoke of restrictions being placed on foreign correspondents. He detailed what he knew of the covert, steady and relentless build-up of munitions, which remained in strict contravention of the Versailles Treaty. He had no idea who would run it, but he had to do something.

He thought of Inge. As the hours passed he had a growing desire to see her. Though she would repulse him, he longed to hold her and convince her that the events leading to Hans's death had been part of a fatal web that had enmeshed them.

According to Khan, Hans was to be accorded a full Nazi funeral with torchlit cortège, speeches, giant banners flapping: all in keeping with the potent mix of religion and Nationalism that Goebbels connived to serve up for the populace. On such occasions Goebbels' publicity machine was at its deadliest, knowing people loved nothing more than a righteous martyr. There was no way Max would dare show his face in that spectacle, even if he'd wanted to.

The body was to be taken from the mortuary the next day. Prior to burial it was to be driven, swastika-draped, through the streets of Neukölln. The SA would be watching her apartment block. Would she even be there? Already there were articles in *der Völkische Beobachter* about Hans, including a snapshot of him in a Brown Shirt before a *Schloss* in Bavaria. Inge was being taken care of by the Party, Khan said.

He had had an attack of remorse. Rhiannon was right. Alcohol solved nothing; its taste of oblivion could only ever be transitory. He could claim it was understandable when your world came crashing down around you, but that was just an excuse. Now, more than ever, he had to get out and fight not only for what was right, but for survival. One look at the beautiful, pale and haunted face of his beloved Rhiannon had been more than he could stand.

His ferocity for the Geli Raubal story, his stab at blocking the Nazis had made him rash. Now he needed to be cunning. The SA were known to have set up a ring of surveillance around Berlin, they were keeping tabs on all their opponents: Social Democrats, Communists, Trade Unionists, fervent Catholic and Evangelical Churchmen, and of course prominent Jews. The Nazi SA were poised to strike whenever given the command. There was an uneasy quiet in the city. Whatever he did next it would need to be well thought through.

He left Wilmersdorf while Rhiannon was still sleeping. He wanted to be out early on the streets, before it was light. He'd muffled himself as best he could, but it would be hard to keep his guard up the whole time. The day before, in and out of a haze, he'd frequented the usual journalist haunts. No one needed a freelance. There was a terrible freedom in all this, he felt uprooted and exhilarated. In Berlin he could only write for *Immer Freiheit*. It was time he called on Dieter.

Fifty eight

Rhiannon devoted extra time to her appearance, applying her make-up with care, adding a dash of rouge to her cheeks. When she presented herself to Miss Stonebridge in the main office, the other greeted her with an expression more severe than normal: 'So you're back, are you?'

'Good morning, Miss Stonebridge. I did send a sick note via Mr Khan.'

'Yes, we received it.' Rhiannon sat down without being asked to in the brown, cabinet-lined room. She could see from Miss Stonebridge's in-tray was piled so high it was on the verge of toppling. Miss Stonebridge propped her chin on her open palm and appraised Rhiannon in a way that unsettled her.

'You are aware, I suppose, of the rules governing married women in the Civil Service?' When Rhiannon showed puzzlement the other went on. 'Strictly speaking a woman may not work in the Civil Service once she is married, but as you went onto the temporary staff list we were able to make an exception. But expectant mothers are another case.'

Rhiannon started. 'I beg your pardon?'

'I said expectant mothers…'

'But I've only just found out. I'm only a few weeks gone. I wasn't going to let people know yet.'

'It's a pity you didn't think to tell your doctor that. It states quite clearly on his note that you have been unwell, indisposed, due to your condition.'

'Oh, but surely I can still work? I'm fine now. I really am.'

Miss Stonebridge moved the ink blotter around on her desk. 'It makes no difference I am afraid, Mrs Dienst. It is not

I who think up these regulations. I only apply them. I am sorry but I will have to serve you notice forthwith. Three weeks is all I can grant you. I'd like to offer more but I can't. To tell the truth you turned out better than I thought you would. But rules are rules.'

Her eyes gripped Rhiannon's, rendering her powerless. Not now, she pleaded inwardly. Why hadn't she thought to steam open the doctor's letter? It had all been moving far too fast for her. 'I need this job,' she said simply. 'More than ever.'

'It's not possible. It can't be helped.' Miss Stonebridge stood up to indicate the matter was now settled. 'As I say, it is not of my making.'

Rhiannon banged away on her typewriter, making up for lost time and batting away useless tears. Memos danced nonsensically in front of her eyes. She tore one out of the roller and crumpled it into a ball, which she lobbed in fury into the wastepaper basket. She rattled on, refusing to leave her chair until her allocated heap of documents was cleared. At lunchtime she filed with others into the canteen. Khan was over the other side. He beckoned to her, lifting his tray bearing steak and kidney pie and a pot of tea. 'Join me?' She nodded. They looked around for a free spot on one of the long tables and were silent while Khan tucked into his meal. Mindful that money would soon be scarce Rhiannon had taken a bowl of soup and several slices of bread, which she finished in no time. She looked at Khan's precise movements as he cut the meat, at his jaw working. He inhaled deeply. 'What's it like being back at work?'

When she raised her shoulders in a huge shrug and let out a gasp of exasperation he said: 'Not so good, eh?'

'It's complicated.'

'How come?' She glanced around at the other tables, at young women with fine nylon stockings and smart outfits

353

busily chatting without a care in the world. All around her was a subdued, ordered world of people in employment with plates piled high. Oh, for a little of their security.

'You look sad, Rhiannon. Is anything the matter?'

'I suppose you'll find out soon enough. But please, promise not to say anything – to talk to others about it.

'Scouts' honour.'

She gave a little laugh. 'I doubt you were ever a scout, you're too devious. But the long and short of it is Miss Stonebridge gave me the sack.'

He looked as taken aback as she had felt. 'But why?' Anger flashed across his dark eyes. 'Whatever for?'

She fiddled with her soup spoon. 'I'm pregnant.'

'Oh, I didn't know.' He frowned and looked down at the ground, visibly shocked.

'I only just found out myself.'

'But why did you tell her?'

'I didn't. The sick note did. It didn't even occur to me that the doctor would write that. In fact, I wasn't really thinking. Right now I can't think straight. I didn't realise it would be a problem. I've never worked for the Civil Service before.'

'I see.'

'It's the last thing we need at the moment. You heard about Max?'

He nodded.

'A good enough reason to leave the city, I suppose.' She gave a little laugh. 'Don't look so stricken.' She reached across and grasped his hand. 'Oh Khan.' He continued to stare at the ground.

As she re-entered Khan's apartment block in Wilmersdorf she noticed the caretaker's door was ajar. As she passed he called out. 'Frau Dienst!' Hearing her name was a shock. She had met the caretaker only once before, on that first distraught night after Max disappeared. Intrigued, she followed as the man beckoned her into his office. The walls were lined with keys. She glanced at the Nazi swastika attached to the interior glass. He caught her eye. 'Don't mind that,' he said. 'Got to keep the chumps off my back.'

She started, unsure what to say. He reached into his jacket pocket, glanced around and pulled out a grubby Communist card. 'You look astonished…'

'You wanted to speak to me, you said.' His face in the half-light looked hollow, shadows playing over his forehead, making her uncertain of his expression.

'A word of warning, that's all. I wanted to catch your husband or Herr Khan, but they haven't come back yet. Things in this block have been pretty quiet but this morning I noticed something…'

'What was that?' she shot back.

'A few men – Brown Shirts – having a snoop round.'

'That's pretty normal these days, isn't it?' she said, as calmly as she was able. The man with his rancid smell of grease and tobacco was making her uneasy.

'You may think I'm not supposed to, but I do know who your husband is, and why he is here. I just wanted to warn you. I am not the only one who knows. You are not safe here. There have been others around – Indian, I think – asking about the comings and goings of people in the house.'

'Why should that be of concern to me?' Her voice was truculent. 'If you let me pass now, I'd be grateful.'

'Frau Dienst, hear me out.'

She held her breath.

'Your whereabouts have become known. Various groups are pulling together, sharing information. If I were you, I'd find somewhere else to stay.'

She pushed past him, no longer able to breathe in the tiny space.

Outside he watched her through the pane.

'Here,' he said, catching her by the arm. 'Give this to your husband. It's from someone he knows.'

She hesitated then nodded and took the envelope.

Inside the apartment she wandered through the rooms. The others were not yet back. She looked around at the silken cushions and languid, colourful Klimt print, then kicked off her shoes and slid to the ground. Her heartbeat was racing as if preparing her for flight. She could feel the plush pile of the carpet beneath her feet, her legs. She stroked it with the palm of her hand, it was soft like an animal's fur. She thought of Vicky and her fox capes. She thought of the spongy warmth and resilience of a lamb's coat before shearing.

She had had enough. 'You're not safe here' reverberated inside her. She took a shower, letting the warm water run over her, through her hair, down her back, careless of the waste; she would wash out the hunger-drawn faces and angry young men that crowded her brain. She changed into a skirt and loose jumper and lay on the bed, letting her tiredness seep into the eiderdown.

Khan was the first to return. She told him about the caretaker. 'How well do you know him?' she asked.

'He hasn't been here long. The last one retired a month ago.' Khan had an alarmed expression, frowning more than usual. 'A lot of these caretakers have joined the Nazis. Some have been planted in strategic parts of the city. It's a good way to keep an eye out.'

'He showed me his Communist card,' she said.

'Did he? What else did he say?'

'I gave you the gist. He did say some of the types hanging

around were Indian. That's when I started wondering about your man Basu...'

Even as they were speaking they heard the front door click open. Max came in. His eyes were gleaming. 'I hit the jackpot,' he said.

'And I've been dismissed,' she declared, piqued that he looked so pleased with himself when she felt so wretched.

'What are you talking about?' The look of disbelief on his face was enough to make her relent. She explained.

'That's not all. Here!' She gave him the letter.

Max spread out the crumpled sheet and read it then screwed it up and tossed it towards the wastepaper basket. 'Someone in the Indian Nationalists sent a warning. Apparently Sri Mihir Basu betrayed our whereabouts.'

'Oh God!' Khan had gone deathly quiet. He looked suddenly ill.

'We were moving from here anyway,' said Max. 'We knew it wouldn't be safe for long.' He raised his shoulder. 'I guess this warning is valid.'

'It *was* Mihir Basu!' Rhiannon was no longer able to contain herself. 'He's a Nationalist. Hasn't he been toadying up to the Nazis all along? You said you went to see him again.'

'They rebuffed him. I thought I had some leverage...' When Max looked askance at Khan, he continued, though less sure of himself. 'It all comes down to what lens, what viewpoint you're taking. There has always been a question mark hanging over him.'

'When did you last see him?' Max cut in.

'I saw him yesterday. I went back to his place again today but he's cleared out. Left his former apartment, lock, stock and barrel. No one seems to know where's he's gone.'

'Still in Berlin, though?' asked Max.

'I haven't a clue.'

Fifty nine

After much persuasion Franz Jacob had given Max a microfilm of the Geli corpse. He had kept it on him the whole time as there had been no chance to conceal it the night before. No one but him should know about it. Khan left for the embassy, saying he would see what he could do about getting them out of the city. Rhiannon had gone to fetch fresh rolls for breakfast. He noticed the crumpled bed and the sink piled high with unwashed dishes from the night before. It was unlike Rhiannon not to tidy up. He wondered how she was. For himself he minded not a jot about uncertainty – he had lived with it as a student – but he did mind for her. These days she was looking increasingly drawn.

The roll of film was tiny. He rummaged in the bedroom for a sewing kit. One of his old jackets of worn tweed – something he'd picked up in Britain – would be ideal. The cloth was bulky and it had a large hem. He rifled in the drawers on Rhiannon's side of the bed and eventually unearthed needle, thread and scissors. He set about stuffing the microfilm into the lining. With his large hands and lack of experience he fumbled, pricked himself but managed to do it.

Over breakfast he sat, elbows propped on the table, thinking. Rhiannon's head was bent. He wanted to reach out and touch it. Now, more than ever, he was aware of the need to protect her. There was nothing else for it: they would have to leave the city as soon as possible, yet even as the decision hardened it sent him into tumult. Would it be that simple? Just hop on a train to Paris or Hamburg or Hanover? Cut ties and disappear? Several people had confirmed that the SA ring had encircled the city with unofficial roadblocks. Trains left by the hour but there might well be men posted on the lookout in every mainline station.

'We need to get our things together,' he said. 'Just the essentials.'

She looked up from her coffee, puzzlement giving way to a sudden clearing in her face. 'We're leaving then?'

'Very soon. Just a couple of things I need to see to first.'

'Then I'll go and tell them at the embassy. See if they give me anything.'

'No,' he said distractedly. 'It's not necessary. The fewer people who know the better.'

She gave him a sharp look then took the dishes through to the kitchen.

Even as Max sifted options to escape he had the irrepressible urge to see Inge. On the surface he and his sister remained enemies, yet it was impossible to stay away from her. He must give her one last hug. Must convince her that events leading to Hans's death had been a horrible accident, see if there was anything he could do for her.

What was more he must go today.

He headed towards the centre. He wandered by the *Landwehrkanal* in the Tiergarten. The black water, clogged with fallen leaves, was near to freezing. He walked through the trees towards the *Siegessäule*, mulling over the best way of contacting her without drawing attention to himself. He decided the least he could do was to find a hat to cover his forehead and a coat with a collar. In the streets around the Ku'damm he searched out a pawnshop. Here he fumbled among the rails of cast-off clothing; they smelled stale and were moth-eaten but he couldn't be fastidious. He bought dark glasses and a voluminous coat and fished out a hat.

The apartment block where Inge lived appeared deserted. Twice he wandered up and down the street, eyeing other passers-by and glancing up towards her floor. A creature of habit, she left every afternoon round this time to pick up a few groceries and take Anna for a short walk to the park. If he hovered in the shadows by the corner of the street, there was less danger of being spotted. Although there was a surprising air of normality with no men on guard, he placed little credence in the apparent calm. His enemies were sly creatures. Members of the SA could be watching from a neighbour's window or be perched up on a balcony somewhere.

He resigned himself to waiting on the street corner, took out a newspaper and leaned against a shop window. A man left the apartment block. Max recognised him from the past. The man peered at Max as he passed, then muttered a garbled: *'Guten Tag'* and continued down the street. Max glanced over his shoulder; the café three shops down appeared ill-lit and half empty: it would be a good place to speak to Inge. He saw her approaching. She was alone and looked pale as death.

'Max! What the hell!' she said when he caught her by the arm and whispered that they should go into the café. Unable to speak, she followed him. He ordered two coffees then sought out the least conspicuous spot, sat down and yanked the hat from his head.

'Inge, I – I had to see how you were.'

'What…?'How dare you!'

'How are you?'

When she did not answer he asked where Anna was. Inge's face had a sickly pallor and shadows lurked round her cheeks and neck.

'You have some nerve…'

'I had to come. I had to see how you…'

'Then you know about Hans?' she cut in, her voice flat. Comprehension lit her face. 'Of course you know. Of course!'

'It was an accident, a scuffle.'

'Max, just let me go, will you.'

'Inge…'

'I have nothing to say to you…'

'Listen…'

'They told me what happened. You were helping with their enquiries. A bunch of ruffians came. That…'

'No Inge, it wasn't like that. In the end he was protecting me. One of the other guards killed him. Whatever they say. You have to believe me. I heard the shots but I didn't know he was dead until yesterday. I had to break out. They were going to kill me.'

'I wish they had!'

'You don't mean that.'

'Hans is dead and my child will have no father.'

'Where is Anna?'

'Anna! Anna! Anna! Anna is with a neighbour. But what about me, Max? What about me?' Her eyes were shrill in her white face.

The waiter brought over the drinks and they sank into silence. She looked as if she were about to faint. 'Oh Inge, this is the last thing I wanted.' He tried to take hold of her hand but she pulled it away. He tried to shift his chair nearer to hers but she leaned back and gave him a cold, hard stare. Though she struggled against him, he caught hold of her wrist. 'Inge, listen to me. It's true what I just said. He was trying to save me and they killed him!'

'I don't believe you.' The words, close to his ear, shocked him into releasing his grasp. He winced. There was no listening. She broke free, banged against the table as she stood up. He got to his feet and attempted a rough embrace. She gave a muffled cry. 'I don't want to see you again! Do you hear? I have no brother. No brother and no husband.' She lurched away from him then stumbled and fell back against him. He held her and for a moment she allowed herself to be held. He could feel her suppressing a sob, her body tightening.

There was nothing more he could say to her. There was nothing to assuage her loss. Perhaps in time there might be words: careful, well-chosen words, to steal past the barrier of bleakness. But for now entry was firmly denied. Shaken, guilt-ridden, confused, he paced away from the block. He barely noticed any glances he drew from passers-by. He returned to the Zoo area and took off in the S-Bahn for Dieter's allotment land.

When he arrived the usual bunch of men were hovering round the brazier playing cards for pfennigs. They ignored him. It was a blustery day. The view over the allotments was sharp, the ground still bare, the huts and sheds with an abandoned air. It took him just an instant to realise something was wrong. Aghast, he stared at the blackened heap, the gap, smouldering remains. He rushed over to where Dieter's shed had stood. The wood-burning stove alone remained proud and undamaged amid the debris. All else was ashes.

He looked around. In one corner something shifted. Moving closer he caught sight of the crazy old woman of the hedges. Her hair was tangled and her eyes bright with wild dreams. With a sickening sense of the inevitable Max followed to where she was pointing. The apartment block, which housed Dieter's office, loomed across the gardens. She turned to her shrivelled patch of ground. 'Back to work,' she said. 'The children have to eat.'

Slowly, unwanted tears streaking his face, Max walked in

the direction of the apartment house. He felt sick to his stomach. Werner, he thought. It would have to be Werner, the former office boy. Had he done it? Had he? Who else would have betrayed Dieter? Despite his banter Dieter trusted those he trusted. In the Berlin of today one should trust no one, not even oneself. Max held back in the shadow of a tree, observing the entrance, looking up towards the attic. He could see little. Then he noticed the ground floor door was gaping open.

He approached, looking all around for signs of activity or violence. Several minutes he waited, attuning his ears to every sound, his eyes to every flicker. Nothing. He moved closer. He took in the wider view, back over the allotments, forwards over the interconnecting streets and other buildings. Nothing. He stood at the base of the building by the door, which had been wrenched from its hinges and swung awkwardly in the wind. From the stairwell came no echo of feet or voices. He crept upwards, heart racing.

The office had been broken into, the desks toppled, the phones torn from their sockets. The files had been emptied or scattered. He paced around surveying the damage. His foot brushed against pieces of the dancer lamp smashed against the wall. He stooped to retrieve a shard and ran his finger down the edge. Dieter's muse! The sight pierced him. Dieter would have fared no better than this lamp if he'd been around at the time of the raid. He picked up a sheet of paper from the floor. It was part of his last article for Dieter, scrawled over with his own notes. He lit a match and set fire to the sheet. He dropped it in dying flames into the waste paper basket where it curled and crinkled.

Sixty

As Khan knocked on Robert Denning's office door he braced himself, the less he had to do with his boss these days the better. Denning opened and responded with a nod of his head. 'Oh, it's you. Grab a seat, will you. There are a few bits and pieces we need to tie up.' Khan glanced around. It was some time since they had worked together here. The room looked as though a hurricane had blasted through it. Denning was in his shirt-sleeves, flushed and anxious. A plant wilted, neglected, on the windowsill.

'I wrote the reports you asked me to. We're more or less up-to-date,' Khan said, clearing a space for himself on one of the seats.

'You've nothing else to tell me about Mihir Basu?'

'It's all in the notes,' Khan fired back, rather too quickly. The very mention of Basu rankled. He looked at the stacks around him. 'That is, if you can find it. I left a copy on your desk yesterday when I couldn't find you. I didn't know where you'd gone…'

'Really? I read it. Is that all you have to say? Seems a bit thin to me. I thought you'd got further than that. You went a few times, didn't you?'

Khan nodded. He could think of nothing else to say. He wanted shot of the whole damn business. He wanted shot of Robert Denning, who increasingly seemed to him a shallow, self-seeking idler, keen to score points. 'Basu is going nowhere fast,' he murmured, in conclusion.

'Crazy he might be,' retorted Denning, 'but any danger to the Crown must be followed. We need to know as much about him as we can.'

'He's gone,' said Khan. 'Gone. His apartment is deserted. He went yesterday I believe. And I have no idea where…'

Only now did Khan acknowledge to himself how easily he'd been duped. He'd been sold down the river merely so Basu could show himself as an ally and willing partner in the ghastly Nationalist Movement. Blood was thinner than water. The Indian connection had proved as useful as a broken drainpipe.

'Come on, Khan – where's he gone to? You must have some idea?'

'No, actually, I don't.'

Robert Denning's cold fish eyes looked across at him, appraising. Inwardly Khan winced. Denning leaned back: 'The two dead Nazis are to be given a hero's farewell. Tomorrow, I believe. I hope to God the British embassy will in no way be compromised…'

'You know that Max Dienst got the sack?'

Denning scratched the side of his cheek. 'Not surprising in the circumstances.'

'If they needed to get out quickly – leave the city. What would you advise?'

Denning stared at Khan but gave no response.

Khan looked at the floor. 'You said you wanted to see me.'

'Yes. As I said, we need to do a few handover reports.'

'I thought we'd done most of that already.'

'Yes, but in case there's a change of government here we need to make recommendations.'

'What sort of recommendations?'

'You know a lot more people than I do.'

'Do I?' Khan baulked at imparting the list of names and details of the network he'd built up over previous months. By now most of them were pretty useless anyway.

'Contacts, I mean. Points of reference.'

365

'Befriending the Fascists? I don't believe it's you saying this.'

'It's not our pigeon to make policies, only recommendations.'

Khan glanced around at the piles of paper, at the shredded reports, at the in-tray marked urgent, as the disarray of their months of work was being hastily sifted, sorted, selected, discarded and concealed.

'How we can help get our friends out of the city if need be?'

'We can't get involved in personal cases...'

'You wanted information and Max Dienst went out there and got it. But when he got into trouble you dropped him. Don't we owe him some sort of loyalty?'

'He's a Communist – a Communist, Khan. Our government has no truck with Communists.' Denning got to his feet, exasperated. 'I've got to go. Can you write up a list of...'

'I don't think they'd be of much use.'

'Just do it, will you?' He picked up two folders lying on the desk and moved swiftly out before Khan could delay him further.

Khan gathered up a nearby heap of typed sheets and thrust them into the air so they sailed, planed and fluttered this way and that. He stared at the chaotic ticker-tack of memos, reports, recommendations and gave a loud snort of derision, tipped over another pile with his foot and contemplated his next move.

He needed to get hold of a car. The friend whose car he had borrowed previously was out of town. An embassy car it would have to be. So he went through to the office of the bureaucrat who dealt with embassy transportation, inventing a plausible scenario in his head. A stickler for protocol, the man acted as if the cars were his own. By a stroke of luck he was not at his desk, though his secretary was hovering nearby.

'I need approval for an embassy car as soon as possible,' he said with as much authority as he could muster. She studied him over her spectacles. 'Mr Robson is at a meeting.'

'I need it for urgent embassy business,' he stated.

'May I ask what…?'

'You may not, Miss…'

'I do not believe you are on the list, Mr Khan.'

'But Robert Denning is.'

'You are not Mr Denning.'

'Look, just sign the chit, will you?'

'I can't do that.'

'You'll hear more about this.' He stormed away from the desk, mind racing. In the garage where the cars were stored the car keys were kept under the surveillance of the concierge. He knew the man. He had once given him a bottle of schnapps at Christmas, knowing that he might one day help oil a few wheels. He found the man dozing in his cubicle. If he was careful, he didn't even need to implicate him. He crept past him and lifted the nearest bunch from the hook. The man shifted in his seat, grunted. Khan slid past him into the recesses of the underground car park. He was stepping over a boundary where they'd be no turning back. He gave a little shrug. Loyalty – what was loyalty? One of the keys opened the hinged door. His hands were shaking as he slotted it into the lock. In the car he fired the ignition and sped toward the exit. The last thing he saw was the concierge racing behind the vehicle, waving his arms.

Sixty one

The end, when it came, surprised her with its quickness. The funeral of Hans and his fellow Nazi guard stirred things up. Tens of thousands of mourners crammed the streets of Neukölln. All orchestrated, said Max, and a gross exaggeration. She was not so sure. They had written about it in the Nazi Press, she saw the headlines as she passed men selling copies of *der Angriff* in the street. There was even a flyover, organised by Göring. No opportunity was to be lost, the flag of the martyrs was hoisted high. Though she longed to see Inge, knowing her world collapsed, her options severed, she held back. Her presence would not salve her wound. Max had tried. Inge would have to wait. Max said they had to leave the city as soon as possible and who was she to argue when this was the very thing she had longed for the last month.

Things were pushing towards resolution. She had given her notice to the embassy in a letter. Miss Stonebridge had been away in Dresden. She was relieved to evade her employer's frown of disapproval but disappointed to have to wait for the final settlement of her salary.

Khan had been busy: from somewhere he had procured a car though he didn't want to talk about it. She suspected it was not quite above board. She ensconced herself with bags and coats in the back of the spacious Mercedes. Max said little about just why and how it had all in the end coalesced into the decision to take flight. The southwest was the safest, Tilda had told Khan. A few country roads remained free of surveillance, the roadblocks of the SA not as systematic as they led people to believe.

The car smelled of petrol and worn leather. They were travelling light. She had abandoned what would not fit into their two suitcases. She choked back the unsaid goodbyes, to Hannah and Uschi and those at the embassy she enjoyed working with. No time.

Piled up with what they could grab from their belongings, Max was stuffing envelopes into the depth of his clothes, rushing, frowning; urgency blotting out the need for explanations. No time. All must be put together now to break through the barriers. She had the name of a friend of the Pastor Neuman, given days before, should they need shelter outside the city. Crammed now into her handbag, along with passports, papers, notepaper with an embassy letterhead. Just in case.

It was a misty evening. After the cold bright day, a swirling moisture, low-level cloud concealing the moon, bringing shadows closer. Even now as they travelled through the streets the air seemed to close behind them like a wake of water. A wake, she thought again of Hans' funeral and Inge, alone now, so alone. Her head was throbbing.

'Are you all right, back there?' Max turned to her. His face was tight with anxiety. He had told her about Dieter. His face was hardened through the tears he could not shed, the fear mounting through his breath. He told her he could only suspect the worst. His office had been ransacked, he had been given away by the old woman of the hedges, by the office boy Werner who had skulked in the Schöneberg office. Tilda said there had been more raids on the Communists. Several had been shot. In Thüringen the Nazis had lost so many votes in the December election that they were furious. They would take revenge, wherever and whenever they could. Berlin was to be theirs.

They were leaving the city through Reinicken, then through Potsdam, out towards the ring of watching SA. It would be thinner there, said Tilda, with barely a roving boy scout to contend with. Their passage would be safe.

'I feel terrible,' Rhiannon wanted to say but didn't. They were on the run she knew not where. The mist was swirling. It was so dark, the road twisting ahead, a biting moist dank air crept into the bones. An owl hooted through the layers of gloom. There were few cars on the road. A headlight swung along the road surface, swerving round the bend, eyes gleamed in the dark among the thickets, the trees. An animal crossed the road. Slinking past fast disappearing, black into black.

'Wild boar,' said Sid. 'These woods are full of them.'

'I thought it was a wolf,' said Rhiannon quietly.

'We'll soon be clear.' Khan sounded calm, rational. Inside Rhiannon was screeching, sister to the owl, her eyes piercing the gloom. 'Another five kilometers,' said Khan. Max said nothing, stern behind the wheel, concentration focused ahead, bringing them through. They had come a long way. She feared the road ahead.

She had dreamt this before. They would not be clear, they would not be free. A fire was burning which could not be put out, a conflagration behind and in front of them, a pyre of hatred. Max had Jewish blood. Max was an object of hatred. They would take him and kill him. He would not escape. It was decreed. She had read it in her dreams, in her destiny.

A sickness black as night was upon her. It weighed against the optimism she heard in the men's voices. They would not come through. The car was gaining speed.

'Tilda said this was the best road,' she heard Khan repeat. 'Our best chance.' Perhaps their only chance, she thought darkly. They rounded another bend, trees thick on either side, not far to go now and they would be out from the city away into the country. She breathed deep, dared hope, dared snuggle down into the coats piled under her, to doze off and wake elsewhere.

The car was slowing down. Max and Khan were muttering, she barely caught what they were saying. She saw the men in boots ahead, the dogs yapping around them, the clouds of breath dissolving into the greater mist. A motorbike was propped against a tree.

'A roadblock,' said Khan. 'I don't think it's anything to worry about. It's unofficial anyway.' She caught the tremor in his voice. They came to a halt. Two men were blocking the road, one walking now to the centre, waving his arms gesturing to them to stop completely. 'Look,' she heard Khan say. 'It's best if I handle this. I'll get out. I have the papers. That'll see us through. There are just two men and two dogs. I'll speak to them...'

'Is that wise?' Max was saying.

'I'm a British subject, don't forget – as good as anyway – and a member of the diplomatic corps. They won't want to cause me any problems.'

He sounded confident. A shiver ran through her. Nothing was certain these days. The whole world had become trigger-happy.

'I could speak to them,' offered Rhiannon.

'No,' said Max. 'Rather me than you...'

'You won't. Your face is known. Let me handle this.'

Rhiannon was silent, her insides shrieking, her dream awake in her now – the impossibility of escape. A light swung from a tree. The SA, paramilitary Brown Shirt, strode over. He had a bland stupid expression. Max pulled up his collar.

'Papers!' shouted the man without preamble.

'Good evening, and to whom do I have the honour of speaking?' Khan as always sounded remarkably calm.

'We're checking everyone leaving the city.'

'Indeed?' responded Khan. 'And on whose authority?' Already he had opened the car door and was walking towards the man with a torch with the dog barking and straining at its leash, leaping up, keen for blood.

'Down!' shouted the man and for a moment the dog was subdued. There was a temporary hut to keep the guards warm. Khan walked with the man towards it all the time talking, talking. Max killed the engine. She shivered, drew her coat closer round her, her heart an angry drum. She felt ill.

Khan was returning to the car, all smiles. Max engaged first gear, pressed down on the accelerator and they moved slowly forward. Khan gave the guard a wave.

'Diplomatic immunity. The car is registered. We have safe passage.'

They accelerated forward, emitting a cloud of exhaust fumes and swaying. 'But I don't know how long for,' he murmured when they had plunged back through the forest. 'Someone has alerted them. They are on the lookout. But for now we are safe.'

'And if they check with the embassy – you'll be covered, will you?'

Khan said nothing. She looked behind. A motorbike kicked into life was zigzagging behind them. It took off in a different direction. She had seen it all before. They were on their way. Gunshot rang out. The night was swallowing the torch, the motorbike, the trees swerving in front of the screen swallowing all. It was her nightmare. They struck on, into the night.

'They'll be no more now,' said Max. 'We're on our way. We've cleared the city boundary.' She lay back and closed her eyes.

Author's Note

This book is a work of research and imagination. Over time it has undergone several drafts and versions. At the centre of the book is the conundrum around the relationship between Adolf Hitler and his niece, Geli Raubal, and the mystery surrounding her death in 1931 at the age of 23.

Whilst this is not a work of history and at times I have deviated from fact for the sake of the story, I have attempted to evoke the atmosphere and conditions of the period. In this I have drawn on books and diaries written at the time and since. I was also lucky enough to talk to eyewitnesses of this turbulent time. Bernard Herzberg, who fled Nazi Germany in 1933 and died in London in 2007, gave generously of his time in recounting his experience of the period. Lily Segal, a schoolgirl in 1930s Berlin, kindly shared her diaries and letters with me.

While Christopher Isherwood's *Berlin Stories: (Mr Norris changes trains* and *Goodbye to Berlin*) helped me set the scene and journalists such as William Shirer in *Berlin Diary*, Joseph Roth in *What I saw. Reports from Berlin 1920-1933,* and Sebastian Haffner's diary: *Defying Hitler,* give a visceral sense of what life was like under the rise of Nazism, Ian Kershaw's works and especially *Hitler (1889-1936) Hubris* provided an invaluable historical framework. Joseph Goebbels' diaries were also very instructive. In exploring the Geli Raubal dimension Ronald Hayman's *Hitler and Geli* was most enlightening, while the historical novel *Hitler's niece* by Ron Hansen made Geli real to me.

In the creation of this book I would like to acknowledge those who have helped me along the way. Broo Doherty, literary agent, read an early draft and encouraged me. David Llewelyn, literary scout and editor, helped breathe life into the story. Anne Garside, historian, shared her wealth of historical knowledge and anecdote. Richard Davies of Parthian's understanding of story and structure, second to none, helped me finally lick the book into shape. Lastly a big thank you to Glen Peters, my nearest and dearest, for bearing with me.